Also by Tarah Benner

Exposure

Book Two of The Fringe

By Tarah Benner

ISBN 978-1512299007

www.tarahbenner.com

*To Dad, for refusing to play the devil's advocate
and encouraging me to go for this.*

one

Eli

Fighting is the best way I know to turn a cadet into a killer. · You can give cadets guns, but all the target practice in the world can't make them bent on survival the way a fight can. To hone that killer instinct and reprogram years of good behavior, you've got to get cadets in the ring and make them fight their way out.

There's something about the smell of sweat and feeling the power in your fists that unleashes the monster inside. That's what we're working toward, at least.

"Concentrate, Harper!" I yell, smacking my gloves together. The sound reverberates along the cinderblock walls and sounds harsher than I intended.

She had just dropped her hands, and I had sunk my hook right into her jaw.

"I am!" she growls around her mouth guard, shaking her head and rolling back into her fighting stance.

I'm holding back, but I shouldn't be. Still, it makes me feel like shit when Harper shrinks back, reeling from my punch. I feel like shit around Harper most of the time these days.

We've been at this for hours, sweating in the dingy training center while the heavy bags stand guard along the wall. Even the gym rats abandoned the weight benches and the track an hour ago. Now the training center just smells like stale sweat mixed with bleach.

"Keep your hands up," I remind her.

"Yeah, yeah," she mutters, faking a jab and coming in with a cross.

It's pretty fast, but she overuses that combo. I block her easily and drive her back across the mat.

"You've done that a hundred times already. Try something else."

Two weeks ago, I might have let her have that one, but we don't have time for any more confidence-building bullshit.

I only have two days left before she's sent out to the Fringe. She's dynamite on the simulation course, and all her tracking and navigation skills are right where they should be, but the fear and desperation in her eyes has become more pronounced with every passing day.

I need her to snap out of it. I can't take her into a war zone scared shitless. That's when cadets freeze and forget everything they learned.

Harper was born tough, but that's not going to be enough on the Fringe. When it's you or the drifters out there, you have to be prepared to pick yourself every time — even when that means hurting someone else. You can't just run away. Sometimes, you have to stand and fight.

That's why I've been pushing her around the ring all day: I need her to switch to offense.

"You're thinking too much," I say. "Don't think. Just react."

I misdirect my jab and then throw a cross and a hook to the body. She slips and absorbs the worst of my hook with her arm, but she steps right into my uppercut. I wince as my glove glances off her chin.

"Son of a bitch!" she yells, staggering backward.

"Fight, Riley! Come on!" I yell. "You're better than this!"

That pisses her off, which is exactly what I need. But I'm unprepared for the animalistic yell that bursts out of her throat.

Without warning, Harper launches herself across the mat and swings a wild overhand right. I block it automatically, but she doesn't use one of the combinations we've worked into muscle memory. She's going off book.

I don't have time to block her double jab to the nose, and she doesn't stop when I cover up. Her long dark ponytail flies back like a whip, and she unleashes a wild storm of punches to my head and body. The fighter in me is screaming to shut her down, but I just keep my gloves up and let her hit me.

She's angry, which is good. At least anger I can understand. It's been my primary emotion lately. Harper needs this. Hell, I need this. It feels like penance.

By the time she tires herself out, my arms and sides are throbbing. Her shoulders sag, and she drops her hands.

"You done?" I ask, a little afraid to drop my guard. After how much I've yelled at her over the last two weeks, I wouldn't put it past her to break my nose.

"Yeah."

I drop my gloves and bend my head to look into those startling gray eyes. "Where was that an hour ago?"

She shrugs, and her lower lip juts out in a rigid scowl.

"That's the aggression you need to neutralize a threat." I lower my voice, deadly serious. "Do whatever you have to do to end them and get out."

She swallows and nods. The silence stretches between us. I can tell she's hurting, but Harper tries to kill her vulnerability with anger and aggression.

Still, the look on her face reminds me so much of that night on the observation deck that it hurts. She kissed me, and I pushed her away. I can't get involved with a cadet, but I've regretted it ever since.

Harper worked hard to trust me after I destroyed the case Constance built to frame her for Sullivan Taylor's murder. Little by little, she managed to chip away at my asshole persona, but I destroyed it in one night.

That's what happens when you fake it for so long: You become that person.

"Your punches are getting stronger," I say, desperate to break the silence. "And your shooting's coming along. You know everything we cover in training for a first-year cadet. I think you'll be okay."

She lets out a harsh laugh. "You must be relieved."

I stare at her, put off by her sudden change in tone. "What's *that* supposed to mean?"

"Nothing."

"No! If you have something to say, say it."

"It's nothing. You did everything you could, okay? You won't have the death of another cadet on your hands."

"Is that what you think?" I ask in disbelief.

"Why else would you be training me?"

"I'm training you so you have a shot at *living!*"

"What about the other cadets? They're going to be deployed soon, too."

"The other cadets don't have a hit out on them," I say, trying to rein in my temper.

"Whatever. That's not why you're doing this."

I roll my eyes. She is something else. "Really? Okay. Well if you know so much about me, tell me why *you* think I'm wasting my time on Recon's most annoying cadet."

"I don't know, Eli."

"No, no. You obviously have an opinion, so . . ."

"You're just training me so you won't have to live with the guilt!"

Rage flares through me, burning its way up my chest. I take a step toward her, backing her up against the wall.

"So I won't have to live with the guilt?" I repeat incredulously. "I live with the guilt every fucking day!"

"I know!" she yells. "If I get killed out there, you'll feel responsible. You think it's your fault I'm here. You carry around every death like it's your personal debt to pay. But that's your shit, Eli. Nobody's making you do this."

The look on her face makes me feel sick to my stomach. She really thinks I don't care about her, and I have nobody to blame but myself.

But in two days, it won't matter. We'll have to operate as a unit, and I can't leave this festering between us.

I take a deep breath, trying to force myself to speak calmly. "You're right. Nobody's *making* me do this. I do this so I can sleep at night. And if you live long enough to train cadets yourself, you'll understand. Taking away the blame doesn't make it any less shitty when one of the kids you're responsible for is shot in the head right in front of you.

"I'm sorry about what happened the other night, but you need to get your shit together. It's not just your ass that's on the line, you know. I need you watching my back, not moping around trying to figure out a way to get back at me. That sort of thinking is going to get us both killed."

Her eyes grow wide, and a dark flush starts to spread up her neck. I know she hadn't been thinking about her role in all this — what I was risking by going out there with her.

Not like it matters. Constance is trying to get rid of me, too.

When the founders first built the compound, they created the secret espionage unit and spread those people out among all the sections. They wrote Constance a blank check to preserve the human race — even if that meant sending those with bad genes out into the Fringe to die early.

Unfortunately, the only person we know for sure is working for them is Jayden, and she knows I know the truth.

If word spread that the VocAps scores were rigged and that Constance had Sullivan Taylor killed, people would riot. Now Jayden is trying to tie up loose ends by sending me and Harper right into a hot zone of drifters.

The realization that we're both screwed takes the fight right out of Harper. I'm simultaneously relieved and disappointed.

I love it when she gets all riled up. It reminds me of that night in my room. It's not the same look she had the night she kissed me for real, but I know I'll never see that look again.

"I'm sorry," she mumbles. "I shouldn't have said that."

"It's fine."

"I've been training hard."

"I know."

"I'm not going to be dead weight out there. I swear."

I nod, fighting every urge to reach out for her. I hate yelling at Harper.

"I've just been really distracted, and I feel like things won't ever be the same."

Now there's the understatement of the century.

I sigh. "You don't have to be embarrassed about that."

"About what?"

Oh shit. She wasn't talking about the kiss.

"Uh —"

"You think I'm distracted because I . . ."

Her face bleeds into a deeper shade of crimson, and I grapple for some way to salvage the conversation.

"No, I —"

"I'm distracted because I'm going to be *dead* soon, you idiot."

"Sorry! I shouldn't have assumed that's what you were saying."

I can't backtrack quickly enough, and I briefly wonder when she stopped calling me "sir" and started calling me an idiot.

"Oh, *really?*" she yells, her voice dripping with sarcasm. "You shouldn't have assumed that my death would overshadow me feeding your enormous ego?"

"Sorry! I'm sorry, okay? That was a bad night for both of us."

I have no idea how I always manage to say the exact wrong thing, but Harper has an almost supernatural ability to make me act like a moron. Her eyes are the only part of her expression that indicates her rage has gone from mildly out of control to deadly.

I've only seen that look once — right before she punched Jacob Morsey in the face. But that realization comes too late.

Her fist flies out so fast my first instinct is to be impressed by her speed and power. That's right before I hear the slight crunch of cartilage and feel the crushing pain radiating from the bridge of my nose.

"I'm sorry it was so terrible for you!"

For a second, I just stare at her in disbelief. Then my eyes start to water from the blow, and I feel the hot drip of blood gushing down my face. Harper chucks her gloves at my head and then turns on her heel and storms out of the training center.

I cup my gloved hand over my nose and slide down the grimy wall. I definitely deserved that, and part of me was prepared for it when I threw her in the ring.

Still, I know that outburst won't be enough to dampen all the pent-up aggression Harper is dying to unleash.

Nudging my nose, I suddenly wonder if volunteering to go out on her first deployment was a mistake. Venturing out into the desert with someone who wants to kill me certainly isn't the brightest move. And with an arm like that, Harper might be more dangerous than the drifters.

two

Harper

Storming out of the training center, I don't even think about where my feet are carrying me. I shouldn't be wandering around the compound alone, but I'm in such a bitchy mood, I almost want someone to jump me so I can have the pleasure of smashing my fist into their face.

I pass several Recon people on their way to dinner, and my bedraggled appearance captures quite a few stares. I know I must look like hell. My tank top is drenched in sweat, my hair is falling out of its ponytail, and I have crazy eyes from dealing with Eli the arrogant ass all evening.

The fact that he assumes my embarrassment over kissing him is a bigger issue than my first deployment is the worst kind of ego trip.

I've spent nearly every waking moment training with Eli over the past two weeks — ever since Jayden decided to send me out to the Fringe early. Hanging out with him *has* been agonizing ever since that night, but only because I'm mad at myself for messing everything up.

Being called out on my anger feels like a huge slap in the face because he's right. I can't afford to focus on our issues.

It isn't until I'm fuming in the corner of the megalift that I notice the other tier-three workers glowering at me.

Since the board announced that half a dozen Recon operatives have gone AWOL, tier three has been a pressure cooker of hostility and distrust. Fights have been breaking out left and right among Recon, ExCon, and Waste Management workers, and the tension is palpable in the small space. I set my jaw and force myself to ignore them until the lift dings and everyone spills out toward the smell of food.

When I reach the canteen, the first thing I see is Celdon slumped in the mess line wearing a wrinkled white blazer. At first I feel relief, but then I realize he's gone on one of his benders and he's not in his right mind.

He's yelling at the line cook — a big guy with a beard he used to be friendly with — and making a huge scene.

When I get closer, I see his blond waves are matted with grease and a faint reddish stubble has taken residence on his chin. His eyes are so bloodshot and unfocused that he doesn't even notice me approaching.

Ever since Constance detained and tortured him, he's been constantly burned and aggressive with everyone in his path. But I can't recall ever seeing him this mean-spirited.

"All I'm saying is . . . where the fuck is my sweet potato?"

"I told you. We're out of sweet potatoes," says the man behind the counter, clearly trying to control his temper. He won't lash out at a tier-one worker, but it's obvious he wants to.

"I don't believe you!" snaps Celdon.

In one jerky motion, he lunges across the glass partition and grabs the larger man by the front of his blue apron. The people waiting in line are staring, and one Systems worker pushes her child behind her to shield him from Celdon's craziness.

"Why is everyone messing with me?" he slurs. "Trying to stick it to me? Huh? Is that it?"

"Celdon!" I yell, grabbing a fistful of his blazer and tugging him back.

He twists around on shaky legs, and it takes several seconds for his eyes to focus on me.

"Oh, look who it is," he huffs, wrenching his blazer out of my grip and trying to smooth the dingy lapel. "Come to babysit me?"

"Is there a problem here?" drawls a familiar voice.

I cringe. Forcing myself to take a deep breath, I turn toward the voice and lock eyes with the most unwelcome person I can imagine.

Paxton Dellwood is standing in front of me with his pelvis thrust forward and feet planted wide to show he's in charge. He has his perfect blond hair slicked back like a prep school bully, and he's swinging his electric nightstick from his belt. Ever since Paxton was placed in Control, his arrogance and entitlement have increased tenfold.

To my delight and horror, Celdon scoffs and rolls his bleary eyes. "No, there's not a problem here, Officer Asswipe."

"Well, clearly there is. You're holding up the line and causing a disturbance."

"Your fugly uniform is causing a disturbance," Celdon mutters.

I swallow back the laugh that's threatening to burst out of my mouth and tug lightly on Celdon's arm to pull him back to the mess line.

At this point, I don't even care that he's burned. I just want to extricate him from this situation before he gets us both arrested.

"Do I need to take you in?" asks Paxton, unable to keep the enthusiasm out of his voice as he fingers the handcuffs at his belt. "I think a night in the cages might get you to simmer down."

That was the wrong thing to say. I'm not sure if it's the reminder of being detained and tortured by Constance or the drug he's on, but that comment flips Celdon's aggressive switch.

Before I can stop him, he lunges at Paxton's perfectly coiffed hair, all arms and legs and rage.

"You little prick!" he yells, spraying spit in Paxton's direction.

"Celdon! Stop!" I growl, yanking him backward.

"I'll have a go at anyone who gets in my way! I don't give a fuck who you are!"

Now at least half the canteen is staring, and the Systems mom is giving us a *really* dirty look. I tighten my hold on Celdon.

He's skin and bone — and totally untrained — but he's *tall*. He manages to pull me forward as he struggles to get to Paxton, and I do the only thing I can think of to keep him from spending the rest of the night in the cages: I sweep his legs out from under him and slam him onto the floor like a rag doll.

Excited jeers fill the room, and I feel a little sick. Celdon seems too stunned to react, but Paxton gives me a cruel smile and stalks off to resume his patrol.

When I release Celdon, he glares up at me with eyes full of betrayal.

"Thanks a lot, Riles," he says in an embarrassed voice. He groans and stumbles to his feet, still tugging at his blazer as if that will fix his bedraggled appearance.

"What were you going to do?" I murmur. "Punch out Paxton Dellwood?"

"It's what you would have done before you lost all your nerve."

"Not now that he's a controller! You would have been arrested!"

"Better than being laid out and humiliated by my best friend."

The guilt starts to rise up in my stomach, overshadowing my worry and irritation. "I'm sorry. I shouldn't have done that. But you were losing it, and I didn't know what else to do."

"Whatever."

He tries to turn away from me, but I grab his arm. "Hey!" I lower my voice. "What are you *on?*"

"None of your goddamn business."

This time he turns all the way around, and I catch a glimpse of a tiny bulge in his breast pocket. Before he can stop me, my hand shoots out and snatches it out of his blazer.

The tiny clear vial feels unnaturally warm in my hand. It's half full of an electric blue powder that makes my stomach turn over. I shove it in my pocket before anyone can see and then look around anxiously.

"What the fuck?" I growl.

Celdon's usually soft, mischievous eyes go cold. "Give it back."

"No! Are you out of your fucking mind?"

He reaches toward me, but he's too slow, and I knock his hands away easily.

Normally Celdon spends his nights in Neverland getting burned on harmless uppers, but this is surge — highly addictive, very illegal, and very easy to overdose on.

"Give it back!"

"No! What is wrong with you? This stuff is dangerous."

His expression darkens. "It's fine. I'm fine. Just leave it alone, Harper."

"Fine? This is why you're acting *insane,*" I hiss.

"No, I'm acting insane because I've had the freaking rug pulled out from under me!"

"This isn't like you," I snarl, jabbing a finger into his bony chest. "You always knew when to stop, but you've gone completely off the rails."

"Who cares? It's not like they're going to let us live anyway."

"You don't see me drugging myself into a coma, though."

"Fuck you," he snaps, looking livid. "You've always been so much better, haven't you?"

I take an automatic step back and stare.

This isn't the Celdon I know. This is an ugly, terrible side of him I've never seen before. "What are you talking about?"

"It means I'm not like you. You've always been able to deal with everything. You've never hit rock bottom."

"Celdon —"

His eyes glaze over, and for a moment, it looks as though he's staring right through me. "Your bid was almost the best thing that ever happened to me."

"What?" Now he just sounds delirious.

He looks up at the ceiling, a sad smile playing on his face. "I thought maybe you would lose it . . . that maybe you'd be just as screwed up as I am. But you just keep going."

I open my mouth, but no words come out. There are no words for what I'm feeling.

His shoulders deflate, and he hangs his head and shuffles past me. "Later, Harper."

I watch him dump his tray and leave the canteen, completely oblivious to all the people still watching me over their food. I turn around to scan my ID and grab my tray, blinking furiously to keep the tears from welling up in my eyes.

As I wheel around, I spot Eli watching me from across the room. He looks serious and a little sad, but that could be my imagination.

"Hey . . ." says an uneasy voice from behind me.

I whip around, prepared to go another round with Paxton or Celdon, but it's just Lenny. She's smiling in an uncomfortable way that tells me she saw everything that just happened.

"Why don't you come sit with us?" She nods back toward a

table full of Recon cadets.

I spot Bear and Kindra and Blaze in the mix and smile gratefully. I may never have wanted anything to do with Recon, but I'm glad to have Lenny. Since Eli has been working with me one on one for the past two weeks, I've barely had a chance to talk to her outside of normal training.

"What was all that about?" she asks under her breath.

"Just a friend of mine. He's had a rough couple weeks."

"He's probably worried about you being deployed."

I don't have the energy to lie, so I just shrug and slump down between her and Bear. I wish it were as simple as that.

"Are you doing okay?" asks Bear in a low voice. He's still sporting a broken nose and a black eye from the tier-three riot, which makes him look deceptively intimidating.

I nod and shovel a spoonful of quinoa in my mouth so I don't have to talk about it. You'd think I'd just been diagnosed with a terminal illness the way everyone is looking at me. Suddenly, their first deployments seem wonderfully far away.

"You'll be all right," says Kindra dreamily. "The stars show something important in your future."

Lenny rolls her eyes, and I take another huge bite of food.

"You guys excited to party tonight?" asks Blaze, oblivious as usual to all the drama.

"What?"

"Your cherry-popping party."

I nearly choke on my food. "*What?*"

"It's tradition," says Bear with a grin. "They throw a party before cadets' first deployment. It's supposed to be a big blowout."

"That seems a little . . ."

"Sick?" Lenny offers.

I grin. After everything with Jayden and Constance, throwing a party for a mission meant to kill me does seem a little messed up. It's almost like a preemptive funeral.

"It's supposed to be good luck," says Lenny. "You're the only one going out early, so *you're* the guest of honor."

I shift a little in my seat, already uncomfortable at the prospect of all that attention.

"What are you going to wear?"

"I don't know." My brain can't even compute an appropriate wardrobe choice right now.

"You gotta look hot. It could be the last thing you ever do." Lenny quirks an eyebrow at me, not realizing her joke hit a little too close to home. It only takes her a couple seconds to pick up on her mistake and cover it with a laugh. "I'm only joking! You'll be fine. Come on. I'll help you get ready."

My stomach still feels empty, but my appetite shrinks with every sympathetic look I get. So I get up and follow her out of the canteen.

These parties sound just as stupid as Bid Day Eve parties, but I actually want to participate. Between the rigorous training and the stress of everything with Constance, nothing sounds better than getting drunk with a bunch of strangers.

* * *

Back in my compartment, I let Lenny raid my closet while I shower off the grime and sweat from training. By the time I dry off and apply a little bit of makeup, Lenny is nearly hyperventilating over some of my outfits.

I let her borrow a tube top from my closet and a pair of heels that bring her up to my height. I don't have any idea how to tame her unruly red curls, so we just let them run wild down her back.

At first, I pull out a pair of tight black pants and a top. But after a little pestering, Lenny convinces me to wear my hair down and don a slinky black dress Celdon once persuaded me to buy from the commissary. I guess there's no reason I can't look hot — even if I'll be dead soon.

Once I'm dressed, it feels like a bit much, so I throw my fake leather jacket over it and swap my heels for boots.

Following the gentle rumble of activity toward the emergency stairwell, I wonder if Eli will make an appearance. He probably thinks these parties are a waste of time, but I try to psych myself up as Lenny leads me down the tunnel.

At first I think she's taking us to Neverland, but then she makes a sharp turn down a maintenance tunnel that runs adjacent to the Underground platform.

Darkness envelops me as we push our way through, but the wave of noise seems to be getting louder. The tunnel narrows the farther we go, and I suddenly feel a little claustrophobic.

I place my hands on the walls to reassure myself that they aren't closing in. Then somebody touches my shoulder, and I jump.

I look behind me, but it's just some other Recon recruit I don't know. Judging by his hazy eyes, he's been pre-gaming down in Neverland.

Just when I can't take the confinement any longer, the tunnel opens up, and we're hit by a wave of sound.

I'm standing inside what looks like the very bowels of the compound. The whitish walls are unfinished, exposing a tangle of pipes and wires snaking up between the concrete beams. It's lit by a few strips of florescent lights suspended from chains, and someone has dragged two enormous speakers into the center of the room.

Bodies are packed in just as tightly as they are down in Neverland, but they're all fully clothed. And instead of grinding up against each other, most people are shouting conversations over the noise, laughing, and drinking.

A few people spot us, and the room erupts into cheers as they recognize me. I try to smile, but I'm sure it looks more like a grimace.

Lenny shoves a drink into my hand and pulls me toward the spotlight in the middle of the room. I hadn't noticed right away, but the crowd is congregated around a makeshift ring, where two Recon guys are going at it.

Judging by their playful grins, this isn't a real fight. One of the guys throws a right hook, and the other one lets it hit him.

Lenny lifts her arms into the air and cheers, as though she's been a Recon fan girl her whole life. The other cadets join us around the ring, and pretty soon I'm having a good time.

The fight comes to a bloody end when one guy strikes the other straight on the nose, and the crowd yells and stomps their feet.

Looking around at the messy tattooed people, I feel a pang of warmth in my stomach. They did this for me. Somehow, I can't imagine Systems coming up with anything like it.

Then a guy in front of us stumbles to the left, and I catch a familiar set of blue eyes watching me from across the room.

"Eli's here," I half yell to Lenny.

"No way!" She whips around and stares openmouthed at him. "I never thought he would come to these things."

But Eli's leaning against the back wall with a drink in his hand. His casual posture makes him look relaxed, and I'm probably the only one who notices the tightness to his gaze.

"Here she is," says a loud voice behind me. I turn just as a huge muscular guy grabs me around the arm and hauls me toward the ring.

I realize it's Miles — the guy Eli grew up with. I've only ever seen him in his Recon uniform, but tonight he's wearing a pair of baggy cargo pants and a tight black T-shirt. He steps up onto the outside edge of the ring and helps me up, too.

Clinging to the rope so I don't tumble back into the crowd, an uneasy feeling creeps over me. I sure as hell hope he doesn't expect me to fight anybody. In this dress, there's no way I could avoid flashing the whole world.

"Here's our guest of honor," Miles booms. "Harper Riley!"

The crowd's cheers are loud enough to rattle the walls, but I'm only focused on one spectator. I catch Eli's eye from the back of the room, and he nods in approval.

"The day after tomorrow, she'll go out to defend our compound . . . kick some drifter ass . . . and make us proud!"

The crowd goes crazy. As he yanks my arm into the air, a feeling of helplessness swamps me.

These people have been out there, but none of them know what I'm walking into. The drifters are mobilizing, and Recon operatives are disappearing faster than Jayden can replace them. Everyone in the room thinks they've just gone AWOL, but I know better.

A deafening wave of bass blares from the speakers around the ring, and a few people start jumping up and down to the beat.

The somber part of the evening is over. Miles releases me, and I'm met by a storm of backslaps and rough, calloused handshakes. I realize they're being nice to me because they think I'm one of them now, which makes my throat burn with guilt.

I make a beeline for the other cadets, but my path is blocked by a solid and very familiar chest. "Hey."

I follow the faint hint of a six-pack up until I meet Eli's piercing eyes. His gaze travels down to my short dress and back up again, and a slight flush sneaks up my neck when I remember Eli's weakness for legs.

"Hey," I say, feeling like an idiot. "I didn't know you came to these."

He quirks an eyebrow. "Why wouldn't I?"

I shrug more dramatically than I meant to. I'm starting to feel a faint buzz from the drink I downed, and it's making me even less coherent than usual. "It just doesn't seem like your kind of thing."

"You think I'm no fun?"

I counter his mock-offended tone with an eye roll. "I *know* you're no fun."

He lets out a quick, full-body laugh that makes me smile. Eli rarely laughs, and the sound sends a surge of warmth through my whole body.

"Well, tonight's your night. And you're my partner out there. I couldn't miss it."

The way he says those words surprises me. I can tell it means something serious to go out on the Fringe with someone, and it hits me what a huge sacrifice he's making. Trained or not, I know I'm unprepared to fend off an army of drifters — and this is no ordinary mission.

Blushing a little, I struggle to meet his gaze dead-on. "Well, thank you . . . for everything. I'm glad you're coming. And I'm sorry for . . . you know . . . punching you in the face."

"It's okay. It happens."

I open my mouth to ask how many other cadets have hit him, but somebody in the crowd staggers into me and shoves me toward Eli.

I throw out an arm to stop my fall — planting my palm on his chest. He reaches out to steady me, glaring at the rugged bearded guy. When he looks back at me, I realize we're barely a foot apart. I'm still touching his chest, and his hand is wrapped around my upper arm.

I drop my hand, but he holds on.

"You're going to be okay, Harper. We'll get through this."

That steals the last bit of air in my lungs, and suddenly the room seems to fold in on me. I'm overwhelmed by the mass of bodies pressing in around us, the loud music, the stress from the last two weeks, and the impact of Eli's words.

Just then, the crowd moves back. I hear a few yells and whistles from near the ring, and I know somebody started a real fight.

I try to take some deep breaths, but it doesn't do anything to calm my racing heart. Just when I can't take it anymore, the wall of bodies rolls back harder. People stomp on our feet to get out of the way, and I jut out my elbows to hold my ground against the wave of people.

The same guy careens into me again, and I pitch forward.

"Hey!" Eli yells, catching me before I face-plant on the floor.

He pulls me back up to my feet and reads the panic in my eyes. My old phobia has kicked in hard, and I'm struggling against the dizziness and heat creeping up my chest and face. I hate crowds, and getting jostled and pushed back in the small space is unleashing my worst fears.

A look of concern flashes across Eli's face, and he tugs me back toward the entrance.

That dark tunnel is the last place I want to go, but it's the only area with no people.

By the time Eli cuts through the thick crowd, my breaths are coming in fits and starts. Normally I would be embarrassed for him to see me like this, but I'm too preoccupied with the choking fear that's cutting off my air supply.

We reach the dark tunnel, and Eli's luminous eyes appear very close to my face.

"Are you okay?"

I nod, yanking off my jacket to cool down. "I don't like crowds."

He takes the jacket from me and drapes it over an exposed pipe. "Does this happen a lot?"

I shake my head and struggle to find enough air to answer. "Only when I'm under a lot of, uh . . . stress."

I don't see him reach out, but I feel his hands on my arms, rubbing up and down in a soothing motion. My bare skin tingles where he touches me, and I try not to read anything into this gesture.

He sighs. "I'm sorry. I should have realized how scared you'd be this week. I should have been . . . nicer to you."

"It's okay. It's not just this. I . . . I'm worried about Celdon. He's on surge now . . . acting completely psycho . . . and I don't know what to do."

"Yeah." Eli grimaces. "I saw you guys in the canteen. Nice takedown, by the way."

I raise an eyebrow.

"He'll be okay. Just focus on getting through the next week."

Those words make me want to throw up. I can't imagine being out on the Fringe for a whole day, much less an entire week.

"Do you really think we're going to make it that long?"

My question is barely audible, but I know he heard it. His hands tighten on my arms, and I suddenly wish I could see his expression.

"You can't think about that," he says gruffly.

"How do you *not?*"

He's silent for so long I think I must have made him angry. But when he finally speaks, his voice is low and scared. "I just can't."

Maybe I'm imagining it, but it seems as though he's moved closer to me. I can feel the warmth of his breath on my face and sense the rise and fall of his chest.

Purely on instinct, I tilt my chin up toward his face.

Then his hands are gone, and I hear him backing up.

He clears his throat. "Everything will be fine, Harper. Just get some sleep tonight. Tomorrow we'll have our briefing, and then . . ."

"Yeah."

"Don't drink too much."

"Got it," I say, trying to keep the disappointment out of my voice.

Typical Eli — backing away when it gets too personal. That's how it's been ever since I've known him.

After my panic attack and those stolen minutes with Eli, the last thing I want to do is return to the party. So I take my jacket and stumble back down the dark tunnel alone, truly sad for the first time that my days in Recon may be numbered.

three

Harper

The next day is a complete blur.

I wake up early for our briefing with Remy Chaplin and make my way down the deserted tunnel alone. The cadet wing is littered with evidence of last night's party, and I'm sure all my friends are still sleeping off hangovers.

When I arrive, Eli's already sitting in a chair across from the undersecretary. They're chatting easily as though they're good friends, but I can tell from Eli's stiff posture that he isn't a fan of Remy's.

He introduces me without meeting my gaze, and I sink down in front of a three-dimensional projection of the Fringe. It looks pretty harmless in its holographic bubble, but there's a nasty-looking red area that says otherwise.

Remy is cold and businesslike as he tells us about a possible drifter stronghold in a town a few miles outside the cleared zone. He speaks with authority, but I can tell he has no idea what's really going on.

There will be a gang of drifters in that town — guaranteed — but Eli and I won't be able to rely on any of the information Jayden provided. I'm sure it's all part of Constance's plan.

I just nod and let Remy's words wash over me, trying to numb myself to the anger eating away at my insides.

He gives us a simple mission: to perform drifter "cleanup" on the town and report on their technological capabilities. I try to hold back my scowl when he explains that it will require us to infiltrate their base. By his tone, you'd think he was sending us to the commissary to buy socks, but his meaning is clear: Let's see what you can discover without getting killed.

When Remy dismisses us, I take off without a word. Eli follows me into the tunnel, but I quicken my pace.

"Hey! Riley!" he calls.

I cringe but pretend not to hear. I don't want to talk to him until I have to. He probably feels awkward about what happened at the party, and I don't want to watch him withdraw all over again.

I lose him in the massive crowd headed to the canteen. But instead of following the other Recon workers to breakfast, I go right back to my compartment.

I still have training today — Eli in the morning, afternoon, and evening — but I don't plan on going to that. I don't have the energy to fight like my life depends on it with the threat of the Fringe looming over me.

Instead, I revert to my oldest coping mechanism: chipping away at one of my side projects to distract myself. It's one I haven't touched since before Bid Day — a slick little application to automatically optimize my intracompound stock portfolio. I'd counted on having a lot of money to invest back then, but now that I make a pittance in Recon, it seems more valuable than ever.

I get some music playing on my interface and down two Energelz. They'll give me a massive crash later, which is the only way I'll get to sleep tonight.

Nostalgia washes over me as I fall into old habits. I haven't had a coding marathon since the week before Bid Day, but they were a regular part of my weekend ritual in higher ed.

There's something soothing about writing code — the way it

sucks me in and leaves no room in my head for anything else. For once, my mind feels sharp and clear. There's no Eli, no Jayden, and no impending deployment.

The hours fly by. Besides a short break for lunch, I don't leave my compartment for the rest of the day.

At seventeen hundred, a quick knock on my door shatters my awesome flow, and I stagger across the room to open it.

I'd been expecting Lenny to show up to wish me luck, and my heart sinks when I see Eli standing there with a rucksack slung over his shoulder. He's wearing an expression he usually reserves for when he's pissed at me. But as he takes in my outfit — tank top, sweats, messy ponytail — I catch a flicker of amusement in his eyes.

"You blew off training today."

"Sorry," I say, stepping aside so he can come in. He shouldn't be hanging around outside my compartment — even if he's only here to admonish me for skipping. Jayden already thinks there's something going on between us, and I don't need any more drama in my life.

Eli looks taken aback by my apology and follows me inside, towering over my small bed in the cramped space.

"How are you feeling?" he asks in a low voice.

That's a stupid question.

"Okay."

He throws me a skeptical look and makes his way over to my computer, taking in the line of empty Energelz with a disapproving look.

"You working on something?" he asks.

"Yeah," I say, a little more defensively than I meant to. "It's an app."

A look of confusion darts across Eli's face, and I feel a little bashful as he bends down to examine the lines of code marching across the monitor.

"It's for *me*, okay?"

He lifts an eyebrow and lets out a long stream of air. "You are too talented to be here, Harper."

I tilt my head to look at him, but I'm too worn out for this weird exchange. "Why are you here?"

"I thought I'd help you pack."

I give him a blank stare. This is so unlike him.

"Nobody ever helped me," he says, cracking a grin. "I always either packed so much that it weighed me down or not enough and ended up hungry the last two days."

He unzips the bag and starts unloading supplies: dehydrated ration packets, a big bag of water with a tube for drinking, new filters for the masks to trap radioactive particles, and ammunition. He even has a tiny first aid kit, a pocketknife, a solar charging station for my interface, and a device I don't recognize.

"What's this?" I ask. The device is made of heavy-duty plastic and has a little screen.

"Your dosimeter. It measures your exposure to ionizing radiation. You'll wear it when we go out."

I nod and set it back on the bed, trying to ignore the pang of dread in my stomach.

"You shouldn't count on the checkpoints being fully stocked," he says, grabbing the rucksack hanging in the back of my closet. "You won't be able to carry enough water to last more than a day or two, but it's good to bring as much food as you can."

When he emerges from the flurry of clothes clutching one of my uniforms, his eyes linger on the flimsy black dress I wore to the party. He swallows once, and I watch in astonishment as he rolls the uniform into a tight cylinder and arranges the supplies in my rucksack.

"There," he says. "That should hold you for a week."

"You only pack one uniform?"

"Trust me. You won't want the extra weight. Better to be dirty and sweaty than too slow."

Too slow. I cringe at the implication of those words. "What about the hazmat suit they gave me?"

He shakes his head. "No point bringing that. It's way too hot out there to wear it for more than an hour or two. And it doesn't block the really damaging radiation anyway. Just wear your mask so you aren't breathing in any radioactive particles."

Sinking down on the bed, the full weight of tomorrow finally hits me. Eli makes a jerky motion, as though he wants to sit down next to me but thinks better of it. The awkward weight of what we're about to do hangs between us, and he clears his throat and shoves his hands into his pockets. "Get some sleep, okay? And drink plenty of water. We need you hydrated."

I nod mutely, wondering when my hydration became a joint concern.

He grabs his rucksack and heads for the door but stops short, looking conflicted. "Harper?"

"Yeah?" My voice sounds too high.

"You're gonna be okay." He glances over his shoulder, his eyes burning into mine. "I'm not going to let anything happen to you."

I open my mouth to say something, but he clears his throat and leaves before I can get the words out. When the door closes behind him, there's a light warmth in my chest that's fighting against my mounting panic.

I don't recall changing clothes or setting an alarm on my interface. When I fall back on my bed, the heaviness of fatigue overtakes me, and I quickly succumb to a deathlike sleep.

* * *

I wake up before the morning train comes barreling through the tunnel outside my window. It's oh-four hundred — two hours before my deployment.

I run the shower cycle on repeat for several minutes, savoring the feeling of clean, hot water pelting my body for the last time. I change into my fatigues and pull my hair into a tight ponytail, taking extra care with the holster I've never used before. There's a place for ammunition, my handgun, the dosimeter, and other accessories Eli never told me about.

Despite all our extra training, I feel incredibly unprepared for what I'm about to do. They're dressing me up to die.

I down as much water as I can stomach and head up to the canteen with my rucksack over my shoulder. The tunnels are completely deserted, and there are only a handful of guys manning the canteen at this hour.

Since it's my deployment day, I get a free breakfast on the compound. It's nothing like typical Recon fare. The portions are twice the size I usually get, and there's a perfect hardboiled egg resting next to my oatmeal. I'm sure they think it's nice to give us a taste of the finer things in life before we head out to the Fringe, but it just seems cruel somehow.

After I finish, I slowly make my way down the tunnel toward the double set of doors everyone usually avoids. I've never even been this far down the wing, but I know I'm in the right place when I see a familiar silhouette against the frosted-glass door.

Eli has his back to me as he stares out the window. Hearing me approach, he turns, and I see him swallow once to keep his expression neutral.

It doesn't work. I can read the fear and dread in those expressive blue eyes and the hard set of his jaw.

"Did you eat breakfast?" I ask.

"I had something in my compartment."

I nod, cringing inwardly at the awkward silence that falls between us. There's nothing to say. There are no words for how I'm feeling.

Eli's eyes widen as though he just remembered something and reaches around to pull an extra rifle off his shoulder. "This is for you," he says. "I cleaned it last night. It's the one you used on the sim course."

"Oh," I say, slightly taken aback. "Thanks."

It seems weird to say "thanks" for a gun, but he shrugs and smiles anyway.

Down the tunnel, quick footsteps echo off the polished floor.

I turn. Remy Chaplin is striding toward us in his imposing tan suit. I've never seen a man achieve such a close shave. His dark skin is so smooth that it gleams, and his jacket and pants are pressed to perfection.

Jayden is skulking along behind him. Even at oh-six hundred, she looks annoyingly put together. Her hair is swept back in a stylish bun, and she's wearing a crisp high-collar shirt under her officer's uniform. I wonder if she sleeps at all or if she's just a robot that Constance powers down at night to conserve energy.

Her sharp eyes find mine, and she sneers. She *loves* having this power over us.

Remy is completely oblivious to the silent power struggle going on between me and Jayden, but I feel Eli stiffen beside me.

"Good morning, Lieutenant . . . Cadet Riley."

"Good morning," we echo.

"We've already gone over your objectives for the mission. Do you have everything you need?"

"Yes, sir," says Eli.

"Good. Let's get on with it, then," says Remy, clapping his hands together and reading off his interface. "Cadet Riley, are you exiting the compound of your own volition, fully aware of the risks of the Fringe?"

Eli warned me about this part — the part where I basically give the board permission to send me out to die.

"I am," I say in a hollow voice.

"And do you understand that you are a free agent on the Fringe and that the compound bears no responsibility for any harm that may come to you?"

"I do."

"And do you understand that you are bound by law to reveal whatever you may find wholly and truthfully to your commanding officers — but never discuss your findings with any compound civilians?"

"I do."

"Thank you."

He turns to Eli, who rattles off the whole spiel from memory.

The sick feeling in my stomach intensifies, and I close my eyes to rein in the sudden nausea.

"Good luck," says Remy. "Strength as one is strength for all."

After we salute, I glance up at Eli's face. The easy smile he had for me just moments ago is gone, and I'm shocked by the severe expression that's replaced it. It's not anger I'm detecting; it's fear.

Remy cuts between us and punches a nine-digit code into the keypad behind me. There's a beep and a slight hiss, and the doors retract to reveal a small entryway with a low ceiling. There are sliding doors on either side leading to the postexposure cham-

Exposure

bers and a huge set of doors right in front of us leading out into the Fringe.

A hunched ExCon man in a hazmat suit is already waiting for us. This is all happening too fast.

Eli steps into the chamber and meets my gaze. I follow his lead and have just enough time to send a withering glare in Jayden's direction before the doors beep again and shut behind us.

A red laser passes through the door as it locks, but I can still see the blurred outlines of the commander and undersecretary through the frosted glass.

I undo the heavy black mask from the clip on my rucksack and pull it down over my face. Eli dons his mask, too, which makes him look like an alien.

"Brace yourselves," says the ExCon man. He lifts his bushy eyebrows at Eli, silently daring him with a contemptuous stare. But I'm in no mood for his shit.

"Let's just get on with it," I snap, my own voice playing back to me through the mic on my mask.

Eli glances in my direction, his expression unreadable.

The man glares daggers at me before pulling a flimsy paper mask over his mouth and stabbing the keypad with a gnarled finger. I wonder if his only job now is to guard the entrance to the compound. He can't be older than forty, but he looks like hell after a lifetime of body-deteriorating service on the Fringe.

As soon as the doors begin to retract, I feel a rush of heat. A gust of warm air blows into the chamber, stirring my hair and making me gasp. I've never felt wind before — at least not that I can remember.

"Ready?" asks Eli, just loud enough for me to hear over my pounding heart.

I don't answer him, but somehow my feet start carrying me

forward.

We step outside, and the Fringe unfolds in front of me in all its terrifying glory.

Barren desert stretches in every direction as far as I can see. The spectrum of color is amazing. From my view inside the compound, I was always struck by how monochromatic the Fringe seemed: burnt orange or brown, depending on the time of day.

Now it feels as though I'm seeing the desert for the very first time. It's a vibrant mix of fiery orange, shell pink, deep green, and maroon. The ground is cracked in places, as though the earth is pulling itself apart, and the orangish dirt is punctuated by scrubby little bushes.

I look up and instantly wish I hadn't. The pale blue sky is dizzying. I've spent plenty of time staring at the sky from the compound, but I've never stood directly beneath it, waiting for the atmosphere to swallow me whole.

Then the heat hits. The warmth that felt almost pleasant in the chamber is suddenly overwhelming. The sun is beating down on my face with terrifying intensity, and when I suck in a breath of dry air, it feels thin and harsh in my lungs. Beads of sweat spring up all over my forehead.

"Okay?" Eli asks.

I realize he's been staring at me this entire time. I must look like an idiot. To him, it's just another day. I'm sure his lungs are working just fine.

I force a shaky breath. "Yeah."

"We should get moving," he says in a low, gentle voice. "We have a lot of ground to cover, and it's going to get hotter."

I can't imagine how that's possible. I spent my whole life in air-conditioned comfort. I have no experience battling the elements.

"Come on."

Forcing my feet to move, I follow Eli away from the compound. I try to get my bearings, but everything I learned in training seems to have evaporated from my mind. Then I glance behind me and trip over my own feet. The compound looks enormous. Aside from pictures and drawings in my compound history textbooks, I've never really seen what it looks like from the outside. Now that I have, I'm amazed that such a structure could be manmade.

With the sunlight reflecting off thousands of ceiling-to-floor windows, it looks like a tall silvery box planted right in the middle of hell.

It's strange to think about all the people working inside to keep the place functioning. They don't know that they only do what they do because Constance made it that way. Hardly any of them can comprehend what lies beyond the thick layer of glass that separates them from the drifters.

The Fringe is quiet except for the steady shuffle of our feet and the whistle of the wind. I wish Eli would say something. The silence only heightens my paranoia.

The farther we walk, the hotter I get. I start to unsnap my long-sleeve overshirt, but Eli glances over his shoulder and shakes his head.

"Keep that on as long as you can. Your skin isn't used to the sun. You're going to burn."

"I use the UV rooms all the time."

"It's not the same. Those are designed to give you a short, healthy dose of ultraviolet light." He reaches into his belt and withdraws a small tube. "Put this on your face. Otherwise, you're going to be red and crispy tonight."

His choice of words is a little alarming — particularly when the sun feels as though it could literally cook me alive. I take the tube and rub some of the thick white stuff on my exposed skin. When I hand it back to Eli, his hard look cracks, and he lets out a full-body laugh. The sound coming through his mic is jarring after the tense silence, and I freeze when he turns to face me.

"Not like that."

Before I can react, he reaches out with both hands and cups my face in his rough palms. The skin-to-skin contact is shocking.

His eyes crinkle in a slight smile as he rubs my cheeks with the pads of his thumbs, blending in the white stuff. It's such a dramatic change from serious, survivalist Eli that all I can do is stare as he touches my face.

When he's finished, he rolls his eyes, but I can tell he's still smiling. He turns back around and continues in the direction we were walking, and I can't stop staring.

What the hell was that all about? Eli hasn't been subtle about distancing himself from me — even in training. I guess it takes a panic attack or the threat of sunburn for him to let himself act like a human being.

I abruptly push the thoughts of Eli out of my head. With miles of desert ahead of us and an army of drifters waiting, Eli should be the last thing I'm thinking about.

We walk for another ten minutes, and then Eli stops and flips on his interface to scan the terrain map. Standard protocol kicks in from training, and I pull up the image on my own interface.

The map overtakes my field of vision, showing a simplified picture of the landscape around us. The image ripples like a sheet as my interface superimposes it over the actual desert.

There are dozens of pulsating red dots on the ground around us. To my right, there's a blinking green dot hovering over Eli's head like a halo.

We've reached the perimeter.

"Remember, the red things are land mines," says Eli.

Even if I forgot everything else from training, there's no way I could forget that detail.

"Stay close."

I wait for him to move, but he seems to be steeling himself for something.

"Harper, once we pass through here, all bets are off. I don't know what's waiting for us."

My heart speeds up, and I feel my palms start to sweat. "I know."

"Are you ready?"

I nod and fall into step right beside him.

It's reassuring to be able to see the land mines myself, but Eli still watches me as we chart a careful course around the blinking red dots. When we reach two mines that are clustered together, Eli draws an arm around my shoulders and guides me around them.

With every passing second, my breathing becomes heavier and more labored. Eli still hasn't released me, and part of me wonders if he's as scared as I am.

It's strange. I didn't think Eli was afraid of *anything*, but his posture changes as soon as we clear the mines.

Instead of walking with his back ramrod straight as he usually does, he's fallen into his fighting stance. His shoulders are hunched — every muscle poised for action — and his head is moving on a swivel.

If a drifter materialized out of thin air and charged toward us, I have no doubts that Eli would pounce and break his neck with his bare hands.

"Stay alert," he murmurs.

As if I could be anything else. My heart is hammering in my chest, and I keep wiping my sweaty palms on my pants to maintain a strong grip on my gun.

Eli's used to this, and I envy the self-assurance that years of experience have given him. No amount of training could have prepared me for the paralyzing fear, the overwhelming size of the Fringe, or the intense heat.

Suddenly, my interface makes a sad beeping sound, and I almost have a heart attack.

"What the —"

"Comms are down," mutters Eli. "It always happens right about here. We're out of range."

"Oh. Right."

"On the plus side, Constance can't spy on us anymore."

I don't find that thought as reassuring as Eli does. I hate the idea of not being able to message anyone, but really, we're on our own out here no matter what.

I can still make out the compound on the horizon, but it looks tiny. To anyone watching from the windows, we would have disappeared into thin air.

Eli clicks his interface once and glances down at me. "Take a drink. You don't want to get dehydrated."

I reach behind me for the hose connected to my water pack, and as soon as I slurp down a few gulps, I realize how thirsty I am.

After a few seconds, Eli nudges me. "Take it easy. That's going to have to last until tomorrow."

I stop and focus on the horizon again.

In the few seconds I've been preoccupied, a fuzzy shape has materialized in the distance.

"Is that a town?"

Eli's jaw goes rigid. "Yep. Make sure you're locked and loaded. I don't know what we're going to find here."

A jolt of fear shoots down my spine, but I try to mentally prepare myself.

I've had training, I think. *I know what to do.*

But my arms are stiff and tense, and my legs feel like jelly. I force myself to mimic Eli's steady breathing to coax my body out of panic mode.

In and out. In and out.

I'm so focused on the town that I barely notice the rock formation looming on our left. It's just part of the landscape — a crack in the otherwise flawless line where the sky meets the earth.

But then, without warning, a gunshot ruptures the silence.

four

Eli

My body reacts to the gunshots before my brain has time to process what's happening.

Adrenaline spills into my bloodstream. My senses sharpen, and my heart kicks into overdrive.

I grab Harper around the shoulders and yank her into a crouch. Her face is white and terrified behind her mask, eyes searching for the source of the gunshots.

"Run!" I croak.

She runs. Her movements are clumsy from shock and terror, so I reach out and grab hold of her arm. My legs burn as I charge toward the town, pulling Harper with me.

We're still a few hundred yards away from the nearest building, but it's our only chance. I can't make out the sniper taking cover behind the rock formation. And since he got the jump on us, there's no way I can take him out before he hits us. He had the advantage of surprise, which is everything on the Fringe.

I push harder. I'm running at a full-out sprint, and miraculously, Harper is keeping up. I'm sure it has something to do with the fact that I'm practically ripping her arm out of its socket, but she's fast.

Another gunshot shatters my eardrums, but whoever is shooting is no marksman.

We're getting closer to the town. I can make out the faded signs and the lumpy shapes of abandoned cars.

Behind me, Harper staggers, and the arm I'm pulling on goes slack.

I panic. *Is she hit?*

She's still moving — half running, half falling. I don't see blood. She must have tripped, but there's no time to feel relief.

In one quick motion, I yank her upright, and we're moving again.

Another shooter has joined in the game, and I hear a bullet whizz past my head. He knows what he's doing.

I consider returning fire, but I know it won't do any good. I still can't see them through the glare, but they have a clear view of us.

So close. I can read the sign for Dave's Diner in peeling red letters: *Steak. Pizza. Hamburgers.*

I stumble on a protruding rock, and my dosimeter flies off my belt. It skids along the ground in front of us, and then the ground breaks in two.

The explosion throws me backward, and pain shoots up my spine as the force of the blow slams me into the ground.

Suddenly everything is upside down. My ears are ringing. My entire body is burning in pain, but all my limbs are still intact.

I roll over onto my side, looking around desperately, but I can't see anything through the cloud of dust. It stings my eyes, so I clamp them shut and start feeling around.

"Harper!" I yell.

Dust coats my throat, and I choke on her name again.

Nothing.

"Harper!"

Where is she? She can't be dead. She can't be —

Then I hear a cough, and she says something I can't quite make out. Gratitude rushes through me at the sound of her hoarse voice.

Fumbling around in the dirt beside me, I find her hand. She squeezes back, and I stagger to my feet and pull her up.

She's choking on a cough, but if she's standing, it must mean she still has two legs.

Now that I'm upright, I realize how dizzy and sick I feel. My heart is pounding, and every cell in my body is thrumming with nervous energy.

As the ground in front of me moves in and out of focus, my eyes fall on a broken piece of plastic. It's half-obscured by dirt, but I recognize it instantly as a piece of a compound land mine. My dosimeter must have triggered it when it hit the ground.

If it hadn't — if I'd triggered it instead — I would have gotten my legs blown off.

I click my interface once, but it shows no buried land mines in the area. The drifters must have figured out how to keep us from tracking them.

As the dust clears, I pull Harper toward the buildings. There's an overgrowth of brush along the road, and it snags at my ankles and almost makes me lose my footing.

I trip up the curb and yank Harper behind the first building I see, flattening my body against the rough brick as I collect my breath.

The shots have stopped, but it won't be long before the drifters realize their mine didn't finish us off. I give myself two seconds to breathe and then raise my rifle and take a quick scan of our surroundings.

The buildings are scattered at random intervals out here, growing into denser clusters of restaurants and businesses near the center of town. A bent street sign sticking out of the concrete reads "Shell Street," but that doesn't help me any.

I'd bet money that there are drifters hiding out here, but they're waiting for us to show ourselves first.

Harper's breath is coming in sharp gasps, but she's still alert enough to raise her rifle and cover me as I check around the corner.

Seeing no movement, I glance over and motion for her to follow. Her eyes are wide with shock, but she's holding it together. We make our way from one building to another, stopping to clear every street corner.

In its day, this was probably the bad part of town. We pass a dilapidated Quik Loans place, a crummy mini mart, and a pawn shop that's been completely looted.

Most of the windows facing the road are broken, and every shadow of a cash register or shelf looks like a drifter. I don't like the idea of taking cover on the ground level, so I head for a two-story motel down the street.

The building looks deserted. The curtains are drawn over the grimy windows, and the faded teal doors give the place a tacky retro look. I shoot up to the rickety walkway and kick down the door closest to the stairs.

I clear the room and pull Harper inside, securing the chain lock and the dead bolt.

That's when the weight of everything hits me: We were almost killed, and it was all my fault.

I was so focused on prepping Harper to enter the town that I completely ignored the obvious threat. Of course the drifters would have lookouts stationed between the perimeter and the town. They know where we come from, and they know what we do to drifters who gather near settlements.

Still panting, I turn my attention to Harper. She's looking around the outdated motel room helplessly, as though she has no idea whether to feel relieved or scared shitless. I've never seen her so out of her element.

"You okay?" I ask, undoing her mask.

Stupid question. She just got shot at. Of course she isn't okay.

But Harper gives a shaky nod. She moves to sit down on the dusty bed, but I steer her away from the window and pull her down onto the floor against the wall. She's breathing rapidly and looks too pale.

Sitting down beside her, I pull the rucksack off her shoulder and check her over for injuries. Apart from a few cuts from flying debris, she's otherwise unharmed — well, except for the obvious trauma. I can tell she's in shock because she still hasn't said a word.

"It's okay," I say. "Breathe."

Her wild eyes dart from the faded desert print hanging on the opposite wall to the gaudy teal-and-burgundy bedspread. She's trying to ground herself by latching on to something physical, so I pull off my mask and meet her gaze.

As soon as she transitions from panic mode to awareness, she snaps.

Harper's eyes crinkle closed, and when her head dips forward, something inside me shatters. I put an arm around her and draw her tightly against my side. She folds in on herself, trying to hide her silent tears, but I can feel the warm wetness against my neck.

"Hey . . . hey. It's okay," I whisper. "You're okay. We made it."

I don't know what I'm saying. Words are spilling out of my mouth, completely bypassing my brain. She's not the first cadet to start crying after a traumatic experience like that, but I don't see just another scared cadet. All I see is Harper.

For once, she doesn't try to act tough or push me away. If anything, the quaking in her body intensifies as she cries, and she lets herself fall into me. My chest aches, and I pull her closer even though I shouldn't.

I talk without thinking, spewing out nonsense. I think I say something about the land mine and tell her about my first deployment, but I'm not even listening to myself. It doesn't matter what I say. She just needs a second to recover.

Once she calms down, I take the opportunity to check my own body for injuries. I have a few cuts like Harper's, but there's no shrapnel embedded anywhere, and all my limbs still work.

Running a hand through my dusty hair, I take a deep breath and try to gather my thoughts. We can't stay here forever. The drifters will know they didn't manage to finish us off, and they'll come looking for us. I don't know this town well, which puts us at a serious disadvantage.

I click my interface and pull up the map Remy showed us back at the compound. It's displaying a large concentration of drifters in this area, but he never warned us that there would be drifters stationed *outside* the town. I should have assumed there would be, but I was not on my A-game today.

Suddenly, I remember we had a mission. We were supposed to clear the area and check out the drifters' technology setup. And after their little trick with *our* land mines, even I'm curious about their capabilities.

"Are you okay?" I ask again.

"Yeah. I'm fine," she says, pulling away from me and dabbing her eyes with the back of her hand. "What's the plan?"

I stare at her for a moment, amazed at how quickly she's managed to pull herself together. "Uh . . . we need to clear the area. But take your time. They don't know we're here yet."

She fixes her ponytail with shaky hands and meets my gaze. "I'm all right."

Exposure

"Are you sure? Because you *were* shot at and blown up —"

"I said I'm *fine*, Eli," she snaps. Her eyes have narrowed to match her scowl, and I see that familiar Harper toughness resurfacing.

"Okay."

Chastised by my calm tone, she grimaces. "I'm sorry. I didn't mean . . . Thank you for getting me out of there. I'm okay. That was just —"

She breaks off. *Horrifying. Traumatic. Fucking crazy. Take your pick.*

Harper looks as though she might cry again, so I nod. "You're handling this really well."

Her mouth tightens, but she pulls on a look I know means she's all business again. "So how are we going to do this?"

"How would *you* do this?" I ask. My instructor impulse is so automatic I don't even think about it, and it's strangely comforting when Harper rolls her eyes.

"We need to maintain the element of surprise — take them out one by one without raising the alarm. That's our only chance."

"Good. That's exactly what we're going to do." I beam the map to her interface and trace a route in the air with my finger so the line appears on her copy. "I say we take the road behind this place and work our way around the perimeter. They'll be concentrated toward the center of town, but we should take out their lookouts first."

I pull out my handgun and the silencer. Harper's eyes grow wide, and I know she's contemplating the fact that she may actually have to kill someone today.

That isn't something I've thought about since I was a teenager, but seeing the weight of it in her eyes makes me think about it now. I don't want her to see this side of me, but it's inevitable.

And the more I can speed this up, the better chance we'll have of getting out of this town alive.

Dragging in some air, she retrieves her own handgun. I peer out of the window, but there's no sign of movement.

We don our masks again, and I open the door and lead us out onto the walkway. The boards creak underfoot, loud enough to attract the attention of anyone lurking nearby, but we don't encounter a single living soul. The crumbling parking lot is completely deserted, and the only movement is the shredded state flag flapping in the breeze.

I signal Harper to keep going, and we press our backs against the building. This town is slightly larger than the ones I'm usually assigned to patrol but just as run-down.

The cluster of fast-food restaurants near the highway means it was probably some sort of hub before Death Storm. Now, the roads have been overtaken by brittle-looking tufts of weeds, and most of the signs are broken and faded from the sun.

As we approach one of the restaurants, the sinister dancing cheeseburger mascots follow us with their dead eyes.

Then I catch a flash of movement around the corner. I make eye contact with Harper and jerk my head toward the gaudy red-and-white brick construction.

With Harper covering me from behind, I sneak in for a better view. That's when I see him.

There's a lookout stationed on the corner, wearing faded jeans and a cutoff black T-shirt. He isn't much older than me, but his skin is dark brown and leathery from spending too much time in the sun. Every inch of him is covered in dirt and grime, and he's been stuck here so long that he's grown bored and oblivious to his surroundings.

I move with such stealth that he never sees my chokehold

coming. He only has a second to react to the blind panic before I plant the silencer against his temple and pull the trigger.

It happens in an instant, but the darkness that settles over me will last forever.

His dead weight crumples in my arms and feels impossibly heavy. I lower him to the ground, trying not to look at his face.

I glance at Harper. She's staring at me as though she's having an out-of-body experience.

I'll never forget that look. I feel the weight of every kill I've ever made in her astonished gaze: the guilt, the horror, the emptiness that sucks you dry. It's the worst feeling in the world.

She can't believe what a monster I am, and she's terrified she may have to become one, too.

I turn away as quickly as I can and lead us around the outskirts of town.

I don't look back, and I don't look at Harper. I can't bear to see that expression again.

I try not to think about the man on the corner. I'll replay that moment over and over back at the compound, but I can't afford to dwell on it now.

It takes us about thirty minutes to reach the opposite end of town. We don't encounter another living soul the entire time. I'm starting to wonder if they've all gathered elsewhere to regroup.

Then I catch a flash of movement outside an abandoned body shop. There's a man pacing around the open garage, but he hasn't spotted us yet.

I grab Harper's arm and jerk my head in his direction. Her eyes grow wide, and she follows me along the side of the road to a filling station across from the shop.

We duck behind a dusty gas pump, and I zoom in with my interface to see how many men we're dealing with.

I only see one guy pacing under the "Qual y Cust ms" sign and another moving just inside the garage, but that doesn't mean there aren't more. Both men are older than the first guy I took down, but they're on high alert.

I could take them both out myself, but if there are more I don't see, we'll be screwed. I don't want to make Harper a killer on her first deployment, but I might not have a choice.

Fighting the wave of despair washing over me, I steel myself for the question I should never have to ask her.

"Do you think you can . . .?"

"Yes." She doesn't look at me, but her deadpan tone tells me she understands what she's agreeing to.

"All right. I'll go in from the front and take out the first guy. That will give you the element of surprise to go around back and take out the second. Got it?"

She nods, silent as she processes the plan.

"Shoot the drifter, not me. If there are more guys inside, get down before they start shooting. I'll take out as many as I can. And if we're seriously outnumbered, you run."

"What about you?" There's an accusatory look in her eyes that tells me she knows I don't plan on retreating.

"Don't worry about me." I summon up my most command-ing tone. "Retreat. That's an order."

She looks away without agreeing, but I just ignore her because we don't have time to get into an argument. The man inside the garage just called the other guy over, and they're both preoccu-pied. It's now or never.

"Let's go."

We shoot across the street, and Harper tails me to a rusted-out pickup truck near the edge of the parking lot. I crouch down just under the busted window and get eyes on my target.

"They're still inside," I whisper. "Go."

I don't want to put her at risk, but this plan gives us the best chance at a clean escape from this town. No drifters, no surprises. Plus, Harper is smart and clearheaded under pressure. If any cadet could handle this, it's her.

I watch as she disappears around the corner of the body shop, praying she'll stay out of sight until I have a chance to finish this guy.

I take the silencer off my gun and count to three. I need to wait until Harper lines up her shot so that when I shoot the first drifter, her target will be distracted enough to give her an opening.

Squinting to the far corner of the garage, I see a sliver of Harper's face and the barrel of her gun.

This is it. There's no room for screwups — no time to second-guess myself.

In one fluid motion, I fly out from behind the truck and dash across the parking lot. I stop in front of the garage and shoot the first man I see.

He collapses onto the ground, and I scan the rest of the garage for threats.

The second drifter wheels around at the sound of my gun. There's another shot, but he doesn't go down.

Harper missed. We hadn't planned for that.

I catch her look of horror, and she steps out from her hiding place to line up a better shot.

What happens next happens so fast I don't have time to react.

A third drifter steps around the corner where Harper was just hiding. He grabs her by the throat and sends her gun clattering to the ground.

I move closer to get a clean shot at him, but by the time I get into position, he's got her in a tight bear hug with the barrel of his gun pressed against her temple.

"Drop it!" he yells in a deep, guttural voice.

I freeze. I can't shoot him without putting Harper in jeopardy. This isn't what we planned for. Harper getting killed wasn't even an option.

The blood is pounding in my ears as I try to formulate a plan. It's the loudest sound I've ever heard.

The drifter that Harper shot and missed bends to retrieve her gun and points it straight at my chest. It doesn't matter, though. The only gun I'm worried about is the one pressed against Harper's head.

"Drop it, or she dies!" yells the drifter holding her. He's wearing a filthy white shirt and cutoffs, but with a gun in his hand, he looks capable enough.

Harper's eyes are fixed on me, steadfast and fearless. She isn't struggling. She isn't panicked. Even with a gun pressed against her temple and a gun pointed at me, she still believes I can somehow get us out of this.

"Let us go, and we'll turn around and leave your town right now," I say, fighting to keep my voice steady.

"Yeah, right. Leave you to kill the rest of us on your way out?" says the drifter closest to me. He raises the gun a fraction of an inch. "I don't think so."

"We won't. You can take us to the border."

"You think we haven't run into your people before?" he asks. "You're like rats. There's an endless supply where you came from."

"I'll tell them to leave this town alone."

"Nice try. But if you were a general, you wouldn't be here, would you?"

"This isn't a negotiation," says the man with the gun on Harper. "Drop it. Now."

"What are you going to do with us?"

"Now!" he shouts, pushing the gun into Harper's head. She lets out a tiny gasp, and fear flashes in her eyes.

"Okay!" I shout. I don't need this guy getting trigger-happy so close to Harper.

"Nice and easy now," says the man closest to me.

Slowly, I bend at the knees and lower myself into a crouch. I can see the man next to Harper watching me closely. This is our only chance.

Just as I predicted, his hand follows his gaze. He drops the gun ever so slightly and moves away from her by about an inch.

It's a long shot, but there's no other way out of this. I make eye contact with Harper, begging her to be ready to fight.

If this doesn't work, she's going to die. But if I don't try *something*, she's as good as dead anyway.

Moving with speed I never knew I had, I jerk my arm back up and shoot the man in front of me.

The sound nearly shatters my eardrums, and a horrible, gripping emptiness sucks the air out of my lungs.

He falls to the ground, his eyes glassy and lifeless, but there's no time to dwell on that.

I jerk my gaze up, dread heavy in my gut, and see Harper struggling with her captor. I was too preoccupied to notice how she got from point A to point B, but she has her drifter's wrist twisted painfully at his side as she tries to wrestle his gun away.

I aim at the drifter, but they're moving too much for me to get a clear shot.

When the man shifts his weight and pulls Harper to the ground, my heart feels as though it might beat right out of my chest.

His elbow shoots out, connecting with Harper's sternum. She whimpers but doesn't let go. If anything, she becomes more ferocious.

I stand paralyzed with indecision. I don't know if I should dive in to help or stand ready to shoot.

I never have time to decide. It's over in less than two seconds.

Somehow, Harper wrestles the drifter's gun away and pulls the trigger.

The sound reverberates through the garage, and a thick cloud of tension settles over everything.

When the ringing in my ears subsides, I expect silence, but the drifter is still alive. He's gasping and choking like a drowning man begging for air, struggling body and soul to stay alive.

Harper must have missed his heart, and now he's bleeding out slowly.

I've never been able to make someone suffer like that. I've never had the stomach for it.

I aim my gun to finish him for her, but Harper pulls the trigger again and sends him down to the dark depths for good.

More than anything, that's the thing I wish I could unsee. Watching Harper take her first life is the only thing that even comes close to the agony of my first kill.

The hand holding the gun drops to her side, and she looks up at me with a frantic gleam in her eyes.

"It's okay," I croak, lowering my gun and moving toward her.

I recognize that expression. All the adrenalin coursing through her veins is overwhelming. The first life-or-death fight I ever engaged in, it felt as though I'd taken speed. My heart was racing, I couldn't catch my breath, and my muscles were burning with enough energy to flip a car.

Harper's enormous eyes go to the drifter's face, as though she needs to reassure herself that he's dead.

"Don't look at him," I order.

But she can't tear her eyes away.

"We need to move," I say. "Somebody will have heard that. They'll send backup."

Harper doesn't give any sign that she understood. She's still staring at the man, simultaneously relieved and horrified by what she's done.

I want to say something to comfort her — something to erase the last ten minutes — but there's nothing I can say. Even if she never saw the drifter's face, he'd come to her in her sleep.

It's over for her. She can never come back from this. She'll always know what it's like to watch a bullet pull the life from another human being.

You never forget your first kill.

five

Harper

As Eli leads me away, a single thought is running through my head on repeat.

I killed someone. I took a life. Someone is dead because of me.

I thought I would feel a horrible, debilitating guilt the first time I killed a drifter, but I just feel sick and numb all over.

If I hadn't shot that man, he would have killed me. But we ambushed them.

I could have walked away, but I didn't.

The image of his empty expression is seared into the back of my eyelids. He was a person — just trying to survive like me — and I ended his existence.

It's eerily quiet as we complete our circuit around the edge of town. We don't encounter any more drifters, but Eli is still tense and alert. His shoulders are stiff, and I can see the rigid lines of his back through his shirt where every muscle is clenched. He's still coming down from the fight.

I'm not sure how he maintains that intensity. As soon as we killed the drifters, the adrenalin burned through my body, leaving me completely drained. I'm not sure I could defend myself again if I had to.

Eli checks every building as we make our way toward the center of town. The shops and restaurants are more concentrated here, which makes it a painfully slow process.

I try to help by covering him, but my body is running on

autopilot. My brain can't seem to muster up the instinct to care whether I get out of here alive. If a drifter jumped out and shot me point blank, I would certainly deserve it.

The longer we walk, the louder the silence becomes. That's all it is out here: death and silence and emptiness.

In the compound, I never felt truly alone. There was always someone breathing on the other side of the wall or talking down the tunnel. Here, we're on our own.

Endless miles of desert stretch in every direction, reclaiming the roads and buildings. Dust obscures the pavement, and little tufts of desert grass line the parking lots and snake their way under car tires.

I want to lie down on the ground and let the dirt suffocate me slowly so I won't have to feel anything ever again.

Eli leads us into a dilapidated little building that's connected to several other businesses. I can't tell what type of store it used to be. The dusty shelves are completely empty, and the cash register is smashed into a million pieces.

He gives me a concerned look I've only seen a handful of times and pulls me down behind the counter. Watching me carefully, he tugs my rucksack off my shoulder, and I go limp as he checks me for injuries and rummages in my pack for an energy bar.

"You need to eat and rehydrate," he says.

I don't feel like doing anything, but I take a sip of water anyway. The energy bar tastes like gravel in my mouth, so I just put the other half in my pocket for later.

Eli finds some food for himself and starts chowing down, but he never takes his eyes off me.

I wish he'd stop staring. I just want to disappear.

"I'm sorry," he says finally. "It shouldn't have gone that way. I should have been more careful."

"It's not your fault."

"It *is* my fault. I didn't see the other guy. I shouldn't have sent you in there, but you . . . handled it."

Handled it.

I shudder. Because of me, that man is gone. Because of me, the people he loved will never see him again.

Eli is still talking. "We need to get to the center of town and find their bunker. We need to know what technology they have access to out here. They're advanced enough to disable our land mines. Who knows what else they can do."

I nod, trying to refocus on our mission. One of the reasons Jayden sent me to do this was because she knew I'd be able to report on their setup accurately. Even if we survive, it won't be a total bust for Constance. At least they'll get some intel out of it.

I'm not sure whether it would be better to bring back a full report this time or not. If we tell them everything they need to know, they may decide to kill us and be done with it. But if we don't, Jayden will send us out again.

Normally, that thought would give me a jolt of fear, but I just feel empty inside. And when you're empty, fear has nothing to latch on to.

"We should at least find out everything we can," says Eli, reading my mind. "Once we know, we can decide what to do with the information. If we find what we came for, at least we'll have a bargaining chip."

"Okay," I say in a flat voice. "Let's go."

He looks worried, but I pull my mask back on before he can argue. We creep out of the building, and I cover him as he darts around the corner.

Each business we pass looks more run-down than the next.

Most of the windows were shattered long ago, giving us an unobstructed view of the enormous interiors. It seems ridiculous that people once lived in houses large enough to fit ten compartments.

It didn't do them any good once the bombs started dropping.

This place wasn't a direct target during Death Storm, but it must have been one of those towns people fled to in the weeks that followed. They left the cities, but they couldn't outrun the nuclear fallout. Most people here died slowly of radiation poisoning, but some of them didn't.

I only learned about the drifters when I joined Recon, and I still can't fathom how they survived. Our enemies had been threatening nuclear war for decades. And while the U.S. government was confident no nation would initiate war and risk ultimate destruction, the compound's founders weren't.

People wrote off the first generation as a doomsday cult, but the attack on Washington, D.C., that launched Operation Extermination sent a whole new generation to the compounds. By the time Death Storm began two decades later, the compounds were at capacity. My parents and I were among the lucky few who made it in, but most people were left on the outside to die.

As we approach the center of town, I catch a glimpse of movement near a huge rustic-looking restaurant. The weathered wood exterior is covered with old license plates and street signs, and there's an enormous porch with a red overhang leading to the entrance.

Some of that old urgency creeps back inside me. It isn't quite fear, but I'm relieved just to feel *something*.

The front door slams, and Eli pulls me behind a dented truck to survey the scene. He taps his interface to zoom in on the restaurant and the adjacent convenience store.

"I think this is it," he breathes. "I'm gonna go around back and see if I can get a better vantage point."

Something familiar stirs inside me, thrusting me back into the present.

"No!" I whisper, grabbing his arm.

I don't want him to leave. Something inside me just *knows* it's a bad idea. My self-preservation instincts may have abandoned me, but I still have enough of myself left to worry about Eli.

"I'll be right back," he says. "If I'm not back in ten, find somewhere safe to spend the night and then get back to the compound."

"Eli —"

"I'm serious."

"Don't go over there."

"I'm not letting us get ambushed again," he says fiercely. "We almost didn't make it, and I . . . I wouldn't have been able to live with myself if they'd . . ."

He's struggling to get the words out, but I don't need him to finish. I know the toll all those cadets' lives have taken on him, and I know he lives in constant fear of losing another. So I force myself to nod, and he hunkers down to creep behind the nearest dumpster.

Glancing back at the restaurant to make sure the lookout isn't watching, he darts across the street and disappears behind the building next door.

As soon as I lose sight of him, my heart starts pounding. I check my interface to note the time, though I have no intention of leaving.

The next few minutes are the longest of my life. I keep waiting to hear gunshots or the panicked yell of people inside the restaurant, but it's dead silent.

I check my interface compulsively, and every minute that drags by compounds the fear unfurling inside me. It mixes with the nauseous feeling I've had since the garage, leaving me tense and clammy despite the oppressive heat.

Eight minutes in, I hear a muffled wail and then a *thud*. Terror roots me in place, and I don't know whether I should run straight toward the source of the noise or take Eli's concealed path.

Deciding to risk exposure, I spring out from behind the truck toward the building where Eli disappeared. I don't feel my legs burning or the dry air hitting my lungs. Every single part of me is focused on finding him.

Eli may have given me orders, but he also risked everything to come out here with me. No matter what he's said or done to push me away, Eli is my friend.

I throw my back against the hot stucco and try to formulate a plan, but my brain has left my body to fend for itself.

I clench my fists and prepare to run into the restaurant to shoot anyone who isn't Eli. It's a stupid plan, but I can't just abandon him.

Just as I take a step out into the open, I feel a powerful arm snake around my waist. A hand knocks my mask askew and clamps over my face to muffle my involuntary scream.

As unfiltered Fringe air hits my lungs, I have to fight another source of panic: I'm breathing in radioactive particles.

I bite down on the fingers and taste salt, shooting my elbow back to connect with my attacker's abdomen. He grunts and slams me against the building.

My fighting instinct kicks in automatically, giving me an unexpected surge of strength. But then I see Eli's blue eyes protruding over the top of his mask, and my arms go limp.

He jerks his head once, and I choke on my breath of relief.

Gasping for air, I yank the mask back down and try to calm my racing heart.

I'm fine. Eli's fine. We're safe.

My mantra doesn't help.

Eli still has me pinned against the wall, but he releases me quickly and gives me a disapproving look.

"What did I say?" he growls.

"Ten minutes," I pant. I click my interface and, sure enough, it hasn't even been ten minutes yet.

I want to defend myself *and* give him hell for making me worry, but orders are orders and Eli is Eli. There's no justification for disobeying him and abandoning the plan.

Luckily, we're both too relieved to be angry.

Once my heart rate has returned to normal, Eli motions for me to follow him.

We crouch down and make our way up the front steps. There's a body tucked behind a trashcan, and I recoil at the sight of his head hanging limply from his neck.

Another kill, another life.

I wonder how many drifters have been murdered in service to the compound. Regardless of the threat they pose, it seems like a high price to pay for security.

Apparently this guy was the only drifter guarding the restaurant, because Eli is calm as he leads me inside.

Momentary blindness sets me on edge, but when my eyes adjust to the dim lighting, I can make out a dozen or so tables pushed against the outer walls. The interior is cluttered with framed posters and more street signs, and the shelves near the front boast an impressive selection of coffee mugs and other knickknacks for sale. It reminds me of the commissary, though I don't know why a restaurant would sell anything other than food.

Part of me wants to stop and look at everything, but Eli leads me straight back to the kitchen. The floorboards groan underfoot, and I tense a little with every step. He pushes the swinging door aside and holds it open for me.

There's nothing unusual back here — just stacks of boxes, pots and pans, and defunct cooking appliances coated in a thick layer of orangish dust. But then Eli jerks his head toward another door and signals for me to be quiet.

There's something in there. I can feel the excitement radiating from him. He opens it slowly, and I follow him down a dark staircase. My heart is pounding, and halfway down, an earth-shattering *creak* nearly dislodges it from my chest.

Eli freezes, and we both wait.

Nothing.

Eli turns on his interface, flooding the dark basement in blue light. I flip on my interface, too, and the added brightness reveals an astounding sight.

We've wandered into what looks like an outdated command center. There are several computers and other equipment I don't recognize trailing wires around the room. I run my hand over the aged keyboard, and I'm shocked when it comes away dust-free.

People have been here recently, and they're using this setup as drifter headquarters.

"What is all this stuff?" asks Eli.

"I don't know. Was that lookout the only . . .?"

"Yeah. The rest must have left for a while."

I catch his meaning. Whoever has been using this basement could be back at any moment. I fall into action and start pouring over the equipment, taking pictures of everything I see and recording notes on my interface.

It doesn't look as though they have any kind of Internet connection, but they clearly have power. There's an old-fashioned two-way radio, and I wonder briefly whom they could be communicating with.

I hit the power button to boot up the computer so I can see what kind of software they have installed, but the sound of voices coming from outside makes me freeze.

Eli's face mirrors my own panic, and he gestures toward the door.

I turn off the computer quickly and follow him back toward the stairs. I have no idea how I hear the footsteps over my own pounding heart, but it sounds as though they're still out in the main restaurant.

I stay close behind Eli as we fly up the stairs and into the kitchen. I can tell from his cool expression that he had planned on this happening.

Instead of kicking down the door and opening fire on the men, he moves toward a concealed exit I hadn't even noticed. At least we won't have to shoot our way out.

He throws the door open, and I'm strangely relieved when I feel the blast of hot Fringe air on my face. He shoots across the street, back toward our original hiding place, and I follow him at a run.

In one motion, he hauls me behind the truck, and we sit leg to leg, catching our breath. My heart is pounding against my ribcage. I want to get back into that basement to learn more about the drifters, but going back in there right now would be foolish.

Still, I'm glad to have something to distract me from the darkness that's taken root inside me. As long as I have a mission, I can keep moving.

When my breathing evens out, I notice the heat is not nearly as oppressive, and the sun is beginning to sink on the horizon. I hadn't even realized how long we'd been out here, and part of me can't believe I survived my first day on the Fringe.

"Come on," says Eli. "We need to find a place to settle in for the night."

Bracing myself for the nerve-wracking journey, I follow him back toward the outskirts of town. I have no idea where he plans on sleeping, but I know I won't be able to close my eyes for a second — not out here.

The town is silent as we make our way around the corner of buildings and duck behind parked cars. We still don't know how many drifters might be roaming around here, so we don't let our guard down for even a second. I can tell from Eli's stance that he still doesn't think we're out of danger.

There's a post office I don't remember passing before, and I'm a little surprised when Eli lets himself in. He scans the small room for any signs of life and then pulls off his mask and mops his sweaty face with his sleeve.

"We're staying here?"

"No. Let's check out the upstairs."

I hadn't even considered what was above the post office, but Eli's powers of observation are leaps and bounds ahead of my own.

Sure enough, there's a steep flight of stairs in the back leading up to more offices and two apartments. Most of the doors are locked, but one creaks open when Eli turns the handle.

"Wait here," he whispers.

I hesitate, but then he shoots me a deadly look that says he won't put up with a repeat of the restaurant stakeout incident.

Eli disappears through the door, and I try to remember to breathe.

He's only gone about twenty seconds, but it feels like forever.

My nerves are already stretched to the breaking point.

Finally he ushers me inside, and I enter through the small kitchen. It's obvious no one has been here in a while. There's a thick layer of dust covering the countertops, but the modest apartment was obviously well cared for. Cheery lace curtains are drawn over the small window, and Eli pulls them aside to peer out onto the street below.

"Why did you pick this place?"

"We'll be more protected up here than on the ground floor," he mutters. "And it's got a nice view."

An uncomfortable silence falls over the homey kitchen when I realize that to Eli, a "nice view" means a good vantage point for shooting drifters.

He opens up all the cabinets, but they're empty except for a few odd dishes and spices.

To distract myself, I wander into the next room to explore. The living room walls are completely bare, but there's a ratty couch, an old TV, and a red velvet recliner that still has the imprint of a thousand naps worn down the middle.

Off to the side, there's a tiny bathroom and a room with a lumpy double bed and a battered chest of drawers. There are very few personal items left in the apartment, but I can see where the wallpaper is faded around the outline of picture frames and a clock.

Once I finish exploring, I join Eli in the living room and sink down onto the scratchy couch. The sun has almost set, and faint golden light is filtering in through the dusty windows.

Now that the immediate danger is gone, I realize how beat-up and exhausted I am. My face feels tight and dry from sunburn, and my hair is a ratty mess. But the real problem is the agonizing black hole expanding in my chest. I've never felt anything like it

— a void where nothing good could ever exist again.

I clasp my dirty hands together, as though holding on to something might help me summon a normal emotion.

Eli still hasn't stopped moving. There's a lot of zipping and unsnapping as he unpacks his rucksack, retrieves two ration packets, and starts preparing one of the unappetizing "just add water" meals.

"You should rehydrate," he says for what feels like the hundredth time. "You haven't had enough water today."

"You said we had to ration everything."

He grins. "I can't exactly carry you back if you pass out from dehydration. Besides, we're restocking tomorrow."

I sigh and start to drink.

He checks and rechecks his rucksack, taking stock of our remaining energy bars and ammunition.

Watching Eli work, I realize how on edge he is. He brought me up here to feel safe, but he doesn't. His handgun is still tucked in its holster, and his rifle hasn't left his side.

His hands are stiff as he tips the seasoning packet into our meal, as though he's just waiting for someone to charge in here and start shooting.

"How did you *live* like this?" I blurt out.

Eli's shoulders stiffen. He doesn't raise his head to look at me, but he knows what I'm referring to. Eli was brought into the compound when he was fourteen, but I've never asked about his childhood.

For a moment, I think he's going to shut me out or yell at me for prying. But when he meets my eyes, his gaze softens.

"Honestly, I don't remember most of it," he says, running a hand through his dark hair. "I think I've blocked out the really bad stuff."

My face heats up, and I instantly feel terrible for ambushing him. I couldn't have picked a worse way to bring it up, but his response makes me feel as though I have to ask a follow-up question.

"What happened to your parents?"

"They were killed when I was eleven."

By his matter-of-fact tone, you'd have thought he was reporting the weather, but it still feels like a punch to the stomach. I wish I hadn't asked, but there's no going back now.

"Who killed them?" I whisper.

Eli shakes his head. "I have no idea. It was just a random attack. Things were chaotic back then. Salt Lake City was one of the last places hit by Death Storm, so most people had time to flee. My family had left the city, and there were a lot of bad people who were trying to claim territory.

"Somebody broke into the house where we were staying, and my parents told me and my brother to hide."

Eli stops for a moment, and the expression on his face tells me he still doesn't understand how it could have happened.

My stomach clenches with dread. I shouldn't have asked. Now he's going to shut down, and it's my fault.

"We'd had looters break in before to steal food, but . . . this was different. Normally, my dad would have told my mom to hide with us. I should have known something was off."

He swallows, and for a moment, I don't think he's going to continue. His face is frozen in the shadows, and the silence feels heavy and tense.

"I think they thought they could slow down whoever it was so that we'd have time to get away. I don't know . . ."

Every word he adds just compounds the sinking feeling inside me. I already know how this ends.

"Owen and I hid in the den, and then I heard my mom scream. I tried to run out there, but Owen held me down. He was a lot bigger than me then."

He swallows thickly, and I can tell the next part is hard for him to get out.

"There were a few gunshots. I couldn't see anything, but I knew she was dead." Eli shudders. "Then I heard my dad. He let out this loud sob. I'll *never* forget that sound. Then they shot him."

He looks up at me, his eyes dark with regret. That look — that helpless, guilty look — cuts me to the core.

"I heard them leave, and Owen ran out into the living room. They were just lying there."

"Your parents?"

"They'd shot them point blank. There was nothing I could do."

"You were only eleven," I murmur.

"I know." Eli lets out a sigh, biting the inside of his cheek. "I couldn't believe they were dead. Owen was pulling on my arm, telling me we had to run. I wouldn't go with him, and he took off. I tried to run after him, but it was *so* dark . . ."

Eli looks away, and when he speaks next, his voice is so quiet I can barely hear it.

"He ran right into them. I heard the shot, but I kept going."

I don't want him to finish. I can see what it's costing him to relive it, but he doesn't stop.

"I couldn't see a foot in front of me. I tripped over something . . . fell down. It was a person, but I didn't get it. I didn't understand why someone would just lie down like that. I thought maybe they were playing possum. But then I realized it was Owen." He clears his throat. "Owen's body."

"Eli . . ."

"I got up, and I ran. I couldn't go back there and see my parents' faces."

I stare at him, searching for something to say. "I didn't even know you had a brother."

"I don't anymore."

Eli's voice is hollow, but he isn't shutting down. He seems relieved to get this off his chest, and it occurs to me that this could be the first time he's told the story.

"I should have stopped him. I could have gone with him right away, and he might've missed the shooter."

"You don't know that," I say, my voice cracking.

He bites the inside of his cheek, but his expression seems lighter now that he's gotten it all out.

"Where did you go then?"

"I lived on the streets for a while, sleeping wherever I could. It wasn't uncommon then. There were plenty of orphans bumming around, and the gangs took advantage of that."

"Gangs?"

He nods. "One day, a guy called Freeman who I'd seen around came up to me and said I either had to come work for him or get the hell out of the neighborhood. I'd wandered into their territory without realizing it. I should have turned around and walked away right then, but . . ."

"You joined the gang?"

"I just didn't want to be by myself anymore." He shrugs. "It was nice at first. Freeman let me stay at his house, gave me plenty to eat. Most of the guys were older, so they'd just make me run errands for them and deliver messages. It wasn't that bad."

"And you stayed with them until you were fourteen?"

"N-No," he says, averting his eyes. His next silence is the longest yet, and I start to wonder if the conversation is over.

"About a year after I joined them, they had me make my first kill. I don't even know why I went along with it. I guess because, by then, I trusted those guys. They just pointed to a man on the street and said, 'follow him home and kill him.'

"I figured they'd never ask me to do it unless it was really important — unless this guy was a real threat, you know?"

He drags a hand through his hair and tugs on it, which tells me this probably bothers him more than anything.

"I did follow him back to his apartment, but I chickened out. I was afraid to go inside and see where he lived. I thought seeing his apartment would somehow make it more real."

I wait with bated breath, dreading the horrible conclusion.

"I shot him in the street and took his wallet. They needed proof he was dead. I opened it up. Inside, he had some credit cards, a driver's license, and this picture of him, a woman, and a kid younger than me.

"He wasn't some gangster who was shaking Freeman down. He was just a *guy* — some random guy they thought would be an easy mark for me. And I shot him right outside his apartment."

"Eli . . ."

He glances up at me, and I'm startled by the pain in his eyes. "I never gave it to them. I never went back to Freeman's house. I was so . . . *ashamed.*"

"I'm sorry." It seems so inappropriate, so inadequate, but I have no idea what else to say.

Without thinking, I reach over and put my hand over his. He winces as though I startled him, and when he looks up, I'm not sure if he's really seeing me. He's looking at me so hard it feels as though he's looking *through* me.

But then he seems to come to his senses, and I see him trying to put up his walls again. "I don't know why I just told you all that," he says, looking angry with himself. "I never tell anyone that stuff. There's no point."

"Sure there is."

He shakes his head. "Don't say I should talk about it because it makes me feel better."

"Does it?"

"Yeah, but it's not something I should ever feel better about."

"Eli, you were just a kid."

"I know that. I just . . . I just wish I could take it all back."

I don't know what to say to that. There's no convincing Eli that he shouldn't blame himself for his parents' death or that he was put in an impossible situation.

"How did you end up in the compound?" I ask finally.

He bobs his head slowly, as though he's trying to return to the present.

"That winter, I got pneumonia. There was a free clinic near where I was staying. A lot of people were dying of radiation poisoning.

"While I was waiting, this man showed up who seemed . . . off. He looked like military, but not any branch I'd ever seen before. He sat down next to me, and we got talking. He started asking me all these questions about my health . . . where I'd lived . . . my parents . . .

"When he found out I was on my own, he asked if I'd like a chance to live in one of the compounds. I didn't really trust the guy, but I was tired and sick. At the time, I was squatting in some abandoned apartment with no heat, and he made the compounds sound like heaven. So I said I'd go with him."

"He was Recon."

"Yeah."

I hesitate for a moment. "Are you glad you went?"

"Every day."

He glances up at me and grins at my surprised expression. "Look. There's a lot I hate about that place. But once you've been starving and cold without a place to sleep . . . you'll take anything else."

He bends his head and returns his attention to our forgotten food.

I realize there's so much I don't know about Eli — so much I wrote off as part of his personality. But he's been through truly horrible things in his life, which makes the goodness in him even more remarkable.

We eat in silence. As the last scraps of light fade from the room, exhaustion hits me all at once, and Eli takes my yawn as a cue to clean up our dinner.

"You take the bed. I'll take the couch," he says.

I nod and start shuffling toward the room, still reeling from his story.

Halfway to the door, I stop and turn back to him. "I'm sorry about your parents . . . and Owen. You shouldn't have had to go through that."

He meets my gaze and tries to smile, not quite managing it.

I leave the door cracked and lie down on the bed. When I finally shut my eyes, I can't banish the horrific images my mind conjures up.

I see a much younger and terrified Eli, hiding with his brother as his parents are shot. I see him falling onto his brother's dead body . . . Eli shooting a man in the street. In my semiconsciousness, the man's face morphs into the man I shot today. His eyes are blank and lifeless.

As exhaustion overtakes my body, my thoughts turn into nightmares, and I sink into a horrible, restless sleep.

six

Eli

Soft whimpers coming from the next room wake me in the middle of the night. I hadn't planned on drifting off, but as soon as I sank down on the lumpy old couch to keep watch, my eyes drifted closed.

My hazy brain tries to place the noise, but I don't immediately remember where I am. Then the dark apartment comes into view, and I realize I'm on the Fringe with Harper.

Without thinking, I leap off the couch and barge into the bedroom. I don't even realize I've pulled out my gun to scan the room for threats until I spot her.

She's curled up in a ball on the bed with the covers wrapped around her legs. Her dark hair is everywhere, and her face is contorted in fear and anguish.

My heart clenches. She had a hell of a day. She made her first kill, and then I went and unloaded my entire fucked-up life story on her. No wonder she's having nightmares.

I don't know what to do, but my feet carry me toward her automatically.

"Hey. Harper. Wake up," I whisper, sinking down beside her and tugging her shoulder gently. Her skin is burning hot from sunburn.

She wakes with a start and lets out a little cry.

"It's okay. It's just me."

Her breaths are coming in short gasps. When she's alert

enough to recognize me, her tear-streaked face scrunches in confusion.

"Eli?"

"It's okay. You were just having a nightmare."

Before my brain can catch up with my body, I'm putting an arm around her and tucking her head into the crook of my neck. She shudders, and I squeeze her while her breathing returns to normal. She feels so good in my arms that I instantly feel guilty for holding her.

"What was it?" I ask.

"We were running from those men at the body shop," she whispers. "They grabbed me and shot you . . . and Celdon was there. They made me watch while they tortured him. I've never seen him in so much pain." She shivers. "It doesn't even make any sense."

"The things we're scared of don't always make sense," I murmur.

"In my dream, when I turned you over . . . you had this look on your face." She stops and shakes her head. "Like it was my fault . . . like I could have stopped them."

I tighten my grip on her, and she stiffens. "Is *that* what you think? That it's your fault I'm out here?"

"It *is* my fault," she says, as though I'm an idiot for asking. "You came out here with me."

"That was my choice, Harper. None of this is your fault."

She shakes her head a little. "It was just a dream."

"It's okay . . . I have nightmares, too, sometimes."

She pulls her head back a little, looking up at me with tears in her eyes. "You do?"

"I see the men I killed and a lot of my old recruits — the ones who died out here. I had a lot of horrible dreams right after they bid on your class, actually."

"Really?"

"Yeah."

"Was I ever in one?"

I swallow. "Yes."

I have no idea why I keep blurting out the truth, but it's going to get me into trouble.

"When was this?"

"Right after I met you."

She falls silent, and for a moment, I wonder if she's drifted back to sleep.

"Eli?" she asks finally.

"Hmm?"

"Will you . . . stay in here?"

Her voice is so quiet that I'm not immediately sure I heard right. But when she looks up, she's giving me a raw, questioning look that says she just asked for something she shouldn't have.

I can't believe she just asked me that. After everything she watched me do today and everything I just told her, she shouldn't even want to be in the same room with me.

But she does.

Since I can't seem to unstick my throat, I just nod. She scoots down on the bed, giving me plenty of room to lie beside her.

I want to slap myself for being so careless. I know I shouldn't, but I don't want to leave her side.

Keeping plenty of distance between us, I move down so I'm half lying next to her, half propped against the headboard. I tell myself I'm still keeping watch, but I'm really just watching Harper.

When she rolls onto her side, we're close enough to spoon, but I don't reach for her. I don't trust myself when her shoulders and back are exposed in that tank top, her scent is everywhere, and her face is flushed from the sun.

It feels wrong to be lying beside her without having her in my arms, but I force myself to do it.

With her just a few inches away, I fall asleep within minutes, and for once, I dream of good things.

* * *

I awake to the feeling of sunshine warming my body. Light is streaming in through the battered blinds, alerting me to the fact that I'm in bed with someone I shouldn't be, and my body is responding . . . inappropriately.

Staring down at Harper's unconscious form, I'm startled by my own happiness. In her sleep, she rolled even closer, turning onto her other side so her head could rest against my shoulder. She has an arm draped over my waist, and I smile a little at the sight of her lying there.

I've never seen Harper asleep, and I'm instantly captivated. Her normally fierce expression is relaxed, and her sleek dark hair is everywhere. It's twisted around my forearm and spilling over my chest, as though I was running my fingers through it in my sleep.

Then the realization punches me in the stomach: We're on the Fringe. This isn't a lazy Sunday in bed. We shouldn't even *be* in bed. God knows what time it is.

Pulling the covers back up to my waist, I nudge her arm. "Harper. *Psst.* Harper."

She wakes with a start, and her eyes widen when she sees me lying next to her. She yanks her arm away as though I burned her and sits bolt upright in bed. "Uh . . . sorry about that."

I hold the covers a little tighter to my midsection and clear my throat. "Uh . . . it's fine. We should get going."

She nods quickly, a little flustered, and reaches up to pull her hair into a ponytail. Watching her lift her silky hair off her flushed neck is doing nothing to alleviate the situation down south, so I leave the room while she gets dressed and pace around to try to clear my head.

Coming out here with her was a bad idea. I pushed her away that night on the observation deck because it was the best thing for both of us.

Harper is still my cadet, and it's inappropriate for me to be having the thoughts that are running through my head. More importantly, they're a distraction from our mission, and distractions get you killed.

When I hear the bedroom door open, I begin rummaging around for some energy bars to eat for breakfast. Harper wanders out fully dressed, watching me as though she wants to say something.

I don't want to hear it. Whatever it is will just make this even more awkward, so I hand her one of the bars and start chugging my water. We'll need to replenish our supply today before we return to the restaurant to poke around.

"Ready?"

She looks slightly alarmed. "For what?"

"We need to swing by the nearest checkpoint to get more water."

"O-kay," she says, biting into the energy bar and watching me carefully.

She knows why I'm acting weird, which just makes it worse.

I make myself busy rearranging the supplies in my pack as she eats. Then I make the bed and get rid of our trash to erase any evidence of our presence here.

Once there's nothing left for me to clean or organize, I pull on my mask. Harper doesn't say anything, but she follows my lead and tucks the last empty wrapper into her pocket. If any drifters wander up here, they'll never know we're using the apartment as our safe house.

I raise my rifle to check the street for drifters before leading us outside. We slept later than we should have, which means the sun is already oppressively hot.

Still, this morning doesn't seem as bad as yesterday. Maybe it's because we got a full night's sleep, or maybe the lightness of my shoulders is from waking up next to Harper.

She seems to be in slightly better spirits today, too. She no longer looks dead inside, which is something.

I lead us around the perimeter of town, charting a careful path between buildings and ducking behind cars in case we're ambushed. Harper follows my every move, mirroring my watchful stance as though she's been doing this for years.

We reach the edge of a residential area, where a few small houses are spaced at uneven intervals along a dusty road. They're surrounded by burnt-looking grass, sun-faded swing sets, and rusty chain-link fences.

Down the road, a large, expensive-looking facility occupies almost an entire block — some kind of manufacturing plant, by the looks of it. Beyond that, there's nothing but empty desert.

Staring out at the wide expanse of land gives me a slight prickle on the back of my neck, but I shove that feeling aside and focus on reaching the checkpoint.

It's about a mile outside the town — in the opposite direction of the compound — which puts a mile of desert between us and fresh water. I don't like the exposure, but without any rock formations or buildings to hide behind, the drifters have an equal disadvantage.

Since there are no landmarks, I flip on my interface and pull up a map of all the Recon checkpoints in the area. It shows me and Harper as moving green dots and the checkpoint as a larger, pulsating blue beacon.

I beam the map to Harper, and she moves a fraction of an inch closer to me as the empty landscape unfolds around us. She doesn't like the lack of cover any more than I do, and she keeps glancing over her shoulder to make sure we aren't being followed.

Every moment we walk, the sun seems to grow hotter and hotter. I yank off my overshirt and imagine us gorging ourselves on water after this. It has to be the longest mile I've ever walked.

As we shuffle along, the blinking blue dot expands slightly. It's the only sign that we're getting closer. Every square foot of desert looks exactly the same to me — every crack in the earth, every dried-up little bush — and the sun doesn't seem to have moved at all from its position.

Suddenly, the dot starts blinking furiously, letting me know we're right on top of the water source. I drop my gaze to the ground, looking for the protruding spigot.

There seems to be a higher than normal concentration of desert grass, so I push it aside to look for the pipe.

Nothing.

The dot is still blinking furiously on my interface, so I pace a small circle around the area. I don't see anything at all.

Frustrated, I get down on my hands and knees and feel along the ground. Harper is watching me with a puzzled expression, but if she thinks I led her out to the middle of the desert on a wild-goose chase, she doesn't say so.

Then my hand hits something solid. I push aside the brush

and run my hand over a tiny piece of pipe sticking out of the ground.

My heart sinks. Where there should have been two feet of pipe and a handle for pumping water, there's only the stump of a pipe that someone has welded shut.

"No," I growl, feeling desperately in the dirt next to it. My fingers graze hot metal, and I hurriedly brush the dirt away.

"Help me out with this," I say.

Harper bends down and starts clawing at the dirt with me. Between the two of us, it only takes a few minutes to reveal the metal trapdoor. I brace my fingers under the lip and pull, but it doesn't budge.

I try again — putting my back into it — but the door stays shut. I keep pulling with everything I have, as if I can somehow wear it down. I just can't look up and face Harper's confused expression.

Finally I stop and run my hand along the edge of the door. That's when the realization sets in: The drifters broke our spigot and welded the trapdoor shut. They purposely cut us off from our supplies so we wouldn't be able to stay here.

But they couldn't have found it by accident. This location would be impossible to stumble upon, and they have no reason to be out here in the first place.

They must have followed us last time. Either that, or someone from the compound gave up the location.

The thought of a Recon operative giving information to the drifters is ridiculous, so that only leaves the possibility that they've been watching us for a while.

"They did this, didn't they?" Harper asks finally.

I nod, unable to form the words. Fury is building inside of me, mixing with the panic and helplessness I always feel on the

Fringe.

"Is there another checkpoint?"

"Not near here," I sigh. "The closest one is five miles away."

Harper reaches into her rucksack, hefting the water bag in her hands. She's almost out, and I'm on empty. It's possible we could make it to the next checkpoint, but if it's been compromised, we could be in a lot of trouble.

"We need to go back," I say. "Let's check out the restaurant one more time and then head back to the compound."

Jayden won't be happy when we return early, but I'm not about to risk our lives on a gamble. I'll gladly take whatever punishment she doles out.

Harper gets to her feet and replaces her water bag. Her hands and knees are covered in dust, adding to her unkempt appearance, but her brow is still set in an expression of absolute faith. You wouldn't think I just led her a mile out into the desert without any water to show for it.

We march back to the town at a much slower pace, both of us trying to conserve our energy. By the time the buildings emerge from the heat haze, we're both exhausted and defeated.

I squint up at the manufacturing plant, wondering if my eyes are playing tricks on me. There's something sticking out over the top of the sloped roof. It could be a vent or a piece of debris, but it doesn't look right.

Then it moves, and I realize it's a person.

I freeze and grab Harper's arm. Someone is watching us from the roof, and I'd bet he's got us in the crosshairs of his rifle.

Hot fear surges through me like molten steel.

"What is it?"

I stiffen for a second — caught on the edge of indecision — and then shove Harper out of the line of fire.

She can't see what I see, but she hears the gunshot. The bullet hits the ground next to her, emitting a small cloud of dust exactly where she was just standing.

"Run," I breathe.

For once, Harper doesn't put up a fight. We take off at a sprint toward the nearest structure, the mounting panic constricting my lungs.

The drifters couldn't have caught us in a worse place. Running for the houses puts us right out in the open, and on the other side of the plant, there's a long stretch of road with nothing but an old warehouse and an abandoned carwash for cover.

My legs are burning, but I force them to go harder.

Harper is panting alongside me, and I swing her around the corner of the warehouse.

We're out of the sniper's range for now, but the smooth-sided structure doesn't provide much protection. I don't know where else they might have snipers stationed, so I tighten my grip on her hand and make a break for the run-down old carwash.

The broken blue "EZ Wash" sign is only thirty yards down the road, but it might as well be a mile. I don't know if we're going to reach it.

The sniper shoots and misses again, but my entire body seizes as I imagine hot lead ripping through my back.

The sound of our feet slapping against the bone-dry concrete floor of the carwash is a welcome relief. Somebody tore out the hoses and pipes long ago, but it provides good overhead cover and gives me the ability to scope out our surroundings.

I stick my head around the corner and try to line up a shot, but I can no longer see the sniper.

"Where are they?" Harper gasps. "I didn't see anyone."

"On the roof of that huge building," I groan. "He barely

moved. I almost didn't see him."

I don't want to think about what would have happened if I hadn't.

"What do we do?" Harper huffs.

I don't answer her right away. I'm still trying to calm down enough to formulate a plan.

"Stick to the edge of town," I say finally. "We'll have to go around to get back to the compound."

Harper's brow crinkles in confusion. "The compound? I thought we were going back to the restaurant . . ."

"Not anymore. They could have shooters anywhere. We'll never make it in and out of there alive."

I know we have to move. It's only a matter of time before they find us. Everything inside me is screaming to stay put, but sometimes you have to fight your natural instincts to survive.

"We'll go that way," I say, pointing at another warehouse two hundred yards away. "Stay right with me, okay?"

She nods, and we take off at a crouched run. I don't hear any more shots, but that doesn't mean there isn't another shooter just waiting for us to cross his path.

Once we leave the town, it will be open season for the drifters, but I don't see another option. We can't risk staying here.

We take off again, and when we reach the warehouse, Harper collapses onto one knee to catch her breath.

"We have to keep moving," I pant, trying not to sound unsympathetic.

"I know, I know."

She takes a couple beats to recover and then gets to her feet.

Harper may talk back, but she's a perfect soldier in the field. She takes orders without question and can keep pace with me despite my longer stride. She must be tired, but she won't admit it, let alone whine.

Our next sprint is slightly farther — from the warehouse to a filling station. All I can hear is my feet hitting the dry earth and the sound of our labored breathing.

Then a bullet whizzes past my head and shatters the window of a car six yards in front of me.

"Go! Go! Go!" I yell.

We're both already sprinting, but Harper picks up the pace. My body is running on empty, but all I feel is my heart hammering against my ribcage.

I tear around the corner of the building just as another bullet ricochets off the sandstone-colored brick.

My heart falters. I lost my grip on Harper.

I yell her name, but it only comes out as a croak. I yell again, my stomach filling with dread.

Then she stumbles around the corner, clutching the stitch in her side.

"Shit!" I breathe, dragging a hand through my hair. Relief and fear are competing for my attention, and I don't even give her a chance to catch her breath before pulling her toward the opposite corner of the building.

My body is completely spent, which means hers must be, too. I point around the corner to the diner we passed on the way into town. There are two lonely cars rusting along the side of the road, which could provide a bit of cover if the sniper starts shooting again.

I squeeze Harper's arm once and take off.

It's this leg that really gets me. Before, the adrenalin was powerful enough to stave off the weakness in my legs and the fire in my chest, but I can feel my body slowing down, as though I'm wading through mud.

Harper manages to stay right behind me, but I know she can't possibly maintain this pace.

Miraculously, we reach the cover of the diner, and I nearly collapse against the rough brick in relief.

Harper's face is bright red under her mask, and I can hear her heavy intake of air coming through the mic. I let out a relieved laugh, but she's still too winded to join in.

This time, I set a sixty-second timer on my interface to give us time to recover. It runs out too quickly, and I signal Harper to move again.

I let my interface guide us straight toward the compound, trying not to think about the rifles pointed at our retreating backs.

Once we leave the cover of the buildings, the uneasy itch between my shoulder blades intensifies.

It's supernatural — crazy even — but I know they're watching us. I can sense the eyes on us from some lofty position on the edge of town, a drifter's dirty finger poised over a trigger. I wonder why he doesn't shoot.

Maybe they're going to let us go home after all, I think. *Maybe we're the messengers and they want us to tell the compound to back the fuck off.*

It seems like a plausible scenario, at least. I've almost convinced myself that we're home free. But then a new rock formation comes into view, and another gunshot shatters the silence.

seven

Harper

The shot reverberates through the air, and every muscle in my body seizes violently.

For a second, I'm frozen in place. Eli and I are still standing, but we're about halfway between the town and the cleared zone with no cover.

We don't need to speak. We just run.

Another shot fires — cutting cleanly between us. Eli crouches down automatically and then pitches forward and takes off again at a sprint.

My feet move without any direction from my brain, which is good because my mind is paralyzed with indecision.

Should we keep running or hit the deck? We're completely exposed out here, and the only reason the shooter hasn't hit us yet is because we're moving targets.

Eli flips on his interface to get a read on the perimeter, but I just focus on his back.

He picks up the pace, glancing over his shoulder every few steps to make sure I'm right behind him.

My back is still tense, waiting for a bullet to tear into my shoulder blades, but the feeling is returning to other parts of my body.

My legs are slow and rubbery, and my skin is giving off an alarming amount of heat. My chest is burning from the lack of oxygen, but I know we can't stop.

I have no idea how far we are from the cleared zone. Half a

mile? A mile? Eli doesn't seem to have slowed his pace, but I can tell by his form that he's exhausted.

Then another shot pierces my eardrums, making my heart go haywire. I push my legs harder — telling my body to speed up — but then Eli lets out a strangled yell.

He stumbles, slowing considerably, and I almost career right into him. He's still moving, but he's clutching his thigh, where a dark pool of blood is seeping through his uniform.

Suddenly I'm thrust back into my nightmares, with Eli dying right in front of me. My panic seems to have reached its upper limit, though, because instead of freezing, my mind sharpens.

"How bad?" I pant. My voice doesn't sound like my own. Nothing seems to be connected to my body anymore.

"They just grazed me," he growls. Eli is gritting his teeth in pain, but he clamps his palm over the wound and staggers forward. "Come on."

To my amazement, he keeps limping toward the perimeter at a good clip. Hands shaking, I flip on my interface and feel a surge of relief when I see we're only a hundred yards away from the mines.

I brace myself for another shot — this one meant for me — but apart from Eli's ragged breathing, the desert is painfully silent.

I lead the way through the mines, navigating with more confidence this time. Eli's still going strong, and he's coherent enough to force me to walk ahead of him — presumably so he can protect me from any stray bullets.

We clear the mines, and I loop an arm under his shoulders to help him limp the last two miles to the compound. The sun beating down on us is somehow hotter than before, and Eli's face grows paler with each step he takes.

He's losing too much blood.

After a few minutes, I stop and kneel down on the ground in front of him.

"What are you *doing?*"

"We need to stop the bleeding," I say, giving the hem of my overshirt a sharp tug. A rip starts, and I keep pulling until a section of it tears free. It's a crappy bandage, but there's no time to fish around in the pack for the first aid kit.

"I'll be fine."

"No, you won't. You're losing too much —"

Eli stiffens and draws his gun so fast, I think he's about to shoot me.

Instead, he aims over my shoulder and fires.

I whip around just in time to see a figure in dark clothing collapse onto the ground.

"What the hell? Is that . . .?"

"It's not possible," Eli murmurs. His face has gone stark white.

Before I can even process the fact that Eli shot a drifter in the cleared zone, he takes off toward the body. I follow him at a jog, marveling at how fast he moves for a guy who was just shot in the leg.

The man is lying facedown on the cracked earth, but Eli yanks him onto his back and starts fishing in his pockets.

His face is too tan for his complexion, tight and rough from a lifetime spent in the sun. He's wearing a black T-shirt and a pair of camo utility pants, and there's a rifle lying beside him in the dirt.

"Nothing," Eli mutters, having finished his search of the man's pockets. "How the hell did he get past the mines?"

"They removed some, didn't they? That equipment they have must be able to read the signals the mines emit."

"But if they figured out how to breach the perimeter, where are the rest of them?"

"Maybe it's just him."

"No way. If they're using the setup we found, this is an organized effort. This guy was the canary." Eli's eyes darken. "They're doing recon of their own."

That thought gives me a sick feeling in the pit of my stomach. There's only one reason the drifters would be performing recon on the compound: to prepare to launch an attack.

"We have to get back," says Eli. "We have to report this."

He sets off toward the compound at his normal speed, but after a few paces, he bends at the waist and clutches his leg again.

Without a word, I kneel down and wrap the piece of my shirt around his thigh. The blood soaks it instantly, but I tie it off anyway.

Gripping him under the shoulders, I stumble toward the compound with Eli in tow. My heart is pounding so hard I can feel it in my throat, and Eli's entire body is tight and alert.

"I wonder if anyone saw anything."

"I doubt it," groans Eli. "Most people aren't really looking for anything out here." He winces from the pain. "To them, it's all just backdrop. The Fringe doesn't even feel like a real place."

I shudder. *If they only knew.*

The farther we walk, the heavier Eli gets. I know it isn't a good sign that he's leaning on me more, but I don't look down.

I don't want to see how bad his leg is because I won't accept the possibility that I might not be able to get him back to the compound.

His breath is coming in short gasps now. His face is tinged with pain and sunburn. Deep creases are forming in the corners of his eyes, and every time he cringes from the pain, it feels like a swift kick to the gut.

I glance up at the dizzying sky — the sun that's cooking us alive — and gain a new appreciation for how much I hate the Fringe.

Eli takes another step, and his leg gives out. I push against him with everything I have left, but my back screams in protest. I'm not strong enough.

Just as I'm about to collapse onto the uneven ground, I catch a flash of light in the distance. It's only sunlight reflecting off the compound's windows, but it dominates the horizon like a gigantic beacon, calling us home.

"We're almost there," I croak, unsure if Eli can hear me. My voice sounds very far away.

"Uh-huh."

I chance a look at Eli. His jaw is locked in a pained expression, and his eyelids are drooping closed.

"Come on!" I yell at him.

His weight is staggering. He's still moving his feet, but his injured leg is limp and weak. It reminds me of the time I had to drag a drunk Celdon up to his compartment from Neverland.

We're *so* close, but I doubt anyone can even see us approaching. No one is looking for us. If I stopped and lay down right here beside Eli, we'd both bake in the sun until we were eaten by vultures.

No one would see us. No one would care.

But the image of Celdon in his stupid mesh shirt languishing in Neverland wakes me up.

It's not just me and Eli out here. There are people *in there* — people I left behind. I can't just give up. Not when we're this close.

I force my feet to keep pulling us toward the compound. I can see the airlock doors, and I'm sure we're close enough now for the ExCon man on duty to spot us on the security feed.

Our reflections in the brushed-steel doors stare hopelessly back at us, and I almost don't recognize myself.

I've become a wild creature with tangled hair and the face of a killer. Eli is a shell of the guy I knew. The Eli I trained with was indestructible, but the Eli draped around me looks like someone on the verge of death.

Suddenly his weight seems to double. My legs wobble, and I realize he's passed out. As much as I want to keep holding him up, his weight is too much for me.

My legs buckle, and for three paces, my momentum is the only thing keeping us both upright.

Just as I'm about to collapse, the airlock doors open, and two ExCon men in masks and hazmat suits jump out. They grab Eli under the arms, and when his weight disappears, I feel as though I could float away.

I'm dizzy, and when someone pulls me forward, my vision goes all spotty.

Voices echo in the chamber around me, and I hear the loud hiss of the airlock doors as we're sealed in the radiation chamber. The voices instantly grow louder — reverberating in the small space — and my eyes strain to adjust to the sudden darkness.

"Help him!" I meant to shout, but my voice comes out scratchy and weak.

Hands grip my arms, forcing me into a tiny side chamber lit with a sickening blue light. The door slides shut, but I can still see the men holding Eli upright through the tiny window. His face is way too pale.

"Somebody help him!" I yell again, banging my palm against the window. I need them to understand, but no one can hear me.

Then I feel a gentle gloved hand grip my upper arm. "Harper! It's all right."

I recognize that voice. But before I can make out the person in the hazmat suit, the old plumbing creaks, and I'm pelted with freezing water.

For some reason, that sends me over the edge, and I start to panic.

"They have to take him to the medical ward!" I shout through the deluge of water. "He's lost too much blood!"

Tears are streaming down my cheeks, and my voice sounds hoarse and insane. The water stops, and the hands reach for me again.

"No!" I scream, feeling scared and ridiculous. "Let me go! I have to tell them!"

"Harper! Harper! It's *me*."

I force myself to focus on the person in the suit. Through the condensation on the face shield, I see the outline of black-rimmed glasses.

"Sawyer!" I croak, feeling immediate relief. She'll make sure Eli is taken care of.

"You're okay," she says in a soothing voice. "You're okay. Everything's fine."

Her gloved hands grip the collar of my overshirt and pull, unsnapping all the buttons in one fluid motion and pulling it off me. I shiver as she strips me down to my shorts and tank top and climbs out of her hazmat suit.

I almost laugh at the sight of Sawyer in her med intern outfit — scrubbed up as though it's just another day.

She ushers me through the door on the other side of the chamber, into a dimly lit tunnel, where a gurney is waiting.

"Are they taking him to the medical ward?" I ask.

"Yes," she says, threading an arm around my waist and pulling me toward the gurney.

"I can walk," I mumble. "Can I see him when the doctor's done?"

Sawyer releases me, shaking her head. "They aren't going to let you see *anyone*. Not for a while."

I glance around. The panic is back in full force. "Why not? What's going on?"

"What *happened* out there?" she demands.

Now that the suit is gone, I can read the anxiety in her eyes.

I bite my lip. "You know I can't tell you anything."

"I'm not stupid, Harper," she hisses. "This is the third mission this month where Recon has turned up early or not at all. Eli got blown up the last time, and now he's been shot!"

"Shh!" I glance around at the deserted tunnel to make sure we're alone. "Give me your interface."

She looks confused but pulls it off her glasses and hands it over. I know I'm being paranoid, but I wouldn't put it past Constance to spy on Sawyer, too. I flip it on, but the telltale blinking red dot isn't there. They aren't recording her conversations, at least.

"Harper!" she snaps in a whisper. "What's — going — on?"

I grimace, and when Sawyer speaks next, her voice is so low I can barely hear.

"There are others out there, aren't there?"

I've been sworn to secrecy, but I feel weak and worn down after everything. And Sawyer already knows.

I nod once, and her eyes widen in shock.

"Somebody broke through the cleared zone," I murmur. "We don't know why, but we think they're staking out the compound."

"*Who?*"

She wants me to say it.

"The drift — er, survivors."

"Survivors? How many?"

I shrug.

"How are they alive after all this time?"

"I don't know."

"The radiation alone —"

"I don't know how they're alive," I snap. "Nobody does. But our job is to kill them, and they're trying to kill us."

Sawyer is staring at me as if her entire world is crumbling around her. "I can't believe this."

"You can't say anything," I plead. "I'm not supposed to tell you."

"How could they do this?" she whispers. "Just leave those people out there?"

"I don't know."

"They've just been lying to everybody. They've been lying for *years.*"

Somewhere down the tunnel, a door slams. Before I can respond, Sawyer looks around anxiously and shoves me onto the gurney. She replaces her interface and pushes my shoulders down until I'm lying flat.

"Sorry," she murmurs in a choked voice. "I have to strap you down. You came in a little hysterical."

She pulls the soft restraints around my shoulders and ankles and then covers me with a sheet. I don't like the feeling of the material holding me to the gurney, but at least it's just Sawyer.

She pushes me down the tunnel to the freight lift, and we shoot up through the compound. I shiver violently on the gurney, partly from the cold water and partly from the stress of being shot at.

I can't believe we saw a drifter in the cleared zone. Eli was shot. My nerves are stretched to the breaking point, and I feel as though I'm teetering on the edge of a total meltdown.

The lift dings, and the doors open up into one of the clean, brightly lit tunnels of the medical ward. The friendly scuff of nonslip shoes mixes with the steady beep of monitors. The noise is a pleasant change from the silence of the Fringe, but it looks too nice and orderly after everything I just experienced.

As we venture farther down the tunnel, the usual medical disinfectant smell mixes with the stench of vomit. That sets me on edge, and I try, unsuccessfully, to sit up.

I know I must look nuts, but the nurses we pass don't bat an eye at seeing a cadet strapped to a gurney. That's when I realize where we are: the postexposure wing.

One door we pass is wide open. In the sickly yellowish glow of florescent lighting, I catch a glimpse of an emaciated man about my age. His head looks too large for his body, as though the rest of him has wasted away from the radiation.

In that second, his eyes find mine. A shiver rolls through me when I realize that look is his way of saying, "You're next."

Sawyer wheels me into a private room and forces me to strip again. Once she's confident I'm free from radioactive dust, she gives me a shapeless gown to wear, takes my vital signs, and draws some blood in quiet, businesslike Sawyer fashion.

"How's Eli?" I ask.

"I don't know yet," she says, consulting her interface with a tense expression. "They're still working on him."

She removes the sensor from my arm and meets my gaze. "I have to go now. I'm sorry. You don't have any life-threatening injuries, so I have to let them debrief you."

"No! Don't go!"

I'm a little shocked by my own desperation, but being with Sawyer is the only thing holding me together.

"I have to," she says. "I'm sorry. I promise I'll come check on you. And I'll find out what's going on with Eli."

"Okay."

Sawyer leaves me alone in my room, and not a minute later, I hear another knock.

The visitors don't wait for me to answer before barging in. I'm not surprised to see Remy Chaplin again. As the undersecretary, he's tasked with making sure no Recon operatives spill the beans about what's really going on outside the compound.

But when I see Jayden skulking behind him, I shrink back into my pillows. She's wearing a familiar predatory expression that makes my stomach clench, and she's pissed.

"What's going on?" she yells as soon as the door swings closed.

"Eli's been shot," I blurt out. "And there's a drifter *inside* the cleared zone."

Her face blanches. "*What?*"

"We just saw the one, but they are definitely performing some kind of drifter recon."

"Drifter re —" Jayden stops and shakes her head. "Start from the beginning, Riley. You aren't making any sense."

"They figured out how to remove our mines. They've repurposed them beyond the perimeter. They almost blew us up! They figured out how to deactivate the signals so they don't show up on the map. We can't even get a read on them once they've been transplanted."

Jayden and Remy exchange a knowing look that irritates me, but I keep going.

"I got a look at their tech setup, too. It's not very advanced, but they're definitely organizing."

I stop, remembering what Eli said about deciding what information we want to give away.

What am I doing? I need to shut up until I talk to him because I am way too frantic to think clearly.

"Did you perform your assigned patrol, Cadet?" asks Jayden in her most patronizing tone.

"What? Um, yeah . . . We went to that town, like you said."

"And what is its status?"

I stare at her in disbelief.

Why the hell is she asking me about some stupid town when drifters are staking out the compound as we speak?

"Cleared," I lie, just trying to speed this part up. "But —"

"That will be all, Riley," she says, holding up a hand. "I've heard quite enough."

"What are you talking about?"

"It's clear you're suffering from severe stress — probably caused by leaving the compound for the first time."

"*What?*"

Yeah, I'm stressed. But since when has Jayden given a fuck about my well-being?

Then she turns her striking dark eyes on me in what I imagine is her most sympathetic expression. "It's nothing to be embarrassed about. Nervous breakdowns and hallucinations aren't uncommon among cadets who are deployed before they're ready. Just relax. We're going to see that you're under constant care until you feel better."

"Constant —"

"Supervision, Riley. Just until we can be sure you aren't a danger to yourself or to others."

"I'm not a danger to myself . . . and I'm not going to tell anybody. But you need to listen to me!"

"Don't worry," she says, and I'm positive I'm not imagining the tiny evil smirk twitching on her lips. "I'm sure the doctors can help you sort out what's real and what's . . . How should I put this? A figment of your imagination."

"*Are you serious?* You're worried I'm going to tell the whole compound about the drifters, so you're going to lock me up so I seem *crazy?*"

I glance from Jayden to Remy, fury and disbelief fighting for dominance. She looks smug, but Remy's expression is grave.

He doesn't think I'm crazy. He's scared shitless.

"Please don't share these, uh, *hallucinations* with anyone else, Riley," says Remy in a quiet voice. "We don't want to start a panic over nothing."

I open my mouth to retort, but Jayden cuts me off. "Rest up," she says, patting my leg. I want to smack her in the face. "We need you back at full strength for your next deployment."

Next deployment? Eli was shot less than an hour ago, and Jayden's already thinking of our next mission. That's when it hits me: Constance never meant for us to come back. They were sure the drifters would finish us off for them.

Now that we've returned, they're not going to let that happen again. And Jayden's going to make damn sure I don't have the chance to tell anybody what we found.

They file out of my room, and I stare at the door for several seconds in shock.

Sawyer reappears a moment later, and I can tell by her expression that I'm not going to like what she has to say.

"What's going on?"

"He's stable," she says in a breathless voice. "They just moved him to his own room."

"I want to see him."

She shakes her head. "You can't. Nobody can see him until he's been debriefed. And anyway . . ." She trails off, and I can tell she's dreading whatever she has to say next.

"What is it?"

"I have to move you to the psych ward," she says, looking torn. "Head physician's orders. Jayden got to him."

"*For how long?*"

Sawyer takes a step toward me, eyebrows raised. "Until you take back whatever you *think* you saw. Maybe not even then."

"They can't keep me there forever," I say indignantly.

"They can keep you there as long as they want — at least until they need you again." Sawyer's eyebrows creep impossibly higher. "I've seen it."

So this is what happens to Recon operatives they consider a risk to the compound: They lock them away until they're confident they won't tell anyone what they saw.

Shocked into silence, I let Sawyer summon an electric wheelchair and steer me down the tunnel in my hospital gown toward a wing I've never visited before. It looks like all the others in the medical ward, except the walls aren't made of frosted glass. They're completely solid and only have a tiny window near the top of the heavy steel doors.

I shiver. It reminds me of the interrogation room Control tortured me in.

But when Sawyer swipes us in, I see that the inside is nearly identical to the other rooms. There are no padded walls or restraints on the bed, and they've even left me a pair of shorts and a black tank top to change into.

"I had Lenny bring up some of your clothes," she says.

"Can she visit?"

Sawyer shakes her head. "You aren't allowed visitors, but I'll come check on you. And I'll keep you updated on Eli's status."

"Thanks."

Standing there in my hospital gown, it strikes me once again how much my life has deviated from the future I had planned. Nothing is the way I thought it was, and now it feels as though I don't have any life of my own.

I'm one of Recon's "assets" now, and they can do whatever they want with me.

eight

Eli

I hate the feeling of regaining consciousness after passing out. It's not like waking up from sleep. You jerk back to life with a sense of urgency — as if your tired brain knows you were in the middle of something important.

Something like . . . getting back to the compound to warn the others.

Judging by the cold air and the sickly artificial light spilling through my eyelids, I'm not on the Fringe anymore. Harper must have gotten me back somehow.

What had I needed to warn Remy about? My leg?

That can't be right. But there's a sharp pain throbbing from my knee to my hip. My brain is struggling to connect the dots, and I recognize the sluggishness from the last time they had me on pain meds.

Reluctantly, I peel my eyes open.

I'm lying in a hospital bed — again — with a tube shooting fluids into my arm. I'm alone, which means they're either debriefing Harper, or . . .

No. Constance still needs Harper. They wouldn't have killed her. Not yet.

The rational part of my brain is wrestling with all the pent-up fear and paranoia I've accumulated from being on the Fringe, but the paranoid half is winning.

I don't trust Jayden as far as I can throw her, and right now, I have no idea where Harper is. Constance could have thrown her in the cages for safekeeping, for all I know. All the veins in my arms are popping against my skin, and I realize I have the edges of the bed in a death grip.

I take a few deep breaths to calm myself down, but it isn't helping. That relaxation shit never does. The only thing that will help me relax is for someone to come in here and tell me what the hell is going on.

I throw back the blankets and stare down at my legs. The left one is covered in snowy white bandages, and someone has tied my ankles to the bed.

What. The. Fuck.

Bending at the waist, I try to reach the restraints around my ankles and almost rip out my IV in the process. I swear and stab the call button, feeling like an invalid.

Two nurses with bouncy ponytails rush in looking panicked, but they both bite back a laugh when they see me hunched over my knees, hairy legs exposed in the short hospital gown.

"Sorry about that, Lieutenant," says one bottle-blond nurse in a lilting voice. "We don't want you ripping your stitches."

"Stitches?"

As she bends to undo the restraints, it all comes back to me in a rush: the drifters, getting shot, the man in the cleared zone.

"Can you find Remy Chaplin, please?" I snap.

"He-He's right out in the lobby," she stammers. "I'll let him know you're awake."

Now that my legs are free, I can tell putting weight on my left leg would be a bad idea. But I need to tell *someone* what's going on.

A moment later, Remy breezes in as though he's got all day. Behind him — surprise, surprise — is Jayden.

"Well. Good afternoon, Parker," she simpers. "It seems you

can't go a single deployment without some life-threatening injury forcing you back to the compound early."

"That's not why we came back," I say between gritted teeth. "The drifters cut off our water supply. They mean business."

"The backup reservoir?"

"Yeah. But that's not what I wanted to report. There was a drifter . . . in the cleared zone. About a mile and a half from the compound."

Jayden's mouth tightens, but she doesn't look surprised. "That's not possible."

I hesitate for a moment, unsure if I should tell her everything we learned about their operations. "It *is*. They know how to disable and repurpose our mines. One almost blew my legs off."

Remy's jaw has gone rigid, and I can tell I've awakened his worst fears. "Why would they only send one man into the cleared zone?"

"To investigate. To see if it was possible. As a warning. I don't know! There could be a million reasons."

Remy glances at Jayden with a serious look in his eyes. "Commander, since Cadet Riley's story checks out, we should send out another party to patrol within the cleared zone . . . ensure none get within sight of the compound."

"With due respect, Undersecretary, our first priority should be learning more about the drifters' operations. Clearly there are more than we thought, and now they're mobilizing against us. We need to locate their headquarters and terminate their leadership."

Remy gives her a look that would make any lesser woman cower, but Jayden stretches up to her full height and meets his gaze dead-on.

"Our first priority is protecting the people inside this compound, Commander," he says sharply. "And don't you forget it.

Send out the patrol. All intelligence-gathering missions are tabled until further notice. Is that understood?"

There's a long, awkward pause as Jayden sizes Remy up. Then she seems to decide to pick her battle some other way.

"Yes, sir," she says in her most acidic voice. But when she says it, I don't get a twinge of amusement the way I do when Harper responds to orders with contempt. There's a note of warning in Jayden's voice that gives me a chill.

She's planning something, and I'm sure it involves me and Harper going back on the Fringe.

She turns on her heel and leaves, slamming the door behind her.

"Sir, how is Cadet Riley?" I ask.

"Cadet Riley made it back to the compound safe and sound. Dragged you about a mile, is what I heard. She's been making quite the scene ever since she got back."

Yeah, that sounds like Harper.

"Can I visit her?"

Remy's face goes dark, and I see him putting his guard up. "No. No, I'm afraid not."

"Why not?"

"She's not being allowed visitors right now."

"But if she's been debriefed . . ."

"Riley is in psychiatric holding until further notice."

My stomach drops. "*What?*"

"When we went to debrief her, she was hysterical. Her story matches up with what you told us, but . . ."

"So release her!" I yell. "She isn't crazy."

Remy grimaces. "No one said she was crazy. She's just been under a lot of stress, and it seems to be getting to her."

"That's ridiculous! I've never seen a cadet behave so well under pressure."

Remy gives me a sharp look, but then it starts to fray with sympathy.

"With all due respect, she may not have been faring as well as you thought, Lieutenant. Commander Pierce seems to think she's suffered some kind of mental break. We've detained her until we can be sure she doesn't pose a threat to internal security."

"She's not going to go telling people. She wouldn't do that."

"That isn't your call to make, Parker," he says, more forcefully this time. "As far as we're concerned, Riley is a liability. But if you're worried about her falling behind on training, I assure you that we'll have her back as soon as she's stable."

I let out a burst of air between my teeth and slam my head back against my pillows. I can't believe Jayden's getting away with this. It has to be Constance flexing its muscles from on high.

Jayden knows Harper is fine, but she's worried about what she might say to people about the drifters, the bid, Sullivan Taylor . . . any of it, really. She'd counted on us getting killed out there. And now that we're back, she's going to do whatever she can to discredit Harper and cut her off from everyone she knows. I'm sure she's still working on my punishment.

"I hope you recover quickly," says Remy. "We'll need your help locating that command center Riley mentioned."

As Remy leaves, I have the sudden urge to go bang my head against the wall. I don't know how much Harper told them, but I hope she didn't just hand over our bargaining chip.

She wouldn't, I tell myself. *We talked about it.*

But after Remy and Jayden's visit, I'm starting to feel a gnawing sense of unrest.

What if Harper really did snap? I thought her reaction to killing that drifter was normal, and she managed to stay levelheaded even when we were under fire. But what if I only saw what I wanted to see? Is it possible I overlooked obvious signs that she wasn't in her right mind?

Before I have time to think about what I'm doing, I swing my legs over the bed and get to my feet.

As soon as I put weight on my left leg, it buckles underneath me, and I have to grab the swiveling tray over the bed to keep from falling. The flimsy thing tips, sending a pitcher of water flying.

The blond nurse runs back in, panting as though she just ran a mile. "I told you not to try to walk!" she shrieks.

"I need to visit someone."

"You're not visiting anyone," she growls, her friendly demeanor vanishing as her shoes squeak through the puddle by my bed. "Visiting hours are over, and you can't walk."

"Then get me a wheelchair," I groan. "Just get me out of here."

But Blondie is already shoving me back into bed and stabbing a needle in my IV.

"What is that?"

"Commander Pierce says you need to rest, Lieutenant."

"What the fuck?" I yell. "Where's Sawyer? I need to talk to Sawyer."

"She's busy! You can see her when you wake up."

"When I . . ."

But the drugs are already taking hold. I can feel myself slipping away. My last thought is how much I'd pay to get Harper in the boxing ring with this girl before I succumb to sleep.

* * *

By the time I regain consciousness, I've slept the day away. The lighting in the tunnel is dim, and my room is dark apart from a single florescent light over the bed. I feel foggy and slightly nauseated, but that's probably just the meds.

I'm tempted to press the call button again, but I don't know if the nurses have changed shifts yet, and I can't risk Blondie coming back. I can already tell she and I aren't going to get along.

Glancing over at the IV suspended above my bed, I catch a glimpse of a shiny pair of crutches propped against the headboard. A white key card with a number stamped on the side is hanging from a bright red lanyard. I grin.

Only one person could have gotten me a key card for the medical ward, and only one med intern is mischievous enough to spring me from bed rest — someone who's been hanging out with Harper way too long.

I make a mental note to thank Sawyer someday and reach for the crutches.

It isn't easy hoisting myself out of bed or maneuvering around the mess of cords and tubes on the floor, but I manage. I only stop when I feel a cool breeze against my ass.

I groan. I'm not going to see Harper while wearing a hospital gown. I'd never get her to listen to me again. I swing my injured leg over to the fake oak wardrobe in the corner and open it.

One of my T-shirts and a pair of sweats are sitting on the shelf, which means Miles must have paid me a visit. He's suffered through enough breezy gowns to know that the first thing you want when you wake up in the medical ward is your own clothes.

Propping myself up on the bed, I change quickly and limp back out into the tunnel.

Luckily, the Recon recovery wing is deserted this time of night. Most of the nurses and interns on duty are making their rounds, and I've been here enough times that I know exactly where the psych ward is.

The lights flicker on as I go, but no one appears to admonish me for wandering around.

When I reach the door with the number on the key card, I slide it into the reader and wait for the light to turn green. It's dark inside Harper's room, but I close the door quietly and feel my way to the bed.

From the tiny bit of light filtering through the window, I can just make out Harper's face resting against the pillow. She's curled into a ball, with her hair spilling everywhere and her brow furrowed in sleep.

I need to talk to her, but I don't want to wake her. Back when I was a private, sleep was a luxury. During that first year, there were times I wouldn't sleep for days after a mission. So I sink into the chair beside the bed and watch her.

Harper looks much more relaxed in sleep, and for some reason, I'm fascinated. But then she makes a noise halfway between a yell and a sob, and I jump.

She wasn't awakened by her own yell, but tears are streaming down her cheeks. She folds in on herself, crying in her sleep, and something inside me cracks.

Without thinking, I lunge forward and accidentally put weight on my injured leg. A jolt of pain shoots up the left side of my body, and I collapse onto the edge of the bed.

"Harper!" I hiss, steadying myself on the flimsy mattress. "Harper!"

When she opens her eyes, it takes her a second to realize there's someone in the room with her. When she does, she jerks upright with a squeak, and I realize how insensitive it was to wake her like that in the middle of a nightmare.

"It's okay! It's okay! It's me."

Harper drags in a shaky breath. She's panting hard, and I know I startled her.

"What are you doing here?" she whispers. "They said I couldn't have any visitors."

My hand is still on her arm, but I don't move it. "I know. Remy and Jayden told me they put you here. It sometimes happens with new cadets. They're just worried you're going to tell people what you saw."

"They haven't told me when I can leave," she says in a terrified whisper. "They're just going to keep me locked up here until they need me again."

"No. No, they won't."

Not if I have anything to do with it.

But her eyes are quickly filling with tears. I've never seen her this rattled, but the postexposure hysteria is all too familiar.

She nods. "I told them about the drifter in the cleared zone, but now Jayden's trying to make me seem crazy. We have to tell someone who will listen — the board or . . ."

"We can't," I say in a warning voice. "That will only make things worse for you."

"But they could come here."

"Who?"

She glances at the door. "The drifters."

"It doesn't matter. They'd never be able to enter the compound."

"I can't go back out there, Eli," she says, shaking her head slowly. I can tell she's teetering on the edge of a total breakdown. "I can't . . . do that again."

"Don't think about that right now," I say. "It won't do any good."

"I've never been so scared in my life. I . . . I *killed* someone."

"I know."

She meets my gaze, wild-eyed. "I can't go through that again. I won't."

We fall silent for a moment, neither of us willing to admit she won't have a choice.

But when I look up, I realize she isn't at a loss for words. She's crying silently, head bowed. "Maybe I am crazy," she squeaks.

"No," I say firmly. "No, you're not."

I pull her toward me, and to my surprise, Harper wraps her arms around my torso and buries her face in my T-shirt.

Harper — tough, unshakable Harper — is sobbing into my shoulder. My arms tighten around her, and I rest my chin on top of her head.

Her fear fills me with fury — fury at the board, fury at Constance, fury at Jayden for locking her up and making her question her sanity.

Harper's the sanest person I know. Any sane person would have a breakdown after what we did. I should be having one, too, but my insides are tough and calloused from years on the Fringe. Recon and everything that came before sucked out my compassion and made me something less than human.

After a while, I become aware of just how long I've been holding Harper. It's definitely longer than what's appropriate, but I can't make myself let go. She fits perfectly in my arms, and holding her makes me feel as though I can neutralize some of her fear and grief.

She pulls away first, looking a little embarrassed but much more like herself.

"I'm sorry," she says in a hoarse whisper.

"Don't be. Listen." I grip her arm and glance at the door. "I'm going to talk to Jayden to see if I can get you out of here, but you can't give them any reason to detain you longer. Constance is going to be looking for any reason to discredit you. Do whatever they tell you. Eat your meals. Talk to the shrink. Keep asking for visitors, but don't fight with the nurses."

She raises an eyebrow, and I fix her with a stern look.

"What about you?" she asks. "How are you feeling?"

"Not bad, considering I got shot. They just grazed me, though. My leg should be fine in a couple of weeks."

She lets out a burst of air. "We have to get out of here, Eli."

"I know. That's what I'm saying."

"No, I mean . . ." Harper bites her lip and glances at the door to make sure we're alone. "We need to get *out*, out. Out of this compound."

At first, I'm not sure she said what I think she said.

"Leave the compound?"

"Yeah."

"You want to transfer?"

She tilts her head to the side, and I can tell she's nervous about sharing this idea with me. "I thought . . . maybe 119 in Arizona, where the new recruits went after the bidding ceremony."

She holds my gaze hopefully for several beats and then tears her eyes away and focuses on the blankets. "Never mind. Of course you don't have to leave. I'm sure Jayden will lay off eventually. But I'm going to try . . . Celdon and I are going to try. It's too dangerous for us to stay here."

I let out a long, deep breath.

Of course I thought about leaving the compound years ago, after I received a bid from Recon. But my VocAps score was so low I knew I wouldn't receive a better bid anywhere else. I'd never even *considered* leaving after that.

The thought is crazy, but it ignites a flicker of hope inside me. "How?"

"Buy a ticket out."

"Do you know how much those cost?"

"Yes!" she snaps. "But what other choice do we have? Stick around until Constance finds a way to get rid of us?"

"What's your plan?"

"I don't have a plan, okay? Unless Celdon becomes a prostitute, I have no way of getting that much money."

She sounds pissed that I'm poking holes in her plan, but then she cracks a grin.

I can't help it. I laugh.

It rumbles up my chest, and when it escapes, Harper joins in with a nervous giggle. The sound sends an unfamiliar warmth over me that I wish I could feel every day.

When we've both recovered, Harper falls silent. She's still smiling, but I know she's serious about leaving the compound. And she asked me to go with her. She wants me to leave with her and Celdon, her best friend in the world.

The rational part of my brain knows it's only because Constance wants me dead, but the other part is screaming that it's significant.

"Three tickets will cost six grand. Can Celdon get that kind of money?"

I don't know how much Systems workers are paid, but I know it's a hell of a lot more than our stipends.

"He says no. Most of his stipend is automatically deducted for food and his swanky compartment. It would take a year for him to save that much. I have a little money put aside, but we'll want to convert that to 119's credits when we get there . . . for food and rent until we're placed."

"And I'm guessing hacking Finance is out?"

Harper throws me a sharp glance, as though she and Celdon never hacked into VocAps records or anything.

Suddenly an idea pops into my head. "I could fight."

"Fight who?"

"You know . . . take a fight."

She looks skeptical. "You can make that much money from an illegal fight?"

"Well, no. Not from one fight, usually. But if it's a big fight where I've got long odds, I could make quite a bit just betting on myself."

"Is that allowed?"

"It's . . . frowned upon. But I could get away with it if someone bet for me."

She shakes her head. "I can't let you do that."

"Why not?"

Harper goes red in the face, which immediately sparks my curiosity, but I wait patiently for her to answer.

"Because . . . I dragged you into this mess. And you're already hurt. You can't fight with your leg."

I shrug. "My leg will be fine in a few weeks. And you didn't drag me into this."

"Yes I did."

"I let myself get dragged in, and it wouldn't have happened if I hadn't recruited you for Recon in the first place."

She falls silent, and I can tell she's mulling the idea over. Even she can't deny that it's a good one. "A few weeks?"

I nod.

Another grin breaks through her serious expression, causing my chest to ache in a pleasant way. Hell, I'd sign up for ten fights just to get her smiling like that because of me.

"Okay."

A heavy silence falls between us, and I feel strangely giddy for reasons I can't explain.

"Talk to Jayden, will you?" she asks finally. "I need to get out of here so I can watch you get your ass handed to you."

nine

Eli

"Jesus Christ. What the hell happened to you?" asks Miles.

"Got shot," I say, glaring at the beige glob of patient-approved food congealing on my tray.

Miles slams the door and swaggers into my room, looking as though he just sent half the nurses running for the hills. Freakishly tall and rugged from too much time on the Fringe, Miles looks wildly out of place in the shiny, clean medical ward.

He stares at my injured leg and collapses into a chair by the bed. "Can you ever go out there and come back in one piece? I'm starting to think you've got the hots for one of these nurses."

I laugh. "Not a chance."

It's day two of my recovery, and Miles is the first visitor I've been allowed. The doctor came by earlier to examine me and said they wouldn't let me leave the medical ward for a few days. He's keeping me there for "observation," but that's just code for "Jayden doesn't want to deal with you." I know because I've messaged her three times to no response.

There was no point arguing. As my commanding officer, Jayden's orders are law.

"How do they keep explaining gunshot wounds and explosions to a bunch of doctors who supposedly have no idea what's out there?"

"The attending physicians who work on the postexposure unit have security clearance," I say, swinging my leg over the bed and gingerly applying some weight. "They know what we know."

"Guess they don't care."

"Why would they? They aren't the ones who have to go out there."

His face grows serious. "So what's the deal? Jayden's put a freeze on outbound missions. They've just got guys patrolling the perimeter now."

"We saw a drifter in the cleared zone."

"No shit?"

"Yeah." I practice standing without my crutches, which does nothing except trigger a fresh wave of pain. I try pacing around the room, but I'm worn out after only a few steps.

By the time I collapse back onto the bed, Miles is staring at me. "How the hell did a drifter get into the cleared zone?"

"They figured out how to track and disarm the mines."

Miles is too shocked to speak, so I launch into the story of what happened to me and Harper out there. His eyes grow wide when I tell him that the drifters repurposed one of our mines, and he bangs his fist on the bed when I get to the part about our ambush near the border.

That's one thing I like about Miles: He always says the wrong thing, but he is a great listener.

"Shit," he says when I finish.

"Yeah."

"I can't believe they took out our checkpoint. And they're using our own mines against us? They mean business."

I nod, but I have a sick feeling that those things were only the warm-up. And now that the drifters have found a way to breach the cleared zone, we aren't as safe as we always thought.

There's a sharp knock at the door that makes us both jump. He leans back in his chair and tries to look casual as Sawyer strides in with a stethoscope around her neck.

By the looks of her, she's been here a while. Her shoulders are sagged in fatigue, her smooth black hair is falling out of a messy ponytail, and there are dark bags under her eyes.

"So how's Riley holding up?" Miles asks.

He doesn't know Sawyer and Harper are friends, but I'm painfully aware that Sawyer is listening to everything we say as she beams the data from my monitors to her interface.

"Jayden seems to want to keep her here indefinitely."

"No shit?"

"Yeah. In the psych ward. They aren't even allowing her visitors."

"Damn. That's cold. Did she lose it?"

"No," I snap. "She's fine. She's upset — and she never wants to go out there again — but she'll be okay."

He nods, but there's suspicion brewing in his dark eyes. "Wait. How do you know how she's doing if they've got her on lockdown?"

I clear my throat loudly, looking for a way to backtrack. I don't want to get into this with Miles — particularly now, when we have an audience.

To my surprise, Sawyer comes to my rescue.

"They plan to release her in a week," she says.

Miles spins around, as though noticing her for the first time. "Riley?"

"Yeah. And she's showing no signs of radiation sickness." She jerks her head toward my monitors. "Neither are you."

"I've never gotten sick after," I say with a shrug. "But that's good, I guess."

I'm a little surprised that anything about my health is positive, considering how much radiation I've been exposed to throughout my life. And based on the fact that section placements are mostly determined by people's viability, there's a good chance I won't live to see thirty.

Once Sawyer finishes reading my data, she throws me a wry grin and leaves. I breathe a sigh of relief when she disappears and slump back onto my pillows.

"How was she out there?" asks Miles. "I mean, I know she's unbelievable in training, but you can never really tell what a cadet's going to do on the Fringe."

"She was great," I say with a shrug. "I've never seen anyone stay that in control the first time. I mean, she was terrified, but she held it together."

As I talk, Miles watches me carefully but doesn't say anything.

"Listen," I mutter in a low voice. "Do you know who might be looking for a big fight?"

"What?" His face twists into an amused expression. "Are you serious?"

"Yeah. I want to fight as soon as my leg is decent."

"Hey, if you're looking to get out of deployment, all you have to do is ask."

I shake my head. "I don't want to throw a fight with you. I need to win."

"Why?"

"It doesn't matter. I just need a fight with long odds on someone I can beat — a fight that draws a crowd. I need to put a lot of money on this one."

Miles scoffs. "Are you crazy? You just got shot. You'll be lucky if your leg is good to go in three weeks, and you want to stack a fight you have no chance of winning?"

"You know I can win."

"Not like this, you can't."

I let out a frustrated groan. "Look, I need to do this."

"What's going on with you? Are you trying to get yourself put on permanent disability?"

"No."

"Then what is it?"

"I just need some cash. Lots of it."

Miles's scowl softens. "Listen. If you're in trouble, you need to tell me. Whoever's shaking you down, we'll take care of it. Once you're healed up, we'll get a couple guys together, go down there, and —" He makes a smashing gesture with his fist.

"It's nothing like that."

I pause. I know I have to tell him, but it isn't going to be pretty.

"I'm leaving the compound."

"What?"

"Do you remember when Harper was arrested?"

His eyebrows shoot halfway up his forehead. "How could I forget?"

"Well, she wasn't just detained by Control. Constance started watching her. They were torturing her to find out what she knew, and when I gave her an alibi, they started watching me, too."

I launch into the story about Sullivan Taylor's murder and Constance's surveillance, my dread mounting with every word. I'm fully aware that the less Miles knows, the better, but I can't just leave without telling him why.

After everything we've been through together, I owe him an explanation.

When I finish, Miles's face is so still and serious it looks as though it's been cut from granite. He's deep in thought, just as shocked as I was that Constance would eliminate anybody they perceived as a threat.

Finally his serious mask slips a little. "Holy shit. You *like* her!"

I stare at him in disbelief. That was the last thing I expected him to say.

"What?"

"You've got a thing for Riley!" He claps his hands together, grinning like a dog. "It all makes sense now — why you were such a whiny little bitch about training her *and* why you got involved with her bid."

He lets out a hollow, crazed laugh that he reserves for times he thinks I'm doing something truly stupid. "Geez, man! Any other girl! Pick *any other girl*, 'cause this one's gonna get your ass killed."

"That's all you have to say?" I snap. "You don't have any advice about handling Constance?"

"Well . . . I hate to say this, but if Constance wants Riley dead . . . you're not going to be able to stop them. My advice is to stay as far away —"

"That's why I need the fight. Six grand, and we can buy three tickets to 119 and get the hell out of here."

"Wait, wait, wait," he says, fighting a grin. "You're leaving *together?*"

"Harper, me, and her friend Celdon. Constance beat the shit out of him to scare Harper, and he's in trouble now, too. They fucking mean business! They aren't going to let us live if we stay here."

"Well isn't that just one big happy family . . ."

"It's not like that." I feel myself swinging abruptly from nervous to pissed off.

"Then what's it like?" he retorts. "You tell me. You put yourself and me at risk to dig into this girl's bid. You lied to Control for her and almost got your ranks stripped. You went out on the

Fringe with her . . . *knowing* Constance wants her dead. And now you want to have an illegal fight so you can run away with her? Are you stupid?"

"She wouldn't even be in this mess if it weren't for me!" I yell. "I recruited her for Recon. I gave her a death sentence!"

"You know that's not your fault. You were just doing your job."

"It doesn't mean it's not my fault."

"That's fucked up, Eli. You can't go carrying that shit around with you. You can't do this out of guilt."

"I'm not," I sigh. "I —"

"You like her!"

"No," I snap, letting out a burst of air. "I can't."

"Can't and don't are two different things, man."

"Not around here, they're not."

He's silent for a moment. "So that's why you want to move, huh?"

"What? No. It's not like it would be any different there. With our scores, we'll still end up in tier three — probably ExCon this time."

"But you won't be Riley's commanding officer there. Come on. Are you seriously going to transfer compounds for that? You can be with her here. You just have to be careful. Brooke and I don't like it, but we manage."

"I don't *want* that!" I growl before I can stop myself. "It's miserable! You think I want what you and Brooke have? You think I want to be with Harper on the side and sneak around so Jayden doesn't find out? You think I want to give her even more to use against me? No! I won't live like that."

Miles's face goes slack. I know my outburst hurt him, and I deserve to run down to Waste Management and stick my hand in a particle shredder. Instead, I let out a sigh, trying to get my temper under control. "I'm sorry. I didn't mean that."

"Oh, you meant it," he says, his voice quiet with subdued rage. "Me and Brooke aren't perfect. I know that, all right? It's not what I'd pick. But that's the way it is.

"You have to stop worrying about the way you wish things were and just go for it. Things are what they are. I can't marry her, but I still see her every day."

"I know. I shouldn't have —"

"You know what's gonna happen to you and Riley?"

The lines of rage disappear from his face, and the calm, serious look that replaces it is even more terrifying.

"You're going to push her away like you always do, and you're both gonna die."

His words shock me a little, but I drag in some air and remind myself that he's only saying that because he's angry. "I'm sorry."

"Don't be sorry, Eli. Man up. If you want a fight, I'll get you a fight. I'll even train with you once your leg is healed."

"Thank you."

"But you want my advice?"

"Go ahead."

After how shitty I was to him, the least I can do is let him talk.

He meets my gaze dead on. "Don't wait around. You two don't have a lot of time."

ten

Harper

I wait for Eli to come to my room the next night, but he never shows. Sawyer stops by to let me know he's still in the medical ward, but she's assigned to other patients, so she doesn't stay long.

I spend the next few days prowling my room like a prisoner. I do everything Eli told me to do: I eat my meals. I talk to the psychiatrist. I ask for visitors, but I don't push the nurses.

Every day, the shrink asks me the same inane questions. And every day, I answer with the same canned responses that Sawyer coached me on.

How are you feeling?

Fine.

Have you been having any night terrors?

No.

Have you been having any visions about your time outside the compound?

No.

Have you been hearing voices?

No.

Do you ever feel as though someone is out to get you?

No.

How do you feel about your position in Recon?

Grateful.

What's your impression of the compound's leadership?

Favorable.

All that obedience is enough to make me crazy for real, but I won't let Constance break me. I'm just a pawn to them, but if I lose it and start raising hell, they'll use my outburst to justify keeping me here for good.

They're still careful to isolate me from other Recon operatives. When my assigned nurse finally takes me out for a walk around the ward, I'm pretty sure she avoids the tunnel with Eli's room on purpose.

A week after my admittance, the attending physician comes by my room during his rounds. He's a tired-looking man with deep frown lines and salt-and-pepper hair.

When he pulls up my chart on his interface, he lingers longer than usual and lets out a heavy burst of air through his nostrils.

"Well, Commander Pierce seemed to feel you were deeply disturbed by your deployment. She thought you might be a danger to yourself, which is why she recommended we place you under observation."

I open my mouth to protest, but the doctor holds up a hand to stop me. "But from what I can see, your reaction is normal for a cadet. You were overwhelmed and frightened, but you'll be all right."

His words stir a tiny bit of hope inside me, and I sit up a little straighter. "That's good, right?"

"Yes. And your physical health is good, too. You don't seem to have suffered any adverse effects from the radiation exposure."

I hold my breath, positive he can't mean what I think he means.

"How are you feeling?"

"Fine."

"Good. I think it would be all right for you to go back to your compartment, just so long as you take it easy for a few days, yes?"

"Yes!" I say, relieved. "Yes, of course."

He smiles a tight, tired smile. "Very good. Lyang? Lyang!"

Sawyer pokes her head around the door and glances at me. "Sir?"

"I'm discharging Cadet Riley. Please process the request and show her out."

Sawyer beams but quickly schools her expression. "Yes, sir."

I grin at Sawyer, unable to hold it in. The doctor shuffles out, and as soon as he leaves, she lets out a breath of relief.

"Thank god! I didn't think they were ever gonna let you out!"

"You and me both," I groan, hopping off the bed and dragging my fingers through my tangled hair.

"One sec," Sawyer says, ducking out of the room and heading down the tunnel.

She's gone for several minutes, and when she returns, I'm relieved to see she's carrying a fresh set of gray fatigues and my combat boots.

"Thanks!" I grab the clothes from her and start pulling the pants on over my sleep shorts. "I thought they were going to make me march down to Recon in a hospital gown."

"Don't thank me," she says. "Lenny dropped those off for you a few days ago. She and some of the other Recon cadets came by . . . Celdon, too . . . but they weren't letting anybody see you."

"Celdon came by?"

Sawyer grimaces. "He told me everything. He feels terrible for what happened before you left."

"Is he still on surge?"

She shrugs. "I've been working back-to-back shifts here. I've barely seen him."

I nod, mustering up the courage to ask the question that's

been weighing on me for the last several days.

"Did . . . Did Eli come by?" I ask cautiously, trying to sound casual.

Her face cracks with sympathy. "No. Not that I've heard. I'm sorry."

I clear my throat. "Um, that's okay." *I probably freaked him out with my talk of 119.* "How's his leg?"

"It should be okay in a few weeks. They discharged him the day before yesterday."

"Oh." I'm trying to hide my disappointment, but Sawyer knows me too well to be fooled.

"He was talking about you, you know."

"What?"

Sawyer cracks a grin. "He and his friend."

"Miles?"

"I don't know. He was asking Eli about you."

I don't want to probe any further, but I'm dying to know what Eli said. "Asking him what?"

"Just how you were." Her smile broadens. "Eli only had good things to say."

"Really?" I'm annoyed by the glowy feeling expanding in my chest, but I can't seem to stop it.

"Yeah. I think he likes you."

"You don't know the half of it."

"Oh, come on," she says. "You like him, too."

"He's my commanding officer, Sawyer. Nothing can happen."

She rolls her eyes, but she's watching me closely, putting her diagnostic skills to the test.

"But something *has* happened!" she hisses. "I can see it in your face."

I shake my head. "It doesn't matter."

"You guys kissed, didn't you?" she asks, taking on a very un-Sawyer-like girly expression.

"Yeah. And then he shot me down."

Her face falls. "*What?*"

"I told you. Nothing can happen between us."

She looks genuinely disappointed, and I wonder what Eli could have said to earn her affection. Sawyer doesn't like many people.

"That sucks. I *swear* he's into you."

"Yeah, well . . . He didn't even come to visit me."

"He probably knew Jayden wasn't letting anyone see you."

I try to smile. Sawyer doesn't usually go to such lengths to make me feel better, and she almost *never* stretches the truth to spare my feelings. I'm actually a little touched.

I bend down to tighten the knots on my bootlaces and try to push Eli out of my mind. "It doesn't matter. They're letting me go. Let's get out of here before they change their minds."

* * *

Even though the doctor told me to take it easy, one week off after deployment is all you get in Recon. Since he declared me healthy, Jayden will expect me to return to training immediately.

I'm strangely grateful for the return to normalcy. After spending a week locked in the psych ward, there's nothing appealing about *more* rest and relaxation. At least in training, I don't have time to think about anything else. Plus, I really want to hit something.

The next morning, I get to the training center a half hour early and start a slow warm-up jog around the shaky metal track suspended over the floor.

I'm jittery with nerves. It's like my first day in Recon all over again.

As I round the bend, I keep my eyes fixed on the entrance. I don't want to admit it, but I'm waiting for Eli to walk through those doors. Even though he didn't come back to my room, he's the only one who was out there with me and the only one who knows what I'm feeling.

A few minutes before oh-eight hundred, the doors fly open. Lenny, Kindra, Bear, and Blaze shuffle in laughing and joking, oblivious to the fact that drifters are encroaching on the compound.

When they spot me, they grin and wave me down. I take the stairs two at a time, and they meet me at the bottom with a flurry of cheers and questions.

"Hey, you!" Lenny shouts. "Good to see they let you out of the looney bin."

I cringe and throw an arm around her small frame. She squeezes me even tighter, and Kindra envelops the both of us with her thin arms.

I can't believe how good it feels or how fast the five of us have become friends. I've been hanging out with Sawyer and Celdon for years, but I guess the prospect of certain death speeds up the bonding process.

"Oh my god!" Lenny moans, pulling out of the embrace. "I heard Eli got shot!"

"Yeah."

Kindra, Bear, and Blaze make some odd noises of disbelief, and Lenny's eyes grow huge.

"What *happened* out there?"

"I can't really talk about it."

Lenny and Bear exchange a glance, but Lenny covers her surprise with a grin. Kindra is eyeing me as though I could have a psychotic break at any moment, which is funny, considering how coo-coo she is sometimes.

Blaze is the only one who looks the way I feel: sick with dread at the prospect of deployment.

I'm dying to tell them what's really going on out there, but I know they'll never understand until they experience it themselves. Scaring them won't do any good.

"Hey!" belts a voice from the door. "Nobody told me it was caring and sharing time!"

My stomach does a weird flip, and I turn toward the familiar voice.

Eli is standing in the doorway, propping himself up on a single crutch. Even though I was waiting for him, seeing him in training again after our deployment is a little strange.

He meets my gaze for a long second, and I try to suppress the fluttering feeling in my stomach.

"On the line, guys. Come on."

The others scramble back to our usual spot, and I can see Lenny fighting a grin. Even Bear seems good-natured about it. It's amazing how Eli's near-death experience has boosted their affection for him.

The other cadets are starting to shuffle into the training center, and I line up between Lenny and Bear, trying not to stare at Eli.

His face is slightly ashen, but apart from the obvious exhaustion and pain, he looks pretty much like his strong, angry self.

"Five laps around the track," he barks. "Go! Last one back does twenty extra push-ups."

I take off for the stairs at a sprint, glancing at him once over my shoulder. He returns my gaze with a steady, unreadable expression, but I notice he isn't regarding me with the contempt he used to.

My laps are a complete blur, and I pass the others easily. It feels good to challenge my body after a week of inactivity. My legs feel warm and alive, and my lungs are getting that wide-open feeling that only comes from running.

When I finish, I take the stairs two at a time and huff across the room. Eli is standing right where we left him, arguing with Jayden. Seamus, who took over our training during Eli's last deployment, is hovering right behind her like an overeager puppy.

"These are my cadets, Commander," Eli says in his most deadly voice. "I'll train them the way I've always trained them."

Jayden sneers. "Your training methods don't seem to be working, Parker. From now on, Lieutenant Duffy will oversee your cadets."

"What the hell am I supposed to do?" Eli growls, glancing over at me.

I instantly wish I could be *anywhere* else but here.

"This is my assignment."

Jayden stares at Eli's leg with a condescending sneer playing on her lips. "You're not much use to me right now, Parker. Rest that leg. Gathering intel on the Fringe is about the only thing you're good for."

Eli drags in a burst of air, his blue eyes burning with fury. For a second, I think he might combust and lay into Jayden for real, but he just glances at me and pivots on his crutch with a jerky motion that's hard to watch.

Jayden follows his gaze, and her eyes snap onto me. "Oh, Riley. Good to see you're back with us." She's faking a smile, but her tone says she wishes I'd gotten a staph infection and died in the medical ward.

As she whips her head around, I see an idea take hold in her mind.

"Riley, since you're so advanced, why don't you work with Lieutenant Parker one on one after lunch? I've got a special assignment in mind for you."

At her mention of a "special assignment," a tremor of fear shoots up my spine, melding with my hatred and causing my hands to ball into fists. The only thing Jayden considers "special" is something that's likely to kill me.

"Yes, Commander," I say through gritted teeth.

"Hey! Pay attention!" belts Jayden, turning to the four cadets gathered behind me. "Things have changed out on the Fringe. We face a greater threat than ever before. I don't need soldiers anymore. I need exterminators. If you don't have the stomach for it, I suggest you start getting used to the color orange, because I have no patience for weakness.

"Lieutenant Duffy will be overseeing your work until you master the basics of combat. I suggest you work hard. Otherwise, you aren't going to last long."

Jayden lets her withering gaze settle over the red-faced cadets behind me and stalks out of the training center.

Eli stares at us for a long second and then tightens his grip on his crutch and limps out behind her.

* * *

"All right," snaps Seamus, clapping his hands together to get our attention. "Hit the bags. I want to see where we're at with strikes."

Lenny, Bear, and I glance back and forth at each other and then turn toward the line of punching bags along the far wall.

"Not you, Riley," says Seamus.

I stop, and Bear hesitates at my side.

"Did I *say* 'Kelso'?" Seamus snaps.

Bear gives him a blank look and shuffles over to join the others.

Seamus clears his throat and rubs the back of his neck, obviously uncomfortable cracking the whip. Being a hard-ass just isn't his style.

"What is it, sir?"

"Since you've already passed your tests, Commander Pierce wants you training with 2B."

"What?"

"Squad 2B," he says again, pointing over at a cluster of privates working out across the training center.

"But this is my squad," I say dumbly, struggling to process the fact that he's kicking me out of the group.

"Not anymore." His face is set, but I can tell he's uncomfortable. I can only imagine the browbeating he must have gotten from Jayden.

I nod, trying not to appear upset. Eli mentioned Jayden would have a hand in my training once I advanced to the next level, but I never anticipated being separated from my squad.

Glancing once more at my friends going at the heavy bags, I turn and walk over to the cluster of first-year privates.

They're all paired off sparring, and I have the sudden urge to run away. They're clearly more advanced than I am and using moves I've never even seen.

I search their faces for someone I know, and my gaze lands on Miles. He's standing apart from the others, watching one guy take down his partner. I cringe as the other man's back slams into the mat with a resounding *thwop!*

Exposure

I'm so not ready for this.

"Riley?"

"Yeah?"

Miles's eyes narrow. Then I remember that Miles outranks me, and "yeah" is not the greeting he's used to getting from cadets. He doesn't look angry at my lazy response, though. He's just confused.

Then I realize he's the one *leading* the group. He's a private, too, but he's Eli's age and has more experience than the others. I clear my throat. "Sorry, sir. I didn't realize."

"It's okay."

"Commander Pierce and Seamus . . . er, Lieutenant Duffy . . . want me to train with your squad. But I don't think I'm quite ready to —"

He waves off my explanation, as though Jayden's name explains everything.

"It's all right. We'll find something for you to do." Miles looks me up and down, searching for weaknesses. "Hit the weights first. Your arms look like toothpicks. If you're going to fight, I need some meat I can work with."

My mouth falls open, but I recover quickly. I drag my feet over to the weights and sit down at one of the benches.

As I heave the bar over my head, I'm overcome by sudden loneliness. Normally, I'd spend the entire day working out with Bear, Blaze, Lenny, and Kindra, but Jayden has managed to isolate me from nearly everyone.

My pity party is short-lived. Ten minutes into my workout, Miles saunters over and raises an eyebrow. He seems skeptical that the cadet who raises so much hell can lift so little weight.

Without a word, he adds plates to the bar I'm lifting and nods approvingly at the pained expression on my face.

After one set, my arms are starting to give out, and I let out an animalistic grunt to force the weight over my head.

At first I think Miles is just going to watch me in total silence, but then he clears his throat. "Man, that's cold."

"Huh?"

He glances over at the other privates and lowers his voice. "What Jayden did to Eli."

"Oh. Yeah," I moan, hatred flashing through my chest at the mention of Jayden.

"You know training you guys is his life, right?"

"I know."

Miles raises an eyebrow but doesn't respond.

"Eli's *all* about the job," I groan, blinking the sweat out of my eyes. "Looks like that's doing a whole lot of good."

I'm shocked by the bitterness in my own voice but not as surprised as I am when Miles breaks into a disarming grin. He looks much less intimidating with a smile stretching from ear to ear, which is probably why I've never seen it.

He lets out a low chuckle and starts to walk away. "Oh, man, Riley. I can already tell it's gonna be fun working with you."

* * *

Miles is no Eli, but he doesn't take it easy on me, either. He keeps me on the weights for an hour and then runs me through some high-intensity interval training to build power and speed.

Several times, I catch the other privates watching me out of the corner of their eyes, but they never say a word.

I'm sure they know I just returned from my first deployment, but they aren't looking at me with pity. They understand. They know what it's like out there, but I still feel like an outcast. I don't belong in their squad, and Seamus kicked me out of mine.

I'm relieved when the lunch bell rings, and I waste no time bounding out of the training center to catch up with Lenny and the others.

"Hey!" I gasp, fighting through the crowd to reach them.

"Hey," says Lenny, an angry edge to her voice.

"What's up?"

"Seamus," Bear growls.

"What happened?"

"He said I have a month," Lenny snaps. "I have a *month*, and then they're going to deploy me."

"Blaze, too," Bear adds.

"What about you and Kindra?"

Bear shrugs his enormous shoulders. "He didn't say."

That isn't good. I knew Jayden would be pressuring Seamus to pass the others on to the next level quickly, but a month seems like a very short amount of time.

"I don't want to go out there," says Blaze. He glances at me. "I can't do it. I couldn't do what you and Parker did."

I don't even bother asking what he thinks Eli and I did. Rumors have been swirling through Recon about the great Eli Parker and his injured leg, but since we can't share what actually happened, no version even comes close to the truth.

When we reach the canteen, the first person I see is Celdon. He's arguing with the Operations worker in the food line again, but at least he seems to be in his right mind this time.

". . . All I'm saying is that you guys shouldn't put it on the menu if you're going to run out within the first five minutes."

I can't hear the woman's reply, but Celdon tips his head back in exasperation. "Kale? Fucking *kale*?"

I grin despite myself, and when Celdon finally takes his tray and turns, his face fills with relief.

"Holy Christ!" he says, sagging his shoulders.

Before I can react, Celdon abandons his tray completely and crosses to where I'm standing. I half expect some sort of snarky comment — maybe even a sloppy left hook — but he just throws his arms around my shoulders and crushes me to his skinny chest.

I let out the breath I was holding and let myself relax against his rib cage. I sniff, and it smells as though he's showered and done his laundry since our last encounter.

"I didn't think you were going to make it back!" he says, lifting me off my feet.

"Thanks for the vote of confidence," I mutter into his shirt.

"I was so scared, Riles."

"Me, too."

His arms tighten around me, and a shudder rolls through him. "No, really. If I'd known . . . I'm sorry." He puts me down. "I was so out of it. And when I came down from . . . you know . . . Sawyer told me they'd sent you out there. Then you were in the medical ward, and she said you weren't allowed visitors . . ."

When he pulls away, I'm startled to see his eyes are glistening with tears. Everyone is watching us, and he wipes them hurriedly on his sleeve. I suppose it's not every day that a Systems worker hugs a sweaty Recon girl in the middle of the canteen.

"I'm so sorry," he says. "I'm sorry about everything."

"It's okay," I say, squeezing his wiry arm. "I have to talk to you."

He nods and returns to the food line, where he argues with the Operations woman for another two minutes until she produces a tray of food for me. I throw the line I just cut an apologetic grimace and follow Celdon to a table in the corner.

"How are you?" he asks, regarding me with uncharacteristic concern.

"I'm fine," I lie. "I'm . . . I'm all right."

Celdon's eyes bug out in disbelief. "Riles. Come *on*. Lieutenant Sexy got shot. You can't tell me everything's fine."

"How do you know about that?" I hiss.

"I'm not a moron! The guy's hobbling around on crutches." I narrow my eyes at him.

"And also Sawyer told me."

I groan. "She shouldn't have told you that. You're not supposed to know any of this."

If this gets out, I'm going to be in so much trouble.

"Well, I do. So spill."

"I can't," I say, staring pointedly at his interface. Just talking to him when he's wearing it is giving me the uncomfortable feeling we're being watched.

"Oh, this?" he says, tapping the device with a knowing grin. "Don't worry. No malware. And I installed some new security software. Those noobs in Constance aren't getting anything past me now."

I still don't trust the interface, but if anyone has the skills to keep Constance out, it's Celdon.

Reluctantly, I launch into the story of what happened on the mission. I tell him about the drifters hijacking the land mine and shutting down our checkpoint and how Eli got shot.

I leave out the part about me shooting a man, which turns out to be a good choice. By the time I get to the part about the drifter in the cleared zone, Celdon's eyes look as if they might fall out of his head.

"I can't go out there again," I finish. "I can't do it."

"So don't."

"I don't have a choice."

He glances around. "So what are you going to do?"

I swallow and lower my voice so no one nearby can hear. "We're getting out of here."

"How?"

"Eli said he would help us," I whisper. "He's going to fight."

"Fight? Like *fight*, fight?" He fakes a few punches, raising an eyebrow.

"Yeah."

"He *loves* you!" Celdon declares with a smirk.

"Stop saying that! You and Sawyer don't know what you're talking about."

"I know Lieutenant Sexy loves you. He's got it *bad*, Riles."

"Whatever. Now we have a plan. So do you think you can stay out of trouble until we get the money?"

He rolls his eyes. "Riles . . . I've been a fucking saint ever since that day before you left."

I meet him with a look of disbelief.

"I'm serious. I report to Systems, I do what they tell me, and —"

"And you're staying away from the hard stuff?" I cut in. "I can't have you losing your shit when we're trying to make a break for it."

"I know. No more surge. I'm getting my act together. I promise."

Deep down, I'm not sure I believe him. Celdon has been a loose cannon since we were teenagers, but it has to be the truth. I have enough to worry about as it is.

eleven

Eli

Waiting for Harper in the empty simulation course, I pace back and forth like a caged animal that's about to be another animal's lunch. The mechanized drifters are perfectly still behind the rock- and car-shaped obstacles, but their empty eyes seem to follow me around the room.

I've gotten better on the crutch, but I'm still slow and weak. Every time I move, I have to fight the impulse to chuck the thing at the wall and tough it out. My leg is still too messed up to support my full weight on its own.

I don't want to see Harper. I don't think I can look her in the eye after the little display in the training center. There's no one in this compound who can humiliate me the way Jayden can. She gets you right where it hurts every time and digs her heel into the wound.

Harper arrives five minutes early. Even though I was expecting her, I'm still a little taken aback. She looks stronger than ever, but there's a dark, wild look in her eyes that wasn't there before.

As she gets closer, I can see they've been working her hard. She's stripped down to her black tank top, and a few pieces of dark hair have fallen loose from her ponytail.

I try to get my thoughts in check, but it's impossible. After watching over her every night in the medical ward, I've gotten used to relaxed, defenseless Harper. I'm unprepared to face Harper as I've grown to know her: tough, strong, and capable.

That Harper is way out of my league.

"Hey," she calls when she gets within earshot. "How's the leg?"

"It's fine," I say, even though it hurts like hell.

"How have you been?" There's a cautious note in her voice that isn't like her.

When she gets closer, I see that those restless nights have begun to take a toll. Her face is pinched with fatigue, and she's developed deep grayish circles under her eyes.

"I'm surviving."

"I'm sorry about this morning."

I wave it off. I don't want to talk about it, but of course that's never stopped Harper.

"Jayden's a bitch. But you know she only did that to get under your skin."

"I know."

"She's just trying to provoke a reaction from you. You know that, right?"

"Yeah," I say, fighting a grin.

When did Harper get so smart? I knew Jayden was messing with me, but it never occurred to me that there may have been a deeper motive besides showing me who's boss.

"She can't keep you on the sidelines forever. Seamus is a horrible instructor."

Her generous lie triggers a surge of hope inside me, but I dampen it quickly. "She can, and she will."

"No. She's desperate. Remy overruled her, and she doesn't know what to do about the drifters."

"That's never stopped Jayden from getting rid of people who aren't useful to her. She already tried to get rid of us once, and now she's working on plan B."

Harper swallows, fear bursting into her eyes. I instantly feel horrible for being so blunt. We never talked about what she said that first night I came to her room about her fear of the Fringe.

"How are you doing?" I ask.

"Fine."

I tilt my head in disbelief.

"I'm fine."

"Cut the crap, Harper. How are you *really* doing?"

She drags in a shaky breath, trying to get her emotions in check. "I don't want to talk about it, okay?" She glances over my shoulder to break eye contact. "I can't talk about it."

"Okay. But you can't keep all that bottled up inside you, or it's going to come out when you least expect it."

"So I should talk about my feelings? Like you do, you mean?"

"No, not like me."

She lets out a harsh laugh. "What do you care? I'm fine, okay? You'd know that if you came to see me."

I bite back the retort burning on my lips. Of course she doesn't know that I *did* come to see her, and I'm not going to tell her.

"I know you're having nightmares," I say before I can stop myself. "They haven't stopped since we got back, have they?"

She looks taken aback and then defensive. "How would you know?"

"Oh, come on, Riley. You look like hell. I know you haven't been sleeping worth a damn."

"That's none of your business. I'm dealing with it."

"You're not dealing with it at all."

"What is your problem?" she snaps. "I can't figure out who you're supposed to be. When I see you here, it's 'Riley, get on the line,' but out there . . ."

"What?" I'm feeling a little panicky for reasons I can't explain.

"I don't know! You act like a human being sometimes, and I almost forget what an *asshole* you are."

That does it. All the rage and frustration building up inside me overflows, and I can't hold it in anymore.

"What the fuck am I supposed to do?" I yell before I can stop myself. "This is how I am, okay? I'm your commanding officer, Riley. I'm not Sawyer or Celdon. I'm not going to coddle you."

"I don't want you to coddle me!" she snaps. "I don't want anything from you. *Yes*, I've had nightmares every night since we've been back. Every time I close my eyes, I see him. I see the life leave his eyes. I see you getting shot, and then you die, and it's just me out there. I'm afraid to go to sleep. Is *that* what you want to hear?"

I'm a little taken aback by her outburst, and I have the sudden urge to pull her into my arms. But I just stand there, hands hanging uselessly at my sides.

We stare at each other for several seconds, and Harper is the first to break eye contact. She looks as though she wishes she hadn't just laid everything out there.

"I'm sorry," I say, clearing my throat. "I didn't mean anything by it. I just . . . I just want to make sure you're okay."

Harper snaps her eyes back onto mine. "Well . . . I'm not."

I let out a growl and drag both hands through my hair. "Nobody should have to live like this."

"Hopefully we'll be out of here soon."

I nod quickly so she thinks that was what I was talking about. *What the hell is wrong with me?* I need to get it together, but ever since that night on the observation deck, I haven't been able to shut out my thoughts of Harper.

She's definitely not just my cadet. And after my talk with Miles, I can feel myself growing more and more reckless. This whole one-on-one training thing was a bad idea.

"So what's the plan?" she probes.

"Miles can get me a fight," I say, relieved the conversation has turned to something I can talk about.

Harper tilts her head to the side and fixes me with a skeptical, admonishing look that I find sexy for some inexplicable reason. "What kind of fight?"

"Probably against this guy Lopez . . . or someone else they think can beat me."

She crosses her arms and raises an eyebrow. "And can he? Beat you, I mean."

I grin. "He could, but he won't."

"When is it?"

"Probably about two weeks."

"*Two weeks?*" she repeats, looking aghast. "You won't be healed by then."

"I'll take my chances."

"No, you won't. I can't let you do this."

"Oh, yeah?" I laugh, unable to stifle a chuckle at the thought of Harper trying to stop me. She wouldn't be able to hold me back any more than I could get her to drop her dangerous obsession with her bid.

"It still probably won't be enough," I say. "They'll send us out again. You should be prepared for that."

She fidgets and runs a hand over the top of her ponytail. "I can't do it."

Now it's my turn to look skeptical. I know it's insensitive to remind her that she doesn't have a choice, so I don't. But my expression gives it away.

"I won't," she says more forcefully. That wild look is back in her eyes, and as tired as she is, it makes her look slightly insane.

Taking a step toward her, I lower my voice and try to get through the barriers she's scrambling to put up. "Hey. I'll be healed by then. I won't let them send you out with anyone else. We'll get through it."

"I can't!" she snaps.

Her eyes quiver with unshed tears, and her breathing speeds up as she tries to get herself under control. Then something breaks inside her, and she can't hold them in anymore. Tears leak out, and she wipes her eyes furiously.

"Every time I think about going back out there . . . I can't breathe. It's like someone is sitting on my chest, and I c-can't get up. I keep seeing their faces, and every time I close my eyes —" She breaks off, unable to get the words around a silent sob.

This time, I don't think about it. I cross the distance between us and pull her against my chest.

To my immense surprise, she folds her arms around my torso and buries her face in my shirt.

Her whole body quivers as she sobs, and I lower us both to the ground to get the weight off my throbbing leg. With my back against the wall, I squeeze Harper around the shoulders. She nestles deeper into the side of my chest.

I stroke her hair and try to think of something to say, but there are no words to take away what she's feeling. This is the cost of killing another human.

I know she hasn't talked to anyone else about this, because there's no one else who would understand.

Eventually her tears subside, and her trembling stops. She raises her head to look at me, and I realize I still have one arm locked around her shoulders. Even with bloodshot eyes and tangled hair, she looks beautiful.

I glance at her lips, which are parted ever so slightly. I think about that night on the observation deck — that night in my room — and remember what those lips feel like. They're *so* close.

Right at this moment, there's nothing I want more than to lean down and kiss her. I might be able to take her pain away — even if it's only for a few seconds.

I swallow once to brace myself, but Harper is already pulling away and wiping her eyes.

"I'm sorry," she murmurs. "I didn't mean to lose it on you."

It takes a while for me to find my voice. "It's okay. I understand. And you didn't lose it. Losing it would be letting that change you."

I don't tell her that eventually, she will lose it. Eventually, it will change her just as it changed me. I don't want that for her.

She gets to her feet with a fortifying breath and holds out a hand to help me up. I take it, but only because all this standing and moving is killing my leg.

We spend the rest of the afternoon on the simulation course, and I make it progressively more difficult for Harper. She had plenty of practice before the mission, but it doesn't compare to shooting for real.

Now that she's experienced the Fringe, she takes everything more seriously.

Every time she fires, the sound and the kickback hit her deep to the core.

I know she's thinking about the last time she held a gun. I want to tell her we can stop, but the sooner she can numb herself to the horrible feelings it brings back, the better. The next time Jayden sends us out, we won't be able to afford even the slightest hesitation.

By the end of the session, her timing has improved tremendously. She can aim, shoot, and reload faster, and she's becoming a more accurate shot. Harper is exhausted, and I've worn myself out just by moving around all day. We wind down early, and I take her gun to return it to the weapons room.

"How have you been feeling?" I ask. "Physically, I mean."

She gives me a confused look.

"Are you nauseous? Dizzy? Any headaches?"

"No."

"Good. No radiation sickness, then."

"What about you?"

"No. But I've never been sick."

"Never?"

I shake my head. "I've been lucky, I guess. Miles had it bad once." I shudder and realize I've fallen into step with Harper on my way to dinner.

It's easy being around her — especially now that she's stopped fighting every little thing. Climbing the stairs with one crutch takes everything out of me, but the exhaustion is enough to distract me from my worries.

"Did you hear?" she asks suddenly. "Jayden is sending out Lenny and Blaze in a month."

I snap my head around so fast I almost give myself whiplash. "*What?*"

"Yeah. That's all the time they're giving them to finish training."

I swear loudly and bang my fist against the wall. The pain radiates all the way up my arm, but it's nothing compared to the rage flaring up inside me.

Harper looks alarmed, and I realized I've stopped on the bottom step just below the ground level. "Do you think Jayden would really send them out before they're ready?"

"She might not have a choice. We're losing men left and right,"

I say, thinking of the AWOL Recon guys who were never found. "She probably just needs to fill the roster."

"What are you going to do?"

"There's nothing I *can* do."

But Harper's still watching me as though she expects me to say I'll take them out for their first deployments. Part of me wishes I could, but I have enough on my plate trying to make sure Jayden doesn't send Harper out without me.

Lenny and Blaze may not be ready to go out there, but at least they don't have Constance gunning for their death.

I tell myself I did everything I could. I trained them the best way I knew how. I tried to keep my distance. But Jayden will still send them out, and I'm going to lose my cadets even faster than I lost them last time.

I've been here too many times already. The sick feeling is almost familiar now.

Losing them will take one more bite out of my sanity, but their loss will be manageable compared to what I would feel if I lost Harper. I don't think I could *handle* losing her, and it's terrifying to realize that I might not be able to save her.

twelve

Harper

"I flipped him off."

"You did *not* flip him off."

Lenny cringes and nods, burying her rosy face in her hands and banging her head against the table.

"She didn't just flip him off," says Bear, looking from me to Lenny. "It was like a double-bird dance. She kind of, uh . . . danced out of the training center."

I raise an eyebrow at Lenny. "You *danced* out of the training center while flipping Seamus off?"

Her huge green eyes appear momentarily, and she scoffs. "Yeah, you know. Like a 'back it up' type of dance."

"Oh my god."

"He said if I didn't get my shit together, I'd be great target practice for the drifters."

"He has been giving her a hard time in training," says Bear. "He kind of deserved it."

"Still! You better hope he's too much of a coward to go to Jayden. You'd be in serious trouble."

"Oh, whatever," she growls, shoving her tray away from her. "What could they possibly do to me? They're already trying to send me out to die. Seamus can suck it. I don't even know how he manages to give orders with his head so far up Jayden's ass."

Bear and I exchange a look, and he bites back a laugh.

"You have to apologize," I say. "Trust me, you don't want to go pissing anybody off right now. Especially the guy who signs off on the tests that determine when you go out on the Fringe."

Lenny groans. "I know, I know. He's just such a . . . douchebag. I never thought I'd miss Eli, but at least he was a sexy douchebag."

I choke on the sweet potato I'm eating and try to turn it into a laugh. Lenny elbows me in the ribs and raises her eyebrows suggestively and then gets up to dump her tray.

Bear follows her, and the two of them leave to go find Seamus.

As soon as they're gone, Blaze scoots over to fill Lenny's empty seat. Kindra already left to run the extra laps that Seamus assigned her, so it's just the two of us sitting at the long table in the far corner of the canteen.

"I hope she apologizes," he murmurs. "Things are bad enough as it is."

"What do you mean?" I ask, shocked to hear Blaze speaking in full sentences. Most of the time, he just goes along with it when we complain and laughs at our jokes. He's never contributed much to the conversation, but he's nice to have around.

He glances down the table once and lowers his voice so I have to lean in to hear. "I heard Seamus and Jayden talking the other day. They didn't mean for me to overhear, but . . . they were talking about sending me and Lenny out on a mission in a few weeks."

A wave of nausea rolls over me. Judging by the look on his face, that isn't the worst of it.

"What about Kindra and Bear?"

"They aren't going to be deploying them."

"Ever?"

He shakes his head. I should feel relieved, but the grave expression on his face just compounds my dread.

"With drifters in the cleared zone, I heard Remy wants Recon guarding the perimeter 24/7. Jayden plans on sending them out there on patrol shifts every day."

"*Every day?*" I ask in disbelief. "But the radiation . . . constant exposure like that would kill them."

"I know. But right now Remy only cares about protecting the compound, and Jayden doesn't want to stop gathering intel, so . . ."

"So she's going to start sacrificing cadets?"

"I guess she figures they wouldn't be very useful out there anyway. She's probably going to sell it to Remy as a safer alternative to combat for cadets who aren't prepared."

The thought makes me feel sick. The reason Recon operatives are only deployed one week per month is to prevent prolonged radiation exposure, and many still develop cancer in their twenties. But being sent out there day after day? I can't even imagine the effect that would have.

"Don't say anything to Bear and Kindra," Blaze whispers.

"I won't."

They're as good as dead anyway, I think. There's no point ruining their last few weeks of relative peace.

When I leave the canteen, my head is spinning. Bear and Kindra might have better odds of survival staying within the cleared zone on patrol. But when they get sick, their death will be slow and painful.

I shouldn't be surprised that Jayden would use her cadets as pawns. Her loyalty lies with Constance — not the soldiers she swore to protect and lead — but I never thought she'd give them a sentence worse than ExCon.

I feel mired in despair. No matter what I do, I can't escape

Constance. None of us can. Their sphere of influence knows no bounds within the compound, which is exactly why we have to leave.

I don't notice where my feet are carrying me until I'm right at Eli's door. I'm not sure why my first impulse is to tell him what Blaze told me, but I realize that's what we do now. Whether I like it or not, Eli is my partner in crime.

The last week and a half has been horrible, and training with Eli has been the only distraction that can suppress the panic about my upcoming deployment. He's been extra nice since my meltdown on the simulation course, and we've almost been getting along.

I bang on his door, but he doesn't answer. I know he wouldn't ignore me deliberately, so I head to the training center to see if he's squeezing in an extra workout to rehab his leg.

He isn't there, either.

There's only one other place I can think of where he could be, but it's a long shot.

Taking a deep breath, I turn down the dark maintenance tunnel and use the walls to guide myself into the shadows. I've only gone a few yards when the sound of voices reaches my ears. *Bingo.*

There are no fights tonight, so this is the perfect place for Eli to train for his upcoming bout. Jayden would flip out if she knew he was entering an illegal fight, which is probably why he isn't practicing in the training center.

As I draw closer, I can make out Eli's and Miles's voices. They're muffled by their mouth guards, but I can tell that they're arguing.

I slow down and consider turning back. I don't like Eli's anger directed at me, but I *really* don't want to walk into the middle of a fight between him and Miles.

"You don't get it," says Eli, his voice echoing in the empty space.

"No, *you* don't get it. You can't do this."

"I have to."

I reach the opening of the shaft and see them facing off across from each other. The entire room is lit by a few florescent lights suspended over the ring, so they can't see me lurking in the shadows. I know I should reveal myself, but seeing Eli like that freezes me in place.

He's stripped down to a pair of black athletic shorts, with his gloves raised protectively in front of his face. His golden skin is glistening with perspiration, and his chest and shoulders are as well muscled as I always imagined. He's lean and fast, with perfectly cut abs leading down to his shorts.

Then my eyes land on the burns trailing up his right arm from the explosion on the Fringe, and I get a sick feeling in the pit of my stomach. I'm appalled that the drifters tried to blow him up — not once but *twice*. They've left their mark in the mottled pink patches of skin splayed across his perfect bicep and chest. But I don't have time to dwell on that.

Miles throws a punch. Eli checks it and delivers a counterstrike. His punch glances off Miles's face, but Miles returns with a fake jab and a ferocious hook.

They're both wearing protective headgear, but I know from experience that it doesn't do much to dampen the blow of a really powerful hit.

The hook catches Eli in the jaw, and he staggers backward.

They trade a few more strikes, each getting faster and more powerful.

When Eli sucker punches Miles, I think that might be the end of it, but Miles comes up swinging. He drives Eli back with a relentless combination of punches and swings out a leg that connects just above Eli's kneecap.

Eli's face twists in anguish, and his injured leg crumples underneath him.

He throws an angry glare at Miles and scrambles back to his feet. He pushes him across the ring with a few jabs and hooks and a wicked uppercut.

Miraculously, Miles puts a little space between them and gears up for a counterstrike. He uses a jab to cover his switch kick, and Eli never sees it coming.

This time, Miles's shin connects with Eli's thigh — right where he was shot.

Eli goes down hard with a strangled groan of pain, and the impulse to go to him is so strong that my legs nearly run over without me.

"Sorry, man," Miles pants. "I told you. You aren't healed yet."

"Fuck you," Eli moans, clutching his leg.

"You can't do this fight."

Eli breathes in deeply, trying to ease the pain.

At first, I think he might give in, but he gets to his feet and tucks his chin. He tilts his head from side to side and wiggles his shoulders, loosening up with a little movement around the ring.

"I'm fine," he says, smacking his gloves together. "Let's go again."

"You're crazy."

Frustrated, Eli spits out his mouth guard and points his glove at Miles. "If you don't want to help me, I can do it without you."

"How?" snaps Miles.

"I'll get Lopez or —"

"You crazy son of a bitch. You can't do this! Hell, I'll fight.

You can bet on me."

Eli jerks his head no. "It's too risky. If Jayden catches you in another illegal fight, you're screwed."

"What's that bitch gonna do to me?"

"Send you out into the Fringe until you get killed."

Miles stops arguing, and I can tell Eli's warning scared him.

Eli smacks his gloves together again. "Let's go."

"No," I say, stepping out from my hiding place.

Both guys whip their heads around, surprised to have an audience. I suddenly think I should have just kept my mouth shut and made a quiet exit.

"Harper, what are you doing here?" snaps Eli. His ears and neck burn crimson, and he throws an annoyed glance at Miles.

"I was looking for you."

Miles is still staring at me in surprise, but I swear I see the shadow of a grin flit across his stoney face.

Eli's expression immediately turns serious. "Why? What's wrong?"

"Never mind. Eli, listen to him. You can't do this. Your leg is just starting to heal."

"What'd I say?" Miles adds in a smug tone.

Eli scowls at me, and I know I'm going to get the full brunt of his anger later. He doesn't like bickering with me in front of Miles, and he especially doesn't like me and Miles ganging up on him.

"You know we don't have a choice."

I take a few steps toward the ring so I can really look at him. "If you do this, you're going to get hurt worse."

Eli scowls. "Do you have a better plan? Because I don't."

I stare at him for a moment, thrown off by the question . . . and his chiseled arms.

Before I have time to think about what I'm about to say, the words come tumbling out of my mouth. "Let me do it."

"*What?*"

Miles's smile broadens. "This ought to be good."

My brain is working in fits and starts, but then I remember something. "They have amateur fights before the main fights, don't they?"

Eli snorts. "Only when there are two novices who are crazy enough to do it. They never go past the first round. Somebody always taps out or gets too messed up to finish."

"So I'll enter one of those. There has to be some girl who would fight me."

Miles and Eli exchange a glance, and Eli lets out a full-body sigh. He knows I'm serious, but there's another problem.

"Have you seen the girls you'd be up against?" he asks. He's choosing his words carefully, which is *so* not like Eli. "Most of them —"

"— would wipe the floor with your ass," Miles finishes.

Crossing my arms over my chest, I draw myself up to my full height and fix Eli with my most stubborn glare. "Then teach me . . . *sir.*"

Eli's eyes widen in an "I'm going to kill you" sort of way, but I twist my scowl into a sweet smile.

Miles looks me up and down and then looks back at Eli. "This just keeps getting better and better."

Eli squeezes his eyes shut in a grimace, as though my stubbornness is giving him a migraine.

Before I know it, I'm standing in the ring across from Eli, with Miles leaning between the ropes to give me instructions. I'm wearing his sweaty headgear and a pair of boxing gloves that look as though they haven't seen any action in about a decade.

Eli is in his fighting stance, still annoyingly sexy, but his face is all business. If I didn't know any better, I'd be scared as hell, but there's a flicker of concern and pride in those bright blue eyes. He taught me everything I know about fighting, and I know he wants me to put on a good show in front of his best friend.

"I'm not going to use full power," he says around his mouth guard.

I scoff and roll my eyes, but then Eli's fist flies out and strikes me right in the nose. I yell, feeling my eyes start to water, and Eli takes the opportunity to sweep my feet out from under me.

My ass hits the mat with a resounding *smack*, and I scramble to my feet, trying not to be a wimp.

"Never let your guard down," Eli warns sharply, looking as though he already regrets this.

I advance on him before he has a chance to launch into a full lecture. I know he's faster than me, but I throw out a jab anyway.

Eli swats my glove away and takes the opening on my dead side to deliver another punch. His glove hits my headgear, but I'm still a little stunned.

Eli isn't using even a fraction of his power, but it's obvious he's been holding back even more in practice. His fists are faster than I ever imagined.

Within seconds, he has me up against the ropes with my gloves forming a protective barrier between his fists and my face.

"Come on, Harper!" he growls. I can tell he's hating himself for this. "Do *something*."

The element of surprise is all I've got going for me. Eli knows this, and yet he's gotten a little careless. He's right up on me, and he doesn't see my knee coming when it shoots up and drives straight into his abdomen.

He grunts and eases up, giving me the chance to create some

space.

"Nice!" yells Miles from right below me.

I don't waste Eli's momentary distraction. I swing out a wild hook to his face. It's not a very powerful hit, but I feel my confidence mounting.

When I hit him, Eli smiles — actually smiles — and aims a low kick.

I block it with my shin, but he anticipated my movement. He delivers a wicked cross, and I barely slip in time to keep it from smashing straight into my face.

I back away to put some distance between us and step out with a powerful round kick.

Unfortunately, Eli never had a chance to break me of my worst habit. As my hips turn, I lean in — just as Eli's fist flies out.

This one is not as soft as the first direct hit.

I hear Miles groan, and Eli's eyes widen in horror. He hadn't counted on me getting that close, and he hit me harder than he meant to.

My glove goes up too late, and I'm stunned by how painful a real honest-to-god punch to the face is. My nose is throbbing through the back of my skull.

"Harper!"

In an instant, the fighter is gone, and the other Eli is back.

His gloves bat mine away to get a look at my face, but I twist out of his reach to collect myself in the corner. I'm fighting back tears, albeit unsuccessfully. Usually I can stop myself from crying, but it's as though the pain flipped the switch on all my screwed-up emotions.

Somehow Eli is right in front of me again. His gloves are off, and he's pulling me down into a seated position and yanking my gloves off, too.

"I told you this was a bad idea," he growls at Miles, reaching around to unfasten my headgear.

Through the tears, I get a look at his face and shiver. Eli is furious with himself, but I know that's his worst mood of all.

"What are you talking about? She did great."

I glance at Miles and see that he's grinning in approval. A muscle is working in Eli's jaw as he pries the headgear off and searches my face with a worried expression.

"Are you okay?" he asks.

"Y-Yeah," I stammer, still trying to get the waterworks under control.

I'm embarrassed, but Eli's too preoccupied with whatever's going on in his head to make me feel any worse about it.

He produces a towel and mops up the blood streaming from my nose. I freak out a little when I see it soaked with red, and I taste the blood running down the back of my throat.

"This was a bad idea," he mutters. "You're not doing this."

"Sure I am," I say. "Whoever I'm fighting won't be as good as you, and —"

But Eli is already shaking his head. "You're not ready yet."

"So train me," I snap. "I have a couple weeks to practice."

"It's not enough. Some of these girls will have been fighting for a year. You'll barely have four months of training."

"Well, I think you should let her do it," says Miles, coming up behind me and grinning. "I'll help her get ready."

"She's not going to be ready," Eli growls.

"She'll be ready enough. If she can take a hit like that . . ."

"It's not going to happen."

"Come on, Eli," I groan, my voice oddly nasally. "I can handle it."

Eli lets out an aggravated sigh. "You really want to do it?"

I nod, pinching the towel over the bridge of my nose to stem the bleeding.

"Let's wait until we see who she'd be fighting," he says to Miles. "If she's too good, we won't take it."

I shrug, and Eli turns his glare on me. "Harper, promise me. If I tell you that you can't win against this girl, you turn it down."

"Why? If you think I can't win, just bet against me. Either way, we get the money."

Miles grins and cocks his head in amusement, but Eli is worried.

Even though I'm determined to fight so Eli won't have to, something tells me I don't have a clue what I'm getting myself into.

thirteen

Eli

There isn't any place I hate as much as the Fringe, but Neverland definitely comes close. The noise, the people, the lights — everything about it puts me on edge.

Every time I go down there, I keep my eyes fixed on the top of the tunnel, just waiting for it to collapse and crush everyone partying down below.

That's the problem with finding people who run illegal fights: Neverland is their playground. And if you want to fight, you have to meet them on their turf.

I really should go alone, but Shane refuses to sign on fighters without meeting them in person, and he's the guy we want. Most of the illegal fights are disorganized and give measly payouts, but Shane runs a top-notch operation with serious prize money. The trade-off is that you get tougher opponents, more dangerous fights, and a certain amount of indebtedness to Shane.

The thought of taking Harper down to meet him gives me an uneasy feeling, but I shove it aside and pound on her door. Since it's nearly midnight, the cadet tunnel is deserted. I still glance around nervously, though, hoping no one spots me down here.

Harper opens the door dressed in tight black pants, knee-high boots, and a studded jacket. With her hair pulled up high in a messy ponytail, she looks like someone who's not to be fucked with.

"You have to change," I blurt out, striding into the room to avoid being seen in the tunnel.

She looks puzzled and then suspicious. "Why?"

"You look like you're ready for a fight."

Harper shuts the door and cocks an eyebrow. "Isn't that the idea?"

"You look too tough."

"What's the problem?"

My stomach does an uncomfortable flip. I do not want to have this conversation with Harper, of all people.

"Don't take this the wrong way, but Shane only books fights between female novices for one reason."

I hope that will be enough to make her understand, but she's still looking at me as though I'm insane.

"It's not for the fight."

For a moment, Harper continues to stare at me. Then her face turns beet red. "That's sick!" she shrieks. "What? Are they going to make me fight in a mud pit or something?"

"N-No," I stammer, fighting the image of Harper wrestling some girl in a mud pit. "But . . . he's not looking for the toughest fighters, okay? He's looking for hot ones who will draw a crowd. You should wear that dress."

I feel the heat burning a trail up the back of my neck, and I clear my throat for the umpteenth time.

Harper's mouth twists into a wicked grin that makes me want to go bang my head against the wall. "*What* dress?"

"You know, that dress . . ." I'm bumbling like an idiot, and she's enjoying it. "I don't know which one."

That's a lie. I've pictured Harper in that dress so many times I'd know it anywhere.

Scooting around me with a mischievous grin, Harper goes to her closet and pulls out *the* dress. "Turn around."

I pivot to face the bed, and I hear a lot of unzipping going on behind me. My entire body is a heated coil, and I clench and unclench my fists to distract myself.

What is wrong *with me?*

"Better?" she asks.

I turn around. Harper looks so different from the Harper I'm used to. She's a knockout in strappy heels and a black dress that hangs over her shoulders from delicate silk cords. It dips down low in the back and shows off her awesome legs.

"Almost," I murmur.

Without thinking, I reach over her shoulder and hook a finger through the tie holding up her heavy mass of dark hair. I pull, and it all tumbles down over her shoulders. Those legs and that hair combined with her silvery-gray eyes are enough to bring any man to his knees.

I realize I've been staring at her too long and toss her hair tie onto the bed. I jerk my head toward the door, and she follows me out toward the emergency stairwell.

Harper walks much slower in heels, which gives me time to collect myself as we make the descent.

The heavy bass vibrates the walls around us and makes my skin tingle unpleasantly. "Ready?"

She nods, and I shove the door open.

The noise bowls me over instantly, and my eyes struggle to adjust to the flash of white light that washes over the crowd of gyrating bodies. The music is upbeat and trippy, and I imagine half the crowd is so burned they have no idea where they are.

Harper stays close to me as I push through the cluster of couples pressing every part of their bodies together on the dance floor. Every now and then, we pass a concrete column stretching up toward the ceiling that's enveloped by a cluster of people making out and groping each other.

I try to stay close to the wall, but somehow the tide of people manages to jostle us closer to the middle. The music is getting louder, and the crowd is converging to form a mosh pit.

Behind me, I hear an angry growl. I whip around just in time to see Harper getting crushed between two bare-chested guys wearing what look like leather harnesses. They're dancing wildly and have her trapped between them. One guy has a green mohawk and wide gauges in his ears. The other has so many piercings that his entire face seems to be made of metal.

I lunge backward, but their friends have formed a solid wall of bodies, and I have to forcibly shove my way through.

The two leather-clad guys have noticed Harper. She doesn't see me, but I can detect the panic in her eyes.

One guy grabs her arm to yank her toward him, but she pushes him away. She stumbles backward on her heels — right into the orbit of the mohawk guy.

I shove the nearest guy harder to get to her, but Mohawk Guy buckles, and I know he just got an elbow to the gut.

Finally, Harper spots me fighting through the crowd. She throws out her hand, and I grab on and yank her toward me.

"You okay?" I yell.

"Yeah." The adrenalin is still sparkling in her eyes, but clearly Harper can handle herself.

Unfortunately, we've caused a bit of a scene, and the people around us are glaring.

Harper's VocAps score gave her some notoriety in the compound, and I've been in too many fights to get through Neverland unnoticed. They know we're from Recon.

A few guys are talking to each other, glancing in our direction and looking as though they're out for a fight.

I really don't want to deal with it, so I tug Harper through the crowd toward a flight of rickety stairs near the back. She struggles up behind me, and I realize her heels keep getting caught in the metal grating.

Standing in the shadows at the top of the steps is a big beefy bouncer. He holds out a hand to make us stop, and Harper straightens up to her full height.

"We're here to see Shane," I say.

"Shane's not here."

I roll my eyes. "Yeah, right. He's always here. Tell him Eli Parker's got a fighter he might be interested in, will you?"

The bouncer crosses his arms and raises his chin. He's trying to intimidate me, but he's curious. "Shane knows every fighter in this place. Who've you got?"

"Someone he hasn't seen before."

The man looks skeptical but intrigued enough to care. "Where is he?"

I step aside so Harper can come up beside me on the narrow landing. "It's her."

"Name?"

"Harper Riley," she says with a feisty edge to her voice.

The bouncer's gaze flits up and down Harper's body in a way I don't like, but then he jerks his head toward the door and leads us inside.

I've been up to Shane's private room plenty of times, but I'm always shocked by the cramped quarters. It's another remnant of the old Underground — a retrofitted conductor's office that he's turned into a VIP area.

There's a high-backed leather bench that snakes around the perimeter, framed by mirrored shelves of alcohol and a low glass table.

My eyes dart from the two bodyguards posted in the corners to the line of surge on the table. Two leggy blondes with bleary eyes are draped over Shane's lap. Their clothes are so skimpy they may as well not be dressed at all, but they seem completely unfazed by our arrival.

Shane is a tall man with dark hair combed back into a short mullet. He's wearing a black suit, black shirt, and ostrich-skin boots that he must have had brought in from the Fringe. Trading pre–Death Storm relics is illegal but not unheard of, and it's certainly not the only crime Shane partakes in. The drug trade, the sex trade, illegal fights — he has his hands in all of it.

"What can I do for you, Lieutenant?" Shane asks in that slow, mocking voice of his. He smiles lazily, and I catch a flash of silver in his teeth.

"I've got a fighter for you."

He raises an eyebrow. "Who?"

"Me," says Harper fiercely, taking a step toward Shane.

His eyes rake over her intrusively just as the bouncer's did, but she doesn't flinch or shrink away from his gaze. If anything, her posture becomes more defiant.

"I take it you're a beginner."

"Yep."

"And what will you do for me?" he asks.

I get a sick feeling in the pit of my stomach, and every muscle in my body tenses. I take stock of the room again, planning to go for the biggest bodyguard first if we need to fight our way out of here.

But Harper doesn't miss a beat. "Absolutely nothing," she says in that stubborn tone of hers. "Except make you a fuck ton of money."

Shane grins. "Really?" He sounds amused more than anything, which I take as a good sign.

Harper crosses her arms and tosses her hair over her shoulder. "I'm not an idiot. I know you take a cut of everything."

"That is true. And why wouldn't I?" His smile widens, revealing even more silver. "I'm a businessman."

"And I'm a fighter. Do you have a match for me or not?"

I cringe. Harper's attitude was enough to get Shane's attention — maybe even earn a little respect — but you can't push him too far. I've dealt with Shane enough to know that he respects someone who can hold their own, but he still likes to feel as though he's in charge.

"I might," he says lazily. "Let's see what you got."

He shoves one of the blondes off his lap, and she stumbles toward Harper on shaky legs. Harper swats her away impatiently, knowing as well as I do that this girl is too burned to stand on her own two feet, let alone put up a fight.

But Shane doesn't want Harper to fight the girl; he wants Harper to lay her out with her bare hands.

"I'm not going to put on a show for you," she snaps. "I'm not getting paid."

"And I'm not sure you know how things work around here," he says in a menacing voice.

Harper eyes the bodyguards, who don't yet seem to think she's a threat. "I've got a pretty good idea."

Shane stares at her for a long moment, and I can tell he's sizing her up. He likes Harper, but he also wants to put her in her place.

"I gotta hand it to you, sweetheart . . . You've got balls."

Harper glances at me, but I try to keep my expression neutral.

"What the hell. I've got a fight for you. In a month. Beginner fights start just before the main event." He glances toward me for the first time in a while. "Eli can show you where."

"Who would she be fighting?" I ask.

"Marta Moreno."

Horror flashes through me, and I take a step forward to get Harper out of the line of fire. "No —"

"Great," says Harper, shooting me a deadly look as she cuts me off.

Shane continues as though he didn't hear me. "You're not allowed to bet on yourself, of course," he muses. "But I'll pay you two grand for the fight — double if you win."

Now Harper glances at me to see if she should take the deal. I'm too panicked and angry to speak, but I shake my head, hoping that for once she'll listen. She looks uneasy but reaches out to shake Shane's hand anyway.

"Done."

"Great!" he says, flashing her a smile that makes me feel sick. "Remember: You don't get paid until the fight is over. Try to stay alive long enough to collect your winnings."

* * *

Harper and I don't speak as I drag her out of the room and down the stairs toward the swaying crowd. The music seems to have grown even louder in the few minutes we were with Shane, and the pounding just intensifies the fear that's constricting my lungs.

I don't let go of Harper as we navigate through the packed crowd and climb the emergency stairwell back to Recon.

As the music fades away, all I can hear is the *clack* of her heels on concrete. It grates on my nerves.

Every decision she's made tonight, from her shoes to the

fight, has been the wrong one. I just want to toss her over my shoulder and drag her up to my compartment before she can do any more damage, but I force myself to stay calm.

When we reach my tunnel, her continued silence makes me think she must be in shock.

I'm too pissed off to speak out where everyone can hear. Fear and rage are simmering just beneath the surface, and I know all the ugliness is going to spill out as soon as I open my mouth.

I pound in my door code with shaky fingers and toss her into my compartment.

"What were you thinking?" I yell as soon as we're inside.

She crosses her arms and glares up at me. "What is your problem?"

"*My* problem? I don't have a problem, but you sure as hell do now!"

Her eyes bug out a little in surprise. "What are you *talking* about?"

She's looking at me as though I've gone insane, and it annoys the shit out of me.

"The fight, Harper! The fight you just agreed to! I told you not to take the deal. We agreed that if the fighter was too dangerous, you wouldn't do it. I said no, and you took the deal anyway. Why would you do that?"

She stares at me in disbelief. "Are you serious?"

"Yeah, I'm serious!"

"We went there to get me a fight, Eli. Shane gave me a fight."

I let out a primal groan that surprises even me. "He might as well have given you a wheelchair! Do you have *any* idea who Marta Moreno is?"

Harper's trying to hold her ground, but she looks alarmed. "Sh-should I?"

"You would if you'd ever watched a beginner fight! She's the deadliest novice in the compound!"

Harper's face goes pale, which just makes it harder for me to stop the sickening dread pooling in the pit of my stomach. I turn away from her, raking a hand through my hair. "If you'd just listened to me . . . just *once* . . ."

"But two grand is good, right? Even if I lose, that's a ticket right there!"

"You don't get it," I moan. "Two grand is *twice* what you'd normally get in a beginner fight. He only offered that because no new fighter in her right mind would fight Marta for anything less."

Harper's eyes are wide with terror. Maybe I shouldn't have told her that, but she needs to know what she's up against.

Finally, she unsticks her throat to speak. "Wh-what should I do?"

I glance at my computer to make sure we aren't being recorded. There's no red light, but that does little to ease the tension in my shoulders. "The only thing we can do is try to get you out of here before your fight. You can't stay here if you decide to back out. Shane doesn't tolerate broken deals."

Harper looks shaken. I feel bad for yelling at her, but I'm not going to lie to make her feel better. She's in deep shit, and no matter how much she trains in the next month, she's never going to be able to beat Marta.

Harper leaves my compartment quickly, looking defeated in that smoking-hot dress.

I don't go after her. I just pace my compartment until I think I might wear a hole in the floor.

I should never have taken Harper to see Shane. The idea of her fighting is ridiculous — especially since most beginners have been fighting a lot longer than she has.

Before my brain has time to register what I'm about to do, I'm heading back out to Neverland to make another deal.

The only way to get Harper out of that fight is to earn enough money to send her away. And to get that, I have to make Shane an offer he can't refuse.

* * *

"A blind fight? Are you crazy?" splutters Miles.

I didn't tell him about my little visit to Shane last night, but I didn't have to.

Word spread through Recon like wildfire that I would be fighting in a week, fueled by speculation about who the other fighter could be.

Blind fights have become sort of an urban legend in the compound because they're so rare. The best fighters never agree to them because the matchups are notoriously uneven. And when you don't know the guy you'll be fighting, you have no time to prepare any kind of strategy to exploit his weaknesses. It's nearly always a bloodbath.

As soon as Miles heard, he stormed into the training center to pester me during my workout.

"I always knew you were a dumb motherfucker, but I never thought you'd go and do something this stupid!"

"It was the only way to make enough money to get her out of here before her fight," I say, tossing him some focus mitts so he can make himself useful.

"Maybe you don't understand," growls Miles. "You're not going to live long enough to escort her to the next compound. You are *going* to die."

"There aren't many fighters in this place who can beat me."

Honestly, I'm a little pissed that Miles is more afraid of me fighting than Harper.

"And I bet Shane knows every single one of them," he says, bugging out his eyes to make his point. "He runs the fight circuit, Eli."

"Why would he put me up against someone I can't possibly beat? It wouldn't be a good fight."

"Because he's already raking in the dough. I hear he's getting a hundred credits a pop for these tickets. He can make a whole lot of money just by telling people that Eli Parker's fighting again. People are going to expect you to win, but they have no idea who the other guy is."

"I can win," I say, throwing a hard jab when he presents the mitt.

"Maybe if your leg wasn't fucked up. But it is."

For a second, I think he's going to kick me again to prove his point, but he just looks helpless. "How much are you going to get if you win?"

"Ten grand."

Instead of looking shocked and impressed, Miles's face becomes grave. "Are you serious?"

"Yeah."

"Eli . . . you can't take this fight."

"It's too late now."

"Listen to me. You aren't going to win . . . not for that much money."

"I'll be fine." I'm getting sick of Miles's cryptic warnings because they're just piling onto my nerves.

The fight is next week. There's no time to come up with a better plan. Yes, taking the blind fight was stupid and impulsive, but

I didn't see an alternative. Jayden is already plotting our next deployment, and I don't know how long we can outrun Constance's plans for our demise.

Even if I lose, I'll get three grand. It's not enough to get us all out of the compound, but it will get Harper out of here before her fight the following week.

I haven't told her what I'm doing, but I'm sure she's heard.

Part of me hopes she can see that I'm doing it for her, but the other part hopes she's mad enough to skip my fight altogether. I don't want her to see me like that again.

When I fight, I become a different person: the person she watched end another man's life without remorse. Just like going out on the Fringe, it's kill or be killed.

fourteen

Harper

The noise in the maintenance shaft is unbelievable on fight night. It fills up the crowded space and hums from the walls, the pipes, and the floor.

People are packed so tightly around the ring, I'd bet Neverland is cleared out tonight. The crowd is a volatile mix of ExCon, Recon, and Waste Management workers, and the general feeling of distrust brewing among them has charged the air with nervous energy.

These people are aching for a fight.

Lenny is right beside me, bouncing on the balls of her feet, trying to see over the crowd. I know Blaze and Bear are somewhere among the onlookers, too, because nearly every cadet is here to watch Eli fight. He's a legend in Recon, but apparently it's been months since his last bout.

The crowd's roar grows impossibly louder, and I know Eli must have entered.

I crane my neck to look, and after several seconds, I see his watchful eyes peering over the wall of onlookers.

Then I realize what's taking him so long. The crowd is jostling him, trying to toss him back and forth against the other spectators. Miles is right behind him, helping him fend off the ExCon and Waste Management guys, but he's struggling just to break through.

Raw terror flares through me like an electric shock. This

crowd is dangerous. All the resentment from Recon's supposed treachery has come to a head, and the other tier-three workers want to see Eli beaten to a pulp.

Apprehension burns through me when he catches my eye. I didn't berate Eli for taking the fight — I've barely said a word to him all week — but my insides have been a mess of confusion, anger, and fear.

Apparently, the compound hasn't seen a blind fight in more than a year because the last one nearly killed the headliner. Based on the hostile crowd, they must think Eli has a shot at winning, but I can't imagine it's going to end well.

Eli doesn't hold my gaze as he climbs up into the ring. He probably feels like a hypocrite for chastising me about my fight when his is clearly more dangerous, but he also needs to focus.

He's shirtless again, and I can tell that every muscle in his body is tightly coiled, prepared to fight for his life. He has the wary look I saw on the Fringe, and I can tell he's wondering if he made the right decision.

"All you guys need to back up," says a familiar, faraway voice. "Please don't crowd the ring."

Somebody pushes me away from the platform. I jerk my head up to say something rude and take an automatic step back.

Blaze is standing in front of me, but he doesn't look like Blaze. Instead of his Recon uniform, he's wearing black pants and a black T-shirt. He's on crowd control, though I can't think why.

"Hey," I say, still a little dazed. "What are you doing here?"

"Working." There's a hard edge to his voice I've never heard before, and it shocks me more than him weighing in on the Lenny-flipping-off-Seamus incident. He's usually easygoing and friendly, but tonight he's all business.

"You two here to see Parker fight?" he yells over the noise, looking from me to Lenny.

"Yeah."

Blaze grimaces. "You shouldn't have come. He's not going to walk away from this one."

Panic claws its way up my throat, making my voice go weak. "What do you mean?"

He glances over my shoulder. "Shane called in a fighter from retirement."

That doesn't sound as bad as Blaze seems to think it is, but I'm briefly distracted by his mention of Shane.

"How do you know Shane?" I ask.

"He's my dad."

I didn't see *that* coming.

"Last call for bets!" someone shouts nearby.

In a panic, I wave over the scraggly-looking man and beam a hundred credits to his interface on Eli.

"Did you just bet on him?" Lenny asks slyly, a wicked grin spreading across her face.

I nod and try to get my breathing under control. I want to ask Blaze more about the fighter and Shane, but he's already disappeared into the crowd.

"I kind of thought you'd want to see him get his ass beat," Lenny shouts at me. "I heard he's been riding you hard."

"What?" I splutter, feeling my face heat up.

"In training," she says, pausing to cheer and clap her hands in the air. "I heard he's been rough on you."

"Oh." My stomach does an uncomfortable flip. I keep forgetting I'm supposed to hate Eli. It's a strange thought to consider when my insides are squirming with fear for his life. "He's not so bad."

I expect someone to come over a microphone to announce

Eli and the other fighter, but the match is less organized than I imagined. There's no announcement, but I know the second the other fighter enters.

The crowd goes wild, dissolving into a storm of cheers and screams.

Because he's a few inches taller, I see this guy's head before I saw Eli's. As he steps through the crowd, the sick feeling in the pit of my stomach intensifies.

Eli's opponent is a gigantic mass of muscle and tattoos. He has light brown skin, a shiny bald head, and watchful black eyes. He's probably only about five years older than Eli, but his weathered face and the jagged scar under his eye add a good decade to his appearance. He's wearing a look of pure hatred and bloodlust.

I always thought Eli was well built and strong, but he's nothing compared to this guy. He can't possibly be in Eli's weight class.

Craning my neck to see over the crowd, I catch a glimpse of Miles. He's standing beside the ring in Eli's corner, and he looks much more nervous than he should.

Completely forgetting that I came here with Lenny, I start fighting my way through the crowd toward him.

The spectators have squished together, craning their necks to get a good look at the other fighter, so I have to stomp on a few feet and elbow people in the side to get to Miles.

By the time I reach Eli's corner, the other fighter is climbing into the ring. He has a pair of fiendish wings tattooed across his back and ink to spare spanning across his chest and shoulders.

Eli is facing him, moving his feet and rolling his shoulders to stay loose. Judging by his rigid back, it isn't working.

The other man sneers, and the thin mustache over his lip quivers. He flexes, and his pecs ripple as though he's teasing Eli.

"Miles!" I pant, tugging on his arm. He's dressed down tonight in athletic shorts and a tight T-shirt, but he still looks pretty intimidating.

He jerks around quickly — almost as though he expects a fight himself — but relaxes when he sees me.

"You shouldn't have come, Riley," he says. "This isn't gonna go well for him."

"Don't say that! You're supposed to be encouraging him!"

"No, I'm supposed to keep him alive in there, and Shane just made my job a lot harder."

"Who *is* that guy?"

"Angel Lopez." Miles's eyes narrow. "They call him the Death Angel. Eli used to fight his brother, but Angel's been in the cages for two years."

"Shit."

"Yeah." Miles glances up at Angel. "You could say that."

The ref steps between the two fighters, and the crowd erupts into a storm of boos and cheers.

Across the room, I can see Blaze and some other men trying to push people away from the ring, but they're too excited for this fight.

Eli steps into the center to hear what the ref is saying, looking as though he's about to witness his own execution. His body is completely motionless, but I can tell every part of him is thrumming with anticipation.

I can't hear what the ref is saying, but I already know the rules: No kicks to the groin, no eye gouges, no rabbit punches, no biting. Pretty much anything else is fair game.

Angel squares off against him, and Eli rolls his body into his fighting stance. A spark of animosity flashes between them, and Angel's mustache quivers as he sneers.

A bell rings, and he springs into action.

Suddenly I understand why blind fights are so dangerous: Eli knows nothing about Angel's style. He has no idea what Angel is going to do, but he doesn't have to wait long to find out.

As though someone let him off the leash, Angel flies forward with two jabs and a wild right hook. Eli is quick to protect himself, but Angel's fist still barrels into his arm with bone-crushing strength.

I cringe, but it doesn't seem to faze Eli. He throws out a punch so fast Angel never saw it coming. It bounces off his nose, but Angel just tosses him an evil smile.

They circle each other, and I can tell Eli isn't giving Angel as much room as he should. He's much more agile, but Angel moves with speed I never would have expected from a man his size. He isn't scared of Eli — that much is clear. He's enjoying this.

Angel throws a jab. Eli slips to the left. He comes over with a cross, but Eli blocks the worst of it. Angel aims a strike at Eli's liver, but he's already dropped his elbow to his hip to absorb the blow. Angel releases another vicious hook, and Eli ducks.

At first, I think he's just going to evade Angel's blows all night, but then I realize Eli's waiting for him to make a mistake.

Angel's hits are packed with power, which means every movement is huge.

I vaguely remember Eli making me watch Bear's strikes in training, and suddenly, it feels as though I'm watching the fight through Eli's eyes — analyzing Angel's movements, choreographing my next strike.

When the Death Angel goes in for a hook, he winds his arm way back.

Eli takes the shot. He throws a punch at Angel's dead side.

He's completely undefended, and Eli's glove sinks into his face and knocks him back.

The crowd screams, and I know many of them were probably waiting for the great Eli Parker to make a comeback. There's no question he's a phenomenal fighter: fast, agile, and patient.

Once he finds his stride, he starts picking Angel apart. Angel may be bigger, but Eli is more skilled. His eyes miss nothing, and he starts taking more risks — lunging in for a jab to the body and setting up a quick succession of hooks and uppercuts.

I can tell he's poked the sleeping giant, and when Angel lets out a feral growl, a jolt of fear shoots through me.

Eli gets tangled up with Angel on his next hook, and he can't get out of the way fast enough to avoid a nasty cross.

The bell rings, signaling the end of the first round, and the ref shoots forward to push the fighters apart.

There's no need. Eli is already backing into his corner. Miles climbs up, and I stick my head between the ropes for a better view. Miles mops the sweat off Eli's face, and Eli's eyes widen in surprise when he sees me.

"What are you doing here?" he pants around his mouth guard.

My mouth falls open, but I'm unable to form a response with all the thoughts flying around in my head.

"What's she doing here?" he asks Miles, a little dazed and apparently pissed off that I showed up.

"She's probably hoping to see you get your ass kicked," says Miles. "You've knocked her around the ring enough."

"Well, you may get what you came for," Eli mutters, taking a swig of water.

The look in his eyes is terrifying: murderous, but afraid.

"What are you doing?" I shout.

"What I have to do."

I stare at him in disbelief. Even though he's doing okay in the fight, it doesn't take a genius to see that he's bitten off more than he can chew with Angel.

The break ends, and Miles helps Eli to his feet and climbs down.

Eli and Angel square off again, and the bell rings.

Within five seconds, I can tell this round isn't going to be anything like the first. The break seems to have given Angel renewed energy. He looks meaner, hungrier, and a little unhinged. He's grinning at Eli in a creepy way, sweat beading on his mocha skin and sliding off his tattoos.

The two circle each other, and Angel throws a few fakes to distract Eli. Eli doesn't take the bait, and when Angel releases a devastating hook to the body, Eli steps in to absorb the force of the blow.

They trade punches back and forth, and Eli manages to counter every one of Angel's worst hits.

Growing annoyed, he comes at Eli for real. His punches are powerful, but Eli seems to know everything Angel's going to do before he does. When Eli takes an opening to throw an uppercut, Angel's head flies back.

Eli doesn't waste the opportunity. He grabs Angel around the neck and uses the leverage to drive his knee into his abdomen with puke-inducing force.

Angel buckles — folding in on himself — and Eli twists around to capture him in a headlock. Angel rolls his head into Eli's side, but not before Eli's gotten two good punches in.

For such a large man, Angel is surprisingly flexible. He twists his body around and throws his weight to the ground. Eli's strong, but he can't withstand that much dead weight on his injured leg. His knee buckles, and they both go down.

Eli lands on top, but Angel uses his weight to throw him. Suddenly their roles are reversed.

I hear myself half groan, half yelp as he winds up for a punch. His fist connects with Eli's face, and his glove comes away shining with blood. He unleashes several more hits, but Eli's still with it enough to keep his gloves protectively in front of his face.

After a few horrible seconds, Eli bucks his hips, and Angel flies forward.

I recognize that move. Eli taught it to me.

The second Angel's hands hit the mat, Eli grabs one of his arms and yanks it toward his body. At the same time, he throws his hips to one side, dumping the larger man onto the mat and climbing on top of him.

Angel is still stunned, and Eli has a handful of seconds to deploy a series of quick, efficient blows.

For an instant, I think he might finish Angel then and there, but then the bell rings, and the ref rushes to push the fighters apart.

Reluctantly, Eli pulls himself off Angel and starts to back away.

It all happens so fast nobody has time to react. Angel springs up unbelievably fast and releases a savage round kick. It connects with Eli's leg just a few inches above the knee, and I have the sudden urge to throw up.

Eli grimaces and doubles over. I know the pain must be flaring through his leg from his gunshot wound, but he tries to hide it.

The ref yells, shoving Angel away too late. The damage is already done. He's hurt Eli, and now he knows his weakness.

The Recon people in the crowd are shouting and booing, but Angel looks satisfied.

Miles is already in the ring, yelling at the ref and Angel, and I clamber up between the ropes to help Eli. I yank up the folding chair and turn to help him lower his body into it.

He no longer looks angry that I'm here. I can tell he's trying not to show the extent of his agony, but it's evident in his eyes. He grimaces as he spits out a stream of blood, and the look on his face is one of pure defeat.

Taking in his swelling eye and the blood coating his face, I have the sudden urge to call for Miles. My heart is hammering against my ribcage, and it feels as though I'm trying to breathe with a hundred-pound weight on my chest.

Eli looks broken.

For a second, I don't think I can handle it. It hurts too much to see him like this. But Miles is busy yelling at the ref and Angel's cornerman, so I tell myself to suck it up and make myself useful.

I don't know what to do, so I hand Eli his water bottle so he can wash the taste of blood from his mouth and grab a towel to dab at the cut over his eye.

"Fuck," he mutters, rubbing his leg where Angel hit. A muscle in his jaw is throbbing, and I know his wound must be killing him. "Now he knows."

"He already knew," says Miles, appearing over my shoulder and eyeing Angel darkly. "He was just waiting for his chance. You were right up on him. He didn't have room when you were fighting."

Someone near the ring produces an ice pack. I take it and push Eli's shorts up a few inches. He tries to grab my hand, but he's too clumsy in his glove to snatch it away from his thigh.

"Shit!" I gasp, wincing at the blood coming through the dressing on his leg.

"It's fine."

"It's *not* fine. You can't stay in the fight."

"I don't have a choice."

"Eli —"

"Harper, stop," he groans. "This is happening."

"Only one round left," says Miles, bouncing on the balls of his feet. "Think you can hang on that long?"

Eli doesn't answer. He just stands up and pushes me gently aside. The ice pack falls to the floor.

Angel is already waiting for him, a malicious gleam in his eyes. Eli tries to look as though the kick didn't affect him, but I can read the pain in his tight shoulders.

The bell rings again, and Angel doesn't hesitate. He fights dirty.

He throws another round kick, but Eli is ready. He raises his leg to block the kick and slips Angel's punch with a cross.

Angel parries his blow and dives in to deliver a sucker punch to Eli's stomach. Eli folds in on himself a little, and Angel throws out an elbow that smashes right into Eli's face.

I know that move. It's my absolute favorite, and it hurts like hell.

Eli staggers back just a little, and Angel comes at him again with a storm of brutal punches.

Jab, jab, hook to the body, hook to the head, upper cut, and Angel's nasty overhand punch.

Eli doesn't have time to evade each blow or aim his counter-strikes. Fists are raining down from every direction. His gloves form a wall around his face, but I know he still feels every hit to the bone.

He should be going on the offensive, but he's just inching toward Angel, taking his punches and slowly closing the distance between them.

At first I think he's giving up, but then I realize he's closing the gap on purpose. When Eli stays within range of Angel's punches, Angel doesn't have room to throw another kick. He doesn't have room to do much of anything.

It seems to be working until Angel rips into Eli's side with a violent hook.

Eli staggers back, and those few feet are all Angel needs. He turns his body and jerks his knee in for a side kick. It's so quick Eli has no time to react. It slams into his leg — right where he was shot.

Eli's face contorts in pain, and his hand goes instinctively to his wound.

When he drops his glove, Angel takes the shot. He hits Eli in the chin with so much force he can't possibly stay upright.

He hits the mat in slow motion, and Angel aims another vicious kick to his wounded leg.

I feel that kick as though it were aimed at me. Pain flashes through Eli's face for a split second, and then I can't see his expression anymore.

Angel dives on top of him, slinging blow after blow after blow.

It's the sounds that tear me up inside — and the fact that Eli doesn't have a chance to fight back. Desperation and helplessness wash over me, and it takes every ounce of self-control I have not to throw myself into the ring and kick Angel in the head. I've never wanted to end someone quite as much as I want to right now.

Get up, get up, get up, I chant.

But Angel is a deadly machine, and Eli remains motionless.

Come on, Eli. Get up!

He doesn't.

The crowd's screams and cheers are deafening. People are flinging themselves toward the ring to get a closer look, almost knocking me over in the process.

I barely notice. I can't tear my eyes away from the grisly battle. Angel shows no sign of slowing down, and Eli still isn't fighting back.

The Death Angel delivers one more crushing blow, and I realize Eli is finished.

fifteen

Harper

Out of nowhere, the ref dives in to break up the fighters. Someone blasts an air horn to signal a technical knockout, and the ref yanks on Angel's arm to pull him off. One of Eli's gloves is still pinned to his face, but his other arm is lying useless at his side.

When the crowd erupts into boos and cheers, I realize I've been gripping Miles's massive bicep in panic. I let go and clamber into the ring, where a guy dressed like Blaze is already running up to check Eli's vitals.

He's stirring, but he doesn't look right.

"Eli! Eli!" I barely recognize my own frantic voice.

His eyes drift around, but he's still lying on his back. He knows I'm there, but he doesn't make eye contact.

Kneeling down in front of him, I'm shocked to see how bad of shape he's in. His face is swollen and bloody, and one of his eyes is so puffy he probably can't even see out of it. I shake his shoulder, but he's still out of it.

The guy with the med kit helps him sit up, and I want to demand this kid's credentials. There's no way he's Health and Rehab, and Eli needs a real doctor.

"We have to get him to the medical ward," I say in an unsteady voice.

Miles is right beside me, and I can see Blaze's worried face swimming behind him. The two of them grip Eli under the arms and hoist him onto their shoulders. He groans as he's carried out of the ring and into the jostling crowd.

The spectators are growing more restless, jeering and yelling and checking their interfaces for their winnings. Some are already trying to push their way out of the confined space, but traffic is bottlenecking near the narrow shaft.

"Get out of the way!" I yell, ducking around Miles to shove people out of our path.

I get lots of irritated glances from ExCon guys, and a few of them even spit at Eli's feet. He's in no shape to retaliate, so I settle on elbowing them all out of the way as hard as I can.

As soon as we enter the narrow shaft, my lungs seize, and the walls seem to be closing in. It doesn't help that there's a solid mass of people in front of us and behind us. Their voices are magnified in the narrow space, and I'm struggling to get enough oxygen to my lungs.

It's all in your head, I think. *You can breathe just fine. We'll be out soon.*

Finally the crowd breaks free, and we spill out into the main tunnel. Blaze and Miles look tired from carrying Eli, but they don't look even half as bad as he does. One of his eyes is fully swollen shut now, and his nose is engorged to twice its normal size.

They drag him up the emergency stairwell and the escalator and onto the megalift, which is mercifully empty. The doors give a friendly *ding* as we arrive at the medical ward, and my eyes go instantly to Sawyer at the front desk.

"Oh shit!" she yells when she sees us.

I stare at her, completely dumbfounded. I'm sure she would never act so unprofessional if the ward wasn't deserted, but I'm grateful for her urgency.

She summons an electric wheelchair, and Miles and Blaze drop Eli into it. He groans a little as the motion jostles his leg, and Sawyer cranks up the speed on the thing.

"What the hell happened?" she demands, jogging to keep up with the wheelchair.

Miles seems a little surprised by Sawyer's demeanor. No one else says anything, so I answer. "Eli entered a blind fight like an *idiot*."

"*What?*"

Eli turns his head. Even though he can only see out of one eye, I know he's glaring at me. We reach an exam room, and Miles and Sawyer help Eli onto the table.

"It was Angel Lopez," Blaze explains, as though Sawyer has any freaking clue who that is. "Nobody wins against Angel."

"He might've won if it weren't for that damn leg," says Miles.

"Your leg!" Sawyer shrieks, grabbing Eli's shorts and yanking one leg up his thigh.

Eli looks annoyed at having yet another girl practically undressing him, but Sawyer doesn't notice or care. There's even more blood soaking through the dressing than before, and she fixes Eli with a deadly look. "Are you insane? Your leg was just starting to heal."

"It's fine," says Eli gruffly.

"And you look like hell," she adds, producing a syringe and plunging the contents into his bicep none too gently. "This should bring the swelling down pretty fast, but I need to see your leg."

She pulls the bandage off, and it looks as though Eli has ripped his stitches. He sucks in a burst of air from between his teeth, and Sawyer rolls her eyes as though she wants to tell him to stop being a baby. She sprays some serious-looking disinfectant on the wound, and Eli grips the edge of the table so tightly that his knuckles whiten.

"I can't believe Shane brought Angel out of retirement," says Miles.

I glance at Blaze and realize Eli and Miles still have no idea that he's Shane's son.

"You weren't meant to win that fight," Blaze says to Eli. "If you had, there would have been trouble. Pops made a lot of money on you tonight. And not just on tickets. The odds for you to win were insane. Nobody thought he could find a real contender."

"Shane is your father?" Eli asks him, looking just as shocked as I felt.

"I didn't grow up with the bastard, if that's what you're thinking. My mom raised me. She's Operations. Ol' Shane barely claimed me until he realized he could use me for the family business, but he wasn't too happy when I got placed in Recon."

"Son of a bitch," Eli mutters. "That's 500 credits down the toilet."

"You bet on yourself?"

"Miles bet for me." Eli turns to him. "How much did *you* lose?"

Miles clears his throat and shifts uncomfortably. "Actually, I . . . uh, made two grand."

"You bet *against* me?" Eli splutters. I can't tell if he's insulted or impressed.

"The odds for you to win were ten to one. I couldn't *not* bet against you."

"And where is this money?"

Miles rolls his eyes. "I already transferred it to Harper's account for safekeeping."

"Thanks," I say, relieved that we now have nearly enough to get everyone to 119. Blaze looks confused by our exchange, so I decide to change the subject.

"Hey. What do you know about the beginner fights?" I ask.

Eli scoffs in disgust, but I ignore him. He is in no position to lecture me after what I just witnessed.

"You mean the fight you accepted with Marta Moreno?"

I nod.

"I know you're not supposed to win that one," says Blaze. "It's pretty obvious to anyone with . . . eyes."

Sawyer is staring at me as though I've grown two heads, and I realize she isn't used to this side of me. She didn't grow up in the Institute, where I frequently got into trouble for fighting, and she doesn't understand the fight-or-die Recon culture.

"But I *could* win," I say to Blaze. "They wouldn't make it a completely uneven match, would they?"

"You're good, Harper. But Marta is . . . insane. I'd be careful if I were you."

He glances at Eli, who's grown silent in the last few moments.

"I'm gonna go. Feel better . . ." Blaze trails off, and I know he almost called Eli "sir."

I grin at his back, and Miles clears his throat, too. "You gonna be okay?" he asks.

Eli nods.

"All right. I'm getting out of here, too. Doctor stuff gives me the creeps." He turns to Sawyer. "No offense."

Sawyer rolls her eyes, and Miles follows Blaze out.

There's a long awkward pause as Sawyer finishes stitching and redressing Eli's wound. I keep glancing up at him, but he won't meet my gaze.

At least whatever stuff Sawyer gave him seems to be working.

The swelling in his eye has already gone down, and his nose is almost back to its normal size.

Sawyer finishes up and reads the tension in the room. "You should be fine," she says. "But come right back if you get a fever. That could mean infection's set in." She levels Eli with a serious expression. "No more fighting. Stay off your damn leg. Next time, I'm just going to chop it off to save everybody the trouble."

She breezes out of the room, leaving me and Eli alone.

"What were you *thinking?*" I ask as soon as she's gone.

"I could ask you the same thing!" he says, snapping his eyes up to mine. "You think *this* was bad? This was nothing compared to what it's going to be like against Marta."

"I'm glad you have so much confidence in me," I say, feeling a little wounded that no one thinks I even have a shot against her.

"It's not about confidence, Harper. It's about being realistic. She has a lot more experience than you. She's been in real fights, for one thing."

"So have I."

He grimaces. "Your little girl fights in the Institute? Please. You won't last five minutes in the ring with her."

"Coming from the guy who did so well tonight!" I snap. "I can't believe you entered a blind fight knowing how dangerous it would be."

"Really? You can't?" Now he's pissed.

"No, I can't! I can't believe you'd risk your life for something so stupid!"

"Stupid? Stupid?" He looks furious beyond words but somehow manages to find them anyway. "I did this for *you*, Harper! I did it so you wouldn't have to fight Marta! I did it so I could get you out of here!"

Whatever I'd expected him to say, it wasn't that. I take an automatic step back in shock.

"What?"

"If I'd won, we wouldn't have needed the winnings from your fight. It was a long shot, but it was worth it if it meant you didn't have to get in the ring with her."

I just stare at him, utterly dumbfounded.

Eli's breathing hard, and as soon as the shock washes over me, it's replaced by a burning shame.

"I . . . I didn't know," I say quietly, feeling my face heat up.

"Well, you should have." Eli still sounds angry, but his voice has lost that uncontrolled edge. "You should really trust me more."

"I do trust you," I whisper.

"Then trust me when I tell you not to do that fight. I still made three grand tonight. With that and Miles's winnings, it's enough for you and Celdon to get yourselves *out.*"

I shake my head. "I'm not going to leave you here."

"I'll be right behind you. Just another fight or two, and —"

"No. We leave together, or we don't leave at all," I say firmly.

He sighs. Eli should have known I wouldn't take him up on his offer, but he still thinks I'm being stupid. "Just think about it, Harper."

"Okay," I say, even though I've already made up my mind. Eli looks exhausted, and I don't want to fight with him anymore.

"Feel better," I say, crossing to the door. "I'll see you later."

He nods, and I turn to go before I lose it. I'm a tangled mess of emotion: fear, relief, confusion, and a strange warmth spreading through my chest.

Eli entered that fight for me.

It makes sense now, and I wonder how I didn't get it before.

Suddenly I feel a hand clench around my arm.

"Hey —"

Before I can turn around, somebody yanks me backward. I yelp in surprise, but there's no one around. Another hand clamps down over my mouth, and the air tightens in my lungs.

This isn't good.

I thrust out a back kick, but my assailant is too fast.

I'm yanked into a supply closet, and panic surges through me. I swing out wildly toward my attacker and hit something solid.

"Hey! Watch it!" comes a familiar voice from the darkness.

An interface floods the closet in blue light. It's Sawyer, rubbing her shoulder.

"What the hell?" I pant, trying to calm my racing heart.

"Sorry. I didn't mean to scare you."

"Geez! You could have just messaged me or calmly called me over here."

She glances at the closed door. "No, I couldn't."

"What's going on?"

Sawyer's eyes look huge in the reflective glow of her interface. "You shouldn't do that fight, Harper," she says seriously.

I open my mouth to protest, but she waves me off. "I know you're going to do it anyway because you're you. Eli may think he can talk you out of it, but I know better. Just hear me out, okay?"

I sigh but listen anyway.

"I've seen this girl. You really don't stand a chance."

"Not you, too," I growl. I'm getting sick of people telling me I can't win.

"I'm not going to try to stop you," she says. "I know you're going to fight her, and you're going to get hurt."

"Gee, thanks. Anything else you'd like to add?"

Sawyer glances at the door again, completely unfazed by my attitude. "I shouldn't even be telling you this," she whispers. "I could get thrown out of Health and Rehab if . . .”

I lean closer. Sawyer is on the verge of breaking the rules. Now at least I've lived to see everything.

“Marta was in here earlier tonight. She fought before the main event.” She takes a deep breath, and her next words come out in a rush. “She won, but she . . . she had some pretty nasty damage to her eighth left rib.”

Sawyer points to the correct rib on herself and then grabs my hand and makes me feel where it is. “This one right here. Do you feel it?”

I nod, unsure where she's going with this.

“She fractured it in the fight tonight. The attending told her she shouldn't fight for at least six weeks.”

Sawyer looks at me seriously, and I'm struck by the gravity of what she's suggesting.

“I'm not going to target her rib on purpose, Sawyer. What happens if I crack the thing?”

Sawyer juts out her bottom lip and swallows, trying to show she doesn't care but not quite managing it. “She won't be able to finish the fight, that's for sure.”

“I'm not going to do that.”

I'm a little horrified by what Sawyer is suggesting. She shouldn't have told me this at all. It's a breach of doctor-patient confidentiality and all kinds of unethical.

“Do whatever you want,” she says, sounding relieved that she's been let off the hook and won't be responsible for putting another girl in the medical ward. “Just be careful, okay?”

I don't say anything. I just hug Sawyer tightly, marveling at how much things have changed.

I'm not sure if I'm the catalyst for all the crazy shit my friends have been willing to do lately or if it's just the messed-up stuff

Tarah Benner

going on in the compound. But if I had any doubts that things were going to hell, they're all gone now.

– 202 –

sixteen

Eli

As soon as Harper leaves, I begin the long, painful journey from the exam room to the front desk.

Angel really did a number on my leg, but asking to have my crutches back is more than my wounded ego can handle tonight. The pain meds haven't kicked in yet, but I'm determined to make it back to my compartment on my own two feet if it kills me.

I attract a lot of stares wandering through the maze of tunnels. I know my face must look pretty gruesome, but *damn* these nurses are judgy.

I reach the waiting room and freeze. Three controllers are standing at the front desk, arguing with Sawyer. There's a preppy-looking blond guy with a pointed face and two older men whose overgrown guts make it clear they've been sitting behind a dispatch desk too long. She's poking one of them in the chest in a stance that's classic Harper.

I recognize the blond weaselly guy at once. It's Paxton Dellwood — the entitled piece of shit I met when Control dragged Harper in for questioning.

As I stare, all three controllers snap their gazes onto me.

"There he is," Dellwood snarls, jutting his chin at Sawyer in a threatening way.

To her credit, she doesn't flinch, but she throws a worried look in my direction.

"Is there a problem here?" I ask, trying to play off my limp as a cocky stride.

The controller closest to me glances at the other two and then reaches for the cuffs on his belt.

"Eli Parker?"

"Who's asking?"

"Officer Dench. You're under arrest for disturbing the peace and assault."

"What?"

"We, uh, got a tip you were participating in an illegal fight this evening against Angel Lopez."

"From *who*?"

Dench moves to restrain me, but I step just out of reach.

"Doesn't matter," he says. "Medical records confirm it."

"This is bullshit."

Two of the officers are converging now, elbows flared and poised for a struggle. There's no way I can run with my leg the way it is, and there'd be no point anyway.

Before I can come up with a better plan, Dench steps around me and yanks my arms behind my back.

"Eli, I'm so sorry," says Sawyer, cupping her hand over her mouth in horror.

She looks as though she might cry, but I'm too focused on the cold metal cuffs snapping on to my wrists to feel too bad.

"I just entered your injuries into the system. I didn't know . . ."

"It's okay," I say through gritted teeth, resisting the urge to kick the controller behind me.

It's not Sawyer's fault anyway. Everybody knows about the illegal fights. Hell, Shane always pays off a few controllers to break up the crowd. This *has* to be Dellwood's way of getting back at me for making him look like a pussy the last time I saw him.

All the nurses are staring now.

Dench and Dellwood frog-march me to the megalift, and I can feel the smug satisfaction radiating from Dellwood. They force me inside the lift and slam me against the opposite wall.

My already swollen temple makes contact with the cold metal, and for a split second, I think I might black out. But before the doors even close, a hand snakes around the back of my skull and smashes my head into the wall again.

This time, I have enough sense to tuck my chin, but the pain still rocks through the back of my head.

All I can see is Dellwood's gleeful smirk out of the corner of my eye.

"Not so cocky now, are ya?" he snarls.

"Go to hell."

"You're gonna wish you were in hell when I'm through with you."

That's when his fist flies out and smashes into the side of my face. There's no real power behind his punch, but my face is already a pulpy mess, and I feel it to the bone.

Another controller's leg shoots out and connects with my shin, and I suck in a burst of air through my teeth.

They're closing in on me — literally backing me into the corner. This time, Dellwood swings straight at my nose and knocks me back into the wall.

Everything is spinning, but I'm with it enough to notice something hard and solid jabbing me in the side just before an electric shock rolls through my body.

I jerk out of Dellwood's grip into the opposite corner of the lift, nearly knocking one of the other controllers to the ground. I can't fight back — not unless I want them piling more charges on me — but I'm not just going to stand there and take it.

Dellwood says something about me getting my ass handed to

me, and the other controllers laugh appreciatively. I'm only half listening. My brain is running on overdrive, trying to think of a way out of this.

If they really want to charge me for the illegal brawl, I'm screwed. Two hundred people watched me fight tonight, and I have no doubts that Angel's crew would come forth as witnesses. No matter how much they hate Control, they probably hate me more.

Then there's the issue of the three thousand credits that were added to my account. *How am I going to explain that?*

The megalift dings, and Dellwood stops guffawing long enough to grab me by the shoulder and wrench me into the lobby. My eyes struggle to adjust to the dim yellowish lighting in Control, and I cringe when the stench of piss and sweat hits my nostrils.

As he pushes me down the tunnel, I try not to look at the crazed, sunken eyes of all the burnouts and psychos hunkered down in the cages. Several of them bang spoons on the bars as I pass, creating an annoying din that reverberates off the concrete walls.

The cage door groans as Dellwood swings it open, and he shoves me inside with both hands.

I'm too weak to do much to break my fall, so my entire right side scrapes along the rough floor. The door slams, and Dellwood throws one more sneer in my direction before swaggering off to rejoin his sidekicks.

For a second, I just lie there. My shoulder is throbbing, and my face feels as though someone took a sledgehammer to it. After losing to Angel, arguing with Harper, and getting beaten up by a couple glorified security guards, I don't have enough fight left in me to care that I look pathetic.

If Dellwood dragged me in as part of his revenge scheme, there's no way they'll let me call anybody — not Miles, not Harper, not the Recon lawyer. I'm totally screwed.

I'm not sure if I dozed off or just passed out, but when I come to, I immediately get the uncomfortable feeling that someone's watching me.

"Well this is just *pitiful*," says a voice from above me.

I know that voice. I *hate* that voice.

Reluctantly, I peel my eyes open. It's a good thing Sawyer injected me with that miracle serum. Otherwise, I don't think I'd even be able to see.

As soon as Jayden's sharp features come into focus, I wish I would have stayed unconscious.

"What the hell are you doing here?" I slur.

She clucks her tongue and makes a pouty face that looks all wrong. "Now that's not very nice, Parker."

I sit up. "Since when have you cared about being nice?"

"Oh . . . I don't. But you should think about being a little bit nicer to me."

"And why is that?" I'm fighting to keep the edge out of my voice, but Jayden knows she's getting under my skin.

"Because I'm here to bail you out," she says innocently. "After all, I'm still your commanding officer."

"Never knew you to give a fuck where I was."

Jayden's smirk widens, and the realization slaps me in the face: Dellwood didn't arrest me just to be a prick, and Control didn't randomly choose tonight of all nights to enforce the law.

Jayden knew I was fighting, and Constance issued the warrant for my arrest.

"Let me guess . . . you had me brought in."

"I might have."

Bitch.

I nod, fighting the fury that's threatening to spill over.

"So why are you here?" I snarl. "I'm not going to be much use to you like this. You can't send me out to die when I'm locked up."

"I didn't want to have you locked up, Parker," she simpers. "I just wanted you to know that I could."

"Not you," I snap. "Constance."

She gives herself way too much credit.

"No. I hate to break it to you, but Constance doesn't consider you much of a threat anymore. To them, you're just a blip on the radar . . . but I think there's more to you than they know. I like to keep my eye on you."

"You've always liked to keep an eye on me, but I don't think it has anything to do with Constance," I mutter.

Jayden's expression doesn't change. Only her eyes hint that I've struck a nerve.

"Do what you want, Parker. Fight. Get shot so you can return early from deployment. Just know that there's nothing in this place that I don't know about. You can go against me all you want, but there will be consequences."

I roll my eyes, which just makes her angrier.

She leans forward until her face is pressed right up against the bars, and I fight the urge to move away.

From a distance, Jayden always looks flawless. But up close, I can see the cracks in her makeup and the terrifying gleam in those cold eyes.

"Just remember how easy it is for me to get to you," she whispers, "and Cadet Riley."

* * *

I stay holed up in my compartment for the next three days, icing my wounds and feeling sorry for myself.

Thanks to Sawyer's intervention, the swelling in my face disappears quickly, and my nose no longer feels as though it has its own heartbeat. Even after the second beating I took in the megalift, all that's left of that night is a black eye and the lingering pain in my leg.

My ego hasn't been as quick to heal. I feel beaten, panicked, and broken.

I know everybody's talking about Eli Parker's humiliating defeat, and Dellwood and Jayden are probably still reveling in the satisfaction they got from exercising their power. To keep myself from murdering one of them or having to face Harper, I go into full hermit mode.

I visit the canteen during off hours to grab meals to go, and I purposely avoid the training center. Harper messages me several times, but I just tell her I'm sick.

She knows I'm lying, but it doesn't really matter. She takes the hint.

After missing our training session on Monday, I get a very unwelcome summons to Jayden's office. I don't even question why she wants to see me anymore. I just assume the worst.

It isn't enough for her to have me arrested and humiliated. She wants me at her beck and call.

When I get to Jayden's office, I'm shocked to see Harper already standing in front of the enormous desk. She's staring straight ahead, while Jayden is watching me like a cat eyeing a canary.

She drinks in my miserable appearance, from the black eye to my uneven stride, and actually *smiles*.

"Parker . . . nice of you to join us."

"Sorry I'm late."

I'm not sorry.

"Well, you're here now," she says in an acidic voice.

Jayden hates people who make her wait. *Eli, one. Jayden, zero.*

"Take a seat."

I'd much rather stay on my feet, but my leg is killing me. I sink down in one of the huge chairs facing her, and Harper sits stiffly beside me.

"As you know, we're trying a new strategy on the Fringe." Jayden rolls her eyes. "Orders of the undersecretary. Now the patrols within the cleared zone haven't turned up any drifters — no surprise there — so I've decided to take matters into my own hands."

"Really?" I try to keep the sarcasm out of my voice, but Jayden's glare tells me I wasn't successful.

"Yes. I sent another team to the location you supplied to gather intelligence about the drifters in the area. They returned with some interesting news."

My stomach clenches, and Harper's head twitches toward me.

"What news?" she asks.

"The base you found in the restaurant serves as a drifter rendezvous point. Tomorrow, they will return."

"And what do you want *us* to do?" I ask, glancing at Harper.

"This gang is escalating. They may be the biggest threat this compound has ever faced. We need to go straight to the source. I need you to discover the location of their home base."

My heart sinks. Of course she wants to deploy us. I dig my fingers into the fake leather armrests, willing myself to stay calm for Harper.

"Is there a problem, Parker?" Jayden asks, sounding utterly delighted. "Your time in the compound for training cadets means you're due for twice-monthly deployments. And you're the one who requested Cadet Riley as a partner, so unless —"

"No," I growl. "There's no problem. When do we go out?"

"Tomorrow at oh-six hundred."

Harper draws in a sudden breath.

"Something wrong, Cadet?"

"No," I say sharply, glancing at Harper.

Jayden raises an eyebrow. "I wasn't talking to you."

"Harper . . ." I warn.

"No," says Jayden, her mouth tightening into a hard line. "I want to hear this."

Harper closes her eyes. "You can't send him out."

"Harper!" I snap.

I don't want her to say it. If she does, she's going to find out Jayden had me arrested, and I can't deal with that right now.

Harper ignores me. "You can't."

Don't do it.

Jayden's fighting a smile. "Why not?"

Harper's eyes shift to me, and I jerk my head infinitesimally.

"His leg is all messed up again. He doesn't move as fast."

"*Again?*" Jayden prompts, barely able to contain her excitement.

Harper snaps her mouth shut.

"It's all right, Riley. I heard about the lieutenant's little brawl. I also heard he was arrested for fighting."

"*What?*"

"My leg is fine," I snap. "Everything's fine."

"Clearly!" Jayden snaps. "Control dropped the charges because, as far as I'm concerned, that fight never happened. It's absurd to me that my best lieutenant would do something so stupid."

I bite my tongue, just waiting for the other shoe to drop.

"You were arrested?" Harper splutters.

I clench my jaw and avoid her gaze.

Jayden smirks. "I'll be expecting a full report from you two. Find out what I need to know, and come right back. Carry whatever supplies you'll need. If you aren't back in three days, I'm going to assume you were killed in action."

"Should we kill the drifters after we learn what we need?" I ask. I'm gripping the armrests so tightly my knuckles are nearly white.

Jayden inhales deeply, basking in the possibility of bloodshed. "No. Keep them alive. I don't want to spook the others. We'll deal with them when the time comes."

I choose to ignore this morbid statement. "When should we report for briefing?"

"There's no need. The undersecretary is not concerned with drifter activity beyond the cleared zone at the moment."

Great, I think. *Jayden's going rogue, and she's chosen us to do her dirty work.*

Harper is quiet — too quiet.

I know she's worried and pissed off, but when Jayden dismisses us, she stands and salutes as though nothing's wrong and beats me out the door.

I follow her automatically and turn down the tunnel right behind her.

"Riley!" I call, acutely aware of the throng of people rushing to the canteen for dinner. "Hey! Wait up!"

People whip their heads around to look at me as I limp behind her. I'm sure they're all reliving the fight in their minds, because the looks they give me are full of pity.

Harper doesn't slow down. In fact, she quickens her pace, and my leg puts up a fight as I try to match her speed.

At first I think she's going back to her compartment, but she passes the cadet wing and keeps walking until she reaches the training center. It's completely deserted, and I slam the doors shut behind me and follow her over to the far wall.

If I didn't know better, I would think she doesn't even know I'm here. She's found the heaviest punching bag and started wailing on it as though her life depends on it.

"Harper . . ."

"Leave me alone, Eli," she snarls, keeping her back to me as she works the bag. She isn't wearing gloves, and I know the brick-solid canvas has to be destroying her hands. With every punch, her knuckles glow a brighter red, but she doesn't stop.

"What are you doing?" I sigh. "You're going to hurt yourself."

She doesn't listen.

"Harper, stop."

I try to pull her away, but she jerks her shoulders out of my grasp.

"You were *arrested?*"

"It was no big deal. Jayden just did it to show that she could. It was just a power trip."

She lets out a crazed laugh. "Right. It's no big deal. Constance just threw you in the cages for fun. Were you even going to *tell* me?"

"No!" I say without thinking. "Why would I?"

"Because Jayden is escalating! That's bad news, Eli. And it affects me, too. Are they going to have *me* arrested?"

"You're not doing that fight, so it has nothing to do with you."

"That's not your decision."

"No, but —"

"I'm doing the fight."

I pinch the bridge of my nose, willing myself to be patient. Harper is stubborn and reckless, and I know she'd do the fight just to spite me. "Harper —"

"I can't do this again," she snaps, a desperate edge to her voice. "I can't go back out there."

Suddenly, I feel as though I skipped a step going down a flight of stairs. We aren't talking about the fight anymore. It was just an outlet for Harper's fear and frustration.

For some reason, I'm unable to muster the appropriate amount of sympathy. I'm still too busy feeling sorry for myself.

"Look, I'm sorry, but we don't have a choice."

"This is a death mission!"

"It's always a death mission. That's all we're going to get until Jayden gets rid of us. You know that."

"No, Eli. Your leg!" she snaps, stepping back far enough to aim a wild kick at the bag.

The instructor in me winces at her atrocious form, but I'm impressed by her power. Her kicks are fueled by rage, and the heavy bag swings a little more with each strike. Then she aims a low kick — Angel's kick — and I actually cringe.

Before she can wind up again, I step forward and grab her by the shoulders. I try to pivot her around to look at me, but she jerks out of my grip and swings around with a vicious hammer fist. I'm legitimately stunned by the force of the blow when her fist connects with the bag.

"What was I supposed to do?" I ask. "Tell her I'm too injured to go?"

Harper rolls her eyes. "Yes!"

"She still would have sent you."

"It doesn't matter. I can handle myself! I don't need you to be my guardian angel!"

That stings more than I'd like to admit, and I feel my face heat up.

Even in the middle of her meltdown, Harper realizes she hurt my feelings. Her huffy expression dissipates, and she tilts her head sideways. "I'm sorry. I didn't mean that. I'm just scared, okay?"

"I know."

"Look . . . Constance is going to kill me regardless. You can't protect me from everything. But you can protect yourself."

She turns back to the punching bag, but the fight seems to have gone out of her. This time, she doesn't resist when I spin her around.

"I'm going with you," I say in a voice I hope conveys my determination.

Harper won't meet my gaze. She's breathing hard, and a few pieces of dark hair have drifted out of her messy ponytail. Her eyes are bright with anger and adrenalin, and I know I should put some distance between us.

It's not that I think Harper might hit me. It's the fact that she's unstable, and it's making me unstable.

Finally, she says, "If you get killed out there because of me . . ." She shakes her head, looking caught between crying and yelling. "This is all my fault. You were fine before I came along. Constance wasn't trying to send you out on these crazy missions. You weren't entering blind fights like a fucking moron . . . or getting arrested . . ."

"You just make my life more interesting," I say lightly.

Harper *has* turned my life completely upside down, but not for the reasons she thinks.

"Listen. I made a choice to put myself in the middle of all this. It isn't your fault."

When she finally snaps her gaze onto mine, her eyes are deep and glassy like two pools of still water.

"I can't . . . do this again." She shudders, and I wait for her to continue. "I can't go out there. I can't *live* like this. I don't know how anyone does."

I let out the breath I've been holding, knowing what I'm about to say isn't the right response. "It gets easier."

"I don't want it to get easier!" she cries. "This is wrong, Eli! We shouldn't be murdering these people. I don't care what they've done or what they're planning to do. They're just *people*."

For the first time, everything becomes extremely clear.

Harper's right. I never considered what I did for Recon murder. I told myself we were fighting a war. That was the only way I could live with what I was doing, but it's all been a lie.

I blamed myself for every cadet's death, but I never gave a second thought to killing drifters. The full weight of it hits me all at once, and I have to fight just to stay standing.

"We have to do this, Harper," I say, trying to keep the pain out of my voice. "Hopefully this will be the last time. After that, we can leave the compound and start over."

"It's too late," she whispers. "I can't erase what I've done. I can't just forget. Even if we go to another compound, every day I'll think . . . the only reason I'm here is because someone else is killing the last survivors. I can't live with that."

"Yes, you can," I say, desperate for her to understand. "It isn't right, but nothing about this is right. We shouldn't have survived Death Storm, but we did. It's what we do, you and me."

"I don't want to just survive, Eli. I need there to be a point to all this. Ever since we got back, I wake up every day and think . . . what if I just *didn't*? It wouldn't matter."

"It matters to me," I growl.

"But it doesn't matter to me anymore!" she yells. "That's the problem. I need some reason . . . some reason to keep me going."

"Then *find* one," I growl, shaking her shoulders. "Do it for Celdon or Sawyer or . . . Jesus, Harper. Do it for me. I need you!"

She just stares at me in shock, her face frozen in pain and understanding.

I don't know who breaks first. Harper puts a hand on my chest, though whether she wants to push me away or bring me closer, I'm not quite sure. At the same time, I reach up and cup her face with both hands.

Her skin is unbelievably soft, and those gray eyes are burning so fiercely that my fingers have a mind of their own. They work into the lose remnants of her ponytail and bring her lips to mine.

As soon as I taste her, I know I won't be able to stop. This is nothing like the tentative kiss she gave me that night on the observation deck. I've replayed that kiss over and over, and this is something else entirely.

Her lips are hot and just as soft as I remember, but they're more demanding this time. She isn't asking for permission. She's giving in to some long-buried need that mirrors mine exactly.

Unrestrained panic and joy flare through me, igniting every nerve in my body.

We've been teetering on the edge of this for weeks, and I just jumped off the fucking cliff.

I yank the tie out of her ponytail so I can thrust my hands into her silky curtain of hair. I drag my fingers through it, tugging gently as I explore her mouth.

I can't believe this is happening, but I don't question it.

Harper's kisses are just as bold and intense as her fighting. She isn't like any other girl. She doesn't just give in to it; she pulls me toward her and takes what she wants. She bites my lip gently, and her tongue begs for entry into my mouth.

I open my lips for her, and she takes it up a notch. Her hands trail up my chest, leaving goose bumps in their wake. She drags her fingers through my hair, nails skimming my scalp.

I moan and move on to her neck, tasting her and trying to commit her scent to memory: a heady vanilla mixed with a slight tang of sweat.

As I work my way down to her collar bone, she lets out a little whimper that almost sends me over the edge. She tips her head back to give me better access, and I feel it the second she lets go.

Her fist bunches in my shirt, pulling me closer, and the momentum knocks us both into the punching bag as we slam into the wall. She wraps herself around me, and I hoist her up against the wall using my good leg for leverage.

Once every inch of her is pressed against me, I can barely restrain myself. My hand slips up the bottom of her tank top and makes contact with her warm flesh. She pulls me even closer, and my fingers glide over the soft skin below her ribs. She shivers, but then her lips drop down to my neck, and my hands climb up hungrily.

She trails kisses up my jaw, and when her teeth graze my ear-lobe, I want her so bad it hurts. I want to rip off her clothes and maul her right here, but a distant little voice reminds me that I can't.

Reality slowly catches up to my brain.

I can't have her right here. I can't have her at all.

Tomorrow, we'll be going out into the Fringe.

Harper senses my hesitation, and her lips find mine once again. Her next kiss is slower, gentle, lingering. She swirls her tongue around mine and sucks lazily on my bottom lip.

Her fingers brush the stubble on my cheek, and I grab her

face to draw out our last kiss.

One of my hands is still in her hair. The other is teasing the curve of her breast under her sports bra. Her hips are flush against mine, and I can feel her body radiating warmth.

I don't want to push her away and tell her it was a mistake. It wasn't a mistake so much as a moment of weakness, and I want to let her make me weak all over.

She already knows what I haven't said. When she pulls away and meets my gaze with those big, beautiful eyes, I know I don't have to apologize or explain.

When I loosen my grip, she unhooks herself and slides down the wall, back onto her feet.

There's a long moment of silence as we both just stare at each other. Her hands are resting on my chest, and one of mine is still tucked in her shirt. It isn't awkward or uncomfortable; we're just standing there because neither of us wants to break the spell.

I know it has to be me. I'm the one who made a fatal slipup. I'm her commanding officer, for Christ's sake.

I drag in a shaky breath and release her, carefully brushing away a long lock of raven hair.

"Pack twice as much food and water as last time," I say. My voice sounds rougher than usual. "I'll see you at oh-six hundred."

She gives me a shaky nod and then glances down at her feet.

I turn to leave but stop after a few steps. I can't turn to look at her, or I'll lose all my resolve not to scoop her up and carry her back to my bed.

"I'm not going to let anything happen to you, Harper. You just have to keep fighting."

Seventeen

Harper

I'm in a complete daze as I load my rucksack for the mission and drag myself to dinner.

I don't watch where I'm going. I don't taste the food. I don't even know what I'm eating.

All I can think about is the memory of Eli's lips on mine. He left his delicious scent all over me, and I can still feel him *everywhere*.

This was nothing like the first time we kissed in his compartment. That had escalated quickly, too, but it had been an act for Constance.

At least it started out that way.

When I kissed him on the observation deck, that had been a lapse in judgment — more of a question than a kiss — and Eli had pushed me away.

This time, I *know* he kissed me. Or maybe we kissed each other, but there was no misinterpreting that burning hunger in him.

I'm having thoughts I shouldn't be, and it's a good thing he stopped when he did. I wouldn't have stopped. He would have had me half naked before my brain realized we probably shouldn't have sex in the training center — or at all.

Now I understand why relationships among Recon operatives are forbidden. Our moments of weakness have *definitely* complicated our relationship. And instead of thinking about tomorrow, I'm thinking about Eli's rough, calloused hands exploring my body.

I fall asleep as soon as my head hits the pillow and awake before my alarm even goes off. I get dressed, throw my rucksack over my shoulder, and head up to the ground level for a quick breakfast.

When I leave the canteen and reach the airlock doors, I'm not surprised to find Eli already waiting there with his back to me. He turns around when he hears my footsteps, and his eyebrows shoot up as though he completely forgot who would be accompanying him.

I attempt a small smile, but the combination of nerves and dread make it difficult. To my immense surprise, he breaks into an easy grin I rarely get to see, and my heart practically combusts.

"Did you pack enough supplies?" he asks in a serious voice.

I smile for real this time. I should have known that getting hot and heavy in the training center wouldn't stop him from slipping back into serious lieutenant mode.

"Yeah."

In typical Eli fashion, he doesn't seem prepared to take my word for it.

In one quick motion that reminds me of his amazing make-out skills, Eli spins me around and unzips my rucksack. He rifles around in my bag, counting meal packets and hefting the bag of water, and I force myself to breathe normally as he manhandles me.

After a few seconds, he seems satisfied. He zips up my bag and clears his throat as he spins me back around.

"I grabbed your gun from the weapons room," he says, pulling a rifle off his right shoulder and fitting it over mine. The weight of it brings the dread creeping back, but I just nod.

Seconds later, Jayden whips around the corner in her too-tight uniform. She looks cold and stern with her hair in a tight bun, and the style only accentuates her pinched features. Remy isn't with her.

She reads us the deployment disclosure in a crisp, perfunctory voice, and Eli and I answer with a flat "I do."

"Remember that we have operatives patrolling the cleared zone," she says. "Don't shoot any of our people."

"Right," says Eli tersely, reaching around to pull on his mask. I match his movements, and when the mask suctions to my face, my heart rate speeds up automatically.

Jayden punches in the door code, and I realize I'm wholly unprepared for this mission — physically and mentally. I haven't had time to resign myself to the possibility that I could die out there . . . or that Eli could.

But there's no time. We step into the chamber, the doors close, and the surly ExCon man punches in the next code.

It's still dark out on the Fringe, but I feel the oppressive expanse of nothingness as soon as the doors open.

Eli glances over at me. To anyone else, it would just seem like a casual look, but I understand Eli well enough to know he's asking if I'm ready.

I nod and step outside, instantly on high alert for any movement in my periphery. It's still too dark to see more than a few feet in front of me, which I really don't like.

As soon as the airlock doors hiss shut behind us, Eli reaches over and clicks something on the top of my mask. Green light illuminates the ground in front of me, which is how other Recon operatives will identify us in the dark.

Eli leads us toward the cleared zone, moving a little slower than usual on his bad leg. I look for other Recon people, but I don't see a single green light out in the desert.

After half an hour, Eli slows to a stop and checks his interface. We've almost reached the perimeter, so I turn mine on, too.

The mines light up like a Christmas tree, and we navigate around them in silence.

Eli is tense, but he seems less on edge than the last time he brought me out. Maybe he's no longer worried that I'm going to have a meltdown since I got it out of my system last night.

Whatever the reason, I want him to see me as a legitimate partner, not a burden.

But as soon as we clear the mines, his posture changes completely. He rolls his shoulders and drops his weight a little lower toward the ground. I know he's thinking about mines the drifters may have reburied and the ambush we faced last time. My skin is crawling with nerves.

The sun is peeking up over the horizon now, rendering our green lights unnecessary. I feel better that I can see, but it also means we'll be an easier target for the drifters.

I match my breaths to Eli's to slow my racing heart and keep scanning the horizon for potential snipers. It takes much longer than last time to cover the same distance since we're walking instead of running from gunfire.

When we finally reach the town, my wariness has reached honest-to-god panic. It seems strange that we've gotten this far without being accosted.

If I didn't know better, I'd think the town was completely deserted. The dusty cars are lined up like empty cans along the road, and the now familiar sign for Shell Street seems to be guiding us along a private tour. Dave's Diner looks especially bleak with its faded red sign and shredded awning.

The air is disturbingly breezeless. All I can hear is the slight scuff of our feet on the cracked pavement and the unearthly sounds of air coming through our masks.

Eli jerks his head toward the mini mart, and I copy his movements as he hugs the brick wall and moves down the block at a shuffle. He must feel just as uneasy as I do, but he still looks in control.

As we move down the street, my fear is downgraded to alertness. Since we're not in any immediate danger, I'm beginning to notice the blistering heat and my own parched throat.

I don't bother asking Eli if we can stop for a drink, though. Something in the back of my mind is still screaming at me to stay on high alert. Jayden told us the drifters would be here, which means the situation is probably even more dangerous than she let on.

We continue our patrol of the tiny town, and it takes nearly an hour at our slow, careful pace. Every street we pass is clear, and the restaurant the drifters are using as their base looks deserted. There's not a guard in sight, and I begin to feel paranoid that the radiation might have killed them all.

We do one more sweep of the main road and duck into a little diner to regroup. It's one of those '50s-themed joints with tacky neon signs hanging in the windows and teal-and-black booths.

As soon as we're inside, I know why Eli picked this restaurant. Windows fill every wall from ceiling to booth, providing a panoramic view of the main part of town. The windows are intact — not a broken pane in sight — so I take the opportunity to remove my mask and take a deep drink from my pack.

There's a faded, half-broken cutout of Elvis sagging in the corner, and the dusty photos of pre–Death Storm celebrities seem to be staring at me from the walls.

"This is weird," says Eli, more to himself than me.

"You could say that."

We sink down into a corner booth. Staring out the window, I watch a light breeze kick up some tumbleweed. It's the only thing moving out there.

"Why would Jayden tell us to be on high alert if there aren't any drifters?"

Eli sighs and rakes a hand through his hair. "Maybe she's just screwing with us. Or maybe her information is wrong."

We fall silent, watching and waiting.

It drags on for hours, and I feel my alertness slipping into boredom. My annoyance with Jayden is mounting by the second. We haven't seen a single drifter, and I'm starting to wonder if we even will.

Just as I'm about to take a break from our endless watch to eat an energy bar, something shifts on the horizon.

The movement is so small I wonder if my eyes are playing tricks on me. But when I squint through the window, I see a boxy shape barreling toward us. It's far away but quickly gaining ground.

I nudge Eli and tilt my head in the direction of the approaching vehicle. His eyes widen, and he pulls me down a little so we can watch the car and stay out of sight.

"It's headed toward the restaurant," Eli murmurs.

"Let's go!"

"We need to get a closer look first."

I want to scream in exasperation. We've been waiting for what feels like forever, and I just want to *do* something.

But there's a reason Eli Parker has lived through so many deployments. He isn't impulsive like me. He thinks things through.

That's why I follow his lead when he dons his mask and creeps out of the diner. We stick to the shadows, moving down the street toward a dilapidated gas station near the restaurant.

As we approach, I can hear the vehicle idling in the parking lot. It's the loudest thing I've heard all morning.

Eli jerks his head toward the glass door leading into the gas station, and I put my back against the wall and inch closer.

Taking a deep breath, I pull on the door handle and open it slowly to avoid disturbing the bell hanging over our heads.

Eli slips in ahead of me to check for drifters and then grabs my arm and swings me around the dusty counter that still smells faintly of disinfectant. He falls into a crouch, and I kneel down in front of the large window.

From this vantage point, I can see the vehicle clearly. It's a large, boxy car covered in dust — an SUV.

Somebody kills the engine, and three men get out of the vehicle, yelling at someone in the backseat I can't see.

They head into the restaurant, and a fourth man gets out of the SUV. He's wearing a cutoff shirt and toting a huge gun. He walks up to the wooden porch surrounding the entrance, but I don't hear the door slam again. He must be the guard.

"Are we gonna go in?" I ask. "There's only one of them watching the door."

"Let's wait to make sure there aren't more coming."

I let out an impatient huff but don't say anything. I know Eli is being extra cautious after our last drifter encounter, but I'm dying to know what's going on down in that basement.

As we stare out at the horizon, I marvel at the idea of drifters driving around in SUVs. I suppose it makes sense that they would use whatever relics they could find, but it just seems as though all those things should have died along with the rest of humanity.

"Have you ridden in one?" I ask.

He looks at me curiously. "In one what?"

"In a car."

I can't see his entire face, but when his eyes crinkle, I know he's cracking a grin. "Yeah. Plenty of times. Everyone had one back then."

"What's it like?"

He glances at me with a fondness I've only ever seen after I did something right in sparring. "Fast. It's fun. I always wanted to learn how to drive, but I never had the chance."

We fall silent, and Eli quickly regains his businesslike demeanor. It's a good thing, too, because I almost miss the shadow of a lone figure approaching the restaurant from the far side.

He materialized too suddenly to tell where he came from, but he's moving toward the building with a purposeful stride.

"Who the hell is that?" Eli murmurs. "And why didn't we see him?"

Alarm flashes through me when I catch his meaning. We searched the entire town for drifters when we arrived, but we missed him somehow.

The figure disappears into the shadow of the porch, and Eli's anxiousness and curiosity seem to get the better of him. He lets out a stream of air from his nose and tightens his grip on his rifle. "Let's go."

Heart pounding, I slip out of the convenience store behind him and skirt along the edge of the building toward the restaurant. I half expect the guard to jump out and shoot us, but we manage to stay out of sight.

When we reach the corner, Eli pushes me down behind a dumpster. "Stay here," he mouths.

Every shred of curiosity is instantly crowded out by fear. I shake my head, but he gives me a look through his mask that tells me he won't have it any other way. I crouch down onto the dusty pavement and watch as he slips around the restaurant.

He stops, and then — to my horror — he kicks an old dented can lying in the alley.

There's a flash of movement on the porch, and Eli flattens himself against the rough wood exterior.

A burly man in his early thirties whips around the corner. He catches a glimpse of Eli in his periphery, but it's too late.

Eli's arm shoots out, grabbing him around the neck. A blade glints in the sunlight, and he swipes it cleanly across his throat.

As the drifter struggles for his last dying breaths, terror and hopelessness fill his eyes. Blood coats Eli's sleeve, and he carefully lowers the man's body to the ground.

My chest tightens, and the dry air suddenly feels too thin in my lungs.

Looking over the edge of the dumpster, Eli nods. I step out, white-knuckling my rifle and trying to conceal how freaked out I am.

"Stealth," he whispers.

I step over the dead man and pick my way up the squeaky stairs in front of the restaurant.

When we reach the entrance, we each flatten ourselves against the outer walls, and Eli is first to check the view inside. He nods, and I follow him through the door.

Once my eyes adjust to the dim lighting, I see there's no one on the main floor. The restaurant is exactly as it was the last time we were here, only now I can hear voices emanating from between the warped floorboards.

I follow Eli's steps exactly to avoid making a sound. We reach the kitchen, and when he moves toward the basement door, I grab his arm. He wants to listen in on their conversation, and he's prepared to go down that staircase to do it.

He widens his eyes at me in his signature "do what I say"

expression and pulls the door open. Everything inside me is screaming that it's a bad idea, but I trust Eli enough to follow.

Angry voices drift up the stairs. Heart pounding, I step onto the landing and pull the door shut.

"We don't like being set up," says one man. He has an accent I don't recognize, and he sounds furious.

"It wasn't a setup," growls another voice — younger and defiant.

There's a harsh slap — the back of someone's hand — and the first man makes an angry noise in his throat. "Do I look fucking stupid to you?"

"He'll be here," says the younger man.

"He better be. Otherwise, it won't end so good for you."

"What do you want with him anyway?" asks the hostage. "If you have business with Jackson, I'm your guy."

As I listen, I realize there's something familiar about his voice.

"He was supposed to be on cleanup duty at the last location, but his guy on the inside chickened out."

"We don't know what happened to Travis," growls the young man. "He might be dead."

"That's what I call shitty planning. But I'm sure your man Jackson has a backup plan."

"Travis *was* the backup plan, you idiot."

There's a long, pregnant silence, and I would bet the man doing the threatening has a gun pointed at the other guy's head. "For your sake, I hope that's not the case."

I feel a hand close around my arm and nearly jump out of my skin. Eli flashes me a look and opens the basement door again.

I rise into a crouch and follow him back into the kitchen. He makes a beeline for the exit, rifle poised. I quicken my pace, letting my nervous energy propel my legs forward.

When we step outside, the warmth of the open air is a welcome relief. I wait for Eli to say something, but he just leads me back to the gas station without a word.

"Why did we leave?" I ask, yanking off my mask and feeling the rush of fresh air against my sweaty face. "It was just getting good!"

"It was just getting *dangerous*," Eli says. "We stumbled into the middle of a gang deal gone bad."

"But Jayden said —"

"*Yeah.* Jayden wanted us there. She wanted us in the middle of it because she doesn't care if we get shot collecting intel."

"Do you know who those people were?"

Eli's eyes narrow, and he crosses to the streaky window to peer out at the restaurant. "I have an idea."

I watch him, waiting for him to finish. "Well, who?" I ask, impatient to fill in the blanks.

"Back when I worked for Freeman, there were a few major gangs that controlled the area. They fought for territory — territory where they could salvage stuff from before Death Storm: food, medicine . . . all the stuff that was in short supply out here. They made a killing selling it back to survivors."

"So what was all that about?"

"I don't know. But we don't want to get caught in the middle of it."

"We need *something* to tell Jayden."

Eli opens his mouth to protest, but I cut him off.

"You know as well as I do that the *second* we're not useful to her anymore, she's going to have us both killed."

"She's trying to get us killed right now."

I shake my head. "Her curiosity is the only thing keeping us alive. I say we find out what's going on, give her a taste to keep her wanting more, and then get the hell out of the compound."

Eli sighs. He knows I'm right.

"What happens when this Jackson guy finally shows up?"

I can't believe he's actually considering my plan.

"It didn't sound like he was going to show. But if that's what you're worried about, we can just wait until we know he won't."

"That guy could be dead by then. Gangsters are not the most patient people."

"No. They need him. He's the closest link they have to this other guy. If he doesn't show, they'll keep him around just to see what he knows."

Eli stares at me for a moment, thinking through my reasoning.

"All right. We'll wait them out for a few hours. Then if this guy doesn't show up, we'll go back in."

"Okay."

We sink down onto the floor to watch the restaurant, and I try to conceal my excitement. I'm not just proud that Eli listened to my idea; I'm also curious to hear what the gangsters are so anxious about.

Eli passes me an energy bar, and we eat in silence. I don't know why I care what happens to the captive in the basement, other than the odd sense of déjà vu I got at the sound of his voice.

I don't share these thoughts with Eli. If he thinks I'm a little too eager to throw myself in harm's way again, he doesn't show it. I can tell it's killing him, too — not knowing what those men were talking about.

We wait for three hours, my lower body growing numb from sitting on the hard floor.

"Well, our friend may be out of luck," he says finally. "I don't think Jackson's going to show."

I stand up and stretch, my heart pounding a little harder against my ribcage. I wanted to go back, but now that Eli is ready to put our plan into action, the danger of the situation is finally hitting me.

He hands me my mask. "You ready?"

"Yeah," I say, hoping he can't tell how nervous I am. "Let's go."

* * *

As soon as we enter the restaurant, I can tell things have gotten a lot worse for the young hostage in the few hours since we left. The tension is palpable in the voices rumbling up between the floorboards, and thunderous footfalls down below make the shelves of souvenirs rattle.

Somebody in the basement yells, and then there's a loud crash. I pry off my mask, and Eli follows suit.

He shoots me a sideways look — silently asking if we should continue — and I nod.

We've come this far. We can't turn back now — not when we're so close to learning more about the drifters.

We inch through the kitchen and push our way onto the landing again, careful not to disturb the creaky floorboards.

"*Where is he?*" shouts the man down below.

"I . . . don't know." The younger man's voice is definitely weaker than before.

There's another crash — louder this time. It sounds as though somebody flipped the chair over and kicked the man in the side.

I cringe at his guttural yell and shrink back against the wall.

Suddenly, I feel a warm draft behind me that wasn't there before.

Alarm bells go off in my head just as the door to the kitchen flies open. My stomach drops when I see a tall, meaty man standing there in baggy jeans, a black shirt, and a black bandana.

His gaze bounces from me to Eli, and it seems to take a long time for his brain to process what he's seeing.

"What the —"

Before he can finish his sentence, Eli flips the butt of his gun around and whacks the guy under the chin.

The man staggers backward and crashes into the metal shelf behind him. Every muscle in my body clenches as pots and pans bang together.

I finally get my rifle trained on him, but the men downstairs have fallen silent.

"What the fuck was that?"

Eli reacts before I do. He shoots the fallen drifter in the head and then throws himself in front of me and aims his gun at the foot of the stairs. My ears are ringing so badly I feel as though I've gone temporarily deaf.

A weathered brown face pops around the corner half a second before Eli shoots again. The man goes down, and Eli flies down the stairs.

My heart is racing. If there are other gangsters in the area, they must have heard the shots. Hopefully they'll think it was their men.

Eli steps over the crumpled body, but before I even reach him, a bullet cracks through the wall behind him. He hits the deck, and two more shots follow.

My body starts moving before my brain can react. I stumble down the steps beside Eli and raise my head over the half wall at the foot of the stairs. I shoot and miss, and Eli yanks me down to his level.

Another bullet pierces the thin drywall in front of us, just inches from Eli's torso.

He swears and raises up into a crouch, shooting off four rounds. I hear a yell and know he hit at least one of the remaining men. But another bullet close to the head sends him back down next to me, breathing hard.

"There are two more," he gasps, his voice going in and out.

"Whatdowedo?" I ask, the panic scrambling my thoughts.

"Both of us need to shoot at once. You get the guy on the left. I'll get the guy on the right."

I tighten my grip on my rifle, trying not to dwell on the fact that I'm about to kill another human being. Instead, I focus on what I need to do to get Eli out of here alive.

I trained for this, I think. *I'm ready.* One shot. One shot is all I get.

Eli mouths a countdown. On three, I spring up and take aim at the man nearest me. He's also wearing black, though he's skinnier than the last guy.

To my amazement, my bullet hits him cleanly in the chest.

Surprise and pain animate his face for the briefest second before all traces of who he was disappear.

As he sinks down, I glance at Eli's target. His eyes are half closed in a grimace, but when the bullet hits the wall behind him and ricochets off, everything seems to fall in around me.

Eli missed.

Eli — the strongest, best lieutenant I've ever known — *missed.*

It only takes a split second for me to realize just how high the cost will be.

Everything slows down. The man he was aiming for still has his gun raised. I see him zero in on Eli — see the decision on his face to end him.

I'm not fast enough to get a bullet between Eli and the other man. But out of the corner of my eye, there's another flash of movement.

A gunshot pierces my eardrums, and I cringe. I look at Eli, expecting to watch the light leave those beautiful blue eyes, but he's staring straight ahead, looking as though he can't believe what he's seeing.

The man before him crumples to the ground, blood seeping from his leg. Eli finally shoots, and it's a kill shot. The man already knew he was going to die, but there's no remorse on his face — only fury.

My brain is slow to put the pieces together. My eyes drift from the fallen gangster to the young man lying next to him.

He's still tied to a folding chair, one arm locked underneath him. The leg of his cargo pants is pulled up ever so slightly, revealing the black strap of a holster around his ankle. One of his biceps has wiggled free from his ropes, and in his hand is the smoking gun.

Eli trains his rifle on the man but hesitates. He glances at me, and I shake my head once.

"Don't move," Eli growls at the man on the ground — the guy who just saved our lives. He still has his gun raised at an awkward angle, and I have no idea how he managed to hit the other guy in the leg from his bound position.

He doesn't say a word.

Eli crosses in front of me with his rifle pointed at the man's head. I grip my gun harder and follow him, dazed and unsure whether we should kill the guy or not.

Just because he shot the drifter who was going to shoot Eli doesn't mean he's friendly. We just gave him the chance he needed to get rid of his captors.

We take a wide path around the man's legs, and when I get a good look at his face, I suck in a breath of surprise.

His face is swollen and bloody from the earlier beating, but familiarity rocks me to the core.

Under one battered eyebrow, I catch a glint of sharp blue eyes. Even under all the blood and bruises, I can make out the defiant set of his jaw and the same probing gaze.

Only there's no fondness or pride there now. Unlike his doppelgänger, this man wants me dead.

Then his gaze flickers to my left, and those unsettling, familiar eyes widen in shock. He opens his mouth to speak, but he can't quite form the words.

It's Eli who speaks first, and the name that comes out of his mouth is the last I ever expected to hear.

"Owen?"

eighteen

Harper

"Eli?" the man whispers in shock.

There it is again — that familiar voice I couldn't quite place. It's nearly identical to Eli's, but there's an edge to it that makes him sound more dangerous. Even in Eli's angriest moments, his voice never scared me quite like that.

"It's impossible."

Eli's face has drained of color, and his eyes are bright with shock and horror. It looks as though he's seen a ghost, but if he's seeing one, that means I am, too.

Then his gaze narrows, as though he thinks he's being tricked. In one swift motion, he reaches down and yanks the chair back into an upright position, causing the guy to jerk forward. As he settles, Eli kicks the gun out of his hand, and it skitters across the floor out of the man's reach.

Now that I'm looking at him head-on, there's no denying the possibility that this could be Owen — Eli's older brother who supposedly died thirteen years ago.

At first glance, they could be twins, but Owen's jaw is more square, and his gaze is harsher under heavy black eyebrows. He wears his dark hair buzzed, and unlike Eli, he has a pronounced five o'clock shadow. He's also bulkier, with a more rugged, dangerous appearance.

Only their eyes are exactly the same: a deep, piercing blue.

"What's your name?" Eli demands.

"What's yours?"

Eli raises his rifle again, training it on the man's face. "I ask the questions here."

I glance up at him. "Eli . . ."

"Owen Parker."

Eli's eyes widen, but he tightens his grip on his gun.

"You're not my brother," he growls. "You can't be. I saw my brother die. He was *dead*." Eli's voice is wavering now, though whether from grief or confusion, I can't quite tell. "Your men raided my house and killed my parents and my brother in cold blood."

Now it's Owen's chance to look shocked. "You *are* him," he whispers.

"Shut up!" Eli yells.

I don't think I've ever seen Eli lose control, but his wary, confident demeanor is unraveling quickly. His usually steady hand is quivering on his rifle, and he swallows several times before speaking again.

"What are your parents' names?" Eli asks.

"Luke and Ellen."

Eli sucks in a breath, but his eyes are still distrustful.

It's not that he doesn't believe Owen; the problem is he does. I can almost see his world crumbling around him. The grief he carried around for years was based on a lie. Now it's been replaced by a devastating uncertainty.

"Eli . . ." I murmur, reaching up to push the rifle down. He doesn't stop me, but he won't meet my gaze either. He's too busy staring at Owen.

Owen's gaze flickers over me but snaps back to Eli within seconds.

"How are you alive?" Eli asks.

"What do you mean?"

"You were shot," Eli says aggressively, as though trying to reassure himself of the facts.

But Owen shakes his head. "I wasn't. I ran outside and got turned around. I was running, but somebody grabbed me and dragged me off."

"But the body . . ." Eli seems to be racking his brain, trying to recall the details of that night.

From what he'd told me, it had been too dark to make out the person's features, so the body he'd thought was his brother's must not have been.

When Eli looks back at Owen, I'm startled to see his eyes look shiny and bloodshot, as though he's trying not to cry. "Why didn't you come back for me?" His voice comes out as a harsh croak, and my heart aches at his pained expression.

"I *did*. I went back to the house the next day, but you weren't there. I didn't know where you could have gone, but I was determined to find you. I looked for you for *years*."

That seems to take the fight right out of Eli. His shoulders slump, and he turns away from Owen. I want to reach out for him, but it's clear he needs some space.

With his back to us, he sinks down into a crouch and lets his eyes wander unfocused over the filthy floor. One of his hands is resting on his rifle; the other arm is draped over his leg and hanging helplessly in the air.

He lets out several breaths, and I start to worry that maybe *this* is what will finally drive him over the edge.

Years of killing and watching people die have made Eli withdraw completely to protect himself from the pain. He's bottled up every ounce of sadness and hope and love and told himself it was better that way. Then a ghost from his past returns, and none of what he's told himself makes sense anymore.

"Can you untie me?" Owen asks, breaking the strained silence. "We shouldn't stick around. More will come." He glances down at the prone bodies of the men we shot, and I have to hold back a shudder.

This seems to shake Eli out of his stupor. His back is still to Owen, but I see an angry expression cloud his face. "No. You work for *them*."

"Yeah. So? You work for *them*."

By Owen's tone, I can tell he means another "them" — the people in the compound. To him, that's just as despicable.

"We should get out of here, Eli," I say.

His eyes find mine for the first time in several minutes, and a heavy question passes between us.

In that instant, he isn't in charge of the mission. He isn't telling me what to do or trying to protect me. He's asking me to tell *him* what to do.

I glance at Owen, suddenly uncomfortable that he's watching our exchange.

"We should find out what he knows anyway," I whisper.

"Oh, not you, too," Owen groans, shooting me a look of naked disgust. His expression is wildly different from what I'm used to, but he looks so much like Eli that I recoil.

"Watch it!" Eli snaps. He jerks back into an upright position and spins around as though he might backhand his brother. "We do this on our terms or not at all."

Owen lets out an irritated breath. "Fine."

Now he looks and sounds just like Eli.

Eli swallows again, and when he finally gets the question out, his voice is low and husky. "Can we trust you?"

Owen looks a little shocked. "It's *me*."

That doesn't seem to reassure Eli, but he takes a knife from his utility belt and cuts Owen's ropes anyway.

When Owen stands, he's only half an inch shorter than his brother. He's wearing a charcoal-colored T-shirt, olive green cargo pants, and heavy boots that look as if they'd be good for kicking somebody's head in. Side by side, their resemblance is uncanny.

For a moment, they just stare at each other. I think they might embrace or start throwing punches, but neither of them moves. Owen's eyes are tight, but the emotion and history that passes between them is enough to steal my breath.

Finally, Eli seems to realize they have an audience. His eyes flit over to me, and Owen takes notice.

"Where should we go?" I ask, a little intimidated by both brothers.

"I know a place," says Owen. "It's not far . . . and no one will find us there."

Eli looks as though he wants to protest, but we've already been here too long.

Since we don't have a better plan, we follow Owen up the stairs and through the kitchen. He checks to make sure the coast is clear before he heads around every corner.

When Eli and I pull on our masks, he looks a little puzzled. Owen just walks outside — completely exposed — and I wonder again how he's still alive. He doesn't seem sick like any of the Recon workers who've had prolonged radiation exposure, but maybe he knows where the radiation levels are lowest.

We walk along the side of the road in alert silence. Eli hasn't stopped watching his brother. He's got one hand on his gun and the other pressed against his thigh, but if his leg is bothering him, he doesn't show it on his face.

Owen is preoccupied scanning the road. It seems strange for him to be on high alert for drifters, but then I remember that the different gangs don't get along.

I expect him to lead us back to the old motel where Eli and I hid or into one of the other abandoned buildings, but instead, he leads us off the main drag to a narrow road winding around an old warehouse.

Hidden behind that is a row of derelict houses. One of them looks as though the elements have taken hold of it completely. The roof is caved in, and gnarled desert bushes have twisted their way up the porch steps as though they plan to consume it. There's also an adobe structure with all the windows broken in.

The house between them is weathered and neglected, but there doesn't seem to be any structural damage. There are boards over the door and windows, but Owen leads us around to the back door — which isn't boarded — and produces a key.

The door opens with a loud *creak*, and the floorboards give in a friendly way when we step inside.

It's hot and dark in the house, but the faint light filtering through the boarded windows is enough to make out a kitchen with yellow-and-white wallpaper, outdated brown cabinets, and a small oak table.

I yank off the mask and deposit my rucksack onto the floor. Owen pushes past me to secure the house, and I follow in a trance.

The house is old but well cared for, and I wonder how Owen managed to find it. Whoever lived here is long gone now, but they left all the comforts of home: a worn paisley couch and matching recliners, creepy ceramic cat figurines, and thick shag carpeting that clashes brilliantly with the wood paneling.

As I'm exploring the living room, I feel a hand on my arm that makes me jump. It's only Eli, but he's got a wary look in his eyes.

"Stay close, all right?"

"Oh, relax," says Owen. "If I wanted to kill you, you'd be dead by now."

"Don't count on it," growls Eli, turning one of the more aggressive cat figurines away from him on the shelf.

"I'm your brother! Why would I kill you?"

"I don't know. Why did you run off and join the thugs that killed Mom and Dad?"

"I didn't! And I thought you were dead!"

"I was around," snarls Eli. "You can't have been looking too hard."

"Are we doing this now?" asks Owen. When he crosses his arms and glares at me, he looks so much like the big brother who wants to keep family business in the family.

"Whatever you have to say to me, you can say in front of Harper," says Eli.

The sudden warmth that surges through my limbs is doused by Owen's harsh gaze. He's scrutinizing me carefully, as though trying to figure out what the hell I'm doing here. "You his girlfriend?"

"No!"

Eli looks a little nervous. "She's my . . . cadet," he says lamely.

Owen rolls his eyes and sinks down into one of the worn recliners. "Yeah, whatever. You want to talk? Let's talk."

I glance at Eli, who's still standing, ready for a fight. I'm sure he's imagined seeing his brother again a million times, but he clearly didn't picture it going like this.

I sink down onto the sagging couch, and Eli follows suit. He looks over at Owen, studying him as if he can't quite believe his eyes.

"How are you alive? So many people I know died of radiation poisoning. How are the rest of you doing it?"

Owen shrugs. "I just don't get sick. Most of us don't. As long as we stay out of the hot zones . . . we seem to be surviving."

"Who's *we*?"

"Nuclear Nation."

"A gang."

Owen frowns. "Just some guys. They took me in after . . . after that night. They calmed me down, fed me, and I've been with them ever since."

"Those thugs who tried to kill you?"

"No," says Owen in a testy voice. "But Nuclear Nation has been taken over by the Desperados. It hasn't been pretty, but with the cities pretty much gone, everything's a fight for territory." He drags an agitated hand through his short hair, as though it still makes him angry to think about it. "We lost."

"Where do you live?"

"Around. When Jackson has business near the compounds, I stay here. But normally I stay in a nearby settlement."

"A city?"

Owen shakes his head. "The cities are not where you want to be. That's where the radiation is the worst. Little towns like this . . . They got the fallout, but they're in much better shape."

"Why do you stay with those people?"

Owen's mouth becomes a hard line, and I can tell Eli is treading in dangerous territory. "Where else was I supposed to go? I was thirteen. I'd lost my family, Eli. They took me in. It wasn't a hard decision."

"Yeah. I thought I lost my family, too." He glances away, resentment hanging in the air between the brothers.

"And you went straight to the compounds?"

"No." Eli swallows, and I know what comes next is hard for him to admit. "I just bummed around the city, stealing food when I could . . . sleeping in old buildings."

He launches into the story of his time in the gang, leaving out the part about killing the man.

As he talks, Owen drops his guard a little, and I can see the pain Eli's story causes him. It's not much different from *his* adolescence, and I know he's thinking about what it might have been like if he and Eli hadn't gotten separated. Maybe he thinks he failed him as an older brother.

When Eli gets to the part about being tested and brought into the compound, Owen sits up a little straighter, listening with rapt attention.

"I'd heard they were experimenting with bringing people in from the outside, but I never believed it!"

"Believe it," I say. "They brought me and my parents in, too."

Owen grows thoughtful, turning this information over in his mind.

Then Eli's face becomes grave, and I can tell there's a question that's weighing on him even more than his family's past. "Why are your men encroaching into compound territory?"

Owen's eyes tighten. "The compounds are what's killing us, Eli. You have to understand that. I know you live there, but . . . they have to be stopped."

Eli lets out a cold laugh. "You can't stop the compounds."

"Well, they aren't gonna go on like this forever. They've been killing our people for decades, but we're organized now — stronger."

"And you think a bunch of drifters can bring down the compounds?"

"*That's* what you call us?" He throws his head back in exasperation. "Fucking unbelievable. Some of those 'drifters' your people have been killing are innocent families, you know. These people take shelter wherever they can while you guys pick them off one by one. Your waste has been contaminating the groundwater, which makes it damn near impossible for anybody to live out here. It's wrong. It's wrong for the minority to make the rest of us suffer."

"You can't destroy the compounds," says Eli. "And even if you could . . . the people can't survive out here. The radiation would kill them."

"It's killing everyone, Eli. It's just doing it slowly. Why should some people get to live like *that* when the rest of us live like this?"

Eli lets out a worried breath and leans forward. "We don't really have the option of dying slowly."

"What are you talking about?"

Eli glances at me and then seems to decide there's no point not telling his brother. "There are people in the compound who want us dead. They sent us to find the Desperados' location and report back."

"The compound is looking for the Desperados?"

Eli nods. "One of your men broke into the cleared zone."

"The perimeter?" Owen grimaces. "I knew it. I knew when he didn't come back . . ."

A look of intense distress flits across his face, and then his eyes widen in horror as the realization hits him. "Did you kill Emmett?"

Eli stares at his brother, his hand clenched on his bad leg. "One of your men shot me. What was I supposed to do?"

Owen bows his head and puts a hand over his mouth. "You killed him, didn't you?"

Eli clenches his jaw. "Yeah. I did."

There's a long pause. As they stare at each other, I'm overcome with sadness for Eli. He's still in shock, unable to accept that the brother he thought was dead is sitting right in front of him.

Now that he knows Owen is alive, he can't just be overjoyed that the last member of his family is sitting before him. He's marred in a cloud of suspicion, and Owen is still trying to process the fact that his brother is the enemy.

As Owen recovers, I have the sudden urge to run out of the room and leave the two of them alone to work out their issues. If Eli is intimidating, the older Parker brother is downright terrifying.

There's a darkness around him I recognized in Eli, only it's been magnified by a decade of running and killing to survive. Eli probably would have turned out the same, had he lived out his teenage years on the Fringe.

"Listen, I need your help," says Eli. "I need you to tell me where the Desperados are based."

Owen's eyes grow dark with fury. "I'm not going to help you help them."

"You've got to give me something," he says, teetering on the edge of desperation. "If we go back with no information, I don't know if they'll bother sending us out again. They may just decide to kill us and be done with it."

Owen stares at Eli, caught between the urge to protect his brother and his hatred of the compound.

"Something," says Eli. "Give me *something* I can tell them."

"I can give you the location of one of the old rendezvous points. We don't use it anymore, but it will keep your people occupied for a while."

Eli hesitates and glances at me. We both know the risk of

sending Jayden on a wild-goose chase — particularly when it could be us doing the chasing — but it's better than returning to the compound empty-handed.

Finally, Eli nods.

Owen stands up and crosses to an old desk in the corner of the room. He returns with a map and spreads it out on the coffee table in front of us.

"This is where we are," he says, pointing on the map. "If you follow the highway north for twenty miles, you'll reach Fort Sol."

He sits up, and Eli stares at him expectantly. "That's it?"

"How would you know the exact location? Just tell your people you heard of a safe house in Fort Sol. That's reasonable."

"You haven't met our commander."

"I'm sorry," says Owen. "I'm not going to hand over the Desperados and make it easier for your people to kill off every survivor in the area."

The way the brothers are staring at each other, I can tell they've reached a stalemate. Owen storms into the kitchen to fix us something to eat, leaving me and Eli alone.

"I don't like this," he whispers, leaning closer and glancing over his shoulder to make sure his brother is out of earshot.

"What? Not having anything to go on when we report back to Jayden?"

"No. This. Being in this house. My brother —" He stops abruptly, staring at the doorway Owen disappeared through as if he can make him reappear as the boy he grew up with.

His eyebrows knit together, and a muscle works in his jaw as he fights to contain the turmoil raging inside him.

Without thinking, I reach out and touch his knee. He drags in a sharp breath, but I leave it there.

"Eli. You found him . . . the brother you thought was *dead.*

This is a good thing."

"Is it?" His eyes widen. "I'm just not sure."

"What do you mean?"

He drags a hand through his hair, conflict burning in his eyes. "We shouldn't even be here, Harper. What the fuck was I thinking? We're in a drifter's house."

"We're in your brother's house," I correct him.

Eli doesn't answer right away, but he jiggles his foot nervously. "You don't trust him?"

For the first time since I've known him, Eli looks genuinely flustered. "How can I? I haven't seen him in thirteen years! I don't even know who he is anymore!"

"He's still your brother."

His jaw tightens. "No," he says with a note of finality. "My brother died with my parents that night."

A creaking sound behind us makes me jump, and I whip around to see Owen standing in the doorway. His face is completely blank — a familiar Lieutenant Parker poker face — but I can tell he heard everything Eli just said.

"Food's almost ready," he says in a harsh voice. "You guys must be hungry."

I turn back to Eli and see him wearing an identical emotionless expression. It's the most inappropriate reaction, but I can't quite kill the smile that's working its way over my face.

I guess being emotionally closed off is a trait the Parker men share.

I get up to follow Owen back into the kitchen and try to gear myself up for the most awkward dinner of my life.

nineteen

Eli

S itting across the table from Owen is nothing like being back home. A strained silence hangs over us, and the only sound comes from the clang of our spoons against the bowls and the steady tick of the creepy cat clock hanging on the wall.

Harper is sitting between us, looking almost as uncomfortable as I feel. I glance around at the outdated kitchen to distract myself, but the tacky yellow wallpaper and cat-themed accents are almost as disturbing as sitting at the table with Harper and my brother.

Owen's made some kind of rehydrated stew, and he crushes his crackers in the palm of his enormous hand the same way he did when we were kids. He looks as I always imagined *I'd* look when I got older, except maybe a little meaner.

We eat quickly so we won't have to talk to each other, but after a few minutes, Owen drops his spoon and shoves his chair away from the table.

"Fuck it," he mutters.

When he stands, it strikes me just how big he is compared to the last time I saw him. Harper goes rigid in her chair, and I grip my knee to keep my hand from going to the gun in my holster.

It's Owen, I tell myself. *He's not one of them.*

Except he is. I'm just in denial. *My brother is a drifter.*

Owen rummages around in the highest cabinet and pulls out a bottle with a faded black label coated in decades of dust. He slams it onto the counter and pulls out three glasses, tipping about an inch of amber liquid into each.

"I think this calls for a drink," he says, sliding a glass toward Harper.

She sniffs it experimentally. "What is it?"

"Old whisky. Pre–Death Storm."

"You're kidding."

"I've been saving it for a . . . special occasion."

"Or an awkward one," I add under my breath.

Owen meets my eyes, and I see his laugh bubbling up before it shows on his face. It comes out as a harsh, grating cough — as though he's forgotten how to do it.

But when he lets it out, he looks like my big brother again. He laughs with his whole head, and his open-mouthed smile is infectious.

"Drink up, brother."

I tip the glass back and let the bitter liquid burn its way down my throat. It fills me with the warmth of synthetic beer, but it tastes different from compound-produced alcohol. It's raw and flavorful.

Owen kills half the glass in one gulp, and Harper sips hers with a pained expression.

"What? They don't have whisky in there?"

I shake my head, marveling at the sensation it causes in my body. After twenty minutes, I realize he was right. I'm feeling a little less on edge, and Owen is starting to seem like Owen again.

"So what do you actually do?" Harper asks.

"Whatever Jackson needs. Right now, that's sending scouts in closer to the compound to gather intel, shutting down compound reservoirs, and picking off you guys."

"*You* messed with our water supply?"

Owen throws a shifty glance at me — a look I know means he's guilty.

"Son of a bitch!" I yell, too surprised to be truly angry. It definitely has Owen's mark: a subtle "fuck you" to the compound. It's what I would have done if I were a drifter.

Harper keeps talking, asking Owen a lot of questions that seem to catch him off guard. She gets him to tell us about the structure of the gang and how he worked his way up to be Jackson's right-hand man.

The more I listen, the more I realize that up until the Desperados and their leader Malcolm took over, Nuclear Nation played a role very similar to Recon's. They protected settlements of survivors, killing rival gang members, mapping the radiation hot zones, and scouting for supplies.

"So how many survivors are there?" she asks.

"In this region? Thousands. The coastline populations were pretty much destroyed, but there are big pockets in rural areas.

"It isn't easy. The smaller the settlement, the harder it is to survive. Most of their people have to be dedicated to farming and hunting, so they get hit hard when the Desperados come through."

"And now you're one of them," says Harper, eyes narrowing. "Why did you stay when they took over?"

"I didn't really have a choice."

"Because of Jackson."

Owen shrugs. "Yeah. I mean, I owe him my life. But even so, there's nowhere else for me to run. The Desperados are everywhere. I'd never be able to survive on my own, as long as Malcolm and his crew are around."

Harper looks down at her barely touched stew. She and I both understand what it's like to be trapped, and apparently not even the drifters are exempt from being ordered around.

Harper picks up her glass and tips back her head to empty the contents. When she sets it down, Owen refills our glasses and reclines back in his chair.

The more I drink, the sleepier and more relaxed I get. As we talk, it starts to sink in: Owen is right here in front of me. It seems too good to be true.

He doesn't laugh as easily as he did when we were kids, but when he does, it's as though nothing has changed.

Then he finally asks about the compound again, and the darkness creeps back into his eyes.

That's when I remember that we're on different sides.

"Our commander wants to take out the Desperados," I say. "Your men getting into the cleared zone has everybody nervous. Civilians don't know you're all still alive out here, and the leadership wants to keep it that way."

"I suppose that must make it easier to control your people," says Owen bitterly.

"Yeah," says Harper. "Except now we know too much, and they want Eli and me dead. That's why we have to leave."

"Leave?"

"Relocate," I say. "Move to another compound down south — Arizona."

"One-nineteen?" Owen asks sharply.

I glance at Harper, who's nibbling on a stale cracker. "That's the one."

"You shouldn't relocate," says Owen. "Not now."

"Why?" Harper puts down her cracker and gives him a suspicious look.

His thick dark eyebrows knit together, and that mannerism reminds me so much of the way our dad used to look when he was stressed. "I can't say. Just . . . trust me. You're better off staying put."

"I'm not going to stay here and help you destroy the compounds, if that's what you're thinking," I say, sudden irritation clawing its way up my chest.

"I never asked you to!" he snaps. "Do whatever you want."

"Whatever."

"Besides, it seems to me that you're the one who's fishing for information."

I try to shrug off the thick tension that's settled around us, but Owen's always known how to push my buttons. I open my mouth to unleash some of my pent-up frustration, but we're interrupted by a loud banging on the door.

Harper jumps about a foot in the air and has her gun trained on the door before I've even gotten mine out of its holster. Clearly Owen had her more on edge than she let on.

"Parker!" yells a voice. "Open the fucking door!"

Owen is already on his feet, motioning toward the living room.

The stranger bangs again — more insistent this time. I follow Owen with my gun still pointed at the door.

"Who is that?" I hiss, keeping an eye on Harper.

"Not someone you want to meet," he growls, grabbing our rucksacks and striding into the small bedroom. He tosses our stuff into the closet and jerks his head. "Get in and be quiet. Don't come out until I give you the all-clear signal."

Even though my heart is racing, I still find it in me to feel annoyed that Owen is bossing me around again. But I hear another angry "Parker!" from outside and open the accordion doors wide enough to yank Harper inside.

She has the good sense not to shoot me in the foot as I shove her between the folds of clothes to the very back of the closet.

I pull the doors shut and squirm in beside her, putting my body between her and the door.

With my back flush against her chest, I can feel her heart beating wildly against her ribcage. I can barely hear what's going on in the kitchen between the pounding of blood in my ears and the sound of Harper's ragged breathing.

There's the low rumble of male voices — at least three — and I can hear Owen's relaxed timbre above the rest. He always had a way of putting people at ease when he wanted to — even if he wasn't feeling calm.

In the neighborhood, whenever I got into a fight with guys twice my size, Owen could usually talk them down with a few jokes and that easy grin. If that didn't work, he resolved the problem with his fists. Mom would be pissed, but I think Dad was always a little proud of him.

Suddenly the conversation is halted by the shatter of glass.

"*Who the* fuck *was here?*" yells a man.

I cringe and keep pushing Harper back, as though I can make her disappear. She's pressed up against the very back corner, and she squeezes my arm to make me stop.

The visitors found three glasses, three bowls, and three spoons. That's going to be tough to explain.

There's a violent scrape of furniture and a loud *thud*, as though somebody shoved Owen into the table and slammed the side of his head against the wood.

"*Where are they?*" the voice demands. "Who were you talking to?"

"No one!" he growls.

"Bullshit. Somebody killed Santiago and the others. Who came for you? Huh?"

Every muscle in my body is tense, preparing for a fight. Part of me wants to launch myself out of the closet and attack the men, but the other part is waiting for Owen to speak. Even though he's my brother, there's still a tiny, horrible part of me that thinks he's going to sell us out.

"There's no one here!" he yells. His voice is so muffled that it's tough to make out the words, and I would bet money he has the barrel of a gun in his mouth.

I can't take it anymore. I reach back until my hand finds the soft flesh of Harper's side, and I squeeze her once. "Stay here," I hiss.

"Eli —"

But I turn and clamp a hand over her mouth.

"Stay!" I whisper. I push her back again, but she grabs my arm.

"Eli, no! Wait!"

Before she can say anything else, I slip out of the closet and pull the doors closed behind me. I pass Owen's bed and move silently into the living room.

When I settle against the wall jutting up to the kitchen, I hear a nasty *crack*. Owen lets out a muffled groan, and I know they're twisting his wrist to get him to talk.

"Who was here?" the man yells.

As long as I live, I'll never forget the sound of anguish that escapes Owen's mouth as the man tries to break his wrist.

I whip around the corner in one motion and raise my gun. I barely have time to register the men's dirty faces before I shoot the one closest to the door in the head. He staggers back, bumping into the cabinets, and collapses like a puppet on the ground.

The man holding Owen against the table removes his gun from Owen's mouth to point it at me, but he's too slow.

I fire, blowing him back into the wall and knocking the cat

clock off its hook.

By now, the third man has his gun on me, but Owen throws his elbow back in a blur, connecting with the man's face. The guy fires, but his aim is off, and the bullet just cracks the doorframe.

"Jesus," Owen breathes, wiping his forehead and looking at me in shock. "That was fast."

"I've had a little practice," I pant. The ringing in my ears is so strong I can barely hear my own voice.

"You couldn't just stay put like I told you?"

I give him a look to remind him that he'd had the barrel of a gun between his teeth just a few seconds ago.

"I had it under control."

"Yeah, it sure looked like it."

"Well, I sure as hell don't know what to do now!" He looks down at the three dead men spilling blood all over his kitchen floor.

"We'll just drag the bodies out for the buzzards to eat."

"You don't understand," he growls, somehow irritated that I killed the men who were threatening him. "The men we killed in that basement were just low-level guys doing Malcolm's dirty work. These were enforcers. People *will* be looking for them, and now they'll be looking for me."

My stomach sinks. I never thought about what trouble Owen would be in now that we had killed Malcolm's men. He wasn't fighting the Desperados because they're dangerous, and seven dead bodies will definitely make Malcolm question Owen's loyalty.

"I'm sorry," I say, still a little annoyed that I've saved my brother twice and he hasn't even thanked me. "We'll get going. I don't want to put you in any more danger."

"You can't go now," Owen says, his eyes flashing with what

I can only read as panic. "It's not safe. I'm taking a huge risk keeping you here, but that's only because this town is going to be swarming with Malcolm's men tonight after the showdown at the grill."

"And you think it's a good idea to stay here?" I ask incredulously. "If Malcolm has men here like you say, someone will have heard those shots."

Owen opens his mouth, but we're both distracted by a flash of movement from the living room. Harper has emerged from the bedroom, and she's staring at the three dead bodies as though she might be sick.

"Come on," I say, reaching for her instinctively. "We need to get out of here."

"I think he's right," she says in a clear voice.

"What?"

"It'll be safer here. We shouldn't just be wandering around out there if people are looking for us. We're blind right now. I think we'll be safer going in the morning."

Owen shoots me a smug look, and I let out a heavy breath. Harper's made up her mind, and honestly, it makes sense. The fighter in me doesn't like the idea of staying here — I'd much rather take my chances on the move — but I can tell this is one battle I'm not going to win.

After I help Owen move the bodies and mop up the blood, he brings us some blankets.

I lie down on the floor, and Harper takes the couch. I can tell she feels a little uneasy in Owen's house, but she curls into the worn cushions and falls asleep quickly.

I drift in and out. Around oh-one hundred, I'm awoken to the faint *whoosh* of a vehicle on the road.

My eyes snap open automatically, and my spine goes rigid. I

can't tell which direction it's moving in, but the harsh sound of tires on asphalt send me into panic mode.

The car doesn't stop.

They're not coming for us, I tell myself. No one knows we're here.

I wait for several minutes, trying to make my pounding heart behave.

I don't remember being this sensitive to the sound of cars as a child, but out on the Fringe where there are so few humans, any approaching vehicle is cause for alarm.

"Eli?" Harper whispers.

"Yeah?"

"You don't think . . ."

"No. It's all right. They passed." I try to sound reassuring, but my voice is just as scared as hers.

She shifts around on the couch. "It's just . . ."

She never finishes the sentence, and I realize too late it was more of a question.

Nearly a minute passes in silence. Then she says, "I can't sleep."

This time, I get it.

I sit up, looking for her in the dark. Her shadow shifts, but I can't make out her expression.

I move slowly, as though I'm approaching a wild animal, and she turns slightly when I sink down onto the cushions.

There's very little room on the narrow couch, but I stretch out and drape an arm around her waist, steeling myself for rejection as I pull her flush against my body.

Harper drags in a ragged breath, but she doesn't pull away. If anything, she seems to melt into my embrace.

My body has the exact opposite reaction. It's on high alert again as I drown in sensory overload.

Her sweet-smelling hair is draped over the cushions and has somehow managed to wrap itself around my arm. She's giving off a pleasant heat that warms me from the inside out, and every part of her is softer than I expected.

When she lets out a content little sigh, I nearly lose my shit. I tighten my grip without quite meaning to and bury my head in her hair, savoring her little moment of weakness.

For a second, I forget that we're out on the Fringe with an entire gang hunting us or that my brother — the brother I thought was dead — is asleep in the next room.

In that instant, I realize I'd do anything Harper needed me to do. I'd yell at her in training to make her stronger, spend all my free time kissing her, take on a brutal fight so she didn't have to, and hold her when she asked.

I'm in deep trouble.

"'Night, Harper," I whisper.

"Goodnight, Eli."

My body slowly relaxes as her reassuring voice fades into the darkness, and I slip into the most content sleep I've had in a long time.

twenty

Eli

I wake up the next morning instantly aware that I'm spooning Harper.

My whole body is awake, but unlike last time, I don't feel as though I shouldn't be here. My arm is locked possessively around her rib cage — my hand a little higher than it should be — and her arm is draped lazily over mine.

And her leg. Holy shit. One of her legs is locked between mine and wrapped around it, making it so I couldn't move even if I wanted to.

I grin against her hair but hastily school my expression. I don't know why I get the sudden urge to act professional when my hands are all over her, but I do.

Reluctantly, I slide my palm down to her stomach and carefully extricate my leg from our tangle of limbs.

"Hey, Harper," I murmur.

"Hmm . . ."

I bend my head lower on the pretense of whispering something else, but I just nuzzle my face into her hair a little before giving her a gentle shake.

"Eli . . ." She lets out a small laugh and then stiffens as she wakes up and remembers where we are.

She sits up, and I almost slide off the couch trying to put an appropriate amount of space between us.

"This is interesting," says a voice from the kitchen.

I jump and peer over the couch to see my brother leaning against the door jamb, arms crossed in front of his chest like the smug bastard he is.

I clear my throat and reach for my boots, trying to act casual. "Did you hear the car pass last night?"

"Yeah. I told you. They're looking for one of your people. They know you killed Santiago and his guys."

"We need to head back," I say to Harper. "Tell Jayden what we know."

She nods quickly, and I get the uncomfortable feeling that Owen has his eyes on us.

I lace up my boots, grab my rucksack, and head into the kitchen to put some distance between us. Owen follows me.

"You're leaving right now?"

"Soon."

He clears his throat gruffly, but I can tell he thinks he's never going to see me again. There's a good possibility he's right.

"Are you okay?" I ask.

He shrugs. "I'm fine."

His voice is brusque, and his eyes look like Dad's did when he was trying not to show how much he was hurting: tired and bloodshot. Neither one of us wants this to be the last we see of each other.

"What's going to happen when you see Malcolm's crew again?"

"I'll have a better story than I did last night, that's for sure."

But his strained expression makes me nervous. He has *no idea* how he's going to get out of this one, especially if the trust between Jackson's old crew and Malcolm's men is as fragile as it sounds.

"When will you be back?" he asks.

I open my mouth to respond but close it immediately. I don't know what our next mission is going to look like, but if I had to guess, I'd say that Jayden is going to send us to Fort Sol.

"I'll be out again in a month," I say, not meeting his gaze. "But I don't know where I'll be sent."

He nods but doesn't say anything.

Harper appears in the doorway, hair pulled up and her rucksack slung over her shoulder.

"Ready?" she asks.

I bob my head and turn back to Owen. This is it — time to say goodbye to one of the people I thought I'd never see again.

At first, I think he might just slap me on the shoulder like the complete stranger I am, but he throws an arm around my neck and pulls me in for an embrace.

I'm not used to this. I know my arms are too stiff, but it's oddly comforting.

Owen lets me go quickly and clears his throat, looking and sounding just like Dad.

"I'll be in touch," he says.

"What?"

He cocks his head, that familiar mischief in his eyes. "Don't worry, kid. I'll find you."

As I pull on my mask and sling my bag over my shoulder, he sticks his head out the door to check that the road is clear. He steps aside so Harper and I can pass, and she glances back at him a few times as we head down the road.

I only allow myself one look. Owen is standing in the doorway with his arms crossed over his chest, attempting an indifferent look that does nothing to mask the regret in his eyes. His shoulders are hunched protectively under his ears, and I can tell he's grown used to losing people, too.

As we walk away, I force myself to ignore the uneasy knot forming deep in the pit of my stomach. Something is telling me I shouldn't go back — that I would never have gone to the compound in the first place if Owen had been with me — but I can't just run off with my brother.

The compound is my home in ways that Owen hasn't been for a long time. And, as much as I hate myself for it, I couldn't just cut and run from Recon.

But I realize I can't go to 119 with Harper either. I'd be hundreds of miles away in Arizona, and I might not even be placed in Recon a second time. I just found Owen. I can't leave now and risk never seeing him again.

"What are you thinking?" Harper asks.

"Nothing," I lie. "Just stay alert."

We're approaching the main strip of buildings. The town is silent as always, and I don't even get that prickle on the back of my neck that tells me we're being watched.

For once, I feel utterly alone out on the Fringe, but I still go through the motions. I stick to the shadows of buildings, look around every corner, and make Harper stop twice to rehydrate.

When we leave the cluster of abandoned restaurants and gas stations behind, my senses sharpen automatically. The town may have been deserted, but I don't trust the huge expanse of open land we have to cross to get back to the compound.

After walking for half an hour in silence, Harper can't keep her thoughts to herself anymore.

"That's crazy," she says, referring to Owen.

"Yeah."

"How has he been alive all this time and you've never run into him out here?"

"I don't know."

She's quiet for a beat. I can tell she's trying to be polite, but her curiosity gets the better of her. "Is he . . . different than you remember?"

I grin despite the nervous energy thrumming in my shoulders. "I haven't seen him since I was eleven. Of course he's different. Taller, too."

"That's not what I meant."

I take a deep breath, not wanting to admit that our reunion wasn't the joyous occasion I always imagined. "Yeah. He's different. He's . . . angrier. But he's still my brother, you know?"

She nods, looking worried. "What's going to happen to him next time he runs into Malcolm's crew?"

The thought makes my stomach clench, but I shove down my discomfort. "I'm sure he'll talk his way out of it. He always had a talent in that department."

"And if he doesn't?"

"Owen's a grown man," I say impatiently. "He can take care of himself."

"I didn't say he couldn't! But these guys mean business, Eli. Don't you think we should help him?"

"Help him how?"

"I don't know!" she splutters. "Talk to someone. See if it's possible to bring someone in from the outside."

"Are you serious?"

"Once we relocate, I mean. Maybe there will be someone at 119 we can trust."

I shake my head. "The compounds killed the Fringe Program. You know that. I was in the last group they brought in from the outside, and considering we all ended up in tier three, it doesn't seem like an overwhelming success."

"So . . . what are you going to do?"

"I don't know yet."

She lets out an impatient huff, and I can tell she's been holding in her thoughts the entire night. "Eli, we can't let them destroy the compounds. I know he's your brother, but —"

"We don't even know what they're planning," I snap, lengthening my stride to put some distance between Harper and my loud, guilty thoughts.

Owen's warning about 119 makes me think they have plans to attack, but I have a hard time believing the drifters would ever have the opportunity or the resources to succeed. And, truthfully, I feel worse about my decision to abandon Harper than the possibility that I could be complicit in a plan to take down one of the largest remaining human settlements in the country.

"Well, clearly they have more capabilities than we thought. Do you think they'd really do it?"

"Try to take down the compounds? Yeah, I do."

"How, though? If we knew what they were planning, maybe we could —"

"Maybe we could *what*?"

"Maybe we could stop them!"

I round on her, fully aware that our voices are much louder than they should be. "No, we couldn't! Don't you think we have enough issues of our own right now? Or have you forgotten that you're at the top of Constance's bad news list?"

Harper goes red in the face and opens her mouth to speak, but I cut her off.

"Don't make this your personal problem. As far as I can tell, they don't have the capabilities to bring down the compound. One drifter getting into the cleared zone doesn't prove anything. Even if they repurposed all our explosives, they wouldn't be able to pull off an attack of that magnitude."

"Shouldn't we at least . . . I don't know . . . try to get more information?"

"I tried! Owen's smarter than that. He's not going to jeopardize their plans."

"But you're in the compound, too! Would he just let you go down with it?"

"No!" I yell. "Of course he wouldn't! That's how I know they haven't gotten very far." I take a deep breath, trying to calm my own racing thoughts. "He may be a drifter, but I know my brother. He wouldn't do that. Not if it meant killing me."

Harper stares at me for a long moment out of the corner of her eye. She isn't convinced, and if I'm being honest, neither am I.

The empty desert stretches out as far as the eye can see, with nothing except the dunes to our right and the compound far off in the distance. I grip my rifle a little tighter, waiting for enemy fire.

Nothing.

As we walk, the silence grows heavier between us. I keep thinking she's going to be the one to end our stalemate, but she doesn't say a word — not about Owen, not about our moment in the training center, and not about the way we woke up this morning.

I know it's dangerous to leave that hanging between us, especially since we have to continue to work together. I clear my throat to tell her it can't change anything between us, but she cuts me off.

"Don't," she snaps. Her eyes look cool and distant over the top of her mask, but I can tell she's a little off balance.

"Don't what?"

"Don't do your lieutenant thing right now."

"My *lieutenant thing?*"

"I know what you're about to say, and I really wish you wouldn't. Don't ruin whatever happened the other day."

She pauses, and I brace for the worst. I'm not sure if she's going to yell at me or declare her undying love, but I know whatever she says is going to be hard to hear.

"I can forget it happened if you can," she says.

Suddenly it feels as though all the air has been sucked out of my lungs. I wasn't prepared for that, and her indifference hurts more than I want to admit.

"I don't want to forget it happened," I say roughly.

Her eyebrows lift in surprise, and it kills me that I can't see her full expression. "You don't?"

"No!"

Now I'm irritated, and I have no reason to be. I don't know if I'm mad at myself for admitting it or angry at Harper for being so quick to doubt me, but I can't blame her after what happened on the observation deck and everything I've done to push her away since. "I don't want to forget it, but it doesn't change anything."

She nods quickly, avoiding my gaze.

"Things are even more fucked up than usual. We can't have something like this getting us separated if Jayden decides to send us out again."

"You want to see Owen," she murmurs. It isn't a question.

"Well . . . yeah."

She sounds hurt, which is strange, considering she was the one who wanted to blow off our little encounter. I know now is the time to tell her that I can't go to 119, but I can't bring myself to do it. I care about Harper, and planning to bail on her makes me feel like a piece of shit.

Thankfully, my interface beeps softly as we approach the mines. The messaging icon lights up as my device registers the compound's wireless signal, bringing a halt to any meaningful conversation that Constance could use against us.

I focus on the ground in front of me, looking for places where the earth has been disturbed. Nothing seems out of place, so I turn on the map display to navigate around the mines that are supposed to be there.

As we cross into the cleared zone, my heart rate speeds up. I don't know why I expect to run into a drifter, but suddenly my awareness is sharpened by a dark undercurrent of guilt.

What would Owen say if I shot another drifter, knowing it could be one of his friends?

I immediately dismiss the thought. This is my job. Owen's gang has been killing Recon operatives without remorse for years. He has to expect that I'll do the same.

In the distance, I see a flash of movement. Harper does, too, because she jumps a little and grabs my arm.

"Is it . . .?"

I squint through the bright sun and raise my rifle.

The figure is too far off to tell if he's one of us or one of them. I zoom in with my interface and breathe a sigh of relief when the gray fatigues come into focus.

"It's one of us," I sigh.

I loosen my grip on my gun and try to relax my shoulders. I don't have to kill anyone today.

We walk in silence for another twenty minutes, and I focus on the sound of Harper's footsteps instead of the pain in my leg and the dread eating at my insides.

The compound looks taller and more imposing than usual with the late-morning sun reflecting off the windows. I inhale deeply and try to welcome the sight of it, but it just makes me feel empty inside. It isn't *really* my home.

Harper puts a little more distance between us, and I cast one more glance in her direction. Her expression is unreadable, but her silence tells me she doesn't feel great about how we left things.

Only a few yards left. I quicken my pace, anxious to get off my feet and rehydrate.

We reach the doors to the compound, but they don't glide open automatically. I bang on the metal, hoping the security camera is just down or the ExCon guy fell asleep waiting for our return.

"Hey! Open up!" I yell, even though no one can hear me through the thick glass and steel.

"That's weird," says Harper, peering in through the nearest window.

I'm starting to get a weird feeling. In all the times I've ever been deployed and returned ahead of schedule, someone has always been standing by to let me back into the compound.

Unnerved, I pull out my interface and message Miles: *Can you go wake up the ExCon guy? Someone needs to let us in.*

"Is there another door?" Harper asks incredulously.

"Not on this side."

We could walk around to the bay on the opposite end of the compound, but the heat is starting to get to me, and I don't want to be out here any longer than I have to.

As the minutes drag on, I start getting nervous. Maybe this is one of Jayden's power plays — her attempt to show us that she's still in control. Maybe she really intends to leave us out here.

But she was too anxious for more information about the drifters. Waiting isn't her style.

Finally I hear a loud *clunk*, and the doors glide open with a hiss.

I step inside, anxious to get out of the oppressive heat, and the cool air stings my sunburned face. I drink in the comfortable humidity and blink a few times to force my eyes to adjust to the dim lighting of the chamber.

As I squint up at the tall figure in front of me, a familiar face swims into view.

"What the hell is going on?" I ask as the doors glide shut behind us.

"Not much time to explain," grunts Miles, yanking off his mask and glancing behind him at the second set of doors.

"Where the hell is the door operator?"

"A lot of shit has gone down since you left. Nobody knew when you'd be coming back, so . . ."

"Why is no one manning the door?"

Miles jerks his head toward the postexposure chamber again, looking anxious. "ExCon has gone on strike."

"*What?*"

"It leaked out that there were 'hostile survivors' in the cleared zone, and they got pissed that the board was knowingly putting them at risk." He cocks an eyebrow. "Three guesses who the rat is."

Jayden. "Are you kidding me?"

"I wish. People are going crazy. The board doesn't know what to do."

I stare at him, wondering how Jayden could be stupid enough to leak that information.

Then I realize it's her crazy way of putting pressure on Remy. He wouldn't allow her to divert all her resources to tracking down the Desperados, so she created the perfect storm to embarrass the board and cause an uproar.

"I can't believe she'd do that."

"Really? You can't? She's fucking crazy. Nothing she does would surprise me."

The doors to the postexposure chambers slide open, flooding our small space in a creepy blue light.

"Hey! You can't be in here!" yells an unfamiliar voice.

"Cool it," growls Miles. "Somebody had to let them in."

He turns to go but puts an enormous hand on my shoulder and lowers his voice. "Hey! Watch your back, all right? People are going nuts."

"Thanks, man."

Miles raises an eyebrow at Harper — as though he's telling her to keep an eye on me — just as the door on her side opens.

Before the Health and Rehab people can get ahold of her, I pull her in. "We debrief together this time. Don't talk to Jayden or Remy without me."

She nods, looking a little frantic, and vanishes behind the sliding door.

Arms clad in a hazmat suit pull me backward into my own chamber, and cold water bears down on me.

I cough and splutter, squinting through the deluge of freezing water, but all I see are the shiny metal walls closing in around me. When the shower stops, a med intern starts unsnapping my overshirt, and I bat his hands away so I can undress myself. He strips off his hazmat suit, and I see he's a scrawny kid with short strawberry-blond hair and a ruddy complexion.

Shivering in my boxer briefs, I allow him to steer me through the next set of doors toward the waiting wheelchair. I sink into it, and he drapes a heated blanket around me. The chair whirrs noisily as we board the lift, and I can't stop my leg from jiggling with nerves.

I don't like being separated from Harper — not with everything that's going on — but since I'm alone in the lift with the med intern, I might as well see what he knows.

"What's going on with ExCon?" I ask.

"I . . . uh . . . we're not supposed to talk until you've been formally debriefed," he says in a nervous voice.

He looks so painfully awkward I almost feel bad for the kid. This must be his first Fringe retrieval, and they told him we might be unhinged.

"No . . . we're not supposed to talk about what happened when I was *deployed*," I say carefully. I have a feeling this kid won't be too hard to corrupt, but I can't push him. I adjust my tone to sound a little friendlier and try to grin. "They don't care if we talk about what's happening *inside* the compound."

His hands tighten on the wheelchair as he considers my logic, and then he lets it all out in one big breath. "Everybody's freaking out a little. ExCon has gone on strike because they don't want to work if there are hostile survivors near the compound. That's what they're telling everybody, at least."

"Really?"

"Yeah. But I don't believe it."

"Believe what?"

"I don't buy that there are survivors out there."

"You don't?"

The kid scrunches his eyebrows together as though he thinks it's a crazy suggestion. "No! No humans could live out in those conditions. And if there *were* survivors right outside, the board would have brought them in. ExCon just doesn't want to go out and be exposed to the radiation anymore."

"Would you?" I snap, all traces of friendliness gone.

The kid looks away, going a little redder around the ears. "I don't mean to be insensitive, but that's their job. Look at you guys. You go out there. Everybody has a job to do, and I just think . . ."

"You just think everyone needs to stop bitching and get on with it."

He swallows a few times and looks at me to gauge how much he thinks I want to hit him. "I mean . . . yeah. Every role is crucial. We need power, and we need the damage to the compound repaired. What if Health and Rehab just went on strike? People could die."

I chuckle and sit back in the chair. This kid may be naïve, but his honesty is refreshing. Most tier-one workers like to pretend that they feel sorry for Recon and ExCon — or that they don't exist. At least this guy is confident about where he belongs.

The doors open, and the chair automatically rolls out into the Recon wing. The nurses on duty stiffen when they recognize me, but their wariness is downgraded to boredom when they realize I'm not bleeding or in handcuffs. I must be earning quite a reputation in the medical ward.

"Phase two decontamination, exam, debrief, and observation," the nurse rattles off to my intern.

He gives her a stiff nod, and we continue down the long tunnel.

After they put me through another icy shower and give me a clean pair of pants and a T-shirt to wear, the doctor examines me and declares I'm in no danger of immediate death.

It's been nearly an hour since we were brought in, and I'm starting to get a little antsy. Jayden and Remy will have heard about our return by now, and I'm worried they went to interrogate Harper first.

Normally I'd be confident that she could hold her own, but

the last time we returned from the Fringe, Harper wasn't in her right mind. Plus, with everything that's going on in the compound, I wouldn't put it past Jayden to threaten Celdon's or Sawyer's life to speed up the debriefing.

As soon as the doctor leaves, I'm off the bed and flying down the tunnel to find her room. Most of the doors in this wing are closed, but there's a decontamination cart parked outside one. I can see the blurry outline of two people through the frosted glass and detect the low murmur of voices, but they don't sound like Remy's or Jayden's. I'd recognize her grating, condescending tone anywhere.

I try the door, but it's locked.

"There you are!" says a voice behind me.

Shit.

I turn around and come face to face with the ballsy intern who brought me up. He looks both relieved and annoyed.

"You can't just sneak out of your room! You haven't been debriefed yet."

I sigh and take a minute to size this kid up. He's an inch or two shorter than me, but a little broader. Even with my bum leg, I'm confident I could take him down easily, but there's something about the determined set of his jaw and the earnest look in his eyes that makes me want to trust him.

"Sorry," I say, throwing caution to the wind. "Listen, I need to get in there to see my partner."

He tilts his head to the side, looking exasperated. "You know I can't let you do that."

"Please," I glance at the name stitched on his scrubs, "MacAvoy."

"Caleb," he says.

"Look, I know it's against the rules, but she really didn't do well when they brought her in last time. I just need to make sure she's okay. I think she freaked out because they wouldn't let her have any visitors."

His jaw is still set, but I can see a hint of sympathy in his eyes. That's the thing about good kids like him: Compassion is their Achilles' heel.

Finally he lets out a long sigh. "Fine. Just a few minutes, though."

I nod quickly, delighted that Harper and I have corrupted not one but *two* med interns, and he pulls out his access card.

When he swipes us in and pushes the door open, Sawyer and Harper freeze on the other side. They were clearly having a private conversation, and Sawyer's accusing gaze snaps onto Caleb.

"What are you doing?" he asks. He sounds a little judgmental for someone who was just caught breaking protocol.

"I could ask you the same thing, MacAvoy," Sawyer snaps.

He narrows his eyes, and I get the feeling I just stumbled into the war of the interns. I find Harper's eyes, and she looks just as puzzled. I step inside and close the door behind me, ignoring the others.

"Have you been debriefed yet?"

"No."

"Good." I glance at Sawyer and Caleb, wishing they would leave and continue their showdown elsewhere.

"Eli, she needs to rest," says Sawyer, looking at Harper with concern. "You both do."

"This will only take a minute."

Sawyer looks conflicted, but she takes the hint and jerks her head for Caleb to follow her outside.

"I'll knock if I see your commander coming."

"Thanks."

I turn to Harper. "We need to get our story straight."

"Okay. How about we say we heard about their old base when we were listening to the interrogation?"

"Yeah. And then guns started going off, and we got the hell out of there. She can't know anything about Owen . . . or that the drifters are planning something."

Harper bites her lip but doesn't say anything.

"*What?*"

"It's just . . . don't you think we have a responsibility to warn someone? I know he's your brother, but we can't just let them get closer to pulling off whatever they're planning."

"No," I say. It comes out like a growl, but Harper doesn't even flinch. "We wait. If Jayden finds out, she's going to send out a fucking army. Just give me some time to figure this out. If it comes down to it, I'll tell Owen to get the hell out of here and then warn Remy."

Just then, there's a frantic knock on the door.

Harper glances over my shoulder nervously. "You have to get out of here!"

But it's too late for me to leave without being seen. Instead of going for the door, I slide into the closet. It's a tight fit, but there's just enough room for me to wedge my body under the shelves and pull the door shut.

It clicks into place just as Jayden breezes into the room. I try to slow my breathing, but I'm convinced she may still be able to hear it.

"Well, you're back," she says in a clipped voice. She doesn't even bother to hide her disappointment.

"Yep."

"Since you've returned, I take it you have something useful for me."

Harper pauses for a moment, and I cringe at her hesitation. "We learned some . . . interesting information."

"And what is that?"

Harper takes a deep breath and carefully relays the story of us listening to the gangsters interrogate Owen in the basement.

She makes it sound as though he was just a random informant, and I'm impressed by the layer of detail she adds. In Harper's version, Owen pulled a gun on his captors and managed to kill one of the men before getting shot himself.

"And what happened after that?" Jayden prompts.

"They were talking about meeting up with their leader Jackson at a safe house in Fort Sol. I don't know exactly where that is, but it didn't sound too far."

"And why would they be meeting up with him?"

There's another brief pause, and I can tell Harper is scrambling to come up with an answer that will satisfy Jayden's curiosity without revealing too much.

"I think they're planning something," she says slowly.

My stomach drops. Harper's treading in dangerous territory. One slipup, and Jayden's going to know we did more than listen in on a conversation.

"They're the ones who screwed up the checkpoint last month. They're fighting back, but it sounded like they were planning a much bigger undertaking."

Don't do it, I beg silently. Harper has stumbled into a trap, and if she keeps talking, there's a good chance she's going to get tripped up and arouse Jayden's suspicion.

I hear Jayden move closer to her, and I have to strain to hear her next words. "Riley, I need you to tell me exactly what you overheard — word for word."

Harper makes a nervous little noise in her throat. "I-I can't remember exactly. It's the adrenalin, you know? But I do remember them saying that one of their men on the inside had been compromised. They didn't know where he was."

"On the inside?"

"Y-Yeah. But I don't know if he was at this compound or another one."

I want to bang my head against the door. Of all the things for Harper to tell Jayden, that was probably the worst detail. Jayden is already paranoid, and if she thinks there's a double agent in Recon, she's going to tear the ranks apart until she finds him.

I half expect her to drag out the interrogation, but she just sighs. "Thank you, Riley. That was very . . . illuminating."

I hold my breath as Jayden crosses to the door. I wait for her to leave, but she stops short.

"You know, you're lucky, Riley. You and Parker seem to be the only operatives who can survive a trip into the lion's den. It's really quite remarkable."

There's a long strained silence.

"What now?" Harper asks finally, clearly trying to discover if Jayden bought her story.

"I don't know. We'll see if your information proves accurate. I hope for your sake it's the truth."

Harper's careful tone vanishes instantly. "What's *that* supposed to mean?"

I can almost feel Jayden's deadly smirk burning through the closet door. "Never overestimate your usefulness, Riley. There are plenty more cadets. I suggest you keep your head down and your mouth shut."

Harper's shock radiates throughout the room, chilling me to the core. When I hear the sound of the door snapping shut, I wait several seconds to make sure Jayden's really gone.

When I burst out of the closet, Harper is sitting on the bed looking stricken. Her face is pale, and her eyes are wide.

When she finally looks up at me, I can tell we're both thinking the same thing: We just sent Jayden on a wild-goose chase, and when she realizes what we've done, she's going to kill us both.

twenty-one

Harper

"Remember what we talked about," says Miles. "Stay out of her way. Let her do all the work."

I snap my fist against the mitt he's holding and let out a burst of air. "Got it."

"You can't stand toe to toe with Marta. Keep your distance. Focus on wearing her out."

"I know."

He's repeated the same words to me every day since I returned from the Fringe: Avoid getting hit. Run Marta around the ring. Then come at her with a series of fast strikes, and make them count.

Miles grabs my wrists and slaps my gloved hands against my cheeks. "Keep your hands up — no matter what she does. Protect yourself."

Protect myself. If only it were that simple.

The last few weeks have been a blur of panic and fatigue. The morning after my debriefing, Miles was banging on my door to help me prepare for my fight. I'd been so absorbed in my thoughts of Owen, Eli, and Jayden's threat that I'd almost forgotten I'd agreed to fight Marta. Miles hasn't let me forget it once since.

Part of me hoped the fight would be cancelled after Eli was arrested, but no one seems to have heard about his night in the cages. The fact that it hasn't leaked out of Control makes it clear that Jayden was just exercising her power to show Eli who was in charge.

I doubt she'll bother having me arrested. She already proved her point — and she has enough on her plate with the drifters — but I'm still worried I may have taken on more than I can handle.

Unfortunately, there's nowhere to run. Since Eli lost his fight, we don't have enough money to leave the compound, and I can't back out now without incurring the wrath of Shane.

I don't have the luxury of being too scared to fight. That's the only thing that keeps me going as Miles pushes me around the ring. The good news is that if I survive this, I'll be one step closer to getting us away from Constance.

It's almost time for my fight, so he doesn't work me hard. He just puts me through a few drills to drive home the finer points of our strategy and help me focus.

According to Miles, my only advantage is my endurance. Because I'm the underdog, Marta and everyone else will expect me to lose. He thinks she's going to come out swinging and try to end the fight quickly, but if I can outlast her and keep her from landing big punches, I might have a shot.

Feeling a little off kilter, I return to my compartment to change. Miles was spectacularly unhelpful in the wardrobe department, but I follow Lenny's advice and don a black sports bra and shorts. Normally I would wear a little more to train in, but my abs are coming in nicely, and — according to her — it's how all the female fighters dress.

I'm just about to head to the training center to finish warming up when I hear a knock at my door.

I peek through the peephole, and my stomach turns over when I see Eli. He's been conspicuously absent from my training over the past few days, but I don't know if that's because he's boycotting my fight or because he feels too awkward to be around me after everything that's happened.

Pulling a zip-up sweatshirt over the top that now seems too skimpy, I open the door and brace myself for a lecture. Eli glides in without an invitation, his blue eyes raking up my legs and my bare midriff and finally settling on my face.

Today he's wearing low-slung black sweats and a tight gray T-shirt that strains across his chest, and I have the sudden urge to kiss that scowl right off his face.

"Don't do this, Harper," he says.

"What?"

He rakes a hand through his hair and paces in front of me like a caged animal. "Don't do this fight. I have a bad feeling."

"I'm not going to get arrested. Jayden just did that to scare you."

"That's not what I'm worried about."

"I'll be okay," I say defiantly, trying to sound more confident than I feel.

He stops pacing and looks at me dead-on. "You haven't seen Marta fight. I have."

"Thanks for the vote of confidence," I mutter, not bothering to hide my eye roll.

"I'm not trying to shake your confidence. I'm telling you not to do this."

He takes two steps toward me, forcing me against the wall as I try to keep an appropriate distance between us.

"We'll get the money another way. I'll do another fight — an easy one this time."

"I'm not going to back out now."

Eli is way too close. His scent is all around me, making it very difficult to think clearly enough to form a coherent argument.

"Harper, listen!"

Before I can duck around him, his hands shoot out to grab my waist. He pins me gently against the wall and captures my eyes with his, his thumbs tracing small circles on my bare stomach. "I don't want you to do this. *Please*. I have a really bad feeling."

It's so hard to make my thoughts behave with him touching me, but I swallow down my doubts and focus on his muscular chest. It's a little easier than making direct eye contact.

"Eli, I have to. Do you know what will happen if I back out of the fight?"

"*Yes*. You'll be alive, for one thing."

"For how long? Do you really think Shane is going to be happy if I bail?"

"I'll deal with Shane," he says dismissively. "I won't let him hurt you."

I shake my head. "I can't back down now. I . . . I think I might have a shot at winning."

He lets out a frustrated growl and releases me roughly. My skin stings where his hands were, and now the distance between us feels like an insult.

He turns away from me and squeezes his temples. "Dammit, Miles."

"This wasn't his decision."

"He shouldn't have encouraged you! Now you've got this false sense of confidence."

"No, I don't!"

He rounds on me again. "What? You think you're all tough now because you've had a few months of training?"

"Miles says I'm doing really well."

"You *are* doing really well, but you're out of your league right now. Shane knows it. Marta knows it. Everybody knows it but you."

That stings a little, but I'm more pissed off than hurt. "Why do you have to do this?" I snap. "You're my commanding officer. You taught me. You're supposed to be on my side."

"I *am* on your side, but I'm not going to cheer you on when you're making a stupid-ass decision!"

"Thanks a lot."

"You can't win, Harper!" he yells.

Ouch.

His eyes crinkle in regret, and for a brief moment, I think he might actually apologize.

But then he whips around and throws open the door. He glances back over his shoulder, and I get the eerie feeling that he thinks he's looking at me for the last time.

"If you aren't going to listen to me . . . just be careful."

And then he's gone.

Trembling with nervous energy, I head to the training center to warm up. I jump rope and throw a few punches on the heavy bag, trying to subdue the anxiety burning in my core. I don't usually doubt myself, but now I'm feeling uneasy about my decision to fight Marta.

"Well, look at you!" says a voice from the doorway.

I wheel around to see Celdon standing in the entrance, looking comically out of place in his white slacks and blazer.

He nods at my getup. "You look pretty scary."

Something inside me breaks, and I launch myself across the room and throw my arms around his neck. I don't know if it's my imminent ass-kicking, the looming threat of Constance and the Desperados, or Eli's plea that has me feeling off balance, but I'm so freaking glad to see him.

"Now this is exactly the sort of thing we want to avoid in the ring," he jokes into my hair. "Hugging your opponents to death is not how you win the belt."

"There is no belt," I mutter against his shoulder.

"Whatever."

As I pull away, I catch a glimpse of the serious expression clouding his usually carefree smile. "Riles . . . Eli told me he didn't think you should be in this fight."

I groan. "Not you, too!"

"Oh, no. I'm much more optimistic than that broody man-donut. I think you should kick her ass."

"Thanks."

"Just be careful."

"Times up, Riley!" belts Miles from behind him. "We've got to go."

I pull away from Celdon, and my dread returns in full force.

Taking a deep breath, I follow Miles out of the training center toward the maintenance shaft, where I can already hear the anxious crowd.

My lungs constrict as we duck down the narrow passageway, and as we move into the heart of the space, the sound becomes deafening.

Miles pushes people out of the way, trying to clear a path for me in the sea of spectators. But the crowd isn't on my side. I don't recognize most of them, which means they're ExCon and Waste Management. The boos are deafening, and the crowd seems to form a solid wall around me and Miles, jostling us in an attempt to intimidate me.

It's working.

The crowd quickly becomes my own personal hell. I feel the walls start to close in around me, and I clamp my teeth down on my lower lip, trying to rein in my mounting panic.

Suddenly I hear a high-pitched cheer off to the side. In the horde of angry faces, I see Lenny, Bear, and Kindra yelling and screaming. They're waving a sign with my name on it and a crude drawing of me punching out another girl with blood splattering everywhere.

"You're going to be great!" yells Lenny.

She's fighting through the cluster of ExCon guys with those wicked-sharp elbows, but Bear pushes through the crowd easily.

"Yeah!" he calls above the din. "You can kick my fat ass. That's gotta count for something."

I give him a weak smile, but I'm slightly distracted by Miles shoving a drunken Waste Management guy in the chest.

Kindra is being swept along like a buoy in the mob, but every so often, I catch a glimpse of her pale blond hair. She's frantically checking her interface, and I'd bet money she's reading my birth chart again.

"Everything okay?" I yell.

She looks up and offers me a weak smile, completely oblivious to the chaos around her. "I hope you win, Harper!"

The crowd is starting to thin a little, and when I hear cheers behind me, I know why.

Marta is coming in, and the spectators are clearing a path for her.

"My horoscope didn't say anything bad, did it?" I yell. I'm ninety percent joking, but the nervousness in my voice gives away the ten percent that really wants to know.

She smiles weakly but doesn't say anything.

That's not reassuring.

My friends' faces become a blur as Miles pulls me toward the ring. My heart is hammering wildly in my chest, and I focus on taking deep breaths in and out.

When another arm shoots out and grabs me, I nearly swing out a punch before I recognize Blaze.

"You shouldn't be here," he mutters into my ear.

"Well, I am," I growl, squeezing between two lanky guys in orange.

Blaze falls into step beside me, still holding on to my arm and pushing people back like a bodyguard.

"I meant what I said, Harper. You aren't supposed to walk away from this one."

I glance up at his face and am startled to see an uncharacteristic look of anxiety in his eyes. Blaze — the quiet, easygoing one — is worried for me.

"I'm not talking about losing," he continues. "I mean you *aren't supposed to live.*"

Those words hit me like a bucket of ice water, and I stop pushing through the crowd.

He yanks me even closer. "Listen. Jayden paid a visit to Shane."

"What?" I choke.

Blaze's eyes tighten, and he suddenly looks like a guy who knows way more than he should. "I don't know what you did to piss her off, Harper, but Jayden wants you *gone.*"

My stomach drops. If Jayden knew about the fight and went to talk to Shane, that can only mean one thing: She doesn't want me arrested. She wants me out of the picture for good.

It won't be a clean, tragic death from walking into an ambush on the Fringe. Jayden plans to execute me in a messy, public fashion.

No one will question Constance's involvement. Nobody thought I would win this fight anyway.

Blaze's grip tightens on my arm, as though he plans to physically stop me from getting in that ring.

"He's already told the refs," he says. "Nobody is going to stop Marta from fighting dirty. If you go down, she's going to keep hitting you until you're finished."

"And she just agreed to kill me?" I splutter.

Blaze clenches his teeth, his jaw working furiously. "Harper . . . I don't know what power Jayden has over my father, but nobody disobeys a direct order from Shane. *Ever.*"

As we reach the ring, the lights suddenly seem much too bright. Miles turns around and looks at me expectantly, and Blaze releases his death grip on my arm.

"Wait!" I yell. "What do I do?"

He leans in quickly, eyes scanning the volatile crowd. "If you get a shot, take it. Don't hesitate. Finish her."

Then he's gone.

There's no time for me to formulate a plan or back out. Miles shoves my mouth guard between my teeth, and I gag a little as I fit my lips around it.

A few people in the crowd slap my shoulders as I climb up onto the platform, and I hope nobody can see how badly my legs are shaking. I try to get my body under control, but the encroaching crowd is making it impossible.

I scan the mess of dark faces, hoping to find someone familiar to latch on to. I see Celdon cheering near the far corner — the only Systems worker in here — and Sawyer is standing next to him.

I can't help but grin when I see her, mainly because she looks even more out of place than Celdon in her crisp Oxford shirt, peach cardigan, and glasses. She looks nervous, but it isn't because of all the rowdy, tattooed people jostling her in the crowd.

I realize she's nervous for me.

Lenny, Bear, and Kindra have moved to my left, rallying the

handful of Recon cadets who showed up, but Eli is nowhere to be found.

Suddenly the spectators closest to the ring erupt into cheers. Marta didn't have to fight her way through the crowd. She's Waste Management, and she's been fighting for a while. They know her and love her.

As soon as I see her face, her dark eyes find mine. She glowers at me and wrinkles her nose as though she's about to take out the trash.

Her expression is unmistakable: *Get out of my ring, bitch.*

Marta climbs up between the ropes as though she does this every day, and I feel a stab of jealousy when I see how much better her mocha skin looks under the harsh florescent lighting. I feel pale and scrawny in comparison.

She's about an inch shorter than me, but she's packing at least ten extra pounds of muscle — most of it in her shoulders and biceps. An acid green top and high-waisted black shorts show off her chiseled abs, and her dark brown hair is pulled back in a braid, with three corn rows on either side of her face.

The ref gestures toward the center of the ring, but I don't hear anything he says. He looks ordinary enough, but he's on Shane's payroll.

Marta isn't watching him. She hasn't taken her eyes off me once.

I glance over my shoulder at the shadowy crowd once again and spot Miles watching me. Eli is standing far behind him, but he's literally in my corner. That would send a thrill through me if I couldn't see his expression.

When he meets my gaze, I know he was holding back when he visited me in my room. His deep blue eyes are full of sorrow and fear. He isn't just spectating; he's committing me to memory.

Eli doesn't just think I'm going to lose tonight. He thinks I'm going to die.

twenty-two

Harper

The bell is deafening, and I'm immediately hit by a wave of sound from the crowd.

Marta charges toward me, and I realize all the training in the world could never prepare me for what's happening in my own body.

For a moment, I freeze. I can't remember anything — not my combinations, not my own name. My hands are frozen, and my arms feel as heavy and stiff as clubs.

Marta swings at me, and miraculously, I slip to the side. Her glove glances off mine, and I quickly back out of her striking range.

My heart is thundering in my chest. Her fist flies out in a fast jab, but my gloves absorb the brunt of the blow. She delivers a left hook, and my body automatically moves to the side. For a split second, she just stares at the spot where I'd been standing, and I take the opportunity to deliver a fast cross to her dead side.

It wasn't as powerful as it could have been, but Marta is momentarily stunned.

That wasn't the plan. *What was it that Miles said?* Just stay out of her way.

When she rounds on me, I can see why. Fury is pouring off her in waves. This is her ring, and she wants me gone.

As I watch her, it's as though someone turned the volume down on the crowd and dimmed their faces.

It's just me and Marta, and she is pissed.

Before I have a chance to move, her leg swings out of nowhere and cracks mine just above the kneecap.

My leg stiffens as pain reverberates up the bone.

I stagger, and she takes the opportunity to swing a punch at me. This time, I don't move out of the way. I take it right in the forehead, and the burning pain crawls back through my skull.

Dragging myself into an upright position, I barely have time to retreat as she unleashes a storm of punches.

Her glove hits my head, and then she pummels me in the side. Some of her strikes glance off my gloves, but she gets a few over my guard.

One hook hits me squarely in the side of the head, and her left hand follows it with a brutal uppercut.

I fold in on myself, desperately trying to shield my face, and when I fall back against the ropes, I know I have to get her off me somehow.

Suddenly I remember the one time Lenny managed to beat me fair and square. She'd used her position of weakness against me, and I'd never seen it coming.

I push myself back as far as I can, forcing Marta to lean in with her next punch. I lunge to the side at the last minute, gripping her around the neck. Using her body for leverage, I drive my knee up into her abdomen and hear a satisfying groan escape her lips.

That had to hurt like a bitch.

I take advantage of the pain rolling through her and slip away from the ropes. She recovers fast and delivers a sidekick. And *damn* her kicks are powerful.

Pain shoots up my knee, and I feel myself go down. I throw out my hands to catch myself, but I still hit the mat.

Marta fights dirty — just as Blaze said she would. I don't see her foot swing out again, but I feel it sink into my gut.

Mercifully, the bell rings, pulling me back to the dark maintenance shaft.

The crowd is cheering, and it's the cruelest sound I've ever heard. They *like* seeing me hunched over on all fours. They want her to win. I want to puke.

"Come on," says a familiar voice behind me. I feel a warm arm snake around my waist and hoist me to my feet.

Everything is still a little blurry, and I have to focus to make out Eli's face. He holds me tight to his body and deposits me in a folding chair that Miles has put in my corner.

I spit out my mouth guard and feel a cool rag on my face. Somebody sticks a straw in my mouth and squirts some water down my throat. I take it all in passively, unable to process the movement around me.

Eli's hands are gripping my knees. His face is right below mine. He looks . . . proud? That can't be right.

"How are you holding up?"

"She's killing me," I gasp.

"I told you," growls Miles. "Stay the fuck out of her way!"

"Even that doesn't seem to help much."

"That's because she's better than you!"

Eli shoots him a death glare, but Miles rolls on. "Just stay on your feet, and you'll be okay."

I don't have the heart to tell them that Marta has no intention of letting me walk out of here tonight. I just nod shakily and take several deep breaths.

My skin is tingling with nerves and pain. I don't feel like myself at all.

"It's the adrenaline," says Eli, correctly interpreting the manic look in my eyes. "You're okay. Just stay sharp in there."

As if I have a choice.

Before I can even catch my breath, the ref is yelling something at us, and Miles hoists me to my feet. He and Eli jump back down, and I'm alone in the ring again — just me and Marta.

I bite down on my mouth guard and see her flash a nasty smile.

She loves to fight. She lives for this shit.

That's when I snap. All the anger and frustration and fear mix together and blaze through me like Owen's whisky. There's a fire burning in my core, my skin feels electric, and every sense is heightened.

When Marta charges me, I don't even let her get within arm's reach. I load up my leg and shoot it out to connect with her stomach.

She was so focused on my locked arms that she never saw it coming. She staggers back with a groan, and I know I got her good.

But she recovers and tucks her chin to try again. This time, I let her get close enough for the fake jab — jab, hook, a hook to the body that once surprised Miles — but she blocks my hits easily.

She aims another round kick, but I block it and throw a jab that she isn't quite fast enough to avoid. She *does* dodge my hook, and I'm still too excited about hitting her to block the punch she delivers in return.

The pain spreads quickly, melding with the ache from all my other bruises.

Marta takes it up a notch. Her punches are relentless, and all I can do is cover up and retreat.

She doesn't give me a chance to aim a counterstrike, and for the first time since she entered the ring, I realize just how much better she is than me.

I'm so busy blocking and parrying her steady punches that I'm unprepared for her lightning-fast double jab. Her fist crashes into my eye socket, and the force rattles my brain. She follows up with a vicious hook, snapping my neck around and throwing me into the ropes.

She doesn't stop there. She punches me in the stomach, and I half expect her fist to go all the way through me. Instead, I just feel the bile bubble up in my throat.

I go into full defense mode, using my arms to form a cage around my upper body. She's still pummeling me, and I feel myself give up a little.

This is what she's been waiting for. The first round was just her warm-up. This go-round, she wants to break my spirit and humiliate me.

The bell rings, but Marta keeps going. I try to push her off, but my willpower has taken a hit.

The ref moves to pull her away from me, but he's taking his sweet-ass time. People are shouting, and the boos in the crowd are becoming more pronounced.

Finally, the pain stops, and I feel two sets of hands pulling me into my corner.

"Harper! Harper!"

Eli's face is swimming in front of me. My upper lip is wet, and something tells me there are hot tears mixing with the blood trickling from my nose.

"Holy shit," says Miles, mopping my face with the towel.

"Can we call the fight?" asks Eli in a panicked voice.

"No!" I growl. "I'm still in this."

"Harper, she's beating the shit out of you."

"Oh, thanks. I hadn't *realized* that," I snarl back, shocked by the anger thrumming in my veins.

"Listen to me," he says, gripping my arms tightly. "You aren't going to make it another round."

"Harper!"

I can't quite turn all the way around, but I catch a glimpse of Celdon's blond hair as he sticks his head through the ropes. "Do what he says."

"Thanks a lot, guys," I mutter, more to myself than to Celdon. I must really look like shit if he's starting to panic.

I roll my eyes, suddenly noticing that Miles is conspicuously quiet.

"Care to weigh in, *coach?*"

Man, I'm really in a bitchy mood.

Miles shrugs and looks over at Eli. "Now, don't hate me," he says cautiously, "but I think she should hold out. If she can take that kind of beating and still be talking, I think she can last one more round."

"Are you out of your mind?" yells Eli. I've never seen him so pissed.

But it's too late. The ref is gesturing me over, and I force myself to stand. My legs are a little shaky, but arguing with Eli has given me a second wind. I'm actually feeling halfway decent. The pain in my face and stomach has dulled to a slight throb, and I force my feet to move back to the center of the ring.

Marta looks a little worried. As her cornerman retreats, I realize her eye is swelling shut from a cut near her eyebrow.

Did I do that?

Just below the platform, I can make out Shane's angry face.

For the first time, it hits me just how much trouble Marta is going to be in if she lets me walk out of here. Blaze's words float back to me: *Nobody disobeys a direct order from Shane.*

Before I have a chance to form a plan, the bell rings, and Marta launches herself at me like a cannon.

She fakes a punch and swings out with a wild kick. I block it, but it doesn't matter. The impact reverberates up my shin, making me stumble.

That second is all Marta needs. She takes the opportunity to blast me with a jab that makes me see stars and an uppercut that snaps my head back. That's when she swings out an elbow, slicing across my face with vicious force.

Blood spurts out of my nose, and suddenly her arm is around my neck. She drags me down to the mat. I try to shift my body sideways as I fall, but she shoves me onto my back and brings her elbow straight down over my guard.

A low grunt escapes my throat, and I feel the tears sting my eyes. I've never felt so much pain.

Marta is on top of me now, but when she winds up for the punch, I buck her forward and throw my hips, rolling her around and miraculously reversing our roles.

As I raise my arm to bring down a hammer fist, she throws a knee up from behind. It connects with my spine, and the shooting pain rushes through my entire body.

She takes advantage of my momentary paralysis and rolls me over again.

Everything is upside down. I can't hear anything except the blood pounding in my ears, but I see an upside-down pair of glasses and Sawyer's look of horror.

Sawyer. Her voice floats back to me, and I'm simultaneously relieved and ashamed when I remember that Marta has a bad rib on her left side.

No. There has to be another way. I don't want to stoop to her level.

I chance a wild punch to the face as a distraction, digging my elbows behind me to try to squirm out from under her.

Marta swings out with a hard right hook, but I've managed to get my head out of range. Undeterred, she traps my left wrist between her arm and body and twists. I hear a slight crack that preludes the blinding pain.

Before I can consider my decision, my body reacts.

I swing into her with a savage hook to the body and feel my knuckles connect with her ribs.

No one in the crowd even realizes what happened, but Marta felt it.

For a second, she looks as though she's going to be sick. She grips her side, and she's completely undefended.

Hating myself, I swing my right fist straight into her head. She tips sideways, and I take the opportunity to scramble out from under her.

My legs are shaky when I stand, but not as shaky as Marta's. She's dazed and unsteady from the pain, but *damn* that bitch is tough.

When she gets to her feet and tilts her head up to meet my gaze, I know I've unleashed a monster. She launches herself at me, and I lock my arms to defend myself.

The bell rings, and relief pours through me.

The furious roar of the crowd breaks through my foggy state, and the ref steps between me and Marta, looking disappointed that she didn't manage to finish me.

The crowd is a mosaic of angry faces, but my gaze locks on Sawyer. She looks grim but relieved, which basically sums up how I feel.

The ref reads off the judges' decision and hoists Marta's hand into the air.

When the crowd cheers, I feel an unwelcome trickle of disappointment. I know I'm lucky to be alive, but losing still sucks. After all the pain and fear and blood, Marta demolished me.

As a wave of debilitating exhaustion hits, I feel Eli's watchful eyes on me. I stagger out of the spotlight and climb down from the ring, where I'm accosted by a man waiting to transfer credits to my account.

Watching the numbers light up on my interface, I don't feel the pain of my throbbing head or my bruised ribs. All I feel is relief. We finally have enough money to leave the compound.

The crowd is growing restless, and Blaze and the others are barely holding them back. I feel Eli's hands on my arms, inspecting my injuries to make sure I'm okay to travel.

Miles appears in my periphery and mutters something to Eli, whose mouth hardens into a deeper scowl. They seem to come to some sort of an agreement, and they steer me through the restless mob.

I expect us to head back to my compartment, but they drag me up the frozen escalator to the megalift, and Celdon and Sawyer hop in after us. I didn't even see them leave, but I'm still disoriented from the fight.

"That — was — awesome!" says Celdon, appearing in front of me with a wide grin. "You are such a badass!"

I try to smile, but my entire face hurts.

"I have to say, I thought she had you."

"Yeah, me too," says Miles, rubbing the back of his neck as though we just dodged a bullet.

"She did," murmurs Eli.

"Hey, you lost, but at least you're still walking."

Eli's expression hasn't relaxed a bit. "You got lucky."

Everyone falls silent, and I finally turn my full attention on him. His body is still angled protectively toward mine, but his eyes are focused on the corner of the megalift. His jaw is stiff, and his smoldering eyes tell me he's just barely containing his anger.

Thankfully, the lift dings, and Sawyer throws me a guilty look before disembarking. We're on a Health and Rehab level, but the lift hasn't stopped at the medical ward. The brightly lit residential tunnel looks just as swanky as Systems, but the red paneled doors and vintage crown molding give it a pre–Death Storm aesthetic.

"Where are we going?" I ask. My face feels tender and swollen, and it must look even worse than it feels. I could really use some of that magical serum Sawyer injected Eli with.

"My compartment." Sawyer nods at Eli and Miles. "They thought it would be best."

"We don't want to give Jayden any excuse to arrest you," Miles explains. "If you're admitted to the medical ward, it could get her attention."

I open my mouth to tell them that Jayden already knew about the fight, but it doesn't seem like the right time to bring up the fact that she tried to have me killed.

Sawyer punches in her code and leads us inside. Her compartment is just as large as Celdon's but much more welcoming. Instead of the stark, minimalist style of Systems, the Health and Rehab decor is warm and traditional.

The light beige carpeting feels fluffy underfoot, and the windows are framed by floor-length crimson drapes that match a comfy-looking couch. The rest of the furniture is painted in a dark wood finish, designed to pop against the white-and-beige backdrop.

Miles whistles, and Sawyer blushes. I know she's thinking

about how her compartment compares to the shabby Recon living quarters, but I'm too busy drinking in the luxurious surroundings to feel awkward.

I head for the couch, but she grabs my wrist and pulls me into the kitchen area, where the lighting is better. She's already laid out bandages, gauze, ointment, and several syringes on a towel, which makes my chest ache with affection.

"How bad is my face?" I ask, hopping onto the counter and wincing when I put weight on my injured wrist.

"Trust me, you don't want to see," she murmurs, swabbing my brow with some strong-smelling antiseptic. I wince as the stuff finds its way into my lacerations and resist the temptation to touch my battered nose.

"You don't even look like you," jokes Celdon.

"Better or worse?" I groan as Sawyer rubs the ointment deep into the cuts.

"Definitely worse."

I snort and instantly regret laughing when the movement tugs painfully at my skin.

"At least we have another two grand now," I say. "It's enough to get all three of us to 119."

"Three grand," says Sawyer.

"What?"

She grins sheepishly. "I made a bet."

"You bet against me?"

Now I know how Eli feels. Even when it's profitable, it sucks to have your best friend wager against you.

"Hell no. Your odds to lose were crazy. I bet that Marta would win by decision and not TKO. I knew you wouldn't go down without a fight."

"Oh . . . thanks." I hadn't expected that.

"Don't move," Sawyer murmurs, grabbing a syringe and injecting the fluid into my bicep.

"That should bring down the swelling in your face."

Sawyer opens the mini fridge and pulls out an icepack. I apply it to my nose while she goes to work disinfecting my other cuts.

Now that it's quiet, the awkwardness in the room is palpable. Even though Eli has angled his body away from me, he's watching me out of the corner of his eye. Miles and Celdon keep exchanging pointed glances, and guilt is written all over Sawyer's face.

I'm sure she feels terrible about breaking doctor-patient confidentiality and telling me about Marta's rib, but I was the one who acted on that information.

I keep telling myself that I didn't have a choice. She was ordered to kill me, but it doesn't change the fact that I did something horrible.

"Man, I really thought she had you," says Miles, finally breaking the silence. "That girl is hell on wheels, and she wasn't holding back."

"No, she wasn't."

I take a deep breath, steeling myself to tell them the truth. "Blaze found me before the fight. He said Jayden paid a visit to Shane."

"*What?*" Eli rounds on me, and I immediately regret my decision.

"She told Shane to have Marta take me out tonight."

"Jayden wanted her to finish you in the fight?"

"I guess this was a clean way to do it," I mumble. "It's not like anybody expected me to win."

"And you waited until *now* to say something?"

Uh-oh. Eli is pissed.

"He told me right before I got in the ring!"

"And you still fought her?"

Eli is right in front of me now, rage pouring off him in waves.

"I didn't have a choice!" I splutter. "You said yourself that Shane wouldn't just let me walk out of there if I bailed on the fight."

Eli opens his mouth to retort, but Miles cuts him off. "It's true. Walking away just would have made it worse."

"Worse than getting in the ring with someone who's been ordered to kill her?" Eli yells. "Shane probably had the ref in on this, too. They wouldn't have stopped the fight."

Miles looks at me. I avert my eyes quickly, but not fast enough to keep Eli from noticing my guilty expression.

"The ref *was* in on it?"

"That's why he was so slow to pull Marta off her when the round ended," mutters Miles.

"Do you have a death wish?" Eli yells.

"No!" I snap, hopping off the counter so I can square off against him. "But what was I supposed to do?"

"All you had to do was tell me or Miles, and we would have pulled you out of the fight like that! You're lucky you weren't killed!"

"Of course I am. I always am. This isn't the first close call I've had," I say pointedly. I just got beat up, and now all my pent-up anger is shifting toward him. "This is no different than Jayden sending us out into the Fringe, except this time I didn't have people shooting at me."

"It's *completely* different!" he yells.

"How? Either way, it's just Jayden trying to kill me."

He takes two big breaths, but it isn't doing anything to calm the fury blazing in his eyes.

"Out there, I can protect you!" he shouts.

"No, you can't."

Now he looks offended. "I can *try*. Tonight, I couldn't do anything! I just had to stand there and watch that girl beat the shit out of you! Do you know what that's like?"

I don't know how to respond to that. I expected him to say that I wasn't skilled enough to defend myself. I didn't expect him to admit that watching it was hard on *him*.

Everyone is staring at us. Celdon looks alarmed. Miles is rubbing his forehead as though he wants to intervene, and Sawyer is staring at Eli with a slight smirk playing on her lips.

Suddenly I don't care about winning the argument anymore. Eli is still staring at me with those fiery blue eyes, unaware of the fact that he just bared his soul in front of everyone.

"I . . . I'm sorry," I stammer. "It was stupid. But I didn't know what else to do."

Eli's expression softens, and the enormous compartment starts to feel much too small.

"Uh, thanks for everything, Sawyer," I say, flashing her a meaningful look. She knows I'm not thanking her for the first-aid job. "I need to go."

"But I haven't even checked your —"

"It's fine."

I don't hear what she says next. I practically run out of her compartment and tear down the tunnel toward the megalift.

Running away is stupid, but Eli and I were about to get into things that I'd rather not discuss in front of my friends. In typical Eli fashion, he would have pulled away as soon as it got too personal, and my pride has been wounded enough for one night.

Out there, I can protect you.

Eli's made it clear that nothing more can happen between us, but it's incredibly hard to keep my feelings in check when he goes around saying things like that.

When I reach the lower levels, the sight of the dingy Recon tunnel gives me a little pang of comfort. Who knew cinderblock walls and bad florescent lighting could be so welcoming?

I can still hear the roar of the crowd. The main fight must have started, but I don't have any desire to watch it. After climbing into that ring, nothing sounds less appealing than watching another person get beaten to death for sport.

The tunnel is completely deserted, and I quicken my pace a little. I want nothing more than to take a hot shower and crawl into my own bed.

But as I round the corner into the cadet wing, an arm shoots out of nowhere and slaps a cloth over my mouth.

I freeze and inhale automatically, which is a mistake.

A strange, sweet odor hits my nostrils, and I feel myself going limp in the stranger's arms.

The last thought that shoots through me is one of pure terror. Whether this is Shane's doing or Jayden's, they aren't taking any chances this time.

twenty-three

Harper

I wake up in a fog. It's completely dark, and I don't remember where I am or how I got there.

I'm lying on my side, but it's not a normal sleeping position. My shoulder is in agony, and my arm is all pins and needles from being wedged under my body.

When I try to free it, I realize my wrists are bound together with some plasticky material.

Slowly, a memory surfaces, and I realize what happened. Somebody grabbed me in the tunnel and kidnapped me. Someone — perhaps more than one someone — wants me dead.

Where am I?

There's no one around, as far as I can tell. Squinting through the darkness gives away nothing about my surroundings, but my other senses are overwhelmed.

The ground is cold and damp, and a familiar stench is stuck in my nostrils. I smelled it once before, but it takes me several seconds to recognize it.

It's the scent of earth and decay, but there's only one place in the entire compound that smells like that: the dead level.

Panic spills into my body like a toxin, and my breathing automatically goes haywire. Sure enough, I can just make out the shape of a mound nearby. My heart feels as though it might give out on me completely.

I'm lying next to a dead body. I'm lying with the dead.

It's impossible to tell if that person died of natural causes or if he was murdered here in cold blood. After a while, the body will break down and become just another source of organic material for growing food.

Whoever kidnapped me is gone now, but there can only be one reason they brought me here: They want to kill me, bury me, and destroy the evidence.

They literally want to make me disappear.

Don't panic. Don't panic. Don't panic.

Using all my remaining core strength, I roll myself into an upright position. I nudge my interface with my shoulder, and its welcoming blue light floods the creepy open level.

I try not to look at the hundreds of mounds dispersed in the graveyard, but it sends a fresh jolt of fear through me.

I'm going to die here. No one will ever find me.

No. I need to focus. When my dashboard loads, I waste no time.

"Video message Eli Parker," I say into the speaker. The app goes into idle mode as it tries to reach Eli.

My heart is beating too fast, and my ears are piqued for the sound of my captors returning.

The app makes a low *ding*, and a robotic voice tells me that Eli isn't available.

I swear and repeat, "Video message Eli Parker."

Once again, the app tries to reach his interface, but either he left it in his compartment or he isn't answering because he's angry with me.

I glance at the time. It's past midnight, but I don't remember what time I left Sawyer's, so I have no idea how long I've been down here. It could be twenty minutes; it could be two hours.

After the app stops trying to reach Eli, I groan and dictate a quick message to send to him.

Before I can finish, a door bangs open. Light floods into the level, illuminating a slice of ground a few hundred yards away. Then the door slams, and I'm thrust into complete darkness again.

I hear the low rumble of male voices approaching. I can't see them, but they're close by.

I hurriedly whisper two more words and speak to send the message.

The men draw closer, and as their voices pull apart, I hear one of them say "Shane."

Shane is trying to kill me.

He couldn't finish the job for Jayden in the fight, so he had to find another way.

Right now, his men are between me and the exit. I can't escape without being seen, but I *can* buy myself some more time.

I drag in some air and stagger to my feet, struggling with my hands bound behind me.

The soft earth muffles my footsteps, but now I can hear the voices clearly. They're getting closer, but they still don't know I'm conscious.

Careful not to disturb the decaying body in front of me, I step over the mound of earth and begin to run.

twenty-four

Eli

My interface buzzes against my ear, but the sensation is strangely muted by the pounding bass.

I haven't visited Neverland for any reason other than arranging fights in years, but tonight seems like the night to get lost.

My interface flickers on to display two missed messages from Harper, but I ignore them. I don't know why she's trying to reach me, and I try not to care.

For weeks I've been tethered to her as though my life depended on it, and she still didn't see fit to trust me when it counted.

I told her to stay out of the fight — a fight that should have killed her — and she ignored me as if I were nobody. Ignoring *her* for once is liberating.

Tonight, she isn't my responsibility. I'm free to do what I want.

All around me, people are grinding against each other to their own rhythm, completely oblivious to whatever song is blaring through the crackly speakers. The strobe lights make the girls' glow-in-the-dark lipstick and eye makeup pop, which is more off-putting than sexy.

Still, I'm here, and there's no reason I shouldn't try to have fun.

I feel the three little black pills in their neon yellow wrapper with the pad of my thumb and try to relax. I bought them from a sketchy guy in the collapsed Underground tunnel to help me forget, and I have every intention of following through.

There's a girl in a little yellow dress the same shade as the wrapper dancing with two of her friends under a purple strobe light. The material between her thin bodice and short skirt is completely see-through, revealing an intricate tribal tattoo that wraps around her ribcage.

The girl catches my eye under her fake silver lashes, and I stare back.

Her expression is seductive, but there's a strange emptiness in those eyes. She isn't throwing me a silent dare the way Harper would. There's nothing complicated about her. She's just fun and available, and she's not my cadet.

My interface buzzes again — this time with a written message — but I double-click the button without checking who sent it. I already know anyway. Nobody else messages me at midnight.

That message spurs me into action. I need to get Harper out of my head. I need to stop caring.

I told myself I wouldn't let this happen — that I wouldn't get attached. But instead of just befriending my cadet and starting to care whether she lived or died, I fell for her like an idiot.

When I'm within shouting distance, the girl in the neon yellow dress smiles sweetly. I get a pang in my gut that's completely separate from how the rest of my body is responding, but I shove down my guilt and press through the crowd to reach her.

Sticky bodies in rough synthetic fabric brush up against me as I pass, creating a nasty abrasiveness against my skin. It's sweaty and humid and too loud, but that doesn't seem to bother the girl.

When I come within arm's reach, she spins around like a ballerina and presses her body against mine.

Her next move is decisively unballerina-like. She slides down my chest in one fluid motion, grinding her ass against me all the way to my knees. Her long dark hair spills over my chest like crude oil, but it smells all wrong — sickly sweet and floral.

It doesn't smell like *her*, and that's when I know I'm too far gone.

Even down here, Harper manages to hijack my every thought. I can't be around her without feeling paralyzed by lust, but there's something else, too — an intoxicating warmth that starts in my core and spreads to my extremities. It makes me feel light and grounded at the same time.

It's nothing like this.

The girl whips around in a cyclone of hair and presses herself against me. She wraps a spindly arm around my neck and throws her head back.

I know she wants me to kiss her, and I could. I could forget for a few minutes. I could disregard all thoughts of Harper and probably screw her in the middle of the dance floor if I wanted to.

That's when my interface buzzes again, reminding me of the unread message.

I place my hands on the girl's hips and pull her tighter against me so I don't have to see the face that's all wrong. Her lips are too big, and her eyes are soft and unfocused. Looking at her just makes me feel like a piece of shit.

I should just delete the message and pretend I never received it. I should stonewall Harper in training until she takes the hint and reverts back to being my snarky, uncontrollable cadet.

She'd be pissed at me for a while, but she'd eventually forget all my screwups: my moment of weakness in the training center and two glorious nights tangled up together on the Fringe.

Suddenly, the urge to be near Harper is too strong. I won't go to her tonight, but I can at least read what she has to say.

The girl is leaning against me now — probably half passed

out from whatever pills she's been popping — so I let her slide down to rest against my chest while I turn on my interface and pull up the message app.

I see the two missed video messages from Harper and one line of text that makes my heart stop:

Need your help. I've been taken. Dead L

My arms go limp, and the girl makes a noise of protest when she slides off my chest. I see her lips move, but I don't hear a word she says. I'm already shoving my way through the crowd toward the exit.

Harper's words are seared into my brain, and all my frustration is replaced by cold dread and guilt.

I've been taken.

I need your help.

Dead L

What the hell does "Dead L" mean?

She can't be dead if she sent me that message, I reason.

But the sick feeling in my stomach won't go away. Harper was trying to reach me. She needed me, and I was wrapping myself around some burnout in Neverland.

What could it mean?

Leave it to Harper to find a way to tell me where she was so I could save her. If she was interrupted sending the message, "L" could be the first letter of a name.

But that's unhelpful. Harper's smart — much smarter than me. She would have realized her time was limited and chosen her words carefully.

Damn it! She's counting on me to figure this out. She needs me. She's in danger. I might already be too late, and it's all my fault.

She just told me Jayden had hired Shane to do her dirty work.

I knew she was in danger, but I let her leave Sawyer's compartment and go back to Recon by herself anyway. She would have gone straight to her own compartment to rest, but she could have been accosted anywhere in between.

Before I realize where I am, I'm pounding on Miles's door.

He takes forever to answer, but when he does, he only looks vaguely surprised to see me.

"Dead L," I pant. "What does that stand for?"

"What?"

"Dead L!"

Miles rubs his bleary eyes, trying to get on my level of craziness. "What the hell are you talking about?" he groans.

"Harper's been taken," I choke. "She sent me this."

I beam him the message, and his tired eyes widen as he reads it.

"Shit. Is this for real?"

"Yes! Constance has to be behind this. Where would they take her?"

"'L' could stand for 'level,'" he murmurs.

"Dead level," I gasp. Everything suddenly clicks into place, and my breathing comes a little faster. "Holy shit. That's gotta be it, right?"

Miles's mouth is still hanging open, and I'm gone before he can say anything else.

As I yank open the door to the emergency stairwell, it occurs to me that I should have asked him to come.

Who knows who's taken her or how much muscle they brought along. Harper's hell on wheels. They'd need more than one guy to subdue her without making a scene. I could be walking into an ambush, but nothing can slow me down now.

I wind my way up the compound to the level that no one ever

visits. When I yank on the handle, I remember why: The dead level is sealed off from the rest of the compound. Only a handful of Waste Management workers are given access.

The door is locked.

I'm probably only a few yards away from her, and I'm stuck out here.

My mind races, trying to think if I know anyone in Waste Management who would answer a message from me at this hour. I could call Control, but if Dellwood is on duty, Harper could be dead by the time they send anyone down here.

I rack my brain, trying to think like Harper.

If she were in my position, she wouldn't go to the law. She'd just hack her way in.

No. Harper would call for backup.

By the time my brain puts the pieces together, I'm already searching the directory for Celdon Reynolds.

I ping his interface, and his groggy image appears in front of my eyes. He's sitting in a darkened room, and only the top part of his face is visible in the faint blue light.

"Celdon! It's Eli! I need you to override security clearance for me. It's Harper!"

"What?"

"Harper!"

"What the hell are you —"

"Constance. The dead level. Can you unlock it remotely?"

"Well, yeah. But —"

"Just do it," I snap. "They've taken her."

Suddenly, he looks completely alert.

"Give me a minute."

He gets up from his bed, and I hear the frantic crash of keys as he begins typing.

My heart is pounding in my chest, and my skin is on fire.

It might be too late. I wasted a lot of time. I didn't answer when she messaged. She probably died hating me.

No, I scold myself. *She has to be alive.*

"I'm in," Celdon murmurs into his interface. He's not looking at me. His eyes are glued to his computer screen, and I can still hear his fingers flying.

Come on. Come on.

"You're good."

I lunge forward and yank on the door. Sure enough, he managed to unlock it remotely.

Relief and gratitude spill into my chest, and I make a mental note to be nice to Celdon in the future.

If I'm not too late.

I nod at him once and shut off my interface.

As soon as the door swings open, I'm hit with a strange, earthy odor. I recognize the smell, but it's not something I'm used to. It reminds me of fall before I was brought into the compound, but it doesn't have the pleasant, life-giving aroma of dead leaves. It smells fake and toxic.

Part of me wants to go tearing in, fists a'blazing, but I know I should be quiet. They could be armed. I'm not. The element of surprise is my only advantage.

I close the door quietly and move toward the other end of the level. Luckily, the dead level isn't a maze of tunnels dividing the space into compartments, offices, and section facilities. It's one big field of bodies.

There's an artificial chill in the air, but I know if I reached down and dug my fingers into the loose dirt, it would be sickeningly warm from decomposing bodies.

A hundred yards away, I hear a faint whimpering noise and

the low-pitched drawl of male voices. I set off toward the source of the noise, stumbling once on a human-sized mound of earth.

I right myself and shiver. I don't want to think about what they're going to do with my dead body once Jayden is through with me. Even if I die of natural causes, I hate the idea of being buried and used even after I'm gone.

The soft earth muffles my footsteps, and soon I'm right on top of two figures standing over a prone body.

Harper.

"No!" she shrieks, screaming as one of the men reaches down and grabs her by the hair.

Relief and disgust hit me simultaneously. She's alive, and they're hurting her.

For once, I don't think.

I throw myself at the man holding Harper, tackling him to the ground. For a second, we're tangled in a painful knot of knees and legs, but then I steady myself and straighten up.

My fist crashes into his face, and I feel my knuckles graze his slimy teeth. He probably cut me up, but he's going to be in much worse shape.

My arm has a mind of its own as it lays into him once, twice, three more times.

"Who are you?" I yell.

The man leers at me through a bloody mouth. I can see the reflection of his grin in the dim light.

This time, I slam my hand down on his throat. "Answer me!"

But I don't have a chance to continue my interrogation. The other man grabs me from behind, yanking me backward off the first guy.

I growl and swing my elbow back into the man's ribs. He groans, loosening his grip enough for me to turn into him. I can't see what I'm doing in the dark, but I've come alive.

My limbs connect with his shins, ribs, and nose. He stumbles back, and Harper's leg flies out in the dark. She kicks him hard in the kneecap, and he backs off.

At first I think he's going to engage us again, but then he takes off toward the door at a sprint.

That's what you get when you buy your loyalty: a pack of cowards who won't take a hit for you.

I should run after him, but the first guy is recovering.

Rage remakes me as I come at him with everything I've got. I become someone else — someone I've only been a few times in the ring when I lost control.

I don't care that he's not fighting back. I don't care when he goes limp.

"Who do you work for?" I yell.

"Eli!" Harper warns.

My rage turns to desperation in two seconds flat. "*Who is he?*"

I already know it's Shane, but I want him to say it. I should stop, but I don't. There's no referee here.

I wind up for another shot, but Harper throws her hip into me, knocking me to the side.

"Eli! Stop!"

I freeze, the sound of her voice calling me back to my body. The man lying underneath me is out cold.

"You're killing him."

I'm shocked by the low growl that comes out of my mouth. "He deserves to die."

Out of the corner of my eye, I see Harper deflate. "Maybe. But I don't want you to be the one who kills him."

In that moment, those words are about the only thing that could stop me from ending this guy's life.

Shaking with rage, I get to my feet and turn toward her. It's too dark to see her face, but her posture tells me she's hurt and exhausted.

"Let's get out of here," I murmur, gripping her shoulders to steer her around the mounds. She doesn't put up a fight, which worries me a little.

Has she forgotten that I yelled at her earlier? Harper should be furious with me — and she doesn't even know what I was doing when she needed me.

We reach the door, and the light from the emergency stairwell immediately blinds me. It's late, and there's nobody out but us.

The second I catch sight of her battered face and bound hands, that dangerous rage flares up again, ripping through my arms and chest like a shot of fire.

It takes me a second to remember she fought Marta tonight, but there are definitely new bruises blooming around her eye and under her jaw.

I turn her gently and pull out my pocketknife to cut her restraints. As I saw through the plastic, I try to force my voice to sound normal. "Are you all right?"

She nods slowly, and alarm bells immediately go off in my head as her shoulders sag and her head dips forward.

She's so still she could be falling asleep, but when I lean forward to look at her face, it's frozen in a wave of tears.

Suddenly it feels as though the past few hours never happened. I reach around and pull her against my chest, locking her in place with both arms. She doesn't fight it.

"They were going to k-kill me," she stammers, her body shaking against me. A few tears plop onto my arm, and I tighten my grip.

"No. We stopped them."

"You stopped them."

Guilt laps at my insides as I get a whiff of her hair. It's distinctly Harper's smell, and the thought fills me with shame. "I almost didn't," I say thickly. "I was so mad at you tonight that . . ."

She stiffens but doesn't pull away. "That what?"

"That I almost ignored your messages."

She hiccups but doesn't say anything, so I continue.

"If I hadn't come . . . If you . . ." Something breaks inside me, and I grip her tighter. "I wouldn't be able to live with myself."

Harper is quiet for a moment and then says, "You were right. I shouldn't have fought Marta."

After all this, *she's* admitting she was wrong.

"No, you shouldn't have. But it doesn't matter. I'm so sorry."

She turns but doesn't look at me, and I lower my hands to her elbows. She's staring off over my shoulder with a haunted look in her eyes.

"Those were Shane's men. He sent them after me because Jayden ordered him to have me killed."

"Yeah."

"Jayden isn't going to stop, is she?"

"No."

This was a wake-up call — no doubt about it. Harper and I were kidding ourselves if we thought we could outsmart Constance and survive. I should have known that if Jayden didn't get us killed on the Fringe, she'd resort to other measures.

Now that we have the money, there's no reason for Harper not to go to 119. It has to be said, but not tonight. She's shaky and weak, and I need to take her home.

Not caring that it's against the rules, I reach down and take her hand. I lead her down the stairs toward Recon, and she's quiet the whole way there.

I wish she'd say something, because I just keep replaying the horrible moment when I thought I might be too late.

If it hadn't been for Celdon, I would have been, I remind myself. I never would have gotten a controller in time.

I walk Harper to her door and examine her one last time. She is definitely going to have a shiner tomorrow, but the damage will fade. I tell myself that there's no harm done, but that's a generous lie.

I brush her temple softly, careful to avoid her bruises, and her eyes flutter closed.

"Are you okay?" I whisper.

"I'll be fine."

I know she will be. Harper is strong. She'll survive another compound. Hell, without Jayden lurking around, she'll probably run it one day.

While her eyes are closed, I bend down and brush my lips against her forehead. She leans into me, but I pull away gently before I screw up all over again. My mistakes have cost her enough tonight.

"Goodnight."

I stand and watch her until she's safely inside her compartment and the door locks behind her. Those men are still out there somewhere, though I doubt they'll try to hurt her again.

Shane may be dangerous, but he's never messed with me.

twenty-five

Harper

I wake up in the middle of a nightmare and shoot up in bed with a gasp.

I can still feel the men's cold, sweaty hands pushing down on my windpipe, and it unleashes the killer inside me.

I *wanted* to kill those men. I wanted to make them suffer. But it didn't matter how hard I fought. I was losing ground every second.

If it weren't for Eli, I definitely wouldn't be here, and that terrifies me.

"Finally," says a relieved voice from the floor.

I jump about a foot in the air and fling myself out of bed. I'm going for a lamp, a shoe — anything I can use to clobber the intruder — but then a golden head pops up out of the shadows.

"Easy!" Celdon says, holding up his hands and backing away. "Shit. I'm sorry. That was stupid."

When I realize it's him, I collapse back onto the bed and put a shaky hand over my racing heart.

"What are you *doing* in here?" I gasp. "You scared me half to death!"

"Eli messaged me about breaking into the dead level. He said you'd been taken. Then he messaged me after to ask if I'd come watch over you tonight."

I glance at the clock. It's oh-four hundred, which means I've had less than three hours of sleep. The warm feeling blossoming in my chest from Celdon's words is quickly squelched by irritation. "So you broke in here?"

"*Broke* is a strong word. All I had to do was override your key code. It wasn't hard."

"Great."

"It's how I got Eli into the dead level," he says seriously, raising an eyebrow.

I let out a stream of air and drag a hand through my hair. I hadn't realized how close I'd come to dying. If Eli hadn't thought to message Celdon, or if Celdon hadn't answered . . .

"He sounded so worried when he called," Celdon adds. "Riles, it was like . . . like the world was coming to an end. Like he would have walked through fire to get to you."

At those words, the embers of warmth in my chest erupt into a blazing heat that makes me feel fuzzy and off balance.

I knew Eli cared, but hearing it from Celdon makes it more real somehow. And even after everything Eli's said, his actions make his feelings obvious.

Up until this point, Celdon has been patiently watching me absorb this information, but soon he grows restless and comes over to sit beside me.

"Are you going to tell me what the hell happened last night? I mean, not that I don't enjoy overriding high-level security, but —"

"It was Shane," I breathe, my heart rate picking up at the memory of those men's hands on me. "He was trying to have me killed. Those were his guys."

Celdon looks a little sick. "Shit."

"I thought Jayden was bluffing," I mutter, more to myself than to Celdon. "I thought she'd keep me and Eli around to do her dirty work until the drifters finished us off, but if she's hiring hit men . . ."

"We can't stay here, Harper."

"I know."

Talking about leaving the compound with Eli is one thing, but the thought of actually turning my back on the one home I've ever known is terrifying. The compound is familiar to me. I have a life here. I have friends. Leaving will mean never seeing Sawyer, Lenny, or any of the other cadets again.

As though he's reading my mind, Celdon says, "It's better to be missed than dead."

I nod, but it's not until I look at him that I make the decision. His eyes are marred by deep purplish shadows from weeks of sleepless nights, and his sideways smile is strained.

No matter how much I want to stay and fight, I can't continue to put Celdon at risk. Last time, Constance tortured him to get to me. If anything else happened to him, I wouldn't be able to handle it.

Steeling myself for what we're about to do, I take one last look around my dingy compartment to commit it to memory. If I'm lucky, I'll never wake up in Recon again.

"Be ready to leave tonight."

* * *

When I go to find Eli at oh-eight hundred, the first place I check is the training center.

It's Saturday, but lately he spends more time in there going at the heavy bag than anywhere else. His anger and frustration have reached a boiling point, and working out seems to be the only thing that releases some of that tension. It reminds me of how I felt growing up in the Institute. It's why I worked so hard to get out of that place and make something of myself.

But there's no way to get out of Recon except leaving the compound, which is a gamble in itself. With his low viability score, there's a very good chance Eli will end up in Waste Management next time. Hell, I could, too, but his future looks particularly grim.

The training center is deserted, so I head to his compartment instead.

I half expect him to still be sleeping, but his door flies open right after I knock. Eli is standing there in his well-worn jeans and a soft gray T-shirt that strains across his biceps.

As soon as he sees me, his eyes fill with relief. His warm hand wraps around my arm to pull me inside, and he takes his time looking me over to make sure I'm all right.

His gaze lingers on my black eye and the spidery purple bruise under my jaw. He seems to tense with every injury he sees, and I have to look away.

Being in his compartment reminds me of the time we kissed to throw Constance off the trail, and the memory wraps itself around me like a warm blanket.

The compartment is exactly as I remember it, though it's somehow even cleaner. Eli's crisp boy smell lingers in the air. The surfaces of the sleek, industrial furniture are completely devoid of any clutter. His computer is powered down, and I'm relieved that the blinking red light near the camera is conspicuously absent.

The bed looks as though I could bounce a quarter off the tightly tucked charcoal blanket, and my insides tingle at the thought of him tossing *me* onto that bed.

My breath comes a little faster, and I feel the flush creeping up my neck.

"Are you okay?" he asks.

"Yeah . . ." I say, forcing myself to meet his gaze. "Thanks to you."

"Don't thank me," he mutters, stepping back and eyeing me with a haunted expression. "I almost didn't make it in time."

"But you *did*."

I don't understand why he's acting so weird. He's got a crease in his brow and looks as if he's carrying the weight of the world on those shoulders. "I'm okay. Everything's okay."

"No, it's not."

I swallow to keep myself from snapping at him — from shaking him to get him out of this funk. But his agitation just confirms what I came here to tell him. Wallowing in my own fear and guilt about Celdon, I hadn't even considered the constant stress Eli has been under trying to keep me alive.

"We need to leave the compound," I say. "Tonight."

Eli swallows thickly and nods once.

His silence is confusing. I thought he'd be relieved to hear me say that. I thought he'd fly to his closet and start stuffing clothes into his rucksack. But he just closes his eyes. "I have to tell you something."

"Okay . . ."

I have no idea where this is going, but the muscle working in Eli's jaw is making me worry. He swallows, and his gaze bounces from the wall behind me to the ceiling before finally meeting my eyes. His expression is so full of sadness and guilt it hurts my heart.

"I can't . . . come with you."

His words wash over me, and it takes me several seconds to process them. When my brain finally catches up, my stomach drops out from under me. "*What?*"

He shakes his head. "I'm so sorry, Harper. I know we had a plan."

"Yeah. We did. Why are you backing out on me?"

I want to smack myself for sounding so weak in that moment, but I can't help it. I never saw this coming.

"It's complicated . . ." He runs a hand through his short hair and looks a little lost. "Before our last deployment, I thought I was all alone. My family was dead. There was nothing left for me here. But then we found Owen, and . . ."

Of course. Owen. I should have known. Every thought I'd had of convincing him to come with me blows away in an instant. I could never ask him to pick me over his brother.

"I've spent the last thirteen years thinking about what it would be like if he were still alive. I'd imagine what he looked like all grown up . . . if he'd be in Recon like me." Eli swallows, and his eyes are so full of hope it takes my breath away. "Seeing him *alive* . . . it was like a gift . . . I can't explain it."

"You don't have to," I whisper. And I mean it. Of all the reasons to back out of his promise, this is the only one I can't argue with.

"The other compound is hundreds of miles away. If I go with you to 119, I'll never see him again."

"I know."

"I'm so sorry."

I shake my head, trying to unstick my throat so I can speak. "What are you going to do? Jayden still wants you dead."

His expression hardens at the mention of Jayden. "I can handle her."

"How? You saw what she was willing to do to get rid of me. She already arrested you. What's she going to do when she gets bored sending you out into the Fringe?"

"I'll be careful. I still plan on coming eventually. I . . . I've sent an appeal to 119 to consider bringing Owen into the compound."

"You did *what?*"

Panic flashes through me. I didn't know it was even possible to contact another compound's leadership, but Eli doing so is tantamount to admitting to treason. Colluding with a drifter is illegal, and spending the night on his couch is definitely grounds for life in the cages.

"I just told them I suspected my brother was still alive . . . in hiding."

"How did you even contact them?"

Information, the board, and certain Operations workers can message other compounds to coordinate supply shipments and gather news, but most civilians have no way to contact them.

"Celdon helped me," he says with a small smile. "He's scary good at overriding security."

I choose to ignore the fact that he dragged Celdon into yet another illegal mission and focus instead on his crazy plan. "Do you think Owen would even come to 119? He hates the compounds."

"I don't know. Maybe for me. I have to try."

"Right," I say, willing myself not to cry. But I can feel the tears blazing in my throat, and it's tough to look at Eli.

"Hey." Eli reaches out and tugs at my chin, forcing me to look at him. "With or without Owen, I'm going to follow you there."

"You have to," I say thickly. "If you don't leave this place, Jayden *will* kill you. It's only a matter of time."

"I know that," he says in a soft voice. His calmness is making my near hysteria seem even more ridiculous. I can feel the tears welling up in my eyes now and yank my chin out of his grasp so he won't see.

"Hey . . . Harper." He puts his hands on my shoulders and

pulls me back to look at him, concern and regret etched in those beautiful eyes. "It's all going to work out."

I nod, but I'm really just trying to pull myself together. These last few weeks have made me an emotional wreck.

I force myself to get a grip. I don't need Eli. I was on my own before Bid Day, and I was fine. I can take care of myself. I've been doing it my whole life.

But Eli looks conflicted now, as though he's teetering on the edge of indecision. "Maybe if we leave the compound, we'll get placed in another section. Maybe . . . maybe things could be different."

"What things?" I ask, a little annoyed that he's dragging this out. I just want to rip off the bandage and leave so the pain will subside.

He doesn't answer me right away. Instead, he grasps my face between his warm, rough hands and captures my lips with his.

The feeling of his mouth on mine is so shocking it takes me several seconds to react.

Eli doesn't mind. He tastes me slowly at first, as though he's trying to commit me to memory.

Then I finally realize what's happening, and a dam breaks somewhere inside me. Everything I've been feeling spills out, and I throw it all into that kiss.

When I respond, his lips grow more demanding, and he kisses me as though he's been slowly starving himself for days.

That's when the wall between us starts to crumble. Suddenly Constance doesn't exist. Jayden doesn't exist. It's just us.

I reach out and grab the neck of his shirt, pulling him closer. He makes a noise of surprise in the back of his throat and locks one arm around my waist, pulling me off my feet a little and holding me flush against him.

The added weight on his injured leg sends us both crashing into the wall, but that doesn't deter him. The hand cradling my face works its way to my hair and then skims down my back, over my hip, and back up my side. He doesn't miss anything.

He yanks his lips away, and I immediately want them back. But then his mouth finds my neck, and every muscle in my body tightens.

It doesn't take long for him to grow impatient and find my lips once again. Every inch of him is pressed up against me, and a slow burn starts to spread across my skin.

My feet are still dangling a little, but I squirm down to the ground so I can touch him. As my hands drift down his hard chest and abs, I have to fight the urge to unbuckle his belt and shove him onto the bed.

He seems to be reading my mind, because his kisses become even hungrier, and he starts to move me in that direction. With one of his arms still locked around my waist, we pitch backward, and my head hits the pillow.

My stomach tightens, and his hand freezes halfway up my shirt. A smile cracks his face, just inches from my mouth.

"If I get you in my bed, it's all over for me," he says in a rough voice.

"I'm already in your bed."

"Yeah, but if we . . ." He tilts his head. "I might just tell Owen to go to hell, because there's no way I'd be able to let you leave without me."

Disappointment washes over me as Eli climbs off and pulls me back up. He leaves his hand wrapped around my arm, and we both stand frozen for several seconds, staring at each other.

"Please tell me you'll come," I whisper. "Eventually."

He doesn't answer. He just touches the side of my face once

more and kisses me softly, wrapping a strand of my hair around his fingers.

This time I know it's a legitimate goodbye.

Feeling a little shaky, I pull out of his arms and cross the room to his computer. I boot it up and slowly log in to my account.

"What are you doing?" he asks.

"Transferring money to your account for the ticket."

But when I pull up my account statement, a brick drops into my stomach. As I scroll down the list of transactions, I realize a few are conspicuously absent.

"Are you sure Miles transferred that money to my account?" I ask.

"Yeah. Why?"

"It isn't here," I say indignantly. I scroll down farther, trying to contain the panic building inside me. "Neither is the money from my fight or Sawyer's bet."

"*What?*"

"There are no deposits, no withdrawals — no record of the transactions at all."

"That's impossible."

But we both know it isn't. If Constance can use our interfaces and computers to spy on us, surely they can access our financials.

In a flash, he's reading the statement over my shoulder — looking for any trace of my missing credits.

Eli's face goes dark when the realization hits him, and he closes his eyes in frustration. "This is all my fault."

"How is it *your* fault?"

He lets out a frustrated growl. "That day . . . in the medical ward . . . Miles must have had his interface on him. I never checked. I didn't know they were watching him, so I just started talking, and . . . Constance could have heard everything."

Eli swears and pulls me to my feet. He drags me out of the room toward the training center, seemingly oblivious to the fact that they aren't recording us from his computer. He's gripping my hand firmly, as though he's forgotten he's supposed to hide what's going on between us. We fly into the training center, and he slams the doors behind us.

"Harper, you have to get out of here."

"But the money —"

"It doesn't matter. You still have to go — on the next train."

"What about you?"

"Don't worry about me. I'll be right behind you."

I take a deep breath, trying to calm down. "Okay. But —"

"You're going to have to sneak onto the cargo train."

I open my mouth to protest, but he cuts me off. "Better a refugee in 119 than dead. Besides, you have some money left. You can rent a compartment outright and appeal for an emergency placement."

I look around desperately, trying to think of another option. But there isn't one. Constance has worked very hard to make sure I don't go anywhere.

If I want to escape, I'm going to have to run.

twenty-six

Harper

It's amazing how much of a life fits into a rucksack. Other than my computer and lots of clothes, I don't have much to my name.

Celdon meets me at my compartment around twenty-two hundred, dressed in dark blue pants and a thin maroon sweater. It's been a long time since I've seen him out of his white Systems uniform, but he probably won't be placed in Systems where we're headed.

I've traded my Recon fatigues for black pants, boots, and my favorite jacket. Part of me feels like a traitor for leaving my gray fatigues folded neatly in my closet, but I'm hoping to be someone entirely new at 119.

A few minutes later, there's a soft knock at my door. It's Eli, and he looks a little more in control than he did the last time I saw him. His eyes widen when he sees me, but he no longer has that wild, hungry look.

"It's time," he says. "They're loading the cargo now."

"Okay."

"Remember what I said: Wait until they're done unloading at 119. They'll board the train, and you run like hell."

I turn to Celdon. He looks almost relieved to be sneaking onto the Underground.

He picks up his bag and navigates around Eli to give us a moment alone, but Eli doesn't try to kiss me again. He just stares at me with conflict raging in his eyes.

"I'll see you soon . . . right?"

He nods once and forces a slight smile that's *so* not Eli.

My stomach contracts. Something isn't right, but I don't have time to wonder what that might be.

I turn to go, and Eli stiffens. He looks as though he wanted to reach for me but thought better of it.

I don't hesitate. Not anymore.

Before he can stop me, I turn around and reach up to find his lips. They're warm but restrained, and I kiss him slowly to savor the taste of him.

After a while, his hands find my waist and pull me closer, but he doesn't deepen the kiss. It's soft and sweet, as though it's the only way to convey how he feels.

I let myself breathe him in for a few more seconds and then force myself to pull away. He releases me gently, and I give him one more look before stepping out into the tunnel.

Celdon is waiting a few yards away with a wry grin on his face, and I shove him along toward the Underground platform before any snarky comments can float back to Eli.

Even though I have a perfect view of the platform from my compartment window, I've only seen the Operations workers load the cargo onto the train a handful of times. I'm a little surprised by how few there are today.

They load up the last stack of crates, and my pulse quickens when they start trickling onto the train for the journey south.

Sure, I've snuck into plenty of places I'm not supposed to be, but the stakes have never been this high.

Celdon glances at me, and I know he's thinking that this is not the greatest plan we've ever had. One shot is all we get. If we're caught, we'll be arrested for sure.

Finally the last worker boards, and my heart shoots into my throat.

"Now!"

Celdon doesn't need to be told twice. He shoots around the corner and makes a break for the open car.

I sprint out behind him, glancing over my shoulder to make sure no one sees us.

My feet touch the inside of the car, and the smell of new plastic stings my nostrils. The floor is scuffed and dirty, and the lights along the top flicker intermittently.

A voice from the platform startles me, and I pull Celdon into a crouch behind a tall stack of crates. He may have world-class hacking skills, but his "duck and cover" needs work.

There's more yelling, and then, without warning, the doors along the sides of the cars slide closed. The lights flicker off, throwing us into darkness.

"Oh my god," I whisper. "We did it."

Celdon turns, and I can just make out the flash of a grin.

"One-nineteen, here we come."

The train lurches forward, and I feel it moving underneath us. It rolls away from the platform slowly, gradually picking up speed.

I feel a little bit queasy, but not from the motion. I'm shocked our terrible plan actually worked, and the success and anticipation are making me feel sick with nerves.

What will people at 119 say?

What if they just send us right back?

What if they stick us both in Recon this time?

I imagine my route out on the Fringe hundreds of miles away from Eli, our orbits never intersecting.

I quickly dismiss the thought. I shouldn't even be thinking

about Eli. When I get two miles away from the compound, my interface will be useless. I'll have no way to contact him — no way to know he's all right. He promised me that he would come, but that could be weeks or months from now.

He may never come, I remind myself. *He may not even live that long.*

Celdon can sense I'm worrying. With an ease I haven't seen from him in a while, he throws an arm over my shoulders and leans back against one of the crates.

"Relax, will you? We made it."

"We haven't made it until they give us a compartment in 119," I murmur. "They could still send us back."

"They wouldn't do that. As far as they're concerned, once you transfer, you're no longer a citizen of the other compound."

I snort. "I'm not sure sneaking onto the supply train qualifies as a formal transfer."

"Hey. Anywhere is better than home."

I nod and try to relax, but leaving Eli behind has unleashed a gnawing sense of regret in the pit of my stomach.

"He'll be fine."

From Celdon's tone, I can tell he's smirking.

"Who?" I say, trying to be coy.

I can almost hear the eye roll he gives me. "*Lieutenant Sexy.* Your six feet of dark, moody man candy."

"Stop."

"C'mon, Harper. It's me. Who do you think you're fooling? It's *so* obvious. And I saw your sweet little goodbye kiss back there."

I bite the inside of my mouth to keep from snapping at him. I know I'm probably beet red, but thankfully he can't see.

"The best lieutenant in Recon doesn't go out on the Fringe with the Systems-track recruit who — no offense — is a bit of a handful," he continues. "Nor does he bail her out of the cages . . . or take on an illegal fight . . . or get his panties in a twist when she has a relatively minor kidnapping incident."

I want to give Celdon a dirty look, but I'm grinning.

"I can't believe he didn't come," he says.

I shrug despite the painful emptiness inside me. "He had a good reason."

"Name one reason that outweighs getting offed by Jayden."

"You know the reason!" I say, feeling a smack of irritation that Celdon never told me he helped Eli contact 119.

There's a long pause. "No, I don't."

"Yeah, you do. Owen."

"Who?"

My stomach drops. "He told you about Owen," I say, a little defensively. "His brother."

I can feel Celdon staring at me as though I'm crazy, and that sick feeling returns to my stomach.

"The brother you contacted 119 about. He said you helped him . . ."

"I haven't talked to Eli about anything but you. He never asked me to do anything."

Even though I should have seen it coming, that news hits me like Marta's worst left hook.

Eli never contacted 119. He only told me he did so I'd leave the compound.

"He lied to me," I say aloud.

"What are you talking about?"

I take a deep breath. "Eli found his brother Owen — out on the Fringe."

"*What?*"

Celdon looks as stunned as I feel. "Well . . . that's a pretty good reason. How the fuck is his brother still out there?"

"They got separated when they were kids . . . in the raid that killed their parents. Eli thought Owen was dead all this time. But his brother is a drifter now."

"No shit?" Celdon shakes his head. "That's messed up."

He falls silent for a minute, processing that information. "So Eli stayed behind to join his brother?"

"N-No," I choke. "He told me you helped him contact 119 about granting his brother citizenship."

Eli couldn't possibly be thinking about joining his brother on the Fringe. Leaving the compound would be suicide. But if he didn't contact 119, that means he never had any intention of following us to the compound.

Celdon is quiet again, and I can tell he's contemplating how Owen survived all those years. He'd accepted the fact that we weren't the only humans left out there, because we'd survived the Fringe as babies. It was completely plausible that there were others who weren't affected by the radiation.

But the realization that there could be family members out there makes killing drifters much more difficult to swallow. The compound has always treated them as the enemy, but some of them are just like us.

"I can't believe he lied to me," I say again, more to myself than to Celdon.

"He wanted you to be safe."

"You don't really think he's going to join the drifters, do you?"

"No. Nobody does that. He probably just wants to see him again." His face darkens. "If I ever . . . if I ever saw my mom out there —" He breaks off, his nostrils flaring in the shadows. "I'd stick around long enough to ask why the fuck she dumped me outside the compound."

"You don't know that. You have no idea what happened to her."

"Neither do you."

"Even if she did, it's because she wanted you to have a good life. You can't fault her for that."

He doesn't respond, and I know the question that's haunted him his entire life must be killing him even more after hearing Owen survived that long.

A new knot has settled in my chest. Eli's lie sours the last few moments I spent with him. I can't look back on that kiss fondly, knowing that everything that came out of his mouth before was a lie.

I tell myself he did it to protect me — he knew there was no way I'd leave otherwise — but all I feel is betrayal and sadness. For the first time, I realize I may never see him again.

The rest of the trip goes by painfully slow. The train maintains its breakneck speed, but the pitch blackness makes it feel as though we're standing still. The only sign that we're actually moving is a flash of graffiti on the tunnel walls illuminated by the small lights along the side of the train.

An hour later, the movement changes, and I hear the high-pitched whistle of the conductor applying the breaks. I glance at Celdon, and we both move to conceal ourselves better behind the stack of crates.

Gradually, the train slows to a stop. The lights click on, and there's a loud *hiss* as the doors are released. My eyes struggle to adjust to the sudden brightness, and my body feels gelatinous from the sudden lack of motion.

If I were standing, my legs would be wobbling. Instead, I just rest my head against the nearest crate and try to stay calm.

I jump when somebody calls out farther up the train. And

when the sound of heavy footsteps echo down the platform, my heart starts pounding.

I can't believe we're actually here.

Apart from the sounds of workers unloading the crates from the train, it's quiet outside the car. Celdon has gone completely still beside me, and I can tell he's wondering when we should make a break for it. We'll be discovered if we're still here when they get to our car, but it's too risky to run out when they could be standing on the platform.

Plus, since our workers came to exchange goods, it's likely 119 has stationed a few Operations workers and controllers out on the platform to check identification and take inventory of the supplies.

I glance around the crate we're hiding behind, but I don't see anyone out on the platform. People are moving around on the train, and I listen to the workers' subdued voices as they move closer and closer to our car.

Suddenly the floor shakes as someone boards, and there's the loud *clang* of a dolly rolling onto our car.

I hold my breath as his feet disturb the dirt inches from our crate, but he scoops up a different box and backs out onto the platform.

I let out some air and look over at Celdon. His eyes are wide, and he mouths, "Let's go."

I nod and grip the edge of our crate to pull myself up. But it isn't as sturdy as I thought, and it starts to slide off the top of the stack.

We both lunge to catch it before it slides off onto the floor, and it feels surprisingly light as we push it back into place.

Celdon and I exchange a bemused look, and I unsnap the lid and peer inside.

The crate is empty.

"What the —"

A noise out on the platform thrusts me back into the moment. I replace the lid and duck down again, poking my head out just enough to survey the scene.

The worker who was just in our car is still rolling the dolly away from the train, and there's no one else in sight. There's no time to wonder why they would bring an empty crate. I just grab my rucksack and glance at Celdon.

It goes against every instinct in my body to run *toward* the people who could send me back to the compound, but I brace myself for the worst and force my feet to move.

Celdon disembarks right after me, and we sprint across the platform toward the cover of the Recon tunnel. I throw myself around the corner and press my back against the wall, panting hard.

At first, I think the tunnel is deserted. It's dark except for the sparse emergency lighting running along the ceiling.

Then I hear footsteps approaching from the opposite end. Someone is moving in the shadows a few yards down the tunnel.

Back on the platform, there's a loud *crash*.

I peer around the corner and see another worker step off the train. He's wheeling a stack of crates in our direction. We're trapped.

We can't reach the escalator from the platform or get to the emergency stairwell without being seen. The second we run down the tunnel toward Recon, we're going to trigger the motion-activated lights.

"Go!" Celdon hisses.

We don't have a choice. If we're running toward someone, it might as well be in the direction of freedom.

Despite my better judgment, I duck down the tunnel at a sprint. I brace myself for the lights and the yell of the approaching worker, but nothing happens. All I hear is the slap of our feet on tile.

At any moment, someone could open their compartment door and see two people who don't belong, but this wing is empty.

We reach the door to the emergency stairwell, and I pull it open to let Celdon pass. Then the door slams behind me, throwing us into total darkness.

twenty-seven

Eli

After Harper leaves, I lie awake in bed, staring at the ceiling. My body is spent, but I can't shut off my brain.

There's a soft knock at my door, and my stomach tightens in anticipation. All my nerves come alive, and my heart rate speeds up.

Then I remember that Harper is gone, and she's not coming back.

My next thought is that it could be Miles. I touch my interface, and it projects the time against my ceiling. It's oh-two hundred — much too late for it to be anyone else.

Fuck it. I roll over onto my side and try to go back to sleep. I don't want to talk about Harper being gone or what my next move is, because truthfully, I have no idea.

I feel sick about lying to her. By now, she's probably discovered that the last words I spoke to her were bullshit.

There's a small glimmer of hope in my chest that she'll get angry enough to come back here and scream at me, but that thought is quickly extinguished when I remember her lying on the ground in the dead level, seconds away from being killed.

The visitor knocks again, more insistent this time.

I reach over to my interface and send a quick message to Miles: *Go away.*

The knocking stops, and after a few seconds, I get a reply: *What are you talking about?*

Just as it hits me that the person on the other side of the door isn't Miles, I hear the soft beep of someone punching in my door code.

By the time the door swings open, I'm on my feet and have my gun pointed at the door.

The light from the tunnel illuminates a dark head of hair, and my heart turns over.

It can't be Harper. The train hasn't even returned yet.

But then my lights flicker on automatically, and I stiffen.

There's a woman standing in my compartment, but it isn't Harper. She's dressed in a matte-black bodysuit with strategically placed seams and zippers that looks as though it was made for her. Her shiny high-heeled boots bring her close to my height, and her dark brown hair curls at the ends where it flows over her chest.

The door slams shut behind her, and she fixes me with two hawklike brown eyes.

"You should really answer your door, Lieutenant."

I stare at her, my gun still pointed at her chest.

"Don't even think about it," she says, pulling out a compact handgun and training it on me.

She looks oddly familiar, and I realize she's from the class above me. We took a few courses together in higher ed, but her name escapes me.

"I'm Mina," she supplies, solidifying my suspicions that she must be a mind reader. "And you're needed in the upper levels."

"Who the hell are you?" I growl.

"We have a mutual friend," she says in a seductive voice. "Commander Pierce was right about you."

I don't have time to think about what that means. I should be relieved that Jayden is summoning me instead of having Shane send a hit man — or hit woman — to my room, but my pulse speeds up anyway.

By now, Jayden must have heard that Shane failed to terminate Harper, and it's possible she's decided to shift her focus to me.

"What does she want?"

"Relax," says Mina, cracking a smile that does not suit her at all. "She just needs your help with something."

"Yeah. The last few times I've heard that, it's been her trying to kill me."

"Well, today's your lucky day, Eli."

I hate how she says my name, drawing out the "L" so she can caress it with her tongue.

For a few seconds, we just stand there looking at each other. She's hot — no doubt about it — but her looks set me on edge the way Jayden's do. They're both poisonous flowers, beautifully designed to lure men to their deaths.

"Let's cut the foreplay," says Mina, interrupting my train of thought.

"Huh?"

"Let's pretend we both held our guns for a few more minutes and then decided to trust each other long enough to satisfy your curiosity."

"You think I'm curious?"

She fans her long dark lashes. It isn't subtle. "You know you are."

"You first."

"Fine."

With truly alarming speed, she flips her gun around so the handle is facing me. "Go ahead. Take it. You aren't really going to shoot me."

I disarm her cautiously and set her gun on the bed behind me, but I keep my own weapon trained on her.

"You're cute," she purrs, barely moving that pouty mouth. "So serious. You might want to put that thing away before we go out in public. No point freaking people out."

"Turn around," I growl.

She complies, and I'm not surprised to see that the back really is as nice as the front. I grab a sweatshirt from the desk chair and put it on awkwardly, one arm at a time. I can't very well stick the gun in my sweatpants — and there's no way I'm walking into this unarmed — so I conceal it in my open sweatshirt and let her walk out into the tunnel first.

Her heeled boots clack loudly on the tiled floor as she leads me down the tunnel. She looks so out of place in Recon with her skintight suit and perfect makeup, and part of me wishes Harper were here just so I could watch her size up this bitch.

As scary and assassin-y as Mina is, I'm confident Harper could take her in the ring.

"You're Information?" I ask, not bothering to hide my disbelief.

It's no secret that most Information workers are complete nerds — lab rats, scholars, and journalists whose duty is to conduct research, process communication, and archive the history of the compounds.

"That's my day job."

Of course. She's Constance. If I had to guess, Mina is one of the Information wildcards whose job is to monitor everything from interface communication to Fringe intelligence.

"So what do you do for Constance?"

She turns around and fixes me with a sharp look and then pivots quickly and keeps walking as though I never spoke.

Rather than being turned on by her aura of mystery, I find I'm pretty fucking annoyed. She and Jayden get a kick out of watching me squirm, but I don't have time for this stealthy Constance bullshit.

In the harsh light of the megalift, Mina isn't nearly as beautiful. Her tanned skin is unnaturally dark from spending too much time under the UV lamps, and her big brown eyes are surprisingly cold.

The lift stops on one of the upper levels, and the doors open to Information.

It's a stark contrast from the bright Systems levels. Everything here is tuxedo black, with shiny floors designed to look like black granite and recessed lighting along the walls. Each door we pass is illuminated by a single spotlight projecting down from the frame.

She leads me halfway down the tunnel to an unmarked door with a tiny sensor. She scans her ID card, and the door beeps softly as it unlocks.

We step inside, and the heat of the room quickly envelops me. It's full of servers blinking lethargically from ceiling to floor.

Mina turns to a keypad on the wall, punches in a code, and then places her thumb on a sensor. There's another high-pitched beep, followed by a mechanical groan.

At first, I can't identify the source of the noise, but then the nearest server starts to move. It's sliding on an invisible track, revealing a hidden space behind the bank of servers.

Throwing me a smug look, Mina gestures for me to follow her.

I hesitate, wondering if she's leading me to my death, but my curiosity gets the better of me.

I step inside, and my eyes struggle to adjust to the unnaturally bright light of two dozen computer monitors. For a moment, I think we're alone, but then a chair swivels around, and my eyes lock onto Jayden's.

"Nice of you to join us, Parker," she says in that clipped voice of hers.

"He wasn't as fun as you said," whines Mina, crossing to Jayden's side and tilting her head to look at me.

Jayden smirks, and I get a pang of irritation imagining the two of them conspiring against me.

"So this is Constance."

"It's one of our home bases," says Jayden. "It allows us to take advantage of Information's extensive resources."

My gaze bounces around the room. Most of the security feeds are changing constantly, revealing different views of the Fringe and several public places within the compound: the canteen, the main hall, and the megalift. I didn't know there were cameras there, but I should have guessed.

Even more disturbing are the infrared views of darkened compartments. I see a few indistinguishable men tossing and turning in their sleep and couples lying together in bed — completely unaware that they're being targeted by Constance.

By the looks of their compartments, most of them are high-level tier-one workers and board members. I imagine my own compartment flashing on screen, and my skin crawls at the thought of Jayden watching me.

It's sick to think what Constance can get away with when no one knows what's happening.

"Why did you bring me here?" I ask finally.

"I thought it was time you knew the extent of Constance's reach," she says. "I thought it might . . . motivate you to cooperate."

"Haven't I cooperated so far?"

Jayden's mouth twists into a sneer. "More or less. But everything I've asked you to do so far has been relatively tame."

"Tame?"

"The intelligence you gave us was good, but I'm afraid we missed the drifters. They move fast. And I have every reason to believe they are up to something serious."

My stomach clenches, but I keep my face blank. Jayden can't possibly know what I know. Hell, I don't even know what they're planning. How could she?

"Whatever they're up to . . . we can't let it happen."

"So what do you want from me?"

Jayden fixes me with those cold eyes again and without missing a beat says, "I need you to take out their leadership."

For a second, it feels as though all the oxygen has been sucked out of the room. It's too hot in here, and the space is way too small for the three of us.

"You want me to do *what?*"

"Your job is to kill drifters, Parker. I see no problem with narrowing the scope of your duties."

"My job is to kill drifters who are getting too close to the compound! Clean out the nearby towns. This isn't defense. It's an assassination."

Jayden crosses her arms over her chest. "It wasn't a request, Parker."

"No," I say, backing away from her. "I won't do it. Find yourself another hit man. I'm sick of this shit."

Jayden swivels her chair around to face the monitor. She doesn't raise her voice, but I can detect the fury and desperation there. "You aren't in any position to refuse an order from me, Parker. Especially after that *unfortunate* incident with Cadet Riley the other night."

I clench my fists. I can't believe she would bring that up. But

Jayden has no problem admitting what she's done when she knows there will be no repercussions. I have the sudden urge to yank her chair around and choke her with my bare hands.

"Funny how you managed to get there just in time to save the day," she muses. "It seems as though Riley's had a couple close calls lately."

I focus my gaze on each of the monitors, trying to distract myself from my murderous thoughts.

"She's proven fairly difficult to get rid of. I'm starting to wonder if my time might be better spent."

I freeze, and Jayden slowly swivels her chair around so I can see her smug grin.

"Might."

"Why are you bringing this up?"

"I'm not as incompetent as you might think, Parker. If I were truly worried about Riley revealing what she knew about VocAps . . . the bidding . . . I would have smothered her in her sleep weeks ago. But because of her little friend Celdon, I knew she wasn't a real threat."

"Then why are you doing this?"

She smiles. "Because I needed to see how far you were willing to go to protect her."

In that instant, it feels as though Jayden reached out and clamped her icy fist around my heart.

She's been playing me the entire time. All those missions, the fight, the attempt on Harper's life — they were just to see how I would react.

"Turns out, you were *very* motivated to save Riley — much more motivated than the average lieutenant. But we already knew that, didn't we?"

She hits a button on the keyboard behind her, and the monitor closest to me flickers to the training center. But it isn't the live feed. It's a recording.

Harper and I are in the middle of a heated debate, and she's going at the punching bag. I don't have to watch to know how this goes — I remember it as if it were yesterday — but I can't look away.

I yank her around, and then we're pulled toward each other like magnets. My hands are all over her, and I wince inwardly as I watch myself cop a feel.

Jayden hits the button again, and the recording freezes.

"I shouldn't say I'm surprised, Parker. Every once in a while, you get a cadet who's a little more . . . intriguing than the others."

She takes her time raking her eyes up my body. Her expression is clear: She thinks she owns me.

"Why do you care about me and Riley?" I ask, feeling bold. "She hasn't affected my work in any way."

Lies.

"Oh, I care very much. The illegal fights, the back talk, your refusal to train my cadets in a timely manner . . . You've always made it clear that my authority means nothing to you. I was starting to think you had a death wish. But as it turns out, I just didn't know how to incentivize you to behave. Now I do."

My back hits the door, and I feel for the handle. I need to get out of here because if I stay a second longer, there's a good chance I'm going to kill Jayden and Mina.

My murderous expression just eggs her on. "Clearly my threats haven't been effective. But I'll tell you one thing. If you do this for me, I'll call off my attempts on Riley's life."

I stop trying to get away from her, too suspicious to leave. "Why would you do that?"

"It occurs to me that you may be more useful alive after all."

I ease up from the door and walk slowly back toward the monitors. Jayden gives me a satisfied sneer.

Her olive branch hardly matters now that Harper is gone, but I can't give her any reason to be suspicious. If she finds out what we've done before they arrive at 119, she could easily get in touch with compound leadership and have controllers waiting to send them back.

Jayden seems to take my tense expression as a sign that I'm interested, and she pulls up a few images of the Fringe on the center monitors.

"This is Malcolm Martinez and Jackson Mills," she says. "They're the leaders of the Desperados — a brutal Fringe gang. Mills used to lead a smaller gang, but their territory was taken over by Martinez's crew."

Hearing Jayden mention the two men Owen talked about feels strange, and it's even eerier when she zooms in on stills of their faces.

Malcolm has a sharp, pointed head, heavy eyebrows, and wary eyes. Jackson looks more like the star quarterback type: well built with a youthful face that oozes charisma.

They're probably the two most well-protected men on the Fringe, yet Constance knows exactly who they are.

"They're going to be hard to get to, but we need to weed them out. You're going to have to go through this man," she says, pulling up another frozen frame of surveillance footage.

This guy is older. He's dressed better than most of the drifters I've seen, exiting a building in a town I don't recognize.

"We don't know his full name or his current location. He's all over the place, and he uses a different alias everywhere he goes. But he's close to Jackson. He'll lead you to him."

She hits the keyboard again, and the footage starts to play. Another man exits the building on screen, and she pauses the video.

She zooms in slowly, waiting for the image to refocus at every level of magnification until she's satisfied.

"When you get to Mills, you need to take him out, too." She points at a fourth man. "He's just a go-between, but he's respected, and he knows *everyone*. From what I've heard, he could take over if Malcolm were killed."

I squint at the grainy image, and the air freezes in my lungs.

Only a slice of the man's face is visible in the still, but I know that face as well as my own.

It's Owen.

twenty-eight

Harper

Running through 119 fills me with a strange sense of déjà vu. From what I've seen, the layout is nearly identical to our compound, but the walls are painted different colors, and the tunnels aren't as well maintained.

The emergency stairwell is pitch black and has a damp, foul smell that ours back home doesn't. The rust on the railing flakes off in my hand, and my boots splash through small puddles of water on every landing.

There must be a leak somewhere that caused the power outage in the stairwell, but I can't believe Operations hasn't fixed it. Back home, those issues are resolved within hours to prevent further damage to the compound.

Celdon starts to pant after five levels, but we can't risk taking the megalift and running into a controller. Our sweaty faces and wary expressions would raise their suspicions, and we can't afford to be brought in for questioning tonight.

I force my legs to keep moving, even when Celdon falls a little behind.

I hope the board members' compartments are in the same place as they are in our compound. If they aren't, our chances of finding them before the rest of 119 wakes up are slim.

When I reach the landing of the correct level, I lean against the wall to collect my breath while I wait for Celdon to catch up.

It's so dark that he bumps into me when he rounds the corner.

I can't see his face, but I know he's glaring at me.

There's no time to let him recover. I pull the door open and step out into the tunnel. It's running on emergency lighting, too, which strikes me as odd. It's possible the compound is experiencing a mass outage, but I can't ever recall a time when our entire compound was without power for more than a few minutes.

Since I can't see anything outside the small pools of yellowish light, I feel for the wall and use it to guide us down the tunnel toward the area where the board members' compartments should be situated.

The silence makes the hair on the back of my neck stand on end, and the knowledge that we're exploring the exact level that was blown to smithereens in our compound just adds to the eeriness.

I don't like feeling my way through the shadows in a strange place, but hopefully we can find a board member, plead our case, and get a room for the night to await processing. They'll have to discuss our case as a group in the morning, but if we can get one board member on our side, I'm confident they'll grant us citizenship.

When we reach the end of the tunnel, Celdon clicks his interface to illuminate the placards on the doors. I grin. My interface is stuffed at the bottom of my rucksack, but Celdon's is never far out of reach. I'm sure it's already killing him that he can't access 119's network.

I see a placard that reads "Secretary of Relations" and knock. If anyone will be sympathetic to our cause, it's her. I heard on the news that when she campaigned for office, one of her platforms was greater freedom to move between compounds. From what I've heard of her speeches, she seems levelheaded and fair.

We wait for a few minutes, but there's no answer. I knock

again — a little louder this time — but there's still no sound of movement from inside the compartment.

It's possible she's a heavy sleeper, or she could be staying somewhere else tonight. For some reason, the thought of the secretary having an illicit affair sends a nervous giggle through me.

Celdon gives me a weird look, but I shrug it off and move on to the Undersecretary of Vocational Placement. He wasn't our first choice, but if he's anything like Sullivan Taylor, he's a decent human being who actually cares about the young people he oversees. Plus, I'm not above threatening him with what we know about VocAps.

Celdon knocks this time — much more loudly than I would dare in the middle of the night — but he's as nervous and impatient as I am.

My stomach clenches in anticipation as the seconds drag by. I already know what I'm going to say, but it's still nerve-wracking since I have no idea how he'll react.

We wait, but he doesn't answer. The silence from inside his compartment is maddening.

We had a second backup — the Undersecretary of Information — but she doesn't answer either.

This is getting weird.

"You think there's some secret bunker where they're all staying?" Celdon asks loudly.

I shush him and rack my brain to think where they could be. It's possible someone called an emergency board meeting, but that seems unlikely. Anything big enough to warrant rousing the board members at oh-three hundred would have woken other people, too.

My first instinct is to go down to Neverland to ask someone, but then I realize Neverland is something that's probably unique to our compound with the collapsed Underground tunnel.

"Fuck this," says Celdon. "I'm asking someone."

I open my mouth to protest, but Celdon is already banging on the nearest compartment door, which probably belongs to some retired Systems worker. I cringe, an apology already on the tip of my tongue.

But when he knocks, the door swings open, and we both freeze.

I shake my head at Celdon, preparing to make a break for it, but he just walks in as though he owns the place.

I don't hear any startled noises or angry protests, so I follow him inside.

The compartment is completely empty, and it looks as though whoever lived here departed in a hurry. There are old canteen takeout containers everywhere, the bed is unmade, and I can smell rotten food in the kitchen area. There's another smell that sets me on edge, but I can't quite identify it.

"This is giving me the creeps," says Celdon. "Where *is* everybody?"

"Let's check the medical ward. There has to be someone there who knows what's going on."

The medical ward is one place where I know there will be people, and part of me has started to associate it with comfort since Sawyer practically lives there.

This isn't home, I remind myself. *You're never going to see Sawyer again.*

That fills me with new desperation as we make our way down the emergency stairwell.

I brace myself for the flood of questions and protests we'll get once people realize we don't belong there. But when we step into the medical ward, I'm shocked to see that this level is dark except for the glowing red "admittance" sign.

"What the hell is going on?" Celdon asks aloud.

He moves his head so the beam of his interface can travel over the deserted waiting area and the vacant nurse's station.

A shiver rolls down my spine at the sight of all the empty chairs. I've never known Health and Rehab to leave the nurse's station unattended. And it definitely shouldn't be dark.

I walk toward the exam rooms and nearly fall headfirst into something metal. It rolls away and bangs into the wall, and I realize it's a gurney. My heart is beating wildly in my chest.

I grip the metal frame tightly to calm myself down, trying to think.

It's okay, I tell myself. *Everything's fine.*

I push the gurney out of the way, but it clangs into something else.

"Celdon!"

The blue beam of his interface shows he's already right behind me. It moves over the gurney I ran into and down the tunnel, where more gurneys are pushed together in a row.

I squeeze between the wall and the first one and peer into the nearest room. It's empty, and the bed has been stripped of its linens. There's no chart hanging on the bed and no patient.

I keep moving down the tunnel, peeking into the next room, but it's just as empty as the first.

It doesn't make sense.

"Hello?" I call.

My voice disappears in the darkness.

No one answers.

"Something's wrong," says Celdon. He sounds genuinely scared. "Where is everyone?"

I don't answer him. I just wander into the next room and stare at the cabinets against the far wall. They're wide open, and it looks as though they've been emptied.

"What the —"

Celdon is putting it together, and I rush down the tunnel toward the supply closet. It's in the same place as the closet Sawyer pulled me into back home, and being in the darkened replica of our medical ward gives me a chill.

I throw the door open. Sure enough, these shelves look depleted, too.

There's something sinister going on here. I can feel it in my bones.

I bump into Celdon on my way to the waiting area and nearly lose my shit. He's breathing as hard as I am, and I grab his arm and pull him back toward the emergency stairwell.

My urgency to find someone has morphed into panic.

Where is everyone?

As soon as we reach the door, I hear footsteps climbing up the stairs on the other side. I shake my head at Celdon and drag him into the shadows behind a fleet of electric wheelchairs.

He ducks down and clicks off his interface just as the door to the stairwell bursts open.

Part of me is worried about being discovered, but the other part is so anxious to see another human being that I'd gladly brave a night in the cages.

The stranger is also wearing an interface, which casts just enough light for me to see that it's one of our Operations workers from the train.

My heart starts to beat faster. *What is he doing up here?*

His expression is set, which tells me he's not at all surprised to find the medical ward deserted. He doesn't bang into the gurneys or call out for assistance. He just moves toward the exam rooms with purpose.

I wait with bated breath as his footsteps fade down the tunnel, and Celdon gives me a puzzled look.

After several minutes, I hear footsteps again, and the man returns holding a small box. I can't tell what's in it, but I'd bet it's full of the remaining medical supplies.

That's what the empty crates were for. *But why are they looting from 119?*

He yanks the door open again and disappears down the stairs. I let out a sigh of relief and wait a couple minutes until I'm sure he's had enough time to make it down a few flights.

Celdon flips his interface back on, and his eyes look wild in the artificial blue light. He's just as suspicious as I am.

I motion toward the stairs, and we follow the man at a cautious pace. I don't know where he's going, but I want to check the main hall. It's one of the few places in the compound that could fit thousands of people.

There must be some reason everyone is out of their beds in the middle of the night. It's probably the same reason the power is out and why one of *our* Operations workers was in the medical ward.

Maybe the workers received word that people had been hurt somewhere in the compound. Maybe there's been a terrorist attack.

As we pass the Ag Level and hit the first landing for Waste Management, I get a nasty whiff of something I missed on the way up.

The second I smell it, I can't believe it didn't stop me before. The odor is so pungent and so horribly familiar that it's enough to make me instantly nauseated.

It's the dead level.

Last night, I'd had my face crushed into the warm dirt, yet all I'd smelled was damp earth and the slight hint of decay. The stench here is much too strong.

Alarm bells go off in my head, and I take a step toward the door without thinking. Everything inside me is screaming to back away, but my hand is already on the handle.

The door shouldn't be unlocked, but the handle turns easily.

Celdon rounds the corner onto the landing and smells what I smelled a second too late.

"Harper! Don't —"

I open the door, and the putrid odor hits me like an avalanche. I gag and stagger backward, but the smell sears the inside of my nostrils and sticks to the back of my throat.

Celdon chokes loudly and turns to wretch on the bottom step.

"What the fuck?" he yells.

This isn't the stench of a reasonable number of corpses in various stages of decomposition. This is a mass grave.

In a trance, I pull my shirt over my mouth and nose and step inside. The odor is still suffocating, and I have to hold my breath to stay standing.

Celdon coughs and scans his interface across the field, and the bottom drops out of my stomach.

Mounds and mounds of the dead are crammed together as far as I can see. In the distance, the ground slopes upward where bodies are stacked two or three deep.

There must be thousands of people recently buried here. The sight is overwhelming.

Stumbling sideways, I bump into Celdon, who pulls me back out onto the landing with a clammy hand and slams the door shut.

Exposure

As the sound reverberates in the narrow stairwell, we both exchange a look of pure despair. Neither one of us says anything because the truth is too horrible.

One-nineteen can't be our new home. Everyone here is dead.

Author's Note

Thank you for reading *Exposure*. If you've made it this far, it means you've already read *Recon* and possibly the Defectors Trilogy, and I'm extremely grateful that you've followed me along my journey as an author.

This year, I was able to take a big leap to become a full-time writer, which wouldn't have been possible without the support of readers like you. I'm hoping to have much more time to devote to writing books in the near future, so please keep reading them, and tell your friends!

The Fringe series has grown so much in scope since I first envisioned it. It was one of those ideas that takes hold and refuses to be ignored, but I had no idea just how big of a playground the compound would be when I first created it or how real these characters would become.

Eli, for instance, has truly taken on a life of his own. I knew a little bit about his past in book one, but *Exposure* was when I discovered the horrors he faced as a child and, simultaneously, his remarkable capacity for goodness.

His flaws, his willingness to make sacrifices for Harper, and his general "don't fuck with me" attitude make him one of my favorite characters that I've written.

I'm very excited to get to know Owen in book three. Both Parker brothers are intense, stubborn, and natural-born leaders, and I'm interested to see how their different upbringings have shaped them as people. They've spent half their lives apart, and I expect their different paths in adulthood will lead to some interesting ethical disagreements.

Harper also had the chance to show a wider range of emotions in *Exposure*, and taking that ride with her was tough at times. As I wrote, I often had the impulse to rush her through those emotional hurdles, but I had to be patient as she struggled with her fear of the Fringe and the trauma of taking a human life.

Still, I got my badass Harper fix during her fight with Marta. The illegal fight circuit was something I was very eager to revisit in book two because boxing and martial arts have become a personal obsession of mine in real life.

In the past few months, I've been learning the fundamentals right alongside Harper, and I found myself going back to write in cool combinations I'd learned and incorporating some elements of MMA. (I've also become addicted to *The Ultimate Fighter*.)

The style of fighting Harper and Eli use isn't purely kick-boxing or MMA. Elbows, knees, and below-the-belt kicks are allowed. It's three rounds like most MMA fights — and the fighters *can* go to the ground — but I wanted the majority of the fighting to be stand-up because I think it's much more dynamic.

Keep in mind that these are illegal bouts, so more dangerous maneuvers would be allowed for novice fighters. Plus, fighting styles are always evolving.

MMA is relatively new, and it's *extremely* new for women. (The first major U.S. women's event was in 2009, and the first UFC women's match took place in 2013.) By the time the nuclear apocalypse comes, I'm confident we'll have yet another new style.

This book also forced me to explore the political climate that could have led to Death Storm in depth. The prospect of nuclear annihilation was difficult for me to stomach because it's been one of my biggest fears since I was a kid.

When I was in seventh grade, my teacher showed us a film about the bombing of Hiroshima and Nagasaki, which gave me nightmares for years afterward. (Thanks a lot, Mr. G.)

Ever since, I've dreaded the prospect of nuclear war, which made speculating on how it could actually come about that much more terrifying.

Before the compounds existed, the world's nuclear status was well beyond where it is today. (As of this book's publication, nine nations have nuclear weapons: the United States, Russia, the United Kingdom, France, China, India, Pakistan, North Korea, and Israel.) However, world powers suspect Iran is trying to build a nuclear bomb, so it follows that we have not seen the end of nuclear stockpiling.

The attack on Washington, D.C., described in the book would have been the inciting incident that provoked Operation Extermination against the United States' enemies. This is the point where the first-generation extreme "preppers" (Paxton's grandparents' generation) and their compounds gained some mainstream acceptance.

Over the next twenty years, the political climate would have gone from bad to worse, culminating in a barrage of nuclear attacks on U.S. soil from multiple hostile nations.

You can think of the effects of a nuclear attack like a bull's-eye, with the epicenter of the attack zone being annihilated and heavy damage spreading for miles around. The economy, supply chains, and major electrical grids would collapse.

Though the compounds were situated outside these hot zones, the surrounding environment would not be immune to the damaging effects of radiation. Radioactive material is very hard to contain because it can travel by rain and wind and get absorbed by plants and animals.

During and after Death Storm, people living in the U.S. would have migrated away from large cities that could become targets for terrorists. Since the compounds were designed to protect inhabitants from radiation, many people would have sought refuge there after Death Storm.

However, once they came close to reaching capacity, each compound's board would have become more selective about whom they let in. Compound leaders would have been concerned with protecting the community's long-term interests — not saving as many humans as possible.

Overcrowding or a graying population could cause the entire system to collapse, which is why the board experimented with the Fringe Program (more on this to come).

And speaking of a graying population, how about those dead people? In a self-sustaining system, you wouldn't want anything to go to waste. That includes dead bodies.

I thought long and hard about what the compound would do with the dead. Traditional burials or cremation seemed like a missed opportunity for recycling, and neither of these methods is very good for the environment. (Remember, the health of the compound ecosystem is very important.)

So far, the most eco-friendly burial method is one that was developed by a Swedish company called Promessa Organic AB. It involves freeze-drying a corpse and using sound waves to dissolve it into a powder. After that, the powder is dried in a vacuum chamber and converted into soil within six to twelve months.

This is by far the coolest method I've read about, but it produces a byproduct that is, quite honestly, far less creepy than an entire floor of dead bodies in various stages of decomposition.

I wondered if there was any place in the world where they were already attempting to turn human bodies into compost using a more traditional method (think a compost bin). As it turns out, there is.

One woman in Seattle is working on a prototype of an urban death center, which will involve burying people together in a multilevel facility with wood chips and saw dust. Although the dead levels in the compounds are a slightly different approach, it's the same idea: controlled decomposition resulting in nutrient-rich compost. Waste Management would be able to turn this into compost tea, which could be used in the compound's hydroponic growing system.

If you've ever tried your hand at composting, you know overloading the compost heap (as they did in 119) is a very bad idea.

The reality of these concepts might be more than most people want to think about, but I believe it's important to ask "what if?" Not only is that the question that leads to lots of great discoveries (and great books), but I think it could also help us avoid some of the really awful chapters of human history.

I hope you enjoyed *Exposure* and that you'll help me spread the word about the series by leaving a review on Amazon and Goodreads. Reviews help readers discover books by independent authors, and I really appreciate them.

You can also sign up for my mailing list at www.tarahbenner.com to be the first to hear about book three of The Fringe and receive exclusive reader perks.

And, as always, feel free to get in touch to tell me what you thought of the book. I love hearing from readers.

* * *

Did you enjoy this book? Visit www.tarahbenner.com to join my mailing list so you can be the first to hear about book three of The Fringe.

You can also connect with me on Twitter @tarahbenner.

27335880R00244

Made in the USA
Middletown, DE
15 December 2015